M000219974

WHAT
THE
RIVER
KNOWS

ALSO BY

ISABEL IBAÑEZ

Woven in Moonlight

Written in Starlight

Rogue Enchantments
(short story in *Reclaim the Stars* anthology)

Together We Burn

The Storyteller's Workbook
(with Adrienne Young)

WHAT
THE
RIVER

KNOWS

a novel

ISABEL IBAÑEZ

WEDNESDAY BOOKS
NEW YORK

First published in the United States by Wednesday Books, an imprint of St. Martin's Publishing Group

WHAT THE RIVER KNOWS. Copyright © 2023 by Isabel Ibañez. All rights reserved. Printed in the United States of America. For information, address St. Martin's Publishing Group, 120 Broadway, New York, NY 10271.

Designed by Devan Norman
Interior illustrations by Isabel Ibañez

ISBN 978-1-250-80337-5

For Rebecca Ross,
who fell in love with Egypt as I wrote the first draft,
who cheered me on, even as I reached dead ends,
and who swooned when Whit first walked across the page

MAP OF EGYPT

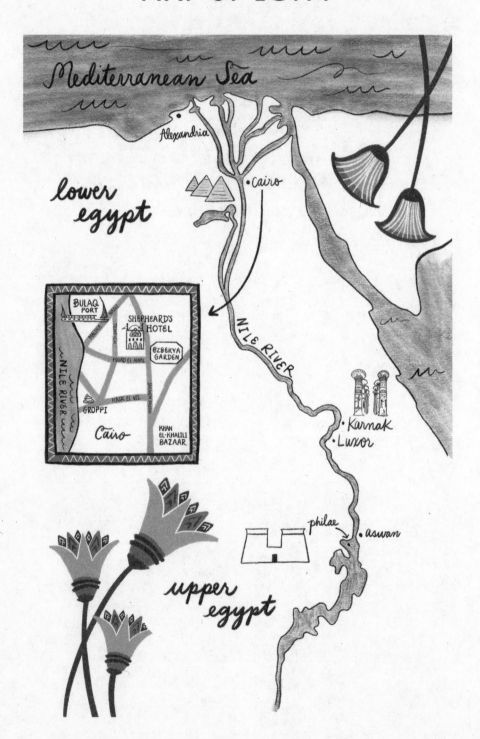

A (BROAD) TIMELINE OF EGYPT

2675–2130 BCE	Old Kingdom
1980–1630 BCE	Middle Kingdom
1539–1075 BCE	New Kingdom
356 BCE	Birth of Alexander the Great
332–305 BCE	Macedonian Period
69 BCE	Birth of Cleopatra VII
31 BCE	Battle of Actium (Deaths of Cleopatra and Marcus Antonius)
31 BCE	Beginning of Roman rule
639	Arab invasion of Egypt
969	Cairo established as capital
1517	Egypt absorbed into the Turkish Ottoman Empire
1798	Napoleon's expedition to Egypt (discovery of Rosetta Stone)
1822	Champollion deciphers hieroglyphs
1869	Opening of Suez Canal
1870	Thomas Cook's first Nile tour
1882	English fleet bombs Alexandria and destroys fortresses
1922	British Protectorate abolished; discovery of Tutankhamun's tomb
1953	Egypt's independence

WHAT THE RIVER KNOWS

PRÓLOGO

Never say you know the last word about any human heart.

—HENRY JAMES

AUGUST 1884

A letter changed my life.

I'd waited for it all day hidden in the old potter's shed, away from Tía Lorena and her two daughters, one I loved and the other who didn't love me. My hideout barely stood up straight, being old and rickety; one strong wind might blow the whole thing over. Golden afternoon light forced itself in through the smudged window. I furrowed my brow, tapping my pencil against my bottom lip, and tried not to think about my parents.

Their letter wouldn't arrive for another hour yet.

If it was coming at all.

I glanced at the sketch pad propped against my knees and made myself more comfortable in the ancient porcelain bathtub. The remnants of old magic shrouded my frame, but barely. The spell had been cast long ago, and too many hands had handled the tub for me to be completely hidden. That was the trouble with most magic-touched things. Any traces of the original spell cast were faint, fading slowly anytime it passed hands. But that didn't stop my father from collecting as many magically tainted objects as he could. The manor was filled with worn shoes that grew flowers from the soles, and mirrors that sang as you walked by them, and chests that spewed bubbles whenever opened.

Outside, my younger cousin, Elvira, hollered my name. The unlady-like shrill would almost certainly displease Tía Lorena. She encouraged moderate tones, unless, of course, *she* was the one talking. Her voice could reach astonishing decibels.

Often aimed in my direction.

"*Inez!*" Elvira cried.

I was too much in a wretched mood for conversation.

I sank lower in the tub, the sound of my prima rustling outside the wooden building, yelling my name again as she searched the lush garden, under a bushy fern and behind the trunk of a lemon tree. But I kept quiet in case Elvira was with her older sister, Amaranta. My least favorite cousin who never had a stain on her gown or a curl out of place. Who never screeched or said anything in a shrill tone.

Through the slits of the wooden panels, I caught sight of Elvira tram-pling on innocent flowerbeds. I smothered a laugh when she stepped into a pot of lilies, yelling a curse I knew her mother also wouldn't appreciate.

Moderate tones *and* no cursing.

I really ought to reveal myself before she sullied yet another pair of her delicate leather shoes. But until the mailman arrived, I wouldn't be fit company for anyone.

Any minute he'd arrive with the post.

Today might *finally* be the day I'd have an answer from Mamá and Papá. Tía Lorena had wanted to take me into town, but I'd declined and stayed hidden all afternoon in case she forced me out of the house. My parents chose her and my two cousins to keep me company during their monthslong travels, and my aunt meant well, but sometimes her iron ways grated.

"Inez! ¿Dónde estás?" Elvira disappeared deeper into the garden, the sound of her voice getting lost between the palms.

I ignored her, my corset a lock around my rib cage, and clutched my pencil tighter. I squinted down at the illustration I'd finished. Mamá's and Papá's sketched faces stared up at me. I was a perfect blend of the two. I had my mother's hazel eyes and freckles, her full lips and pointed chin. My father gave me his wild and curly black hair—now gone over to complete gray—and his tanned complexion, straight nose, and brows. He was older than Mamá, but he was the one who understood me the most.

Mamá was much harder to impress.

I hadn't meant to draw them, hadn't wanted to think of them at all. Because if I thought of them, I'd count the miles between us. If I thought of them, I'd remember they were a world away from where I sat hidden in a small corner of the manor grounds.

I'd remember they were in Egypt.

A country they adored, a place they called home for half the year. For as long as I could remember, their bags were always packed, their goodbyes as constant as the rising and setting of the sun. For seventeen years, I sent them off with a brave smile, but when their exploring eventually stretched into months, my smiles had turned brittle.

The trip was too dangerous for me, they said. The voyage long and arduous. For someone who had stayed in one place for most of her life, their yearly adventure sounded divine. Despite the troubles they'd faced, it never stopped them from buying another ticket on a steamship sailing from the port of Buenos Aires all the way to Alexandria. Mamá and Papá never invited me along.

Actually, they *forbade* me from going.

I flipped the sheet with a scowl and stared down at a blank page. My fingers clutched the pencil as I drew familiar lines and shapes of Egyptian hieroglyphs. I practiced the glyphs whenever I could, forcing myself to remember as many as I could and their closest phonetic values to the Roman alphabet. Papá knew hundreds and I wanted to keep up. He always asked me if I'd learned any new ones and I hated disappointing him. I devoured the various volumes from *Description de L'Egypte* and Florence Nightingale's journals while traveling through Egypt, to Samuel Birch's *History of Egypt*. I knew the names of the pharaohs from the New Kingdom by heart and could identify numerous Egyptian gods and goddesses.

EGYPTIAN hieroglyphs

🦅	vulture	A	⊖	sieve	Kh
	reed	i/y		animal belly	Kh
	arm	a		door bolt	s/z
	chick	u/w		folded cloth	s
	leg	b		pool	sh
	stool	p		hill	K/q
	viper	f		basket	K
	owl	m		jar stand	g
	water	n		bread loaf	t
	mouth	r		rope	ch
	shelter	h		hand	d
	wick	h		cobra	j

I dropped the pencil in my lap when I finished, and idly twisted the golden ring around my littlest finger. Papá had sent it in his last package back in July with no note, only his name and return address in Cairo labeled on the box. That was so like him to forget. The ring glinted in the soft light, and I remembered the first time I'd slipped it on. The moment I touched it, my fingers had tingled, a burning current had raced up my arm, and my mouth had filled with the taste of roses.

An image of a woman walked across my vision, disappearing when I blinked. In that breathless moment, I'd felt a keen sense of longing, the emotion acute, as if it were *me* experiencing it.

Papá had sent me a magic-touched object.

It was baffling.

I never told a soul what he did or what had happened. Old world magic had *transferred* onto me. It was rare, but possible as long as the object hadn't been handled too many times by different people.

Papá once explained it to me like this: long ago, before people built their cities, before they decided to root themselves to one area, past generations of Spellcasters from all around the world created magic with rare plants and hard-to-find ingredients. With every spell performed, the magic gave up a spark, an otherworldly energy that was quite literally *heavy*. As a result, it would latch on to surrounding objects, leaving behind an imprint of the spell.

A natural byproduct of performing magic.

But no one performed it anymore. The people with the knowledge to create spells were long gone. Everyone knew it was dangerous to write magic down, and so their methods were taught orally. But even this tradition became a dead art, and so civilizations had to embrace man-made things.

Ancient practices were forgotten.

But all that created magic, that intangible *something*, had already gone somewhere. That magical energy had been sinking deep into the ground, or drowning itself in deep lakes and oceans. It clung to objects, the ordinary and obscure, and sometimes transferred whenever it first came into contact with something, or some*one,* else. Magic had a mind of its own, and no one knew why it leapfrogged, or clung to one object or person, but not the other. Regardless, every time a transfer happened, the spell weakened in minuscule degrees until it finally disappeared. Understandably, people hated picking up or buying random things that might hold old magic. Imagine getting ahold of a teapot that brewed envy or conjured up a prickly ghost.

Countless artifacts were destroyed or hidden by organizations specializing in magic tracing, and large quantities were buried and lost and mostly forgotten.

Much like the names of generations long past, or of the original creators of magic themselves. Who they were, how they lived, and what they did. They left all this magic behind—not unlike hidden treasures—most of which hadn't been handled all that often.

Mamá was the daughter of a rancher from Bolivia, and in her small pueblo, she once told me, the magia was closer to the surface, easier to find. Trapped in plaster or worn leather sandals, an old sombrero. It had thrilled her, the remnants of a powerful spell now caught up in the ordinary. She loved the idea of her town descending from generations of talented Spellcasters.

I flipped the page of my sketchbook and started again, trying not to think about The Last Letter I'd sent to them. I'd written the greeting in shaky hieratic—cursive hieroglyphic writing—and then asked them again to *please* let me come to Egypt. I had asked this same question in countless different ways, but the answer was always the same.

No, no, no.

But maybe this time, the answer would be different. Their letter might arrive soon, *that day*, and maybe, just maybe, it would have the one word I was looking for.

Yes, Inez, you may finally come to the country where we live half our lives away from you. Yes, Inez, you can finally see what we do in the desert, and why we love it so much—more than spending time with you. Yes, Inez, you'll finally understand why we leave you, again and again, and why the answer has always been no.

Yes, yes, yes.

"Inez," cousin Elvira yelled again, and I startled. I hadn't realized she'd drawn closer to my hiding place. The magic clinging to the old tub might obscure my frame from afar but if she got close enough, she'd see me easily. This time her voice rose and I noted the hint of panic. "You've a *letter*!"

I snapped my face away from my sketch pad and sat up with a jerk. *Finalmente.*

I tucked the pencil behind my ear, and climbed out of the tub. Swinging the heavy wooden door open a crack, I peered through, a sheepish smile on my face. Elvira stood not ten paces from me. Thankfully, Amaranta was nowhere in sight. She'd cringe at the state of my wrinkled skirt and report my heinous crime to her mother.

"Hola, prima!" I screamed.

Elvira shrieked, jumping a foot. She rolled her eyes. "You're incorrigible."

"Only in front of you." I glanced down at her empty hands, looking for the missive. "Where is it?"

"My mother bid me to come fetch you. That's all I know."

We set off the cobbled path leading up to the main house, our arms linked. I walked briskly as was my norm. I never understood my cousin's slow amble. What was the point in not reaching where you wanted to go quickly? Elvira hastened her step, following at my heels. It was an accurate picture of our relationship. She was forever trying to tag along. If I liked the color yellow, then she declared it the prettiest shade on earth. If I wanted carne asada for dinner, then she was already sharpening the knives.

"The letter won't suddenly disappear," Elvira said with a laugh, tossing her dark brown hair. Her eyes were warm, her full mouth stretched into a wide grin. We favored each other in appearances, except for our eyes. Hers were greener than my ever-changing hazel ones. "My mother said it was postmarked from Cairo."

My heart stuttered.

I hadn't told my cousin about The Last Letter. She wouldn't be happy about my wanting to join Mamá and Papá. Neither of my cousins nor my aunt understood my parents' decision to disappear for half the year to Egypt. My aunt and cousins *loved* Buenos Aires, a glamorous city with its European-style architecture and wide avenues and cafés. My father's side of the family hailed from Spain originally, and they came to Argentina nearly a hundred years ago, surviving a harrowing journey but ultimately making a success in the railroad industry.

Their marriage was a match built on combining Mamá's good name and Papá's great wealth, but it bloomed into mutual admiration and respect over the years, and by the time of my birth, into deep love. Papá never got the large family he wanted, but my parents often liked to say that they had their hands full with me anyway.

Though I'm not precisely sure *how* they did when they were gone so much.

The house came into view, beautiful and expansive with white stones and large windows, the style ornate and elegant, reminiscent of a Parisian manor. A gilded iron fence caged us in, obscuring views of the neighborhood. When I was little, I used to hoist myself up to the top bar of the gate, hoping for a glimpse of the ocean. It remained forever out of sight, and I had to content myself with exploring the gardens.

But the letter might change everything.

Yes or no. Was I staying or leaving? Every step I took toward the house might be one step closer to a different country. Another world.

A seat at the table with my parents.

"There you are," Tía Lorena said from the patio door. Amaranta stood next to her, a thick, leather-bound tome in one hand. *The Odyssey*. An intriguing choice. If I recalled correctly, the last classic she tried to read had bitten her finger. Blood had stained the pages and the magic-touched book escaped out the window, never to be seen again. Though sometimes I still heard yips and growls coming from the sunflower beds.

My cousin's mint-green gown ruffled in the warm breeze, but even so, not a single hair dared to escape her pulled-back hairstyle. She was everything my mother wanted me to be. Her dark eyes stole over mine, and her lips twitched in disapproval when she took in my stained fingers. Charcoal pencils always left their mark, like soot.

"Reading again?" Elvira asked her sister.

Amaranta's attention flickered to Elvira, and her expression softened. She reached forward and linked arms with her. "It's a fascinating tale; I wish you would have stayed with me. I would have read my favorite parts to you."

She never used that sweet tone with me.

"Where have you been? Never mind," Tía Lorena said as I began to answer. "Your dress is dirty, did you know?"

The yellow linen bore wrinkles and frightful stains, but it was one of my favorites. The design allowed me to dress without the help of a maid. I'd secretly ordered several garments with buttons easy to access, which Tía Lorena detested. She thought it made the gowns scandalous. My poor aunt tried her hardest to keep me looking presentable but unfortunately for her, I had a singular ability to ruin hemlines and crush ruffles. I did love my dresses, but did they have to be so delicate?

I noticed her empty hands and smothered a flare of impatience. "I was in the garden."

Elvira tightened her hold on my arm with her free one, and rushed to my defense. "She was practicing her art, Mamá, that's all."

My aunt and Elvira loved my illustrations (Amaranta said they were too juvenile), and always made sure I had enough supplies to paint and sketch. Tía Lorena thought I was talented enough to sell my work in the many galleries popping up in the city. She and my mother had quite the life planned out for me. Along with the lessons from countless tutors in the artistic sphere, I had been schooled in French and English, the general sciences, and histories, with a particular emphasis, of course, on Egypt.

Papá made sure I read the same books on that subject as he did, and also that I read his favorite plays. Shakespeare was a particular favorite of his, and we quoted the lines to each other back and forth, a game only we knew how to win. Sometimes we put on performances for the staff, using the ballroom as our own home theater. Since he was a patron of the opera house, he constantly received a steady supply of costumes and wigs and theater makeup, and some of my favorite memories were of us trying on new ensembles, planning for our next show.

My aunt's face cleared. "Well, come along, Inez. You have a visitor."

I shot a questioning look at Elvira. "I thought you said I had a letter?"

"Your visitor has brought a letter from your parents," Tía Lorena clarified. "He must have run into them during his travels. I can't think of who else might be writing to you. Unless there's a secret caballero I don't know about . . ." She raised her brows expectantly.

"You ran off the last two."

"Miscreants, the both of them. Neither could identify a salad fork."

"I don't know why you bother rounding them up," I said. "Mamá has her mind made up. She thinks Ernesto would make me a suitable husband."

Tía Lorena's lips turned downward. "There's nothing wrong with having options."

I stared at her in amusement. My aunt would oppose a prince if my mother suggested it. They'd never gotten along. Both were too headstrong, too opinionated. Sometimes I thought my aunt was the reason my mother chose to leave me behind. She couldn't stand sharing space with my father's sister.

"I'm sure his family's wealth is a point in his favor," Amaranta said in her dry voice. I recognized that tone. She resented being married off, more than I did. "That's the most important thing, correct?"

Her mother glared at her eldest daughter. "It is not, just because . . ."

I tuned out the rest of the conversation, closed my eyes, my breath lodged at the back of my throat. My parents' letter was here, and I'd finally have an answer. Tonight I could be planning my wardrobe, packing my trunks, maybe even convincing Elvira to accompany me on the long journey. I opened my eyes in time to catch the little line appear between my cousin's eyebrows.

"I've been waiting to hear from them," I explained.

She frowned. "Aren't you *always* waiting to hear from them?"

A fantastic point. "I asked them if I could join them in Egypt," I admitted, darting a nervous glance toward my aunt.

"But . . . but, *why*?" Tía Lorena sputtered.

I linked my arms through Elvira's and propelled us into the house. We were charmingly grouped, traversing the long stretch of the tiled hall, the three of us arm in arm, my aunt leading us like a tour guide.

The house boasted nine bedrooms, a breakfast parlor, two living rooms, and a kitchen rivaling that of the most elegant hotel in the city. We even had a smoking room but ever since Papá had purchased a pair of armchairs that could fly, no one had been inside. They caused terrible damage, crashing into the walls, smashing the mirrors, poking holes into the paintings. To this day, my father still lamented the loss of his two-hundred-year-old whiskey trapped in the bar cabinet.

"Because she's *Inez*," Amaranta said. "Too good for indoor activities like sewing or knitting, or any other task for respectable ladies." She slanted a glare in my direction. "Your curiosity will get you in trouble one day."

I dropped my chin, stung. I wasn't *above* sewing or knitting. I disliked doing either because I was so terribly wretched at them.

"This is about your cumpleaños," Elvira said. "It must be. You're hurt that they won't be here, and I understand. I *do*, Inez. But they'll come back, and we'll have a grand dinner to celebrate and invite all the handsome boys living in the barrio, including Ernesto."

She was partly right. My parents were going to miss my nineteenth. Another year without them as I blew out the candles.

"Your uncle is a terrible influence on Cayo," Tía Lorena said with a sniff. "I cannot comprehend why my brother funds so many of Ricardo's outlandish schemes. Cleopatra's tomb, for heaven's sake."

"¿Qué?" I asked.

Even Amaranta appeared startled. Her lips parted in surprise. We were both avid readers, but I was unaware that she had read any of my books on ancient Egypt.

Tía Lorena's face colored slightly, and she nervously tucked an errant strand of brown hair shot with silver behind her ear. "Ricardo's latest pursuit. Something silly I overheard Cayo discussing with his lawyer, that's all."

"About Cleopatra's tomb?" I pressed. "And what do you mean by *fund*, exactly?"

"Who on earth is Cleopatra?" Elvira said. "And why couldn't you have named me something like that, Mamá? Much more romantic. Instead, I got *Elvira*."

"For the last time, Elvira is stately. Elegant and appropriate. Just like Amaranta."

"Cleopatra was the last pharaoh of Egypt," I explained. "Papá talked of nothing else when they were here last."

Elvira furrowed her brow. "Pharaohs could be . . . women?"

I nodded. "Egyptians were quite progressive. Though, technically, Cleopatra wasn't actually Egyptian. She was Greek. Still, they were ahead of *our* time, if you ask me."

Amaranta shot me a disapproving look. "No one did."

But I ignored her and glanced pointedly at my aunt, raising my brow. Curiosity burned up my throat. "What else do you know?"

"I don't have any more details," Tía Lorena said.

"It sounds like you do," I said.

Elvira leaned forward and swung her head around so that she could look at her mother across from me. "I want to know this, too, actually—"

"Well, of course you do. You'll do whatever Inez says or wants," my aunt muttered, exasperated. "What did I say about nosy ladies who can't mind their own business? Amaranta never gives me this much trouble."

"You were the one eavesdropping," Elvira said. Then she turned to me, an eager smile on her lips. "Do you think your parents sent a package with the letter?"

My heart quickened as my sandals slapped against the tile floor. Their last letter came with a box filled with beautiful things, and in the minutes that it took to unpack everything, some of my resentment had drifted away as I stared at the bounty. Gorgeous yellow slippers with golden tassels, a rose-colored silk dress with delicate embroidery, and a whimsical outer robe in a riot of colors: mulberry, olive, peach, and a pale sea green. And that wasn't all; at the bottom of the box I had found copper drinking cups and a trinket dish made of ebony inlaid with pearl.

I cherished every gift, every letter they mailed to me, even though it was half of what I sent to them. It didn't matter. A part of me understood that it was as much as I'd ever get from them. They'd chosen Egypt, had given themselves heart, body, and soul. I had learned to live with whatever was left over, even if it felt like heavy rocks in my stomach.

I was about to answer Elvira's question, but we rounded the corner and I stopped abruptly, my reply forgotten.

An older gentleman with graying hair and deep lines carved across the brow of his brown face waited by the front door. He was a stranger to me. My entire focus narrowed down to the letter clamped in the visitor's wrinkled hands.

I broke free from my aunt and cousins and walked quickly toward him, my heart fluttering wildly in my ribs, as if it were a bird yearning for freedom. This was it. The reply I'd been waiting for.

"Señorita Olivera," the man said in a deep baritone. "I'm Rudolpho Sanchez, your parents' solicitor."

The words didn't register. My hands had already snatched the envelope.

With trembling fingers, I flipped it over, bracing myself for their answer. I didn't recognize the handwriting on the opposite side. I flipped the note again, studying the strawberry-colored wax sealing the flap. It had the tiniest beetle—no, *scarab*—in the middle, along with words too distorted to be called legible.

"What are you waiting for? Do you need me to read it for you?" Elvira asked, looking over my shoulder.

I ignored her and hastily opened the envelope, my eyes darting to the smeared lettering. Someone must have gotten the paper wet, but I barely noticed because I finally realized what I was reading. The words swam across the paper as my vision blurred. Suddenly, it was hard to breathe, and the room had turned frigid.

Elvira let out a sharp gasp near my ear. A cold shiver skipped down my spine, an icy finger of dread.

"Well?" Tía Lorena prodded with an uneasy glance at the solicitor.

My tongue swelled in my mouth. I wasn't sure I'd be able to speak, but when I did, my voice was hoarse, as if I'd been screaming for hours.

"My parents are dead."

PART ONE

A WORLD AWAY

CAPÍTULO UNO

NOVEMBER 1884

*F*or God's sake, I couldn't wait to get off this infernal ship.

I peered out the round window of my cabin, my fingers pressed against the glass as if I were a child swooning outside a bakery window craving alfajores and a vat of dulce de leche. Not one cloud hung in the azure sky over Alexandria's port. A long wooden deck stretched out to meet the ship, a hand in greeting. The disembarking plank had been extended, and several of the crew swept in and out of the belly of the steamship, carrying leather trunks and round hatboxes and wooden crates.

I had made it to Africa.

After a month of traveling by boat, traversing miles of moody ocean currents, I'd arrived. Several pounds lighter—the sea *hated* me—and after countless nights of tossing and turning, crying into my pillow, and playing the same card games with my fellow travelers, I was really here.

Egypt.

The country where my parents had lived for seventeen years.

The country where they died.

I nervously twisted the golden ring. It hadn't come off my finger in months. Bringing it felt like I'd invited my parents with me on the journey. I thought I'd feel their presence the minute I locked eyes with the coast. A profound sense of connection.

But it never came. It *still* hadn't.

Impatience pushed me away from the window, forced me to pace, my arms flapping wildly. Up and down I walked, covering nearly every inch of my stately room. Nervous energy circled around me like a whirlwind. I shoved my packed trunks out of the way with my booted foot to clear a wider path. My silk purse rested on the narrow bed, and as I marched past, I pulled it toward me to grab my uncle's letter once more.

The second sentence still killed me, still made my eyes burn. But I forced myself to read the whole thing. The subtle rocking of the ship made it hard, but despite the sudden lurch in my stomach, I gripped his note and reread it for the hundredth time, careful not to accidentally tear the paper in half.

July 1884

My dear Inez,

I hardly know where to begin, or how to write of what I must. Your parents went missing in the desert and have been presumed dead. We searched for weeks and found no trace of them.

I'm sorry. More sorry than I'll ever be able to express. Please know that I am your servant and should you need anything, I'm only a letter away. I think it's best you hold their funeral in Buenos Aires without delay, so that you may visit them whenever you wish. Knowing my sister, I have no doubt her spirit is back with you in the land of her birth.

As I've no doubt you are aware, I'm now your guardian, and administrator of the estate and your inheritance. Since you are eighteen, and by all accounts a bright young woman, I have sent a letter to the national bank of Argentina granting my permission for you to withdraw funds as you need them—within reason.

Only you, and myself, will have access to the money, Inez.

Be very careful with whom you trust. I took the liberty of informing the family solicitor of the present circumstances and I urge you to go to him should you need anything immediate. If I may, I recommend hiring a steward to oversee the household so that you may have time and space

*to grieve this terrible loss. Forgive me for this news, and I truly lament I
can't be there with you to share your grief.*

Please send word if you need anything from me.

Your uncle,
Ricardo Marqués

I slumped onto the bed and flopped backward with unladylike abandon, hearing Tía Lorena's admonishing tone ringing in my ear. *A lady must
always be a lady, even when no one is watching. That means no slouching or
cursing, Inez.* I shut my eyes, pushing away the guilt I'd felt ever since leaving the estate. It was a hardy companion, and no matter how far I traveled,
it couldn't be squashed or smothered. Neither Tía Lorena nor my cousins
had known of my plans to abandon Argentina. I could imagine their faces
as they read the note I'd left behind in my bedroom.

My uncle's letter had shattered my heart. I'm sure mine had broken
theirs.

No chaperone. Barely nineteen—I'd celebrated in my bedroom by
crying inconsolably until Amaranta knocked against the wall loudly—
voyaging on my own without a guide or any experience, or even a personal maid to handle the more troublesome aspects of my wardrobe. I'd
really done it now. But that didn't matter. I was here to learn the details
surrounding my parents' disappearance. I was here to learn why my uncle
hadn't protected them, and why they had been out in the desert alone. My
father was absentminded, true, but he knew better than to take my mother
out for an adventure without necessary supplies.

I pulled at my bottom lip with my teeth. That wasn't quite true, however. He could be thoughtless, especially when rushing from one place to
another. Regardless, there were gaps in what I knew, and I hated the unanswered questions. They were an open door I wanted to close behind me.

I hoped my plan would work.

Traveling alone was an education. I discovered I didn't like to eat alone,
reading on boats made me ill, and I was terrible at cards. But I learned
that I had a knack for making friends. Most of them were older couples,

voyaging to Egypt because of the agreeable climate. At first, they balked at my being alone, but I was prepared for that.

I pretended to be a widow and had dressed accordingly.

My backstory grew more elaborate with each passing day. Married off far too young to an older caballero who could have been my grandfather. By the first week, I had most of the women's sympathy, and the gentlemen approved of my desire to widen my horizons by vacationing abroad.

I glanced at the window and scowled. With an impatient shake of my head, I pulled my cabin door open and peered up and down the corridor. Still no progress on disembarking. I shut the door and resumed pacing.

My thoughts turned to my uncle.

I'd mailed a hastily written letter to him after purchasing my ticket. No doubt he waited for me on the dock, impatient to see me. In a matter of hours, we'd be reunited after ten years. A decade without speaking. Oh, I had included drawings to him in my letters to my parents every now and then, but I was only being polite. Besides, he *never* sent anything to me. Not one letter or birthday card or some small trinket tucked into my parents' luggage. We were strangers, family in name and blood only. I barely remembered his visit to Buenos Aires, but that didn't matter because my mother had made sure I never forgot her favorite brother, never mind that he was the only one she had.

Mamá and Papá were fantastic storytellers, spinning words into tales, creating woven masterpieces that were immersive and unforgettable. Tío Ricardo seemed larger than life. A mountain of a man, always carting around books, and adjusting his thin, wire-framed glasses, his hazel eyes pinned to the horizon, and wearing down yet another pair of boots. He was tall and brawny, at odds with his academic passions and scholarly pursuits. He thrived in academia, quite at home in a library, but was scrappy enough to survive a bar fight.

Not that I personally knew anything about bar fights or how to survive them.

My uncle lived for archaeology, his obsession beginning at Quilmes in northern Argentina, digging with the crew and wielding a shovel when he was my age. After he'd learned all that he could, he left for Egypt. It was here he fell in love and married an Egyptian woman named Zazi, but after only three years together, she and their infant daughter died during childbirth. He never remarried or came back to Argentina, except for that one visit. What I didn't understand was what he actually *did*. Was he a treasure hunter? A student of Egyptian history? A lover of sand and blistering days out in the sun?

Maybe he was a little of everything.

All I really had was this letter. Twice he wrote that if I ever needed anything, I only had to let him know.

Well, I did need something, Tío Ricardo.

Answers.

———— ✄ ————

Tío Ricardo was late.

I stood on the dock, my nose full of briny sea air. Overhead, the sun bore down in a fiery assault, the heat snatching my breath. My pocket watch told me I'd been waiting for two hours. My trunks were piled precariously next to me as I searched for a face that closely resembled my mother's. Mamá told me her brother's beard had gotten out of hand, bushy and streaked with gray, too long for polite society.

People crowded around me, having just disembarked, chattering loudly, excited to be in the land of majestic pyramids and the great Nile River bisecting Egypt. But I felt none of it, too focused on my sore feet, too worried about my situation.

A fissure of panic curled around my edges.

I couldn't stay out here much longer. The temperature was turning cool as the sun marched across the sky, the breeze coming from the water had teeth to it, and I still had miles to go yet. From what I could remember, my parents would board a train in Alexandria, and around four hours later, they'd reach Cairo. From there they'd hire transport to Shepheard's Hotel.

My gaze dropped to my luggage. I contemplated what I could and couldn't leave behind. Lamentably, I wasn't strong enough to carry everything with me. Perhaps I could find someone to help, but I didn't know the language beyond a few conversational phrases, none of which amounted to *Hello, can you please assist me with all of my belongings?*

Sweat beaded at my hairline, and nervous energy made me fidget needlessly. My navy traveling dress had several layers to it, along with a double-breasted jacket, and it felt like an iron fist around my rib cage. I dared to unbutton my jacket, knowing my mother would have borne her worry in quiet fortitude. The noise around me rose: people chattering, greeting family and friends, the sound of the sea crashing against the coast, the ship's horn blaring. Through the cacophony of sounds, someone called my name.

The voice cut through the pandemonium, a deep baritone.

A young man approached in long, easy strides. He came to a stop in front of me, his hands deep in his khaki pockets, giving an air of someone who'd been strolling along the dock, admiring the view of the sea and probably whistling. His pale blue shirt was tucked and slightly wrinkled underneath leather-edged suspenders. The man's boots laced up to mid-calf, and I could tell they'd traversed miles, and they were dusty, the once brown leather turned gray.

The stranger met my gaze, the lines flanking his mouth drawn tight. His posture was loose, his manner carefree, but with more careful observation, I noted the tension he carried in his clenched jaw. Something bothered him, but he didn't want anyone to see.

I catalogued the rest of his features. An aristocratic nose that sat under straight brows and blue eyes the same color as his shirt. Full lips featuring a perfect bow that stretched into a crooked smile, a counterpoint to the sharp line of his jaw. His hair was thick and tousled, walking the line between red and brown. He impatiently brushed it aside.

"Hello, are you Señorita Olivera? The niece of Ricardo Marqués?"

"You've found her," I replied back in English. His breath smelled faintly of hard liquor. I wrinkled my nose.

"Thank God," he said. "You're the fourth woman I've asked." His attention dropped to my trunks and he let out a low whistle. "I sincerely hope you remembered everything."

He didn't sound remotely sincere.

I narrowed my gaze. "And who are you, exactly?"

"I work for your uncle."

I glanced behind him, hoping to catch sight of my mysterious relative. No one resembling my uncle stood anywhere near us. "I expected him to meet me here."

He shook his head. "Afraid not."

It took a moment for the words to sink in. Realization dawned and my blood rushed to my cheeks. Tío Ricardo hadn't bothered to show up himself. His only niece who had traveled for *weeks* and survived the repeated offenses of seasickness. He had sent a *stranger* to welcome me.

A stranger who was *late*.

And, as his accent registered, *British*.

I gestured to the crumbled buildings, the piles of jagged stone, the builders trying to put the port back together after what Britain had done. "The work of your countrymen. I suppose you're proud of their triumph," I added bitterly.

He blinked. "Pardon?"

"You're English," I said flatly.

He quirked a brow.

"The accent," I explained.

"Correct," he said, the lines at the corner of his mouth deepening. "Do you always presume to know the mind and sentiments of a total stranger?"

"Why isn't my uncle here?" I countered.

The young man shrugged. "He had a meeting with an antiquities officer. Couldn't be delayed, but he did send his regrets."

I tried to keep the sarcasm from staining my words but failed. "Oh, well as long as he sent his *regrets*. Though, he might have had the decency to send them on time."

The man's lips twitched. His hand glided through his thick hair, once again pushing the tousled mess off his forehead. The gesture made him look boyish, but only for a fleeting moment. His shoulders were too broad, his hands too calloused and rough to detract from his ruffian appearance. He seemed like the sort to survive a bar fight.

"Well, not all is lost," he said, gesturing toward my belongings. "You now have me at your service."

"Kind of you," I said begrudgingly, not quite over the disappointment of my uncle's absence. Didn't he want to see me?

"I am nothing of the sort," he said lazily. "Shall we be off? I have a carriage waiting."

"Will we be heading straight to the hotel? Shepheard's, isn't it? That's where they"—my voice cracked—"always stayed."

The stranger's expression adjusted to something more carefully neutral. I noticed his eyes were a trifle red-rimmed, but heavily lashed. "Actually, it's just *me* returning to Cairo. I've booked *you* a return passage home on the steamship you just vacated."

I blinked, sure I'd misheard. "¿Perdón?"

"That's why I was late. There was a beastly line at the ticket office." At my blank stare he hurriedly pressed on. "I'm here to see you off," he said, and he sounded almost kind. Or he would have if he *also* wasn't trying to appear stern. "And to make sure you're on board before departure."

Each word landed between us in unforgiving thuds. I couldn't fathom the meaning of them. Perhaps I had seawater in my ears. "No te entiendo."

"Your uncle," he began slowly, as if I were five years old, "would like for you to return to Argentina. I have a ticket with your name on it."

But I'd only just arrived. How could he send me away so soon? My confusion simmered until it boiled over into anger. "Miércoles."

The stranger tilted his head and smiled at me in bemusement. "Doesn't that mean *Wednesday*?"

I nodded. In Spanish it sounded close to *mierda*, a curse word I was not allowed to say. Mamá made my father use it around me.

"Well, we ought to get you all settled," he said, rummaging around his pockets. He pulled out a creased ticket and handed it to me. "No need to pay me back."

"No need to . . ." I began dumbly, shaking my head to clear my thoughts. "You never told me your name." Another realization dawned. "You understand Spanish."

"I said I worked for your uncle, didn't I?" His smile returned, charmingly boyish and at odds with his brawny frame. He looked like he could murder me with a spoon.

I was decidedly not charmed.

"Well then," I said in Spanish. "You'll understand when I tell you that I won't be leaving Egypt. If we're going to be traveling together, I ought to know your name."

"You're getting back onto the boat in the next ten minutes. A formal introduction hardly seems worth it."

"Ah," I said coldly. "It looks like you don't understand Spanish after all. I'm not getting on that boat."

The stranger never dropped his grin, baring his teeth. "Please don't make me force you."

My blood froze. "You wouldn't."

"Oh, you don't think so? I'm feeling quite *triumphant*," he said, voice dripping in disdain. He took a step forward and reached for me, his fingers managing to brush against my jacket before I twisted out of reach.

"Touch me again and I'll scream. They'll hear me in Europe, I swear."

"I believe you." He pivoted away from me and walked off, heading to an area where a dozen empty carts waited to be used. He rolled one of them back, and then proceeded to stack my trunks—without my say-so. For a man who'd clearly been drinking, he moved with a lazy grace that reminded me of an indolent cat. He handled my luggage as if it were empty and not filled with a dozen sketch pads, several blank journals, and brand-new paints. Not to mention clothing and shoes to last me several weeks.

Tourists dressed in feathered hats and expensive leather shoes surrounded us, regarding us curiously. It occurred to me that they might have observed the tension between myself and this annoying stranger.

He glanced back at me, arching an auburn brow.

I didn't stop him because it would be easier to move my things on that cart but when he hauled all of my belongings out onto the dock, heading straight for the embarking line, I opened my mouth and yelled, "Ladrón! Thief! Help! He's stealing my things!"

The well-dressed tourists glanced at me in alarm, shuffling their children away from the spectacle. I gaped at them, hoping one of them would assist me by tackling the stranger to the ground.

No such help came.

CAPÍTULO DOS

I glared after him, his laughter trailing behind him like a mischievous ghost. Prickly annoyance flared up and down my body. The stranger had everything except for my purse, which contained my Egyptian money, several handfuls of bills and piastres I'd found after scouring the manor, and Argentinian gold pesos for emergencies. Which, I suppose, was the most important thing. I could try to pry the cart away from him, but I strongly suspected his brute strength would prevent any real success. That was frustrating.

I considered my options.

There weren't many.

I could follow him meekly back onto the ship where Argentina waited for me on the other end of the journey. But what would it be like without my parents? True, they spent half the year away from me, but I always looked forward to their arrival. The months with them were wonderful, day trips to various archaeological sites, museum tours, and late-night conversations over books and art. Mamá was strict but she doted on me, allowed me to pursue my hobbies with abandon, and she never stifled my creativity. Her life had always been structured, and while she made sure I was well brought up, she gave me freedom to read what I wanted and to speak my mind and to draw whatever I wished.

Papá, too, encouraged me to study widely, with a concentration in ancient Egypt, and we'd loudly discuss what I learned at the dinner table. My aunt preferred me quiet and docile and obedient. If I went back, I could predict what my life would look like, down to the hour. Mornings were for lessons in running an estate, followed by lunch and then tea—the social event of the day—and back home for visits with various suitors over dinner. It wasn't a bad life, but it wasn't the life I wanted.

I wanted one with my parents.

My parents.

Tears threatened to slide down my cheeks, but I squeezed my eyes and took several calming breaths. This was my chance. I'd made it to Egypt on my own, despite everything. No other country had fascinated my parents, no other city felt like a second home to them, and for all I knew, maybe Cairo *was* their home. More than Argentina.

More than me.

If I left, I'd never understand what brought them here, year after year. Never learn who they were so I *wouldn't* forget about them. If I left, I'd never learn what happened to them. Curiosity burned a path straight to my heart, making it beat wildly.

More than anything, I wanted to know what was worth their lives.

If they thought of me at all. If they missed me.

The only person who had answers lived *here*. And for some reason, he wanted me gone. Dismissed. My hands curled into fists. I wouldn't be forgotten again, tossed aside as if I were a second thought. I came here for a reason, and I was going to see it through. Even if it hurt, even if the discovery broke my heart.

No one and nothing was going to keep me from my parents again.

The stranger with my belongings strolled farther down the dock. He craned his neck over his shoulder, his blue eyes finding mine unerringly amid the swirling crowd. He jerked his chin in the direction of the boat, as if it were a foregone conclusion that I'd follow after him like an obedient lapdog.

No, sir.

I took a step back, and his lips parted in surprise. His shoulders tensed almost imperceptibly. He rolled my belongings a few inches forward, somehow not managing to hit the person in front of him waiting in line to board. The stranger with no name beckoned me with a crook of his finger.

A surprised laugh burst from my lips.

No, I mouthed.

Yes, he mouthed back.

He didn't know me well enough to understand that once I'd made up my mind, there was no changing it. Mamá called it stubbornness, my tutors thought it a flaw. But I named it what it was: persistence. He seemed to recognize the decision on my face because he shook his head, alarm tightening the lines at the corners of his eyes. I spun around, melting into the crowd, not caring a fig about my things. Everything was replaceable, but this chance?

It was a once-in-a-lifetime kind of opportunity.

I snatched it with both hands.

The mass of people served as my guide, leading me away from the tugboats lining the docks. The stranger yelled, but I'd already skipped too far away to make out his words. Let him worry about my luggage. If he were a gentleman, he'd hardly leave them unguarded. And if he weren't—but no, that didn't quite fit. There was something in the way he carried himself. Confident, despite the irreverent grin. Put together, despite the alcohol on his breath.

He seemed aristocratic, born to tell others what to do.

Conversations broke out in different languages, surrounding me in every direction. Egyptian Arabic, English, French, Dutch, and even Portuguese. Egyptians dressed in tailored suits and tarbooshes skirted around all the tourists, hurrying to their places of business. My fellow travelers crossed the wide avenue, skirting around horse-drawn carriages and donkeys laden with canvas bags. I was careful not to step on any of the animal droppings adorning the street. The smell of expensive perfume and sweat wafted in the air. My stomach dropped at the sight of the crumbled buildings and piles of debris, a reminder of the British bombing two years earlier. I remembered reading how the damage had been extensive, especially at the citadel where some Egyptians had tried to defend Alexandria.

Seeing the battered port in person was far different from reading about it in print.

A crowd that'd come from the docks ventured to the large stone building adorned by four arches situated in front of a long train track that spanned outward for miles. The railway station. I clutched my purse and crossed the street, looking over my shoulder in case the stranger had decided to pursue me.

No sign of him, but I didn't slow down. I had a feeling he wouldn't let me go that easily.

Up ahead, a small group conversed in English. I spoke it much better than French. I followed the crowd into the station, sweat making my hair stick to the back of my neck. The square-shaped windows provided enough lighting to see the discord. Piles of luggage were scattered everywhere. Travelers shouted in confusion, calling to loved ones, or running to board the train, while others pushed carts filled with trunks teetering ominously. My pulse raced. I'd never seen so many people in one place, dressed in various degrees of elegance, from plumed hats to simple neckties. Scores of Egyptians dressed in long tunics offered to help with suitcases in exchange for tips.

With a start, I realized I'd lost the Englishman.

"Miércoles," I muttered.

Rising on tiptoes, I frantically tried to sort through the masses. One person was wearing a tall hat—*there*. I skirted through the crowd, keeping a watchful eye, and they led me straight to the ticket office. Most of the signage was written in French, which of course I couldn't read with ease. How was I supposed to buy a ticket to Cairo? My parents warned against speaking with strangers, but I clearly needed help.

I approached them, and broke one of Mamá's rules.

———— ✄ ————

I leaned back against the plush cushion and sniffed the stale air. A layer of dust coated everything from the seating to the storage shelves on top of the benches. The train had looked sleek from the outside; strong black lines adorned with a red and gold trim, but the interior hadn't been updated in decades. I didn't care. I would have traveled by donkey through the desert if it would have meant reaching Shepheard's.

So far, I had the cabin to myself, despite scores of travelers climbing aboard, effendis heading to Cairo to conduct their business affairs, and tourists chattering madly in various languages.

The wooden door of my compartment slid open and a gentleman with a truly spectacular mustache and round cheeks stood in the entrance. His left hand gripped a leather briefcase, monogrammed in gold with the initials *BS*. He startled at the sight of me, and then smiled broadly, gallantly tipping his dark hat upward in a polite salute. An elegant gray ensemble with wide trouser legs and a crisp white Oxford shirt made up his attire. Judging by his polished leather shoes and smart tailoring, he was a man of means.

Despite the warmth of his gaze, a frisson of apprehension skipped up my spine. The journey to Cairo took about four hours. A long time to be enclosed in a small space with a man. Never in my life had I been in that situation. My poor aunt would bemoan the ding to my reputation. Traveling alone without a chaperone was scandalous. If anyone in polite society were ever to find out, there went my unsullied character.

"Good afternoon," he said as he hauled his briefcase into one of the overhead compartments. "First time in Egypt?"

"Yes," I said in English. "You're from . . . England?"

He sat directly across from me, stretching his legs so that the tassels on his shoes brushed against my skirt. I shifted my knees toward the window.

"London."

Another Englishman. I was surrounded. I'd encountered too many to count since disembarking. Soldiers and businessmen, politicians and merchants.

Tío Ricardo's hired man intent on throwing me out of the country.

My companion looked to the closed door, no doubt waiting for someone else to join us, and when the door remained closed, he returned his attention to me. "Traveling alone?"

I squirmed, unsure of how to reply. He seemed harmless enough, and while I didn't *want* to tell him the truth, he'd know it by the time the train pulled into Cairo.

"I am, actually." I winced at the defensive note in my voice.

The Englishman studied me. "Forgive me, I mean no offense, but do you need assistance? I see you're without a maid or chaperone. Quite unusual, I daresay."

I'd have to continue wearing the mourning dress I'd worn for the majority of the trip in order to continue the charade. While I enjoyed the freedom it provided, I missed wearing my favorite colors, buttery yellow and olive green, periwinkle blue and soft lavender. "Not that it's any of your business, but I'm mourning the death of my husband."

His features softened. "Oh, I'm terribly sorry. Forgive my question, it was invasive." A slight awkward pause followed, and I struggled with how to fill the silence. I didn't know my way around Cairo, and any information or insight would be incredibly helpful. But it chafed me to give the impression that I was helpless.

"I lost my wife," he said in a gentle voice.

Some of the tension stiffening my shoulders eased. "I'm sorry to hear that."

"I have a daughter about your age," he said. "My pride and joy."

The train lurched forward, and I snapped around to face the smudged window. The sprawling city of Alexandria swept past with its wide avenues and piles of debris next to stately buildings. Moments later, we left the city clear behind and edifices were replaced with long stretches of green farmlands. The Englishman pulled out a tiny gold pocket watch. "On time for once," he murmured.

"It's not, usually?"

He scoffed with an arrogant lift to his chin. "The Egyptian railway still has a long way to go before anyone in their right mind would call it efficient. But we only recently took up the management, and progress has been lamentably slow." He leaned forward, voice dropping to a whisper. "Though I have it on good authority the station will be receiving newer trains from England and Scotland."

"When you say *we,* do you mean to say the British own the station?"

He nodded, apologetic. "Forgive me, I often forget ladies aren't up to date on current affairs. We seized control in 1882—"

Any compassion I felt for his widowed state slowly eked out of me, one drop at a time. "I know all about how Britain bombarded their way through Alexandria," I said, not bothering to hide my disapproval. "Thank you."

The man paused, his lips tightening. "A necessity."

"Oh, really?" I asked sarcastically.

The man blinked in clear astonishment at my spirited tone. "We're slowly, but surely, reshaping the country until it's more civilized," he said, his voice rising and insistent. "Free from the overreaching arms of the French. In the meantime, Egypt is a popular destination for many travelers—such as yourself." The corners of his lips turned down. "For Americans, as well. We have Thomas Cook's tours to thank for that."

Papá had raged about all the ways Egypt was being *reshaped*. Managed by a foreign country who looked down at the locals, appalled at the audacity that they might want to govern themselves. He constantly worried foreigners would strip and loot every archaeological site before he could visit.

What grated against my skin was this man's assumption that I wasn't up to date on current affairs. And his supercilious tone in the way he explained the horrifying lens through which he viewed Egypt. A country whose raw materials and resources were *his* for the taking. Mamá still seethed about the Spanish mining in Cerro Rico, the mountain full of silver in Potosí. Over centuries, it had been stripped bare.

The town had never recovered.

I fought to keep my tone neutral. "Who is Thomas Cook?"

"A businessman of the worst order," he said with a pronounced scowl. "He founded a company specializing in Egyptian tours, particularly ones that clog the Nile with garish boats filled with loud, inebriated Americans."

I raised an eyebrow. "Britons don't speak in loud volumes or drink?"

"We are more dignified when in our cups," he said in a pompous voice. Then he abruptly switched the topic, probably in an effort to avoid an argument. A pity, I was just starting to enjoy myself. "What brings you to Egypt?"

Though I expected the question, and had an answer prepared, I switched my reply at the last second. "A little sightseeing. I've booked a Nile River tour. Until you mentioned it, I'd forgotten the name of the company," I added with a sly grin.

The man's face turned purple, and I bit my cheek to keep myself from laughing. He opened his mouth to reply, but broke off when his eyes fell to the golden ring glittering as it caught rays of sunlight streaming into the dim compartment.

"What an unusual ring," he said slowly, leaning forward to better examine it.

Papá hadn't told me anything about where it came from. There hadn't even been a note with the package. That was the only reason I didn't cover my ring finger. I was curious if my unfortunate companion could tell me something about it. "Why is it unusual?"

"It looks quite old. At least a century."

"Is it?" I asked, hoping he might give me a better clue. I'd thought the ring an antique, but never did I think it was an actual *artifact*. Papá wouldn't have actually sent me one . . . would he? He'd never steal something so priceless from a dig site.

Unease settled deep in my belly. I was afraid of the doubt rising like steam in my mind.

What if he had?

"May I take a closer look?"

I hesitated but lifted my hand closer to his face. He bent his head to examine it more closely. His expression turned hungry. Before I could say anything, he slipped the ring off my finger.

My jaw dropped. *"Excuse* me."

He ignored my protest, squinting to catch every groove and detail. "Extraordinary," he murmured under his breath. He fell silent, his whole body unmoving. He might have been a painting. Then he tore his gaze away from the ring and lifted his eyes to meet mine. His feverish attention made me uncomfortable.

Alarm whispered into my ear, told me to take my things and go. "Please give it back."

"Where did you get this?" he demanded. "Who are you? What's your name?"

The lie was instinctive. "Elvira Montenegro."

He repeated my name, considering. No doubt searching his memory and tossing it around for any connections. "Do you have relatives here?"

I shook my head. Lying came easily, and thank goodness I'd had a lot of practice. I'd told a frightful many to get out of afternoons filled with sewing and stitching. "Like I said, I'm a widow here to see the great river and the pyramids."

"But you must have acquired this ring from somewhere," he pressed.

My heart thumped loudly against my corset. "A trinket stall next to the dock. May I have it back, please?"

"You have found this ring in *Alexandria*? How . . . curious." His fingers curled around my father's gift. "I'll pay you ten sovereigns for it."

"The ring isn't for sale. Give it back."

"It occurs to me that I haven't told you what I do," he said. "I'm an officer for the Antiquities Service."

I leveled him with my coldest, haughtiest stare. "I want it back."

"This ring would be a marvelous addition to a showcase highlighting Egyptian jewelry. Now, I personally think it's your social responsibility to relinquish such an item in order that it receives proper care and attention. Others have a right to enjoy its workmanship in a museum."

I arched a brow. "The museum in Egypt?"

"Naturally."

"And how often are Egyptians encouraged to visit the museum showcasing their heritage? Not very often, would be my guess."

"Well, I never—" He broke off, his face deepening to the exact shade of an eggplant. "I'm prepared to pay you twenty sovereigns for it."

"A minute ago it was ten."

He quirked a brow. "Are you complaining?"

"No," I said firmly. "Because it's *not* for sale. And I know all about your profession, so I'll thank you not to explain it to me. You're no better than a grave robber."

The man's cheeks flushed. He dragged in air, straining the buttons of his crisp white shirt. "Somebody already stole this from a tomb."

I flinched, because apparently that *was* true. My father had inexplicably taken something and sent it to me. Papá had made it clear to me that every discovery was carefully observed. But what my father had done went well beyond observation. He'd acted against his morals.

He'd acted against mine. Why?

"Look here—" He held up the front of the ring for my inspection. "Do you know what's stamped on this ring?"

"It's a cartouche," I said mutinously. "Surrounding the name of a god or royal person."

The man opened and closed his mouth. He looked like an inquisitive fish. He recovered quickly and fired another question. "Do you know what the hieroglyphs say?"

Mutely, I shook my head. While I could identify some, I was in no way proficient. The ancient Egyptian alphabet was immense and it'd take decades of study to be fluent.

"See here." He lifted the ring to examine. "It's a *royal* name. It spells *Cleopatra*."

The last pharaoh of Egypt.

Goosebumps flared up and down my arms as I recalled the conversation I'd had with Tía Lorena and Elvira. That was the last time I'd heard the name—and it was in connection to my uncle and his work here in Egypt. That ring was a clue to what they'd been doing here. What—or *who*—they might have found. I was done being polite.

I jumped to my feet. "Give it back!"

The Englishman stood, fists on his hips. "Young lady—"

The cabin door opened and an attendant, a young man wearing a navy uniform, appeared within the frame. "Tickets?"

I angrily rummaged through my silk purse until I found the crumpled note. "Here."

The attendant stared between us, dark brow puckering. "Is everything all right?"

"No," I seethed. "This man stole a ring right off my finger."

The attendant's jaw dropped. "Excuse me?"

I stabbed a finger in the direction of the Englishman. "This person—I can hardly call him a gentleman—took something from me, *and I want it back*."

The Englishman drew himself to his full height, straightening his shoulders and lifting his chin. We were facing off, battle lines drawn. "My name is Basil Sterling, and I'm an antiquities officer for the Egyptian Museum. I was merely showing the young lady one of our latest acquisitions, and she became overly excited, as you can see."

"*What*—" I sputtered. "My father entrusted that ring in my care! Give it back."

Mr. Sterling's gaze narrowed and I realized my mistake. Before I could correct it, he pulled down his leather briefcase and produced a document and his ticket and handed both to the attendant. "You'll find evidence of my position detailed on the sheet."

The attendant shifted his feet. "This is very good, sir. Everything seems to be in order."

Fury burned my cheeks. "This is outrageous."

"As you can see, this lady is about to be hysterical," Mr. Sterling interjected quickly. "I'd like to change compartments."

"Not until you give it back!"

Mr. Sterling smiled coldly, a shrewd gleam in his light eyes. "Why would I give *my* ring to you?" He strode to the door.

"Wait a minute—" I said.

"I'm sorry," the attendant said, returning my ticket.

The next second, they were both gone, and that odious man took the last thing Papá gave me, burying it deep into his pocket.

 ## WHIT

For fuck's sake.

I stared after the silly chit, my frustration mounting. I didn't have time for wayward nieces, even if they were related to my employer. My employer who would be none too pleased when he found out I hadn't been able to manage one teenage girl. I dragged an unsteady hand through my hair, my attention dropping to the sizable trunks stacked high on the cart. She'd left without any of her belongings.

Bold move, Olivera. Bold move.

I considered leaving all of it on the dock but when my conscience protested, I let out a rueful sigh. My mother raised me better than that, unfortunately. I had to hand it to Olivera. She won the point, but I wouldn't let her win again. That would be annoying. I didn't like losing, as much as I didn't like being told what to do.

Those days were long behind me.

And yet.

She had the gall to dress like a *widow*. Crossed oceans unchaperoned. Told me off with a firm hand on her hip. A reluctant smile tugged at the corner of my mouth as I studied the brass button I'd nicked from her jacket. It gleamed in the sunlight, an alloy of copper and zinc and first cousins with bronze. Her outraged expression had made me want to laugh for the first time in months.

The girl had personality, I'd give her that much.

My fingers curled around the button, even as I knew it would be better to toss the damn thing into the Mediterranean Sea. Instead, I tucked the keepsake deep into my pocket. I rolled the cart back to the road where my hired carriage waited, knowing I'd made a mistake.

But the button remained safe from my good judgment.

A severe headache pressed hard on my temples and with my free hand, I took out the flask I'd stolen from my older brother and took a long drag of whiskey, the burn a soothing flame down my throat. What time had I gotten in last night?

I couldn't remember. I'd been down at the bar in Shepheard's for hours, smiling and laughing hollowly, pretending to have a good time. God, I *hated* antiquities officers.

But some four inches of bourbon later, I'd found out what I needed to know.

No one knew who Abdullah and Ricardo were searching for.

Not one whisper.

Now all I had to do was deal with the silly chit.

CAPÍTULO TRES

*E*xhaustion dragged at my edges, sucking me down like mud. By the time the carriage pulled in front of Shepheard's, my smart linen dress no longer looked smart or clean. The pressed shirt bore signs of dust and wrinkles, and somehow, I'd lost a button from my jacket. Anger had followed me every part of the journey, simmering under my skin as if my blood were boiling. The driver opened the carriage door, and I stumbled on the steps. He swung an arm in my direction to help me from toppling over.

"Gracias," I said hoarsely. "Sorry, I meant shokran." My throat was raw from arguing. No one had listened to me about my stolen ring. Not the conductor or other attendants or even other passengers. I'd asked everyone I could think to help me, sure that our argument was heard by the cabins on either side of us.

I paid the driver and focused on my surroundings. The style of architecture was so similar to the wide avenues of Paris, I could literally have been in France. Gilded carriages rushed up and down Ibrahim Pasha Street, and lush palms lined the thoroughfare. The buildings were of the same height, four stories high, and studded with arched windows, the curtains fluttering in the breeze. It was familiar when it ought not to have been. Exactly like in Buenos Aires, where streets ran wide like in the paved avenues of Europe. Ismail Pasha had wanted to modernize Cairo, and to him that had meant working with a French architect and fashioning parts of the city to look like a Parisian street.

Shepheard's took up nearly the length of one block. Steps led to the grand entrance covered by a thin metal roof with delicate openings, allowing patches of twilight to kiss the stone floor below it. A long terrace filled with dozens of tables and wicker chairs, adorned by various trees and plants, stood adjacent to the wooden double doors. The hotel was more elegant and ornate than I could have ever imagined, and the people coming out of the front entryway, dressed in expensive clothing and gowns, matched the surrounding opulence.

I walked up the front steps, trying to ignore my disheveled state. The doormen, dressed in kaftans that reached their shins, smiled broadly and together they welcomed me inside. I pushed my shoulders back, lifted my chin, and rearranged my features to look serene, the picture of decorum.

The effect was immediately lost when I let out a loud gasp. "Oh, cielos."

The lobby boasted the grandeur of the most luxurious palaces across Europe, places I'd only heard about. Granite pillars stretched high to the ceilings, resembling the entrances of ancient temples I'd only ever seen in books. Comfortable chairs in a variety of materials—leather, rattan, and wood—sat on opulent Persian rugs. Chandeliers crafted of metal in dark bronze featuring floral trelliswork and a scalloped skirt illuminated the dim interior, washing everything in a haze of warmth. The lobby opened up to another room, equally ornate with tiled flooring and dark alcoves where several people sat reading the paper.

I could picture my parents in this room, rushing in from their day out in the desert, wanting tea and dinner.

This might have been the last place they were seen.

I swallowed the lump at the back of my throat, and blinked away the sudden burning in my eyes. I looked around, surrounded from all sides by people of all nationalities, ages, and ranks. They spoke in different languages, the noise dimmed by the large rugs that had been thrown over the tiled floor. Elderly Englishwomen lamented the horrors of finding an adequate boat for the journey up the Nile as they sipped cold hibiscus tea, unmistakable for its dark purple color. British officers strode up and down the corridor, dressed in their red uniforms, sabers strapped to their waists, and with a start I recalled the hotel also served as the militia's headquarters. Frowning, I turned away from the sight of them.

In the alcove, a group of Egyptian businessmen was gathered around a table, smoking their pipes and engaged in an intense discussion, the tassels from their fez hats brushing against their cheeks. As I walked past, snippets of their conversation regarding cotton prices reached my ears. My mother often returned to Buenos Aires with brand-new bedding, the fabric thick and looking nearly like silk. The plant grew along the Nile, and the production of it was a highly lucrative endeavor for Egyptian landowners.

I spun around, looking for the main desk, as a foppish American with his stalwart briefcase and booming voice bumbled into others, marveling at the decor. Someone yelled, "Burton! Over here!" and the American gave a great start and joined the rest of his party, where he was received with claps on the back. I watched the reunion wistfully.

The number of people who would welcome me home from a long journey had dwindled.

The employees at the front desk eyed me. One of the attendants paused mid-motion at my approach. His dark eyes widened, and he slowly lowered his arm. He was in the middle of stamping a booklet.

"Salaam aleikum," I said uncertainly. His stare was unnerving. "I'd like to book a room, please. Well, actually, I suppose I should confirm that Ricardo Marqués is staying in this hotel?"

"You look so much like your mother."

Everything in me stilled.

The attendant pushed the stamp and booklet out of the way with a soft smile. "I am Sallam," he said, smoothing down his dark green kaftan. "I'm terribly sorry to hear about the loss of your parents. They were decent people, and we enjoyed having them here."

Even after months, I wasn't used to hearing them spoken about in past tense. "Gracias. Shokran," I hastily corrected.

"De nada," he said, and I smiled in surprise.

"Your parents taught me a few phrases." He looked over my shoulder, and I followed the line of his gaze. "I'd have expected to see young Whit with you," he said.

"Who?"

"Mr. Whitford Hayes," Sallam explained. "He works for your uncle, who indeed is staying at this hotel for the night. But he's not here at the moment. I believe he had business at the museum."

So that was his name, the stranger I'd ditched at the dock. I made a mental note to avoid him at all costs. "Do you know when my uncle will be returning?"

"He has reservations for dinner in our dining room. Did you just arrive?"

"This morning in Alexandria. The train unfortunately broke down halfway to Cairo, otherwise I'd have arrived sooner."

Sallam's thick, graying brows climbed to his hairline. "You came to Cairo by train? I would have thought Whit had better sense than that. Always behind and breaking down. You would have had a better time by carriage."

I decided to refrain from telling Sallam the full story. Instead, I brought up my purse and dropped it onto the counter. "Well, I'd like to book a room, please."

"There's no need for payment," he said. "You'll take your parents' suite. It's paid in full until"—he glanced down to check his notes—"the tenth of January. The room has been left undisturbed in accordance with your uncle's wishes." Sallam hesitated. "He said he'd deal with their things in the new year."

My mind spun. I never dreamed I'd sleep in their own bedroom, the one overlooking the Ezbekieh Gardens. Papá talked at length about their usual suite, the lavish rooms and pretty view. Even my mother had approved of it. Neither realized how badly I had wished to see it for myself. Now it seemed I would. This trip would mark many such firsts, things I thought I would have experienced with them. My heart snagged, as if caught on a splinter.

My voice was barely above a whisper. "That will be fine."

Sallam studied me for a moment and then leaned forward to write a quick note on crisp hotel stationery. Then he whistled to a young boy wearing a tarboosh and dressed in forest-green trousers and a soft yellow button-down. "Please deliver this."

The boy glanced at the folded note, saw the name, and grinned. Then he strode away, nimbly weaving through the throng of hotel guests.

"Come, I'll personally show you to suite three hundred and two." Another attendant, dressed in the same green-and-yellow hotel livery, took over the desk and Sallam extended a hand, motioning for me to walk alongside him.

"I remember when your parents first came to Egypt," Sallam said. "Your father fell in love the moment he arrived in Cairo. It took your mother a little longer, but after that first season, she was never the same. I knew they'd be back. And look! I was right. Seventeen years I think it's been since that first visit."

It was impossible for me to reply. Their trips coincided with some of my more terrible memories. I remembered one winter all too well. My parents had stayed a whole month longer in Egypt, and I'd fallen ill. The flu had spread all over Buenos Aires and yet my parents didn't make it back in time to see the danger I was in. They came when I was well into my recovery, the worst of it over. I was eight years old. Of course my aunt had words with my mother—several of them. Afterward, Mamá and Papá spent every day with me. Eating every meal together, exploring the city, delighting in concerts and frequent outings to the park.

We were together until we weren't.

Sallam led me up a grand staircase with a blue rug running down the center. I was familiar with the design, my parents having brought all manner of decor back to Argentina. They favored Turkish tile, Moroccan lighting, and Persian rugs.

We climbed up to the third floor and Sallam handed me a brass key with a coin-sized disc stamped with the words SHEPHEARD'S HOTEL, CAIRO and the room number. I inserted the key and the door swung open, revealing a sitting area that opened up to two additional rooms on either end. I walked inside, admiring the charmingly grouped green velvet sofa and leather chairs sitting in front of balcony windows. Silk-paneled walls trimmed in gold and a small wooden desk with a high-back leather chair underscored the stately elegance. As for the decor, there were several beautiful paintings, a gilded mirror, and three large rugs in a blue-and-mint color scheme adding sophisticated touches throughout.

"This is where your parents slept." Sallam gestured to the room on the right. "The left is an extra space for guests."

But never for me. Their only child.

"Egypt isn't as warm as you might think during the winter. I suggest a wrap over your jacket," Sallam said from behind me. "If you're hungry, come down to dine at the restaurant. Delicious food in the French style. Your uncle will want to see you, I'm sure."

I couldn't help the resentful note in my voice. "I highly doubt it."

Sallam retreated to the entrance. "Is there anything I can get for you?"

I shook my head. "La shokran."

"Nice accent," he said approvingly, and then he dipped his chin and shut the door behind him.

I was alone.

Alone in the room my parents had lived in for nearly half of the year. The last place they'd slept in, some of the last things they'd touched. Every surface drew my notice, begged a question. Had my mother used this desk? Had she sat in the leather wingback chair? Did she last write with this quill? I rummaged through drawers and found a stack of blank sheets of paper, all except one. The top sheet had two words written in a delicate hand.

Dear Inez.

She never got to finish the letter. I was robbed of my mother's last words to me. I dragged in a deep shuddering breath, filled my lungs with as much air as I could, and then exhaled, fighting to keep myself from breaking down. This was a golden opportunity to study the room as they'd left it, before it became cluttered with my things.

The waste basket had several crumpled-up sheets, and I wondered if it took Mamá several tries to think of what to say to me. A sob climbed up my throat, and I abruptly turned away from the wooden desk. I hammered down the wave of emotion, pressing in like a strong tide. Another exhale later, and I was calmer and clearer eyed. I continued my exploration, determined to do something productive. My gaze flickered to my parents' room.

I nodded to myself and straightened my shoulders.

With a bracing breath, I opened their door—and gasped.

Papá's trunks were open on the bed, clothing strewn all over, shoes and trousers lying in piles. The drawers of a lovely oak dresser were open, the items inside tossed around as if he'd been packing in a hurry. I frowned. That didn't make sense—their last note told me they were staying longer in Cairo. The sheets were gathered at the foot of the bed, and Mamá's luggage sat on a chair near the large window.

I walked farther inside, examining the dresses slung over the back of the chair. Clothing styles I'd never seen my mother wear at home. The material was lighter, and more youthful, and heavily adorned with ruffles and beading. Mother's clothing in Argentina, while fashionable, never drew any notice. She wore her modesty with a polite smile and pretty manners. She was raising me to be the same. Inside the wardrobe, rows of shimmering gowns and well-heeled leather shoes greeted me.

I fingered the fabric curiously, a feeling of wistfulness stealing over me. My mother was someone who knew the right way to comport herself; she always spoke eloquently and she knew how to host large parties and guests at the estate. But here, her clothing suggested she was more carefree, less starchy and refined.

I wish I would have gotten to know that side of her.

A sharp knock interrupted my reverie. Probably Sallam wanting to make sure I was settling in. He seemed like the kind of person my parents would have liked. Polite and competent, a good listener and knowledgeable.

I crossed the room and opened the door, an answering smile on my lips. But it was not Sallam.

The stranger from the dock leaned against the opposite wall, legs crossed at the ankle, with my trunks stacked one on top of the other at his side. His arms were folded across his broad chest, and he stared at me, a sardonic curve to his mouth. He appeared to be faintly amused.

"Mr. *Hayes,* I presume?"

CAPÍTULO CUATRO

he man in question kicked off the wall and sauntered into the room. "You're more resourceful than I thought you would be," he said cheerfully. "It's been duly noted, so don't try that shit with me again."

I opened my mouth, but Mr. Hayes pressed on with a smirk. "Before you cast judgment on my language, I'll venture to guess that a young woman who traveled across the ocean, pretending to be a widow, has most likely consigned the proprieties to hell." He bent his knees, his blue gaze level with mine. "Where they belong, I might add."

"I wasn't going to cast judgment," I said stiffly, even though I had been. Mamá expected me to observe the proprieties, no matter what I personally believed. Sometimes, though, rebellion beckoned like a siren, and I couldn't resist.

Hence my being here at all.

"Oh no?" he asked with an irritating smile. Then he ventured farther into the room, leaving the door open behind him.

"Well, *Mr.* Hayes," I said, turning my body to keep him in my line of sight. He seemed like the type of person one ought to meet head on while standing. On the docks, I'd written him off, but there was something different in the way he carried himself now. Perhaps it was his brawn, or the faintly smirking line to his mouth. He looked and felt dangerous, despite his informal conversation. He lazily walked about the room, picking up random objects and setting them down in a careless fashion.

"Thank you for bringing me my bags." And then because I couldn't quite help myself, I added, "That was very kind."

He threw me a dirty look. "I was doing my job."

"So, you work for my uncle," I said. "That must be exciting."

"It certainly is," he said. His elegant accent was at odds with the irreverent edge in his voice. He sounded like a stuffy aristocrat, except for that subtle hint of hostility lurking under the surface, and the colorful language.

He must be a recent hire. My parents had never once mentioned him. "How long have you worked for him?"

"A bit," he said vaguely.

"How long is a bit?"

"Two years or so." Mr. Hayes met my gaze every so often to distract me from his continued poking around. I let him satisfy his curiosity, thinking it might soften him. We'd gotten off on the wrong foot, and if he worked so closely with my uncle—and if I didn't want him to haul *me* to the docks like he had my luggage earlier—then it'd be wise to have a friendly interaction. But more than that, I had questions and Mr. Hayes surely had answers.

I gestured to the couch. "Why don't we sit? I'd love to talk about what work you do and my uncle's latest excavation."

"Oh you would, would you?" Mr. Hayes sat and stretched out his long legs, and idly pulled out a flask from his pocket. He took a long swallow and then held it out to me.

I took a seat on one of the available armchairs. "What is it?"

"Whiskey."

"In the middle of the day?" I shook my head. "No, thank you."

"Does that mean you only drink at night?"

"It means I don't drink at all." I was very careful to keep my voice from sounding interested. Mamá never allowed me to take even the smallest sip of wine. That didn't mean I hadn't tried it, though. I managed to sneak in tastes during one of their many dinner parties right under her nose.

He grinned, and screwed on the cap. "Listen, as pretty as you are, I'm not your friend, I'm not your guard, and I'm certainly not your babysitter. How much trouble are you going to cause me?"

The question almost made me laugh, but I caught it in time. I considered lying, but instinct told me that he'd see through me anyway. "I really can't say," I said honestly. "It might be a great deal."

He let out a surprised chuckle. "You're supposed to be stuffy and boring. A lady well brought up, buttoned up with nary a wrinkle on your gown."

"I *am* a well-brought-up lady."

He assessed me slowly, his perusal lingering on my dusty boots and my travel-stained jacket. For some reason, his observations seemed to irritate him. "But not always," he muttered. "That's terribly inconvenient for me."

I tilted my head, brow furrowed in confusion. "How exactly?"

Now the line of his mouth was thin and humorless, and he remained silent and considering, his gaze never leaving my face.

I squirmed in my seat, unused to such a direct stare. "Am I supposed to apologize?" I asked finally with an exasperated huff. "I'm not your problem. Let my uncle deal with me."

"Actually the fact that you're here at all *is* my problem. At least, your uncle will see it that way."

"I won't apologize for what I did."

Mr. Hayes leaned forward, a wicked gleam lurking in his wolflike eyes. "I didn't think you would. Hence, why you're a terrible inconvenience for me. It would have been better if I found you stuffy and boring."

Were we still talking about the docks? A feeling I couldn't identify rose within me.

It might have been alarm.

"Well, I doubt we'll be spending that much time together," I said stiffly. "But I consider myself warned, Mr. Hayes. So long as you don't cross me, we'll get along fine."

I hadn't meant to make it sound like a challenge, but I instinctively understood that was how he took my words. He seemed to be visibly at war with himself. His body relaxed in slow degrees. When he spoke again, his expression was closed off and remote, his tone of voice almost aloof. "You'll be sent away soon, anyway; it hardly signifies."

He lounged on the couch as if he didn't have a care in the world, or maybe that was the impression he *wanted* to give. My gaze narrowed. There was a directness in his stare, even as his red-rimmed eyes flickered over the room.

"Are we back to that argument?"

"As far as I'm concerned, we never left it," he said with a glance in my direction. "This isn't up for discussion. Your uncle wants you back home and far away from here."

"Why is that, exactly?"

Mr. Hayes arched a brow and remained infuriatingly silent.

"What exactly do you do for my uncle?"

"A little of everything."

I considered kicking him. "Are you his secretary?"

He laughed.

The quality of it gave me pause. "Is your work dangerous?"

"It can be."

"Is it legal?"

His grin dazzled me. "Sometimes."

"Mr. Hayes, whatever you and my uncle are—"

"What's legal and illegal in this country is very fluid, Señorita Olivera."

"Well, *I* want to know what happened to my parents," I said in a low voice. "Why were they wandering around in the desert? What were they looking for? And why wasn't Tío Ricardo with them?"

"Your parents were free to do what they wished," he said smoothly. "They were the money behind the whole operation and weren't often told what to do. The only person who had any sway over them was Abdullah." Mr. Hayes paused. "You do know who he is, correct?"

I'd heard the name hundreds of times. Abdullah was the brains behind every dig site. He was my parents' business partner, the brilliant man who knew everything there was to know about ancient Egyptians. Over the years, my parents would sometimes idly share where Abdullah's team was digging, but they'd never said a word about their latest excavation.

The one that had something to do with Cleopatra.

"Tell me more about the operation."

Mr. Hayes shot to his feet, and I startled. He drew closer to my parents' bedroom, the door flung open, and peered inside their chamber and let out a low whistle. I stood and joined him under the doorframe, once again struck by the discord.

"They weren't messy people. Well, Papá is—was—incredibly absent-minded. But this is something else."

"Yes, it is," he agreed, and for once he sounded serious. "Ricardo isn't messy either."

"I wouldn't know," I said coolly. "I've been in his company exactly one time, ten years ago."

Mr. Hayes made no comment, but silently stepped forward, carefully picking up the discarded clothing. I didn't like a stranger pawing at my parents' belongings, and I almost said so, but a realization silenced me.

He wasn't the stranger—*I was*.

Mr. Hayes knew a side of my parents I'd never seen. Knew them in ways that I never would. He had memories of them I would never be a part of. He worked alongside them, shared meals, and slept at the same campsite.

"Have you been inside the room before?"

He nodded. "Many times."

So, he had more than a working relationship with them. They were more likely to invite a friend inside their private hotel room, and not a work colleague. "Have you been inside since they've disappeared?"

His shoulders tensed. He leveled a look in my direction and stared at me for a few seconds in silent contemplation. Incredibly, the hard line of his mouth softened. "You understand, don't you, that they're gone?"

"What kind of question is that?"

"I want you to comprehend that you'll gain nothing with your questions."

I swallowed a painful lump at the back of my throat. "I will discover what happened to them."

He neatly folded one of Papá's shirts, and gently placed it inside one of the trunks. "It's your uncle who unearths things for a living. Not you, Señorita Olivera."

"But that's my aim, nevertheless."

He kept his attention trained on me and I fought the urge to fidget. If he wanted to intimidate me, he'd have to try harder than that. Despite his size, despite the gun hanging loosely at his side. The handle was engraved with the letters CGG. I hadn't noticed it before, but taking him in from his rough leather boots to the straight line of his shoulders, the unpleasant truth hit me square in the face.

"Military?"

His brows lowered, forbidding. "Pardon?"

"Are you British military?"

"No," he said.

"Those are not your initials." I pointed to the gun in his holster. "I thought your name is Whitford Hayes?"

"It is." Then he abruptly changed the subject. "Put on something frilly and decent and come down for dinner."

First, he tried to send me away from Egypt. Now he was ordering me to dinner. "Stop trying to tell me what to do."

He walked around the bed and stood in front of me, a mischievous glint hidden in the deep well of his blue gaze. The subtle scent of smoky liquor on his breath swirled between us. "Would you rather I flirt with you?"

His confidence, bordering on arrogance, must have come from having never been told *no* in his entire life. My expression remained unimpressed. "I wouldn't bother."

"Right. You're off-limits." He smiled down at me, dimples bracketing his mouth like parentheses. I didn't trust it. "Come down and join me. Please."

I shook my head. "I've traveled all this way pretending to be a widow, and while I probably got away with it, I doubtless won't be able to continue the charade here. Eating with you wouldn't be proper—not without my uncle."

"He's down there."

"Why didn't you say?" I exclaimed.

He abruptly walked out of the room, saying over his shoulder, "I just did."

With an indignant squawk, I rushed to follow him, only to encounter an empty sitting room. He'd made a mess without my noticing. Subtly moving things around; the throw pillows on the sofa no longer sat in the corner, but the middle; and the corner of the rug had been curled back. Deliberately toed aside. I made a sound of annoyance at the back of my throat.

He was already halfway down the long corridor.

"Oh, and Mr. Hayes?" I called out.

He elegantly swung around, and without checking his stride, walked backward. "What is it?"

I strode after him. "I'd like to know what it was that you were searching for, please."

Mr. Hayes stilled. "What makes you think I was looking for something?"

His tone was a little too nonchalant. His easy familiarity felt a touch too practiced, his manners the mark of someone who knew just how handsome he was. He was handling me, and trying not to show it. Suspicion pressed close.

"The rug was overturned, the pillows moved."

"So?"

I stayed silent, his lie hovering between us, creating a palpable tension in the air.

I raised my eyebrow and waited.

He made no comment but regarded me thoughtfully. When it was clear that he wouldn't give me an answer, I let out a long, frustrated sigh. "Can you wait a moment?" I asked. "I must change."

He eyed my dress in amusement. "I don't recall *you* waiting when I asked," he said with a grin. Then he *winked* at me before resuming his long-legged stride down the corridor. That was the smile I didn't trust—I just knew it came with consequences. He was the kind of person who could charm someone while robbing them blind.

I turned around and dragged my luggage into the room—a man of courtesy would have helped me—and quickly rummaged through several gown options. From everything I remember about Shepheard's, their dining room became the central hubbub of society at night. Well-to-do travelers, tourists all the way from America and the metropolitan cities of Europe would be mingling in the grand foyer. For this first meeting with my uncle, I had to look the part. Respectable and capable.

Maybe, then, he'd change his mind about sending me away.

I selected a long-sleeved navy-and-cream striped dress with a cinched waist and corresponding necktie. On my feet were slim leather boots that crept up mid-calf, their only ornament a row of tiny brass buttons. I had no time to fix my hair or even splash my face with water, and for that, I quietly cursed the annoying Mr. Hayes. I locked the door behind me and raced down the corridor, careful not to trip over my voluminous skirt. By the time I made it to the foot of the stairs, my breath was coming out in embarrassing loud huffs.

There I stopped. I had absolutely no idea where to go next. The hotel covered nearly a city block, and from where I stood in the lobby, there were a number of corridors leading to who knew where. I might end up in the gardens or in their laundry room.

I looked around, searching for Sallam, but found no trace of him. My gaze caught on the foppish American I'd seen earlier. He was sitting in an alcove, engrossed in his paper. I walked over. He didn't notice my presence until I was a foot away from him.

He looked up, blinking. He glanced to the left and then to the right, unsure. "Hello?"

"Buenas tardes," I returned in Spanish. "I'm looking for the dining room. Would you mind telling me where it is?"

His brow cleared. He folded the paper and stood, and gallantly offered me his arm. "I would be happy to assist you!"

I took his arm, and he proceeded to lead me down one of the corridors. He was tall, but he kept his shoulders hunched, his lean form lanky. He appeared to be in his early thirties, judging by his unlined face and thick blond hair.

"I'm Thomas Burton," he said, looking at me from the corner of his eyes. A deep blush bloomed in his cheeks. "You have a charming accent. Might I ask for your name?"

I was surprised to again hear myself say, "Elvira Montenegro." I cleared my throat, discomfited. "You're from America, I think?"

He nodded. "New York. Have you had the pleasure of visiting?"

I shook my head. "Not yet."

He smiled shyly. "Perhaps I'll see you there one day."

I returned his smile, somehow knowing that had he come calling at the estate, my aunt would have welcomed him with open arms. So would my mother, come to think of it. He was unassuming and friendly, with kind brown eyes. His clothing told a story of wealth and success.

We reached the entrance of the dining room. He dropped his arm and gazed at me. I shifted on my feet, dismay fluttering in my belly. I recognized that look.

"Would you . . . would you like to join me for dinner, Miss Montenegro?"

"Thank you, but no. I'm meeting family." I kept the smile on my face to soften the rejection. "Thank you for the escort."

I walked inside the dining room before he could reply. It was decorated from top to bottom in the Renaissance style. Arched windows allowed a generous stream of moonlight to touch every wooden table, covered in snowy cloth. The ceiling, painted in a creamy white, displayed a Greco pattern lining the four corners while the walls were adorned in oak panels and sculpted garlands.

Nearly every table held guests and patrons, all chattering among themselves, sipping wine and enjoying their entrees. Like the lobby, the room teemed with people of all nationalities. French tourists marveling over the wine offerings. Pashas and beys in Western clothing paired with the cylinder-shaped tarbooshes atop their heads, speaking in Egyptian Arabic. English soldiers in uniform, their brass buttons gleaming in the soft candlelight.

I took a few hesitant steps inside and the general chatter dropped to a hush. A few people looked me over curiously, no doubt noticing my messy hair and tired eyes. I tucked a few strands behind my ears. Straightening my shoulders, I took a few more steps, my gaze flickering from one table to the next, searching for my uncle.

I found Mr. Hayes instead. He sat near one of the immense windows. I had an easy view of his profile, the hard line of his squared jaw, and rigid chin. His hair looked more red than brown in the soft lighting. Four people sat at the table, and while I didn't recognize the two gentlemen visible to me, there was something familiar in the shape of the man who sat at Mr. Hayes's left.

My feet propelled me toward them as if by their own accord. I skirted around the sea of dining tables and hotel guests dressed in their expensive evening gowns and suits. The journey felt like miles, every step a steep climb up to an unknown summit. Worry dug deep in my belly, taking root. Tío Ricardo might refuse to speak with me. He might send me away in front of all these people—in front of Mr. Hayes, who clearly belonged when I didn't.

I kept moving.

Mr. Hayes saw me first.

He met my gaze, and the corners of his mouth deepened. He looked to be on the verge of laughing. The other two gentlemen observed my approach, pausing their drinking. They weren't hostile, but rather surprised. One of them eyed me over, noting the state of my hair contrasted with the ornate details of my evening dress. He was an older gentleman with white hair and beard, the regal air surrounding him all but palpable. He wore his respectability like a well-tailored cloak. The other gentleman had a friendly face and heavy-lidded eyes. I wasn't nearly as interested in them as I was in the man whose face I couldn't see.

He continued talking, a deep bass to his voice. Goosebumps erupted up and down my arms. I recognized that baritone, even after all these years.

"Sir Evelyn, you're a damned fool," Tío Ricardo said in a hard voice.

Whichever Sir Evelyn was, I couldn't guess. Neither the gentlemen nor Mr. Hayes were paying the slightest attention to my uncle, despite one of them having just been insulted. My uncle's companions were focused on me, riveted by the sight of an unchaperoned girl in a crowded dining room, clearly waiting to address them.

But I was done with waiting.

"Hola, Tío Ricardo," I said.

CAPÍTULO CINCO

My uncle's shoulders stiffened. He gave a minute shake of his head and then half turned in his chair. He lifted his chin and met my gaze. The sight of him, the familiar hazel eyes he shared with my mother, robbed me of breath. I'd forgotten how much they'd resembled each other. The curling dark hair, the smattering of freckles across the bridge of the nose. He had more wrinkles, more gray strands than my mother, but the shape of his brows and the curve of his ears were identical to hers.

Which meant I looked like him, too.

For one breathless second, fury detonated across his face, eyes narrowed into slits, his breathing harsh. I blinked and then his expression turned welcoming, a smile stretching his lips.

Master of his emotions. What a useful skill set.

"My dear niece," he said smoothly, getting to his feet. "Take this seat and I'll request another from—oh, I see they've already anticipated me." Tío Ricardo stepped closer to allow room for an attendant to dart forward, carrying a dining chair. I couldn't quite believe that after all this time, after the long weeks in getting here, my uncle stood not even a breath away. He towered over me, and while he wore his age in every line of his face, his bearing denoted a subtle strength.

His smile still in place, he patted my shoulder in a way that felt almost fond. "You're no longer the girl I remember with dirty knees and scraped elbows."

"Not for some time," I agreed. "You look well, Tío."

"And you," he said softly, "look just like my sister."

The room softened to a hush. I felt, rather than saw, the stares of every-one in the room. Mr. Hayes and the other gentlemen stood, the latter two watching me with unabashed curiosity.

"Your niece," one of the men said in a thick French accent. "*Incroyable!* But this must be the daughter of Lourdes, then." The Frenchman fell silent, a deep blush marring his pale cheeks. His balding head shined in the soft candlelight illuminating the dining chamber. "Forgive me, je suis désolé. I was very sorry to hear what happened to your parents."

"Monsieur Maspero, Sir Evelyn, allow me to present my niece, Miss Inez Olivera. She's come for a quick visit"—I stiffened, but didn't argue—"to enjoy the sights. My dear, I trust that you've met Mr. Hayes?"

Since my uncle had sent him on the errand to the docks, he knew that I had. But I played along. "I have, gracias."

Sir Evelyn inclined his head and we stood as the waiters brought an additional place setting. We sat down once all was arranged for five guests. My uncle and I were squeezed together on one side, our elbows brushing, while Mr. Hayes sat at the head of the table on my opposite side. Book-marked by the two people who wanted to send me packing.

Mr. Hayes eyed the cramped space. "I can switch with one of you."

Tío Ricardo glanced at me. "I'm comfortable, if you are?"

There was the slightest hint of challenge in his voice.

"Perfectamente."

The waiter brought menus printed on buttercream-hued sheets, the pa-per thick and luxurious. Conversation lulled as we examined the offerings, the only sound coming from Monsieur Maspero, who murmured apprecia-tively at the selections. They were extravagant: boiled sea bass, hens glazed in white wine with buttered rice, roasted wild duck paired with a seasonal salad, and Turkish coffee for dessert, with chocolate cake and fresh fruit. I wanted to try one of everything but restrained myself and ordered the chicken prepared the Portuguese way. Everyone else requested the fish, which made me think they knew something that I didn't. The waiter left, promising to bring several bottles of French wine.

"Next time order the fish," Monsieur Maspero said. "Caught fresh from the Nile daily."

"That sounds delicious. I'm sorry if I'm interrupting," I said. "I arrived just in time to hear you insulted, Sir Evelyn."

Mr. Hayes let out a choked laugh. Monsieur Maspero's light eyes darted from my uncle to Sir Evelyn. Tío Ricardo folded his arms, angling his face in my direction, amusement lurking in his hazel eyes. I could only imagine the thoughts that swirled in his mind as he tried to figure me out. But the truth was simple. I deplored empty conversation and my uncle clearly had a reason for dining with people he didn't seem to like. I wasn't going to let my presence distract him from what he was after.

That wouldn't put me in a favorable light.

Before anyone could reply, the wine came and was promptly poured into gorgeous, long-stemmed glasses. Mr. Hayes took a prolonged sip. Not partial to just whiskey, then. Sir Evelyn sat stiffly in his chair, coldly silent.

"You are correct, Mademoiselle," Monsieur Maspero said. "Your uncle sought to offend, and he succeeded. How this will help his cause, I have no idea. But perhaps it's a clever ruse to get what he wants."

"And what is his cause?" I asked.

"Are you going to answer that, Mr. Marqués?" Sir Evelyn asked in a frigid tone. "You've done most of the talking, so far."

The two men stared at each other, hardly moving except to breathe. I took my cue from Mr. Hayes, who remained quiet, his fingers fiddling with the edge of the knife next to his side plate. Finally, my uncle turned to me. "Egypt has been overrun with people who spend most of their lives in grand hotels, visiting many lands but not bothering to learn languages, who have looked at everything, but seen nothing. They ruin the planet with their footsteps, and they disrespect Egyptians by taking priceless historical objects and vandalizing monuments. These two men have the means to improve the situation here."

"Well, you have just said it," Sir Evelyn said. "We are only two men. How are we to keep tourists from defacing archaeological sites? To keep them from smuggling artifacts in their trunks? It is impossible."

Tío Ricardo adjusted his thin, wire-framed glasses. "You set the example by allowing duplicates out of the country. Hardly anything is being recorded or studied or made available to the people here. Thousands upon thousands of objects pertaining to Egyptian history are disappearing—"

"Now, be fair," Monsieur Maspero protested. "I curate the Egyptian Museum myself—"

"Oh, I know all about your *sale room*," my uncle said. "I'm shocked the mummies you've unwrapped over the years don't all have a price tag on them."

Despite Tío Ricardo's mild tone, his polite smiles, I sensed his profound dislike of the two men. It was in the way he clutched his flatware, the way the corners of his eyes tightened whenever either Monsieur Maspero or Sir Evelyn spoke.

Monsieur Maspero flushed, his mustache quivering madly. "You go too far, Ricardo!"

Slowly, I leaned closer to Mr. Hayes. His scent reminded me of the morning mist shrouding the grounds of our estate: woodsy, with the slightest hint of salt and musk. When I was close enough, I cleared my throat softly. He tilted his chin down in acknowledgment without taking his attention off the men arguing.

"Yes?" he asked under his breath.

"Sale room?"

His expression remained carefully neutral, save for the tightening of his jaw. "Maspero allows tourists to buy excavated artifacts in his museum. Statuettes, figurines, jewelry, pottery, and the like."

I blinked. "Historical objects of significance are for sale?"

"Correct."

"To *tourists*?"

"Correct again."

My voice rose. "And the money goes *where*, exactly?"

Their conversation abruptly stopped. All three men shifted in their seat to look at me. My uncle's expression held reluctant admiration.

"Back to the government, of course," Sir Evelyn said, his lips stiff and barely moving. When I had sat down he had regarded me curiously, but now he glared at me with obvious dislike. How quickly I had fallen from grace.

I straightened away from Mr. Hayes with as much dignity as I could muster.

"And the money will eventually end up in Britain. Isn't that how it works, Sir Evelyn?" Tío Ricardo asked with a knowing gleam. "I think it's fair to say that you're becoming a wealthy man."

Sir Evelyn's expression turned stony.

My uncle laughed, but it sounded off to me. As if he weren't actually amused, far from it. Tension gathered in his shoulders. "You say you're only two men, when I know countless valuable artifacts are sold in that room by foreign buyers. No one is worse than Mr. Sterling," Tío Ricardo said. "The man is a deplorable rogue."

I let out a gasp and covered the sound by coughing loudly. No one noticed. No one except for Mr. Hayes.

"Are you all right, Señorita Olivera?" Mr. Hayes leaned forward, intently studying my face. "Did you recognize the name?"

My uncle handed me a glass of water and I took a long sip, biding time in order to carefully think of my answer. Should I admit to having met the vile Mr. Sterling? But to do so, I'd have to reveal what Papá had done. He'd sent me an ancient Egyptian ring, smuggled it out of the country and never explained his reasoning. Tío Ricardo would hardly approve, nor Abdullah. Not to mention what I thought of what he'd done. Papá had lost his senses.

I lowered the glass. "He doesn't seem like someone I would care to know."

"And you shouldn't," Tío Ricardo said. "The man ought to be in prison."

"Now, see here. He's a friend—" Sir Evelyn interrupted.

My uncle snorted. "Because he makes you an obscene amount of money—"

"Who follows the law to the letter—" Sir Evelyn said.

"Laws that you have made as the consul general of Egypt," Tío Ricardo said, his hand curling into a fist around the cloth napkin. "You oversee the country's finances. It is you who has stripped Egypt of any progress instigated by Ismail Pasha. It is you who has closed schools, barred Egyptians from higher education and opportunities for women."

"I notice how you don't mention how Ismail Pasha sank Egypt into debt," Sir Evelyn said dryly. "He's the reason for Europe's involvement in this country's affairs. Egypt must pay back what it owes."

My uncle rubbed his temples, weariness etched into every line that crossed his brow in deep grooves. "Don't start with that. You're deliberately missing the point I'm trying to make."

"Eh, bien. What is it that you want?" Monsieur Maspero asked.

"Gentlemen," Tío Ricardo began after inhaling deeply. "I'm asking that you put my brother-in-law Abdullah in charge of the Antiquities Service. He deserves a seat at the table."

"But that's *my* job," Monsieur Maspero sputtered.

"He's hardly qualified, Mr. Marqués," Sir Evelyn said coldly. "When was the last time your team discovered anything? Every season you and Abdullah turn up empty-handed. You'll forgive me if I'm hardly inspired."

"If we didn't allow a legal way for objects to be excavated and removed from Egypt, then we'd have a rampant return of illegal auctions," Monsieur Maspero mused. "You must admit that my tenure has already seen a marked decrease in objects leaving the country. We must all learn to bend a little, I think."

"Ask my brother-in-law how he feels and then perhaps I'd be inclined to listen to you," Tío Ricardo said. "You know as well as I do that it's impossible to ascertain how many objects leave Egypt's borders since so many are stolen. And you *yourself* have granted permits to the Egypt Exploration Fund."

"They must *ask* before taking anything out of the country," Monsieur Maspero said, outrage dawning. "It's all under the supervision of the Antiquities Service."

Which begged the question, did the Antiquities Service employ any Egyptians? I glanced at Tío Ricardo and his clenched jaw. He was a teapot, filled with boiling water, and nearly ready to whistle. It ought to be Abdullah sitting here, arguing the point. But I understood my uncle's earlier words, his frustration that Abdullah wasn't even allowed a seat at the table.

"Have you forgotten what you do for a living, Mr. Marqués?" Sir Evelyn asked. "You're a treasure hunter like all the rest of them, and a terrible one at that. Bleeding money every month. I've heard of how you and Abdullah run your excavation sites, paying your workers exorbitant sums—"

Tío Ricardo sneered. "You mean a living wage? *No one* works for me for free—"

"—You're a fool dressed up as an archaeologist," Sir Evelyn said, his voice bellowing above my uncle's.

Monsieur Maspero let out a noise of protest. Mr. Hayes narrowed his eyes into dangerous slits. His knuckles brushed the handle of the knife near his dinner plate. I shifted in my chair, my heart thundering wildly. I stared at my uncle, at the stubborn line of his jaw, his clenched hands. Despite my earlier frustration, despite him not wanting me in Egypt at all, my admiration of him grew. I agreed with his words, and even with the ones he hadn't said.

Everyone deserved a living wage. No human ought to be treated as if their work didn't matter, or their choices, or their dreams.

"You're not a fool," I whispered to him.

Tío Ricardo glanced down at me, partly in surprise, as if he'd forgotten I was sitting next to him, practically bumping elbows.

"A *fool*," Sir Evelyn said again, and this time, his words were aimed at me.

I glared at him, my fingers reaching for my glass. I wanted to throw it in his face.

"Whitford," Tío Ricardo warned in an urgent hush.

Mr. Hayes released his hold on the knife and instead lifted his drink and emptied it in one long swallow. He leaned back against his seat, hands folded calmly across his flat belly, a serene expression settling over his countenance, as if he hadn't been contemplating murder one second ago.

Someone approached our table, an older Egyptian with a regal bearing and a shrewd gaze. My uncle noticed where I was looking and glanced over his shoulder, then immediately stood to greet the man. Mr. Hayes followed suit, but Sir Evelyn and Monsieur Maspero remained seated. I didn't know the proper etiquette, and so I remained in my seat, too.

"Judge Youssef Pasha," Tío Ricardo said smiling hugely. Then he lowered his voice and said something only the judge could hear. They exchanged more words and then my uncle and Mr. Hayes returned to their seats. The mood at the table soured further. Sir Evelyn's face had turned tomato red.

"That man is a nationalist," Sir Evelyn said stiffly.

"I'm aware," Tío Ricardo said cheerfully. "He's an avid reader of the newspaper run by Mostafa Pasha."

"Those are the people you are spending time with?" Sir Evelyn asked. "I'd tread carefully, Ricardo. You don't want to find yourself on the wrong side."

"Are you talking of war, Sir Evelyn?" Mr. Hayes spat.

I blinked in astonishment. Until now, he had seemed content enough to let Tío Ricardo take the lead in the conversation. Fury radiated off Mr. Hayes's tense shoulders.

My uncle reached across me and laid a hand on Mr. Hayes's arm. "Sir Evelyn would prefer we all behave like Tewfiq Pasha, I'm sure."

Tewfiq Pasha, the son of Ismail Pasha. I knew little of the present khedive, except that he supported Sir Evelyn's atrocious policies, dismantling whatever progress his father had made in Egypt. I recalled Papá lamenting the man's meek submission to British policy.

Sir Evelyn threw down his linen napkin and stood. "I'm done with this conversation. And if I were you, Mr. Marqués, I'd be careful with your ideas. You might not have permission to dig anywhere in Egypt, isn't that right, Monsieur Maspero?"

"Well, I . . ." Monsieur Maspero floundered.

Sir Evelyn's nostrils flared and then he strode off, spine rigid. He didn't look back as he left the dining room.

"There is much work that must be done," Monsieur Maspero said quietly. "Not all is bad, I think." The Frenchman sighed and stood, going after Sir Evelyn.

Judging by how the conversation went, this evening would have lasting repercussions. I hadn't remembered earlier, but I recalled that it was Monsieur Maspero who allowed excavators to work in Egypt. He accorded licenses as he saw fit.

My uncle might not get another.

"That went well," Mr. Hayes said dryly.

"Would you please—" my uncle began.

"Certainly," Mr. Hayes murmured. He quickly made his way through the numerous tables and chairs, the hushed gossip, and rudely staring hotel guests, and disappeared through the arched entrance.

"Where is Mr. Hayes going?" I asked.

Tío Ricardo folded his arms across the breadth of his muscled chest and studied me. Any trace of his earlier politeness vanished in the space of a blink. We eyed each other warily. Whatever assumptions he'd made about me, I wasn't leaving just because he told me to.

"Are you angry?" I asked in Spanish.

"Well, I would prefer you hadn't disobeyed me," he said. "When I think about the manner in which you traveled here, to a *different continent* . . . what do you think your mother would have said, Inez?"

"I'm here because of them."

Something shifted in his expression, a subtle tug at the corners of his mouth. A faintly discomfited look. "They wouldn't want you here, either."

His words opened a yawning pit deep in my belly. The chatter surrounding us seemed distant. I struggled to find something to say, but my throat had tightened.

His expression turned ruthless. "In all the years that they've come to Egypt, have they ever extended an invitation?"

I could only stare. He knew the answer.

"No, they haven't," he continued. "Their will named me as your guardian, and as such, you are in my care and I mean to go on as they would have wished."

"Your letter left me unsatisfied."

His dark brows rose. "¿Perdón?"

"I spoke quite clearly. What happened to them? Why were they traveling through the desert? Did they not have guards or assistance? A guide?"

"It was an unspeakable tragedy," he said through stiffened lips. "But nothing can be done. The desert eats people alive and after a few days without water or shade or reliable transportation, survival is impossible."

I leaned forward. "How do you know they didn't have any of those things?"

"It's simple, Inez," he said quietly. "If they did, then they'd still be alive."

Two waiters came to the table, laden with steaming dishes. They placed the food before us, correctly remembering who ordered what, and then left us to enjoy the meal.

"Should we wait for Mr. Hayes?"

Tío Ricardo shook his head. "Eat your dinner while it's still hot."

I took several bites, and though everything tasted divine, I hardly noticed. My uncle's behavior cut deep into my skin. While traveling on the ship carrying me from Argentina to Africa, I had dreamed of a reunion in which he'd welcome me with open arms. He was *family*, after all. Together we'd work through what had happened and then he might take me under his wing in the same way he had my parents. His refusal had struck a nerve close to my heart. He wouldn't talk to me, and he didn't want me here. I took a sip of wine, thinking furiously. How could I persuade him to answer my questions about my parents?

I thought about the golden ring Papá had sent, and the way Mr. Sterling had ogled it as if it were a diamond. An idea struck, brilliant like a lit match against shadows.

"Mamá mentioned you have a boat."

My uncle inclined his head. "A recent acquisition."

"And what pharaoh did you name it after?"

"I chose the name *Elephantine*," he said. "After an island near Aswan."

"How curious!" I said, taking another sip. The wine tasted sharp. "I would have thought you'd choose something like . . . Cleopatra."

Tío Ricardo smiled small, and then said, "I have a little more imagination than that."

"A fascinating character in Egyptian history, wouldn't you say?"

He paused lifting his fork to his mouth. "What do you know about her?"

I weighed my next words carefully. My idea felt tenuous; one wrong slip and he might continue to dismiss me. But if I could surprise him, show him that I was familiar with his life's work, and somehow allude that my parents told me more than he knew, perhaps he might let me stay.

I threw down the gauntlet.

"She loved two powerful men and bore them children. She was a brilliant strategist, and knew how to raise a fleet, and she spoke ancient Egyptian when none of her ancestors had bothered to learn." I leaned forward and whispered, "But that's not all, isn't that right, Tío Ricardo?"

"What are you talking about, querida?"

I leaned forward even more, inclining my head. He matched my posture with an amused eye roll. Very slowly, I cupped my palm around my mouth and whispered into his ear, "You're looking for Cleopatra's tomb."

WHIT

I followed the pair into the lobby, taking care to keep far enough away so they wouldn't see me, but close enough that they were still in my line of sight. Not that either of them would expect to be followed. They strode out into the night and paused on the open terrace of Shepheard's, overlooking the busy Cairo street. Four-wheeled broughams carried tourists away into the night, while donkeys with henna-stained manes cluttered the path. I hid in the shadows, near a potted palm, within hearing range of my marks. Neither disappointed my efforts.

Sir Evelyn snapped his fingers and one of the hotel attendants rushed over. He ordered a carriage and the young worker rushed off to do his bidding.

"He's only grown more intolerable," Sir Evelyn muttered. "I don't know how you can bear his arrogance."

"Mr. Marqués is usually quite charming and there's no denying his expertise, or that of his business partner—"

"Who is an uneducated Egyptian."

Monsieur Maspero made a noise of protest at the back of his throat. "I believe he has studied extensively abroad—"

"Not," Sir Evelyn began in a flat voice, "where it matters."

"You mean in England," Monsieur Maspero said in a slightly disapproving voice.

The Englishman didn't notice. "You should take my advice and bar their ability to work in Egypt. They are unpredictable and can't be controlled. If there's another 'Urabi revolt, trust that Ricardo and Abdullah will be in support of it. Them and the disingenuous Mr. Hayes."

I clenched my fists, forced myself to breathe slowly though my blood had begun to riot in my veins. The revolt had been led by Egyptian nationalists, but they lost the battle against Britain two years earlier. And now the country was under England's dominant thumb.

"I can't without grounds," Monsieur Maspero said.

"You have many!" Sir Evelyn spat. "His refusal to comply with our methods, his failing to report any of his findings, his vague and unsatisfying explanations into Abdullah's digging plans. He's a loose cannon who won't play by our rules."

"I'm not convinced his methods are all that untoward."

Sir Evelyn turned to face his companion with an air of disbelief. He seemed to visibly work to restrain himself from shouting, his mouth opening and closing. "If you need proof, I can acquire it."

Monsieur Maspero shifted on his feet, and nervously twirled his mustache. "Here! I believe the carriage comes."

But Sir Evelyn reached out and gripped his arm, his face turning a mottled red. He was like acetone drawing near a flame, readying to explode. His next words were a shout. "Didn't you hear me?"

"I did," Monsieur Maspero said quietly. And then he said something else I didn't catch, not with the noise of another party moving out into the terrace from indoors.

"I have the perfect man in place, and I already have agents at Aswan to assist him. He can gather whatever you need," Sir Evelyn said.

The words set my teeth on edge. Aswan was a little too close to Philae for my comfort. I shifted, drawing out of the shadows, trying to get a better view of the Frenchman's face. But whatever he'd said I missed it. The pair walked forward and down the steps, and ultimately climbed into a carriage. Sir Evelyn turned his head halfway, as if finally realizing they might have been overheard. It didn't matter, he wouldn't see me. And besides, I'd heard enough.

Sir Evelyn had a ready spy on his hands.

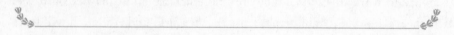

CAPÍTULO SEIS

*T*ío Ricardo slowly leaned into the plush backing of his chair, his
gaze never leaving mine. It electrified me, to have his full attention,
to have surprised him at all. My parents spent every waking moment with
him, and I heard the stories. His indomitable temper, his unfailing work
ethic, his love of Egypt. He breathed competency in every word he spoke.

In my mind, he had become a legend—one that I resented.

He was the one who had lured Mamá and Papá across the ocean like a
persistent and troublesome siren. But meeting him in person as an adult,
I finally understood why my parents had financially supported and helped
him with every one of his excavations.

My uncle inspired their loyalty.

"You believe I'm looking for Cleopatra." Tío Ricardo measured my expression for any signs of weakness. He probably thought I'd been lying.
"What makes you think that?"

"Let's have a proper exchange of information," I said. "You ask a question and I'll answer, and vice versa. I think that's more than fair. Te parece
bien?"

"I'm your guardian," Tío Ricardo reminded me mildly. "I don't owe you
anything beyond seeing to your welfare."

Anger pulsed red behind my vision. "You're wrong. You owe more than
that, and you know it. There's—"

"Oh, thank God," Mr. Hayes said as he approached the table, effectively
cutting me off. I scowled at him, but it went unnoticed. "I'm starving," he

said as he dropped into his seat with a contented sigh and glanced at my uncle. "You were right."

My uncle took this statement without so much as a blink. "Really? How interesting."

"Well, *you* might think so," Mr. Hayes said. "But it means way more work for me." He pointed a fork in my direction. "What's she still doing here?"

I bristled. "*She* is sitting right here and can speak for herself."

"I could hardly send her away without dinner," Tío Ricardo said, stroking his grizzled beard. "Inez thinks that I'm looking for the last pharaoh of Egypt's tomb."

Mr. Hayes swung his head in my direction. A lock of auburn hair fell at an angle across his brow. "That so?"

"Let's stop with all pretense," I said. "I despise it, even more than I hate being lied to. I have information that you need, Tío. I'm happy to share it with you, but only *if* you answer some of my questions."

Mr. Hayes's eyes flickered to my uncle.

"Agreed," Tío Ricardo said.

Progress at last.

I pulled a fountain pen from within my purse. I always kept one on me. The golden ring might have been stolen but I'd had months to study it at length. I knew every line, every hieroglyph. I could draw it in seconds; the resting lion, falcon and feather, staff, and the *shen* ring encircling the symbols, offering eternal protection for the person named within. My napkin would make an adequate canvas and so I unfolded it from my lap and laid it flat on the table. I quickly sketched the symbols that had been stamped onto the surface of the jewelry a thousand or more years ago. Then I laid the cloth in front of my uncle.

They both studied the cartouche and as one, very slowly, looked at me. Tío Ricardo was quietly astounded, his brows nearly reaching his hairline, while Mr. Hayes sat with a thunderous expression until it gave way to a low chuckle. His blue eyes crinkled at the corners when he laughed.

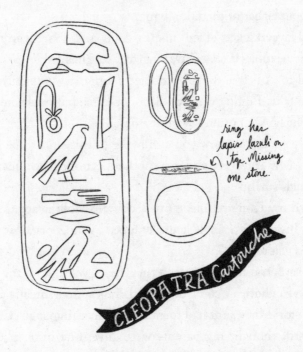

ring has lapis lazuli on top. Missing one stone.

CLEOPATRA Cartouche

"I'll be damned." Mr. Hayes took a swig from his flask. My uncle's eye twitched.

I pushed the basket of bread in Mr. Hayes's direction. "Have some bread with your liquor."

The corners of Mr. Hayes's mouth deepened. He was trying not to laugh at me. I averted my attention back to my uncle.

"And where have you seen this ring?" Tío Ricardo asked in marveling tones.

"Will you answer my questions?" I asked.

Tío Ricardo reached forward and clasped my upper arm. His thumb dug into my skin, and while it didn't hurt, it unsettled me. His face glowed with a feverish sheen. My uncle tugged my arm, drawing me closer. "¿Dónde?"

Mr. Hayes sobered immediately, eyes dropping to Tío Ricardo's hand. My hunch had been right. The ring was important, it might have even belonged to Cleopatra herself. And instead of giving it to Tío Ricardo, Papá had sent it on to me.

Without either of them knowing.

Mr. Hayes kicked at my uncle's chair and Tío Ricardo blinked and shook his head, as if slowly waking from a dream. He loosened his hold. I wanted to pull free, but I remained motionless, wondering at the best course to take. I didn't want to dishonor Papá, but how could I expect my uncle to be honest, when I wouldn't be?

"Did your father show you a drawing of this ring while he was in Argentina?" Mr. Hayes asked after another beat of silence, his attention still on my uncle's hand.

I lifted my chin and made my decision. "Months ago, Papá sent me a package. Inside was a single item." I tapped my finger against the cloth napkin. "This golden ring."

Neither betrayed anything on their faces, waiting for me to say more.

"I don't believe in coincidences." I took a deep breath and continued with my story. "My aunt had mentioned something about Cleopatra, back when I still thought my parents were alive. She implied that you were looking for her, Tío. Upon arriving in Egypt, I have since learned this ring had something to do with the Queen of the Nile herself." I raised my brows expectantly. "Well?"

"Where is the ring?" Tío Ricardo asked. He released me and leaned back in his chair.

I wouldn't answer, not until he gave me more information. "Have you found Cleopatra's tomb?"

My uncle rolled his eyes. "Of course not. Artifacts are strewn all over several excavation sites. Tomb robbers have done everyone a disservice by spreading around their *treasures*," he spat the word, "in various markets. I *personally* have found items belonging to a myriad of noble families outside of their final resting place." From here, my uncle's voice rose to a near shout. "Your father never ought to have sent it out of Egypt, much less relied on the postal service. What would have happened if the mail had been lost at sea?"

It was a good question, and Papá's behavior was so uncharacteristic as to be baffling. I could only conclude that he believed to have a very good reason.

"But it didn't," I said quickly. "Where do you think he found the ring?"

"It could have been anywhere. In another tomb, buried under a pot. He might have bought the damned thing at Khan el-Khalili, for all we know," he said vaguely. "Lord knows stolen artifacts turn up at the bazaar *all the time*."

My pulse thrummed in my throat. If he bought the ring at the bazaar, there might be a record of it. Someone might have seen Papá, might remember him.

"But enough questions," Tío Ricardo continued. "Cayo ought to have given it to me, and if you don't mind, I'd like for you to hand it over. It could be a clue."

"A clue?" I repeated as I sat a little higher in my plush, high-backed chair. "How?"

"You are not a part of the team, querida," Tío Ricardo reminded me.

"I could be if you allowed it," I argued. "I've studied the books my parents gave me. I have passable knowledge of some Egyptian history and I'm familiar with hieroglyphs. The heat doesn't bother me, nor does sand or getting dirty. I made it all the way here on my own—"

"While I'm incredibly proud of your achievements," my uncle began, "my answer is still the same. I need you to trust me on this, Inez."

"But—"

"I grow tired of this," he cut in. "Give me the ring."

I tried not to show my frustration. Any emotion from me might telegraph hysteria or something equally ridiculous. "Well, I, too, grow tired, Tío. I have so many questions. Why were my parents out in the desert? Where were *you* when they needed you? Why did my father send the ring to me? And I want to know why it's a clue in finding her tomb. I'll keep asking until I have all the information I need."

Tío Ricardo rubbed his eyes. "Now isn't the time."

"Do you know the old tales about magic?"

My uncle's eyes snapped open. "*Whitford.*"

"Certainly," I said quickly. "From my father."

"Magic has been slowly disappearing everywhere," Mr. Hayes said. "And here in Egypt, the remnants of magical energy manifested in curious weather patterns—famines, desert storms, and so on—but we have also found that some items, pot shards and the odd sandal, also have the hall-marks of old-world magic. What was incredibly interesting was that the magic *felt* the same between various things found in the same location."

"I'm following you," I said. "You're hinting that Cleopatra's ring is touched by old magic, and I agree with you. From the beginning I felt an odd tingle, or pulse, any time I wore it. I *tasted* it in my mouth." Mr. Hayes's brows rose a fraction. I waited for him to speak, but he remained quietly thoughtful. I pressed on, deciding not to mention that I had also been seeing some of her memories. They felt like . . . diary entries. A win-dow into her soul that was too private to say aloud. "I still don't understand how's it's a clue on finding her tomb, though."

"The magic clinging to the ring can lead us to other items with the exact same kind of enchantment from when it was originally performed. Objects that have the same spell call to one another. That's why it's a clue," Mr. Hayes said. "As to why your father sent it to you, I don't know."

"You have your answers," Tío Ricardo said. "I want that ring."

"So do I." I took a deep breath. "It's been stolen."

Mr. Hayes certainly knew how to handle my uncle and his stormy moods. Tío Ricardo reached into his jacket pocket and tossed a handful of coins onto the table before abruptly standing. His chair toppled over, drawing every eye to him as he stomped out of the dining room, the pair of us rush-ing to follow his quick, long strides. I watched the proud line of his strong back as he led us up to the third floor.

Mr. Hayes dug his hands into his pockets and trailed after my uncle, whistling. By the time we reached the door of my room, Tío Ricardo had calmed down somewhat. It might have been Mr. Hayes's merry little tune. My uncle held out his hand toward me.

Wordlessly, I rummaged for the brass key in my purse and handed it to him.

He walked in first.

Mr. Hayes stepped aside and gestured toward the open doorway. "After you, Señorita."

I swept past and stopped at the sight of my uncle moving things around on the desk. He ruffled through papers, sorted through books. Then he turned away, his gaze snagging on the balcony doors. There he stilled, as if trapped by some memory.

"They always had tea the day before leaving for an excavation site," Mr. Hayes said in an undertone. "Out on the balcony."

Several emotions hit me all at once. A profound sadness for my uncle, who had lost his sister and close friend. His biggest supporters and believers in his lifelong dream—a career in archaeology. Bitterness because I couldn't share in that grief, in a memory that so obviously excluded me. And anger toward my parents, wandering the desert, no doubt after some clue pointing them toward another Egyptian mystery.

How could they have been so careless?

They knew, better than anyone, the dangers of the desert. They'd been coming to Egypt for seventeen years. They didn't take the harsh sands lightly, not with storms constantly brewing, not with the risk of dehydration.

Tío Ricardo wrenched his gaze away and back to me, as if understanding what I was feeling. His attention dropped to my unadorned fingers. A frown ripped through his weathered features, and he began prowling around the room. Mr. Hayes threw himself onto one of the couches and I sat opposite him. He pulled out his flask and took a long sip. He stared into space, capping the bottle absently. It disappeared back into his pocket.

"I think you ought to look on the bright side," Mr. Hayes said mildly. "The ring isn't lost anymore."

"Whitford, use your head," my uncle said. "You know what Mr. Sterling is like."

"I do," Mr. Hayes said coolly. "And now I can go and—"

Tío Ricardo shook his head. "He won't have it on him."

My attention turned to the mysterious Mr. Hayes. He'd stretched his long legs, crossing them at the ankles, his head propped up by one of the overly stuffed throw pillows. He was lounging on that sofa as if at any moment someone were going to feed him with a silver spoon.

"The ring will be hidden away somewhere," Tío Ricardo continued, pulling me from my thoughts.

"It's not impossible," Mr. Hayes said idly.

I watched their exchange in silence, partly because I didn't have anything useful to contribute, and partly because every time I opened my mouth, Mr. Hayes shot me a look of warning. But an idea had just occurred to me, and I thought it was at least worth airing out in the open. "I can make a formal complaint with the police here. If we can have it written down on paper somewhere official that the ring was stolen—"

"Mr. Sterling has many friends with the police. Not to mention the incorrigible Sir Evelyn," Tío Ricardo said impatiently. "If you showed your face there, you'd only be turned away."

"And probably followed," Mr. Hayes added.

"Then what do we do?" I asked.

"We? *We?*" Tío Ricardo asked in a horrified voice. "There is no *we*, my dear niece. You will be leaving Egypt tomorrow."

My blood ran cold. "You're *still* sending me away?"

My uncle faced me, hands on his hips. "You came without permission. I am your legal guardian and I control your money. Whatever you might feel, I'm only thinking of your best interests. I'll book a train ticket for Alexandria at the earliest opportunity. Most likely it will be tomorrow afternoon, so I'll expect you to be packed and ready to depart." He inhaled deeply, the buttons on his starched shirt stretching across his broad frame. "Given your antics, I think it's best you stay in this room. It's quite comfortable and the food here is excellent."

I sat in total silence, a loud ringing in my ear. Was he going to *lock* me in this suite?

"Inez?" my uncle asked.

"I understood the words you said. But I hardly believe them. Am I to be kept in here like a prisoner?"

"Don't be dramatic," he said, waving his hand airily. "You don't know the city. You don't speak the language. I haven't the time or inclination to act as your tour guide. But I'll see that you'll be reasonably entertained."

This was happening too quickly, and panic reared its head. I wanted to speak louder, to somehow sway my uncle. "But Tío—"

My uncle shifted his attention to Mr. Hayes. "In fact, you can keep watch."

Mr. Hayes's face darkened. "Christ."

"If you would just listen—" I began, desperate.

My uncle held up his hand. "I think you've done quite enough, Inez. Don't you? Thanks to you, a priceless artifact is in the hands of the worst sort of human. It's time for bed. Your maid will wake you in the morning to help you dress and pack."

"I don't have a maid."

"It will be no trouble to provide you with one."

Mr. Hayes stood and strode past me without a look in my direction and exited the room without a word. Only my uncle and I remained.

"So this is goodbye, then." I took a step toward him. "If you would just—"

My uncle swooped down and kissed my cheek, and then the other. I stared after him, stunned, as he marched to the door, his long-legged stride eating the ground with every step.

"Tío—"

"Safe journey, querida sobrina," he said over his shoulder before shutting the door with a measured click. I stared at it stupidly, convinced my uncle would return a second later. The quiet in the room might have been as loud as cannon fire. A minute ticked by.

I splayed my hands, flabbergasted and annoyed. "What just *happened*?"

But of course, there was no one to answer me.

CAPÍTULO SIETE

Dawn came outfitted in rosy streaks of light, the thick gauze of the mosquito net enshrouding my bed. Dimly, I heard the last sounds of the Fajr prayer drift into my bedroom from the open balcony. I lay buried under a thick coverlet. Escaping the netting proved to be quite an exercise in patience; it took me several tries to wrench myself free. At last, I was able to untangle myself, veering toward my luggage. I rummaged through several walking dresses to find my favorite cotton robe. Slipping into it, I made my way to the balcony.

Stately green palms stretched out before me, their wispy leaves riding the breeze. The garden looked like a fairy tale against the golden morning light, far-reaching and filled with amber dates and crows fluttering from tree to tree. Beyond, a thousand minarets decorated the old Cairo skyline, beautiful and ornate. And farther still, the great pyramids in the hazy distance. This sight, more than anything else, reminded me I was far from the home I knew. Looking out into the city, I made my plan for the day.

Despite what Tío Ricardo thought or wanted, I would absolutely not be staying inside this room for the whole of the day. I stood in a foreign country, quite alone, and incredibly proud I'd made it this far. If I only had one more day in Egypt, then I was going to make the most of it and find out whatever I could. Thanks to my uncle, I knew where to start. Last night during dinner, he had given me a clue: Khan el-Khalili.

It wasn't much of one, but it was something. If I could locate the shop, I could perhaps have a conversation with the seller, maybe even the owner, and ask them about Papá. Maybe they had more artifacts that belonged to Cleopatra, or at least objects that might have been touched by the same magic as the golden ring. And thanks to Mamá, I knew about the legendary bazaar. A frequent destination for tourists looking to do a bit of shopping.

My mind settled now that I had something to do.

I only had one problem.

The insufferable Mr. Hayes.

I'd have to figure out how to evade his notice to sneak out of the hotel. To pull off something like that would take planning. Time I didn't have.

A soft rap disrupted the still quiet of the early morning. I looked over my shoulder, frowning. I pulled my robe tight across my long nightgown as I walked through the sitting area of the suite and opened the door, revealing Mr. Hayes and a young woman. The former leaned against the opposite wall, in a position so like yesterday I had to remind myself not to get my days confused. A newspaper, written in Arabic, was tucked under his arm. Today he wore wool trousers in dark gray, along with a matching waistcoat. His cotton shirt appeared to be light blue in the dim light of the corridor, and the necktie was undone. And like yesterday, his clothing was appallingly wrinkled and faintly smelled of alcohol.

"You're an early riser," Mr. Hayes commented. "And looking quite fetching *deshabillée*."

A blush warmed my cheeks despite my best effort to appear unaffected by his outrageous compliment. "Gracias," I said. "And I'm not *undressed*."

Mr. Hayes arched a brow. "You know perfectly well what I meant."

"Have you even gone to bed?"

He grinned. "I got several hours of sleep, I thank you for your concern."

I looked pointedly to the young woman at his side. "Aren't you going to introduce me?"

He inclined his head. "This is Colette. She will be your maid for the day."

She inclined her head and murmured, "Bonjour, mademoiselle."

My French was atrocious, but I managed to return her greeting.

"Ricardo has booked your train ticket for this afternoon at five," Whit said. "You'll spend the night in Alexandria, and the boat leaving for Argentina will depart early the next morning. He's still trying to secure a chaperone that will accompany you for the whole of the journey." The corners of his mouth deepened, and an amused glint lurked in his blue gaze. "No more wearing black and pretending to be a widow, I'm afraid."

"It sounds like it's all sorted," I said dryly. "Though you didn't have to tell me about it this *early* in the morning."

"I told you," he said, looking down at his nails. "Your resourcefulness was duly noted. I'm not taking any chances."

I gripped the doorknob and set my mouth to a mulish line.

"Colette is going to help you pack and dress, et cetera, et cetera," Mr. Hayes added around a huge yawn.

I raised a brow. "Long night?"

His smile pulled toward the right of his face, charmingly crooked. Probably like his conscience. "Have you not heard of the bar at Shepheard's? It's legendary. The best of humanity gathered round to gossip, deal, manipulate, and inebriate." Mr. Hayes let out a little cynical chuckle. "My kind of people."

"What an adventure! Since you're packing me off like a crate meant for the post, I guess I won't get to experience it for myself."

"Young ladies aren't invited," he said. "Because of the aforementioned gossiping, dealing, manipulating, and inebriating. Apparently your sensibilities can't handle that level of debauchery."

I found the subtle note of sarcasm in his tone intriguing. I opened my mouth to reply but he looked toward my new maid. Colette regarded me curiously when I tried to tell her in French that I didn't need her services for the day. Mr. Hayes let out a strangled laugh at my probable poor pronunciation.

"I don't need a maid to dress or help me pack," I repeated. "Why bother since I'm not leaving this room?"

"Colette stays," Mr. Hayes said, and then he turned to her and spoke quickly in French. It sounded like he was reciting poetry, and I was *ashamed* of myself for thinking it.

"You're fluent in French," I said in resignation. "Of course you are. What did you say?"

Mr. Hayes smirked. "I warned her of your general sneakiness."

Colette stepped around me to venture inside. I let her pass because I was uninterested in arguing in busy hallways. Everyone in this hotel rose early, it seemed. Guests walked in between our conversation with a polite *excuse me*.

"Now stay put, Olivera."

How were we on such informal terms? My mother would have been appalled. I think I *was* appalled.

"I dislike your mandates."

"I know. Why do you think I do it?" He tucked his hands deep into his pockets, no doubt planning something else that would likely annoy me.

"You're despicable."

Mr. Hayes laughed, and I slammed the door in his face.

After a second, I opened the door again and snatched the paper from his grip, simply to annoy him. He laughed harder as I slammed the door for the second time. By the time I made it back to my room, Colette had already pulled out one of my linen day dresses. She looked it over and nodded and then shook out the wrinkles. She carried herself with a confident air. Her appearance wasn't unexpected—my uncle had warned me after all—but studying her now, I understood that she'd be a hard person to bribe. She struck me as a person who would take her job very seriously.

Admirable of her, but inconvenient for me.

I was going to Khan el-Khalili, even if I had to steal a carriage to do it.

But first I had to figure out a way to dodge Mr. Hayes and his infuriating winks. Behind his easy smiles, I sensed he paid particular attention to his surroundings, belying an intuitive and perceptive ability to read people. And as he took care to mention, he'd noted my ability to worm my way out of hairy situations.

Colette muttered something to herself in French as she pulled out various shoe options.

"Merci."

She smiled at me. "De rien."

Colette secured the bustle around my waist and then buttoned me into the dress. She'd chosen one of my favorite ensembles, perfect for a warmer climate and not so voluminous that I'd struggle getting around. The only thing I hated about it was the standing collar, which itched my neck. Not for the first time, I wished for the freedom of movement accorded to men by their comfortable trousers. My gown consisted of a linen fabric in the softest shade of blue that reminded me of a delicate bird's egg. It had a matching parasol, ruffled and useless save for protecting my skin from the sun. Colette helped me lace up my leather boots and then sat me down to work on my hair. As usual this process took the better part of the morning. The curls wouldn't be tamed and at last, Colette decided on a thick braid that she coiled on top of my head.

"I think you are ready, mademoiselle," Colette said in a clear, accented voice.

She held out a handheld mirror and I studied my reflection. Somewhere in the crossing, I had grown up. There were hollows under my cheekbones. Hazel eyes that didn't hide the grief I carried. Lips that hadn't smiled or laughed in months. I gave it back to her, not wanting to see more, and stood up, feeling restless, yearning to go out and explore.

I was ready.

Crossing the room, Colette at my heels, I opened the door of my suite to find Mr. Hayes lounging in a narrow wooden chair reading a book. He looked up at my sudden appearance.

"I'm hungry," I explained. "Am I allowed food or a scrap of bread, do you think?"

"Such dramatics," he said with an eye roll to the heavens. "I would never let you inconvenience me by dying. I do have some scruples."

"What do you know about scruples, except possibly how to spell it?"

He barked out a laugh. "I'll order breakfast and tea. Or do you prefer coffee?"

"Café, por favor."

"Fine," he said, standing. He looked past my shoulder and switched to French. I understood nothing, but gathered he ordered Colette not to let me out of her sight. "I'll return shortly."

He walked away, cheerfully whistling. When he'd disappeared fully, I shut the door. I had minutes to make my escape. My pulse thrummed in my veins. I gathered my things: purse filled with piastres and my pencil and pad, parasol, and room key. Colette watched me, her eyebrows climbing up to her hairline and her jaw dropping at my quick movements. Before she could say or do anything, I slipped out of the room and promptly locked her in.

She banged loudly on the door, but I didn't turn back.

The lobby teemed with guests heading toward the dining room. But mercifully, there was no sign of my jailor. Mr. Hayes might have already made his way inside, or perhaps he'd gone directly to the kitchens to place my breakfast order. It didn't matter. I rushed to the front desk where Sallam stood, attending to a couple. He turned his face to meet my gaze.

"Can I quickly interrupt, please?"

The couple graciously moved to the side, and I stepped forward, holding out my room key. "I know this will sound incredibly strange but the lock on my door is faulty, and my poor maid is trapped within. Would you mind trying to open it yourself?"

"Of course!" Sallam rushed around the counter, my key tucked in his palm. "Shokran!"

He nodded and said something to an attendant nearby, who went to follow his order.

I turned away and dashed through the grand foyer, and out the double doors. Sharp sunlight hit me square in the face, but I hardly noticed. People sat at various tables situated along the front terrace, and down below the steps, the Cairo street held all manner of activity. Donkeys passed through, carrying travelers and packs alike, while horses pulled all manner of carriages. As quickly as I could, I made my way down to the wide avenue, my parasol swinging.

One of the hotel attendants dressed in the dark green kaftan saw my rapid approach. "Are you in need of transport, Madame?"

I nodded and he quickly secured a brougham, and then helped me climb inside. The driver closed the door and waited.

"Khan el-Khalili," I replied with a nervous glance behind me.

A familiar figure materialized in the open frame of the hotel doors. Mr. Hayes.

He stood scanning the terrace, his fists clenched. My heart slammed against my ribs as I sank back against the cushions, the window only partially hiding me from view. The driver nodded and moved away and the carriage rocked as he situated himself onto the seat, clicking his teeth. The reins snapped against the horse's backside.

I chanced a look in the direction of Shepheard's.

Mr. Hayes stared straight back at me. And he was *furious*.

"Go, please! Yallah, yallah!" I yelled to the driver. "Rápido!"

My transport lurched forward, the momentum pushing me backward. We moved quickly through the thickening traffic, making a turn and then another. I looked out the window, the breeze rustling my curls as my stomach dropped to my toes.

Mr. Hayes was *running* after us.

He nimbly dodged donkeys and carts, skirted around people crossing the street. When he cleared a tall stack of crates, I let out an impressed whistle despite myself. The man could hustle. It seemed no obstacle stood a chance against Mr. Hayes, even willful donkeys and stray dogs yipping at his heels.

Miércoles.

Mr. Hayes met my gaze after a near collision with a vendor selling fruit. He shouted something at me, but I couldn't make out the words. I blew a kiss at him and laughed when he shot me a rude gesture. The only reason I recognized it was because I had made our gardener's son explain it to me after I saw *him* using it against someone else.

The brougham made another turn and came to an abrupt stop.

I turned my head. A long line of traffic stood idle ahead of us. "Shit, blast, *shit.*"

A rush of rapid Arabic reached my ears. Any moment and—

The door flew open and a panting Mr. Hayes stood at the threshold. "You are"—he huffed—"more trouble"—another breath—"than you're worth!"

"So I have been told," I said. "No, don't come in—"

Mr. Hayes climbed inside and sat on the bench opposite from me.

Sweat glistened across his brow. "I had a word with your driver. He's taking the both of us back to the hotel—"

"How dare you!"

"—for your own damned good!"

He glared at me, and I matched the ferocity of his expression with one of my own. I folded my arms tight across my chest, resentful that his brawn took up so much space in the cramped interior. "Remove yourself. It isn't proper for an unwed lady—"

His jaw locked with an audible snap. "Do you see a lady present? If my sister comported herself as you have done, my mother would—"

"My mother isn't here!"

Mr. Hayes fell silent, the color leaching from his face. "I didn't mean . . ."

"I'm not your problem," I continued as if he hadn't spoken.

"For the *hundredth* time, your uncle made you *my* problem."

Our transport pushed forward at a slow crawl. I swiftly glanced at the door, considered my options, and then rose from the seat.

"Don't you get out of a moving carriage," Mr. Hayes snarled. "Sit down."

I pushed the door open, managing to take a hold of my purse, and scrambled out, tripping over my skirts, my arms windmilling to keep balance on the dirt road.

Behind me, Mr. Hayes said, "*Bloody* hell."

I heard, rather than saw, Mr. Hayes jump out, landing neatly by me. A strong, tanned hand steadied me before I toppled sideways on my accursedly long skirt. He held on to my arm as I rearranged my dress, dusting the hem to rid it of any dirt that had blown onto it from my near scrape. My carriage, I noted, continued its trek away from us, carrying my parasol with it.

"Better run if you mean to catch it," I said.

"Not without you," Mr. Hayes said.

I wrenched myself free and waited a beat to see what Mr. Hayes would do. He stayed close but didn't touch me. Instead, he gestured for me to walk onto the path lining the road. I allowed it because it was safer not to block traffic.

Once there, I stood my ground. "I'm not going back to the hotel."

"Have a care for your reputation," he said, towering over me.

"As if you care about mine," I snapped. "I'm just a job to you."

Mr. Hayes didn't bat an eyelash. He might have been made of stone.

"I'm going to the bazaar. If you want to make sure I stay safe, then come along. But don't bother trying to take me back." I poked him in his very broad chest. "I can be incredibly loud and annoying when I want to be."

"Oh, I'm aware," Mr. Hayes fumed, his blue eyes bloodshot.

I whirled and walked on, not caring which direction I went for the moment. But I felt Mr. Hayes's scheming gaze between my shoulder blades with every step I took.

CAPÍTULO OCHO

I was horribly lost. Khan el-Khalili had rudely decided to keep itself hidden, and several of the buildings all looked suspiciously familiar. They were all tall and narrow with sculpted recesses that displayed ornate entrances and front porches. Pale-skinned gentlemen wearing palm-leaf hats strode through the thick crowd as if they owned the dirt under our feet. A grand opera house added a sense of opulence to the busy street. With a jolt, I remembered how Papá had taken my mother to see *Aida,* and they had reenacted the performance for me months later. Mamá forgot the lines, and Papá had valiantly tried to carry on without her, but it only made me wish I could have been there with them. All I wanted was to share memories with them. In the end, we had all sat atop the plush rug in front of the fireplace and talked long into the night.

Grief was like a memory keeper. It showed me moments I'd forgotten, and I was grateful, even as my stomach hollowed out. I never wanted to forget them, no matter how painful it was to remember. I wiped my eyes, making sure Mr. Hayes didn't see, and strode on toward the bazaar.

Or where I imagined it to be, anyway.

Mr. Hayes followed me without saying a word for one block, and then another. When I made a turn he broke his silence. "You don't have the slightest idea where you're going," he said cheerfully.

"I'm sightseeing. I believe the dictionary would say that there's a significant difference."

"In this case, not bloody likely."

He walked at my side, keeping a careful distance while somehow communicating to others that we were together.

"I can help," he said after another moment.

"I won't believe a word out of your mouth."

He blocked my path and folded his arms across his broad chest. And then waited.

"Remove yourself from my way," I said through gritted teeth.

"You're going to have to trust me," he said with a coaxing smile.

I narrowed my gaze.

"Do you want to see Khan el-Khalili, or don't you?" Some of his anger had melted off him, and amusement curled at the edge of his mouth, a secret waiting to be told. His easy manner only inflamed my distrust. I felt as if he were *handling* me again. Accommodating me only until an opportunity presented itself.

My guard remained. "Of course I do."

Mr. Hayes tilted his head toward a street we hadn't traversed. "Then follow me."

He walked away without seeing if I'd follow. A soft wind caressed my cheeks as I deliberated. Then, shrugging, I set off after him. If he tried to trick me, I'd make such a racket that he'd come to regret it. He hadn't seen me at my loudest. He slowed to match my shorter stride.

"How far is it?"

"Not far," he said with a quick look in my direction. "You'll love it."

The street became smaller and with every step, Mr. Hayes seemed to shed the layer of aristocracy that clung to him like a well-tailored cloak. His movements became looser, his long limbs more relaxed. We crossed into a slender lane, lined with what seemed like hundreds of shops. High and narrow houses sat above the little storefronts, the upper stories projecting outward and peppered with windows bracketed by wooden shutters carved in delicate latticework.

"Oh," I breathed.

Mr. Hayes smirked. "Told you."

We were surrounded by a thick, moving crowd, dappled in sunlight from the overhead rafters that occasionally permitted rays of light to pass through. The owners of the various establishments watched the people coursing through the unpaved path, sometimes calling out prices for their wares, sometimes silently smoking. The tourists spoke mostly in English—American or British—and occasionally snippets of German, French, and Dutch reached my ears. We were in the height of an Egyptian season, and it seemed everyone from the known world had gathered onto this same road.

Mr. Hayes led the way through the throng, careful to keep us from getting squashed by the noisy and restless crowd who wandered on foot or on horseback. Women took hold of their children, guiding them while also somehow managing to shop and barter and carry on conversations with their companions at the same time. British officers in their formidable livery marched through the cramped space, keeping order.

To my surprise, Mr. Hayes eyed them with the same level of distrust as I did.

I made him stop every few feet, first to buy lemonade from a seller carrying a tin jar. He filled a brass cup to the brim and handed it to me. The first taste of the tart liquid exploded on my tongue. I immediately bought one for Mr. Hayes.

He lifted his brow questioningly.

"For taking me here," I explained. "Gracias."

"Now your manners are polite."

"I'm always polite."

He quietly said "ha" under his breath. Mr. Hayes drank the lemonade wordlessly and handed the cup back to the seller. It was then I noticed a man eyeing me openly. He wore an expensive suit, and in his left hand, he clutched a cane. Mr. Hayes followed my line of sight and glared. The man took a step in my direction, his smile leering.

"How would you like a boot to the stomach?" Mr. Hayes asked.

His mild tone didn't deceive me. Mr. Hayes was built like an explosive weapon. He towered over everyone, broad in shoulder with lean muscle. The businessman paused, glancing warily at Mr. Hayes. With a regretful quirk of his brow, he moved on.

I looked around the public street filled with shoppers. "What would you have done to him?"

"I would have kicked him," he said cheerfully. "Let's keep going."

"There's never any need for violence."

He shot me a baleful glance over his shoulder.

We proceeded down the road again, and he slid closer to me as we went on. It had been a long time since I'd been this happy, this free. Far from Tía Lorena's well-meaning lectures, far from a daily routine that left me yawning. Far from Amaranta's cold aloofness. My cousin Elvira would adore the bazaar's offerings, loving every nook and cranny. I missed her with an ache, and I suddenly wished that I'd included her on my journey.

But Tía Lorena and Amaranta would never have forgiven me.

Everyone knew Mr. Hayes, and as he passed, shoppers, vendors, and even children shouted greetings. I silently stood off to the side as some of them rushed up to him. He emptied his pockets, handing out piastres and candy. In this part of the city, he was someone else entirely. I tried to pin down the difference.

For one thing, he hadn't tried to flirt with me. For another, he wasn't ordering me around. But it was more than that. He seemed lighter, and the hard edge in his eyes had softened. And instead of trying to trick me, he had led me exactly where I wanted to go.

Nice of him—which wasn't a word that I thought I'd ever think in conjunction with Mr. Hayes.

He caught me staring. "Do I have something on my face?"

I tapped my finger against my mouth. "I'm thinking."

Mr. Hayes waited.

At last, it came to me. "You've dropped the cynicism."

"What?" He looked at me warily. "I'm not cynical."

I stepped closer to him, and he stiffened at my deliberate approach. "You're not fooling me. Not even for a minute."

Mr. Hayes straightened away from me, and his demeanor changed with every subtle correction. Retreating behind the wall he used to keep the demons at bay. His tanned hand reached for his flask and pulled a long sip. "I have no idea what you're talking about, darling," he drawled. A smirk pulled at his mouth, his blue gaze became several degrees cooler.

I pointed to his mouth. "That smile is as empty as your endearments."

Mr. Hayes laughed, and it sounded hollow, a bit forced.

"You know," I said softly, "somewhere in what I said earlier, there was a compliment."

He arched a brow. "Was there?"

I nodded.

He rolled his eyes and pulled me to a vendor wearing a turban and a long kaftan that reached his sandaled feet. His outer robe made me itch for my paintbrush; the braided cloth was gorgeous and incredibly detailed. A sash, tied neatly around his waist, completed his ensemble. He sold gorgeous little stools and cabinets inlaid with mother-of-pearl. Another vendor sold basins and copper drinking vessels, trays and incense holders. I wanted one of everything but kept my purchases to a minimum; for Elvira and Tía Lorena, slippers embroidered with glimmering beads and golden thread I found from a seller carrying several pairs dangling from one end of a long pole. For Amaranta, I bought a ruby-hued sash, even though I knew she'd never wear it.

But nowhere did I see anyone selling jewelry like the piece that was stolen from me. I took care to look through the shops carefully, but nothing jumped out at me. Frustration curled in my belly. Maybe it was foolish to even try looking. My uncle might have made a throwaway comment that I ought not to have taken seriously. He did say Papá could have found the golden ring under a pot, for God's sake.

"Are you looking for anything in particular?" Mr. Hayes asked, studying my face.

"I thought perhaps to buy myself something to replace the ring I lost. It was the last thing Papá gave me."

The hard line of his jaw softened. "It's unlikely you'll find another like it." He pulled at his lower lip, brow furrowed. It cleared when a thought struck him. "Follow me, there might be something else."

We took several turns, revealing a network of alleys opening to more shops, more people, more donkeys laden with tourists. A line of camels walked past, ill-mannered and lodging the occasional spitball at their owners. It soon became clear to me that Khan el-Khalili was divided into quarters, and each place sold similar items. If you wanted hardware, there was a specific section for that. A rug? Try the next street over.

Mr. Hayes led me to an area offering lavish jewelry, half-lit and smelling sweetly of incense. The avenue had narrowed, and it soon became impossible to walk side by side. Mr. Hayes took up the front, and I trailed behind him. At one point, he reached behind me and took hold of my hand. I looked down, stunned at the gesture. His calloused palm engulfed mine. It struck me that in the midst of such delightful pandemonium, he was a steady and calming presence.

I walked past a storefront not unlike its neighbors, but a whisper of something reached me. A burst of energy enhanced by a supernatural element. It sizzled down my spine, made my fingers tingle. My body recognized the distinct flavor of the magic, filling my mouth with a taste of flowers.

Mr. Hayes felt the vibration in my palm and immediately stopped. "What was that?"

"I don't know," I said slowly. "What's over there?"

Mr. Hayes half turned, following my line of sight. "The usual trinkets."

"I'd like to purchase something in there."

He released my hand. "After you, then."

The little shop was no more than a cupboard flung open with dozens of tiny drawers. The vendor sat on a stool within the small space, his head just visible over the counter. He regarded us with an enormous smile that made me want to buy every little thing he had off him.

I walked forward to greet the merchant. "Salaam aleikum."

"What are you looking for?" Mr. Hayes asked.

I closed my eyes, the inner pulse ticking like a clock. "I don't know exactly."

Mr. Hayes said something to the seller who immediately stood and began opening drawers, laying out his items for sale onto the counter. Bangles, earrings, anklets of filigree—absolutely gorgeous, there was no question I was buying it—tusk-shaped pendants and amulets of varying degrees of execution. There were no golden rings available, but I peered at everything, trying to identify where I'd felt that faint whisper. It seemed like I was chasing the last scrap of daylight.

The merchant held up piece after piece, and to each one, I shook my head.

And then I felt it again. The softest beckoning.

Beneath the piles of jewelry laid a small wooden trinket box, absolutely filthy. I pointed to it and the seller raised his brows and muttered something under his breath. He placed it into my cupped palm.

A sizzle of magic zipped up my arm.

An unidentifiable pulse locked into place, a profound sense of recognition. My mouth tasted as if I'd eaten a bouquet of flowers. A shadowy presence loomed in my mind, one woman who stood under a divided sky, half covered with a million glimmering stars and a milky orb casting her skin in a silver glow, the other half inflamed with a blistering heat from the sun. She wore pearls and smelled like roses; on her feet were gilded sandals adorned with jewels.

Dimly, I was aware of Mr. Hayes, who stood close, yet I could not see his face. He might have been speaking to me, but I wouldn't know it. My whole existence narrowed to one focal point, sharp as the tip of a blade. Somehow, I'd been filled with a current that pulsed with a magical force made up entirely of one thing.

Love.

The vendor gazed at me in bafflement when I pulled out my purse. Mr. Hayes looked over my shoulder at the dirty and rusty trinket box.

The shop owner addressed Mr. Hayes, speaking rapidly.

"What did he say?"

"He wants to know if you're sure you want to buy the trinket. It's already been returned once."

"I'm sure."

The shop owner said something else, and Mr. Hayes furrowed his brow in response.

I barely paid any attention. The magic vibrated out from the box in widening circles. Every inch of my hand tingled, as if the blood were stirred in a feverish pitch. The sensation overwhelmed me.

I'd never felt anything like it before, and yet it was brutally familiar to me.

Mr. Hayes watched me closely. "Are you all right?"

"Estoy bien."

His blue eyes were skeptical. "You really want to buy this dirty thing?"

"Sí," I insisted, "and the pretty anklet. Por favor."

Mr. Hayes shrugged and found out the price. After paying the merchant, I followed him down the narrow avenue, hardly looking up from studying my purchase. The scarred wooden box looked to have displayed a charming miniature painting, long since scratched off. It fit in the palm of my hand, and when I turned it on its side, I noticed a long seam running lengthwise from one end to the other. Gently, I tucked both items into my purse, the magic swirling under my skin.

Eventually we emerged from within the narrow streets of the bazaar and when my stomach grumbled loudly, he gave me a pointed look. "We are going back to the hotel for lunch."

The sun's position told me it was near noon. No wonder my stomach growled. "We are doing nothing of the sort. I'm going to Groppi."

"They serve tea and cakes at the hotel, too, you know."

My parents had raved about the establishment, a favorite among Cairo society. And I intended to try it for myself. "But do they have chocolate-covered dates?"

Mr. Hayes smiled, slow, as if he were charmed despite himself. "Your uncle would never forgive me should anything happen to you."

"What's he going to do?" I asked. "Send me home?"

Then I turned away, intent on finding a brougham to take me to Groppi. But Mr. Hayes let out a long, high-pitched whistle, and a second later, transportation was secured. He helped me into the open carriage, and I lifted a brow, waiting to see what location he'd give to the driver.

Mr. Hayes's gaze dropped to my hand clutching the doorknob, making my intentions clear. I would jump out of a moving carriage if he didn't take me where I wanted to go.

"Groppi," he said with a resigned air.

I leaned back against the cushion and smiled, triumphant.

Mr. Hayes studied me from across the carriage. "You don't do that often."

"What?"

"Smile."

I shrugged. "Most of yours are fake, so I guess it makes us even."

"Fake?"

"You heard me, Mr. Hayes."

"Oh, this is about your theory of my being cynical."

The man didn't even have the decency to look in my direction while I rolled my eyes at him. "It's not a theory."

"Why don't you just sit there and look pretty and admire the surroundings?"

I waited a beat, heart fluttering in my chest like a wayward butterfly. "You think I look pretty?"

Mr. Hayes regarded me lazily, his eyes hooded. "You know you do, Señorita Olivera."

He said it so breezily, a compliment for all women everywhere. I wondered how he'd feel if someone gave it back to him. "Well, you quite turn my head. You're so handsome."

His expression turned to one of profound wariness, as if I were a coiled snake about to pounce. "Thank you."

"Truly," I said, fluttering my hand in front of my face. "I have heart palpitations."

He kicked my bench. "*Stop* that."

I fluttered my eyelashes, the picture of wide-eyed sweetness. "Isn't this what you're looking for? I'm returning your flirtation."

"The hell you are," he snapped. "Say one more idiotic thing to me and I'm telling our driver to take us back to Shepheard's."

I relaxed against my seat, laughing.

Mr. Hayes didn't say another word to me for the rest of the ride.

CAPÍTULO NUEVE

*W*henever Mamá came home to Buenos Aires, she took me out for tea at the earliest opportunity. It was just the two of us, sitting across from each other as waiters delivered a steaming pot and matching porcelain cups, along with pastries dusted in sugar and coconut flakes. She would look me over, catalogue how much I'd grown, observe my pretty manners. She wanted to know everything that had happened while she was away. The gossip, news about our neighbors, and especially my aunt's treatment of me.

Which I grudgingly admitted to being doting.

It was my favorite time with her. I knew she was happy to see me, in the same way I was desperate for her, too. She would laugh and smile as she recounted the trip, and I could have eaten every word with a spoon. But as time went on, days turned into months, her smiles dimmed, and I knew it was because life in Argentina, *our* life, wasn't enough.

She missed Egypt. They both did.

As we neared the patisserie, an ache for my parents unfurled. I would give anything to sit across from my mother again, to hear her voice, to have her easel next to mine, the pair of us painting side by side.

Groppi's stately entrance, made of gray stone and pristine glass, loomed at the corner of a busy intersection. Inside, colorful tiles laid in a unique pattern decorated the floor. The buttery scent of fresh-made croissants and nutty coffee wafted into my nose. Mr. Hayes acquired a small round table near the back of the busy establishment. Some of the same faces I'd seen in the lobby of the hotel stared back at me. There was the party of Englishwomen enjoying ice cream, and the foppish American sitting by himself over at the next table, accompanied by his faithful briefcase. Effendis chatted among friends, sipping strong coffee and nibbling on cookies. Curious gazes watched us as we sat down together. I wore no ring on my finger, and a chaperone wasn't trailing after me like the long train of a wedding dress.

"Hark! I believe I see the remnants of my reputation being blown to smithereens."

"You asked for it." Mr. Hayes peered at me from above the edge of the menu. He sat across from me, facing the door. His attention flickered around the room, onto the sheet of paper in his hands, to the entrance, and then to the other patrons dining.

I shrugged. "I'm not from your part of the world, though I certainly know all about the *ton*, and their regimented rules for young ladies. Maybe gossip will travel across the ocean to Argentina, but I hardly doubt it. I'm not really part of society yet. None of the people here know who I am."

"Easy enough to discover your identity," Mr. Hayes countered. "People make discreet inquiries all the time. Letters reach the four corners of the world."

"Then allow me to repeat myself," I said softly. "Since my parents' disappearance, I don't give a damn."

He settled back against the chair and regarded me quietly. "Have I told you how sorry I am?"

I shook my head.

"They were fine people and I truly cared for them." There was no smirk hidden in the line of his mouth or the depth of his eyes. He gazed at me from the other side of the wall he'd erected, completely unguarded. I never dreamed I'd see him look so . . . earnest.

"When was the last time you'd seen them?"

My question shattered the moment. He shifted in his chair, visibly retreating. His voice came out clipped. "A few days before they disappeared."

"How did they seem to you?"

Mr. Hayes folded his arms. "Why put yourself through hell? They're gone, and there's nothing you can do about it."

I flinched. Not one minute ago, I would have expected his flippant remarks. I would have been prepared for his elusive conversation that went nowhere. But then he let me see the man behind his charming smirk. He'd been kind and sympathetic.

His abrupt change wounded me.

"If it were your family, wouldn't you want to know?"

Mr. Hayes dropped his gaze to the table. His lashes were thick, resting against his cheeks like outstretched wings. "Yes, I would."

He didn't say more than that. The waiter came by our small table and took our order; coffee for me, tea for Mr. Hayes. He ordered the chocolate-covered dates and two buttery croissants stuffed with Chantilly cream.

Mr. Hayes began talking about Groppi. He had plenty to say about the establishment, how most of the staff were multilingual, and how in the kitchens you'd find world-class pastry chefs. He pointed out several customers. Some were Egyptian politicians, ministers and the like, others renowned tourists. The place certainly seemed to house Cairo's upper society: Pashas, beys, effendis, well-heeled tourists, and foreign dignitaries.

As he talked, his hands gestured wildly. He was a natural storyteller, hitting the right pauses, pulling me in despite myself. I stared at his face, a study of hollows and sharp lines. His cheeks sloped at a harsh angle, and the curve of his mouth hinted at someone who knew how to tell a lie. Altogether, his face displayed an outward affability that disguised a wary bitterness hidden in the depth of his pale, wolflike eyes.

I pulled out my sketch pad from within my purse. My fingers itched to capture the way he looked right this moment. The portable size made it easy to bring with me wherever I went, and its pages were filled with drawings of my fellow passengers on the steamship and the balcony of my suite, overlooking the gardens. In seconds, I drew the Mr. Hayes I knew the best: a steady stare that didn't fully disguise the turmoil he kept just out of reach. I used a napkin to smudge the harsh charcoal lines, softening the tension he carried across his brow.

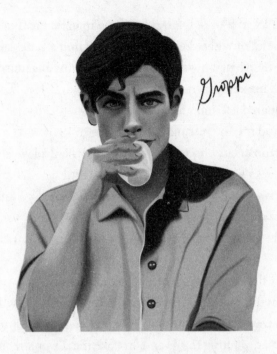

When I finished, Mr. Hayes pulled my pad over to his side of the table and flipped through the pages.

"Not bad," he mused, a smile lifting the corner of his mouth.

"Not bad was *exactly* what I was going for," I said.

"Stop fishing for compliments," Mr. Hayes said, still flipping through my drawings. "You respond to the wrong ones, anyway."

I lifted a brow, but he didn't notice. It struck me, then, that he kept expecting me to act one way and my refusal to do so infuriated him. I vowed not to alter my behavior.

He let out a laugh and held up a page. "Is this supposed to be me? You've drawn my jawline too stubborn."

I regarded the sharp line of his squared jaw. "No, I haven't."

"There are no pictures of you in here."

"What for? I like to draw people who interest me."

He stilled and I realized what I'd said. Frantically, I tried to think of a way to take the words back, but nothing came to mind. A slow realization trickled through my mind, moving like honey. I'd spoken the truth, and whether I liked it or not, Mr. Hayes *did* interest me. For all the things he didn't say, the thoughts he kept hidden behind a quicksilver grin. Despite myself, my attention was frequently caught by his muscled forearms, and the blunt fingers edged around a strong palm. His bottom lip drew my notice, squared off and cut with immaculate precision.

"So, you find me interesting."

I said nothing, curious to see what game he'd play. He was always playing one.

"What is it *exactly* that interests you?" A wicked gleam lit his eyes. He leaned forward, curling over the table, taking up too much space to ignore. His nearness quickened my pulse. "Have you thought about kissing me?"

He uttered that irritating question with a straight face.

But I knew he was drawing battle lines. Firing where he could and warning me away. Resolve hardened me. He chose the way of the mask-wearing charmer, wanting to rile and provoke me. I wouldn't be ensnared in his plan, the same way he kept everyone else continuously at arm's length. His strategy was simple and brilliant; by flirting, he kept the conversation from anything meaningful.

"If you haven't guessed," I began quietly, "I have a lot more in common with my parents than you might think. Like them, I like to discover the truth. Hidden things have always fascinated me. And you, Mr. Hayes, have a secret. It's long since been buried, but I know it's there. And one day, I will uncover it. Mark my words."

He looked down at his fingernails. "Are you sure that's wise?"

"I traveled here all on my own," I said. "Lied through my teeth to anyone I met, disobeyed my uncle at every turn. What makes you think that I'm wise?"

Mr. Hayes lifted his face and glowered at me. "I'm telling you to stay out of my business. You won't like what you find, I promise you."

"I've always been too curious for my own good."

"Well, it's a good thing that you're leaving in a matter of hours."

My mood soured and I abruptly changed the subject. "What brought you to Egypt? You never said."

Mr. Hayes flipped the cover of my pad in place and pushed it back to me. "Duty."

I gestured for him to continue, but our food arrived, and Mr. Hayes busied himself by plucking one of the croissants and putting it on his plate. With little fanfare, he bit into it and moaned. "This is the first thing you have to try."

He cut half of another one and slid it onto my plate. I took a bite and found myself making the exact same sound he did. Somehow, the pastry was both sweet and salty, creamy and decadent.

"Does it live up to your expectations?"

"Everything here has. I can see why my parents couldn't get enough." I looked around wistfully, taking in the various patrons situated around us, enjoying their ice cream and enormous slices of cake. "I wish my uncle would give me more time." I popped another bite of the dessert into my mouth.

"He has none to spare." Mr. Hayes wiped his fingers with a cloth napkin. "We're leaving tonight."

I choked on a date. "What?"

He sat motionless, visibly weighing his response. After a beat he said, "We're to board the *Elephantine* after dinner this evening. Early next morning, we sail for the excavation site from Bulaq."

"Where is that?" I tried to keep my tone neutral, but the idea of them sailing up the Nile without me stung. I hadn't found the shop where Papá might have bought the golden ring. I hadn't discovered anything of note regarding my parents' disappearance.

"Clear across the city," Mr. Hayes said, his voice oddly gentle. "Come now. No need to look as if you've lost your puppy. You can always come back once your uncle's temper has cooled down. He only wants to keep you safe, and he can't be expected to watch over you while running an excavation team."

I bristled. "Why do you and my uncle insist that I'm in some kind of danger? Look around! There seem to be plenty of tourists enjoying the sights. Cairo looks perfectly safe to me."

Mr. Hayes's eyes glittered a frozen blue. "Does it?"

"Did you know you ask a question when you wish to avoid a subject?"

"Do I?"

"Yes. It's unspeakably annoying."

Mr. Hayes rearranged his handsome features into a look of contrition, which I didn't believe. "Sorry, Señorita Olivera."

We stared at each other in cold silence until he grudgingly said, "Cairo *is* perfectly safe. Ricardo isn't worried about that. He has other reasons."

"And they are?"

"You'll have to speak to him."

Everything came back to my uncle. I couldn't tear my gaze away from the large clock hanging on the wall. Every tick forward meant one minute lost. I only had a few hours left to figure out my next move. Otherwise, Tío Ricardo and his team would sail up the Nile without me. My attention swerved away from my irritating companion and to the other people dining around us, filling every available table.

One man in particular seemed very familiar to me. The slicked-back hair, the cut of his coat. I looked closely. The Englishman turned his head, lifting his coffee to his pursed mouth. The man's profile struck a chord deep in my belly. My gaze flickered to his companion. My body recognized him before my mind did, a deep feeling of unease pooling in my belly. Hot anger ran up my throat.

The white-haired gentleman was Sir Evelyn. The man on his right was Mr. Sterling.

And on his littlest finger, he wore Cleopatra's golden ring.

CAPÍTULO DIEZ

I had several options and none of them were suitable. I could stand and yell *thief* at the top of my voice or march over to their table and demand Mr. Sterling return the ring. Logic begged me to use my head, to not draw undue attention onto myself. Mr. Sterling never found out my real name, but if he spotted me now, he might be able to follow me or, at the very least, inquire after my companion.

Mr. Hayes was well-known in this part of the world.

Surreptitiously, I glanced toward Sir Evelyn and the toad-faced Mr. Sterling. This afternoon he certainly looked like one in his green velvet smoking jacket and matching waistcoat. Mr. Hayes followed my gaze and raised his brows.

"Do you see what I see?" I asked in a low murmur.

Mr. Hayes stood. "I'm always aware of my surroundings."

"Well, I don't want him to notice me so it's best if we're off."

"Right." He left money on the table and then took my arm and swiftly led me through the large dining space. "Time to return to the hotel."

We hurried outside and Mr. Hayes strode to the sidewalk and let out another sharp whistle. A carriage pulled up to the curb and after helping me climb in, he settled in the seat across from mine. He gave directions to the driver and we lurched forward.

"Are you going to attempt to retrieve the ring from Mr. Sterling?" I whispered.

Mr. Hayes continued to peer outside, one finger lightly tapping on the window frame. "Have you asked yourself why he's wearing it at all?"

I shook my head. "I was angry and unable to think beyond that. The way he took it from me, the arrogance, quite literally made me see red. You should have heard the way he made me out to be *hysterical*. Someone to be dismissed."

His lips flattened to a pale slash. "Bastard."

I stared at him, aghast. Slowly, he was becoming someone I could call a friend. I wasn't sure how I felt about that. It would be easier if I didn't like him at all. I cleared my throat. "You haven't answered my question."

"If he's wearing it, then retrieving it might be impossible. I'm more concerned that he's *flaunting* it."

I didn't understand his point. "Why does it concern you?"

"With the ring in his possession, he'd know that his best chance in finding Cleopatra's tomb would be to let the magic guide him, as each kind attracts and recognizes its own. Mr. Sterling will have told everyone of his findings and he'll secure a firman—"

"I don't know that word," I broke in.

"A license to excavate. Monsieur Maspero evaluates everyone's applications, and he decides who digs where. Your uncle is under constant threat to lose his for the season."

I shook my head, trying to make sense of the situation. "But with only the ring to guide Mr. Sterling, he'd have to visit every site up and down the Nile. That would take months."

"How much do you know of Cleopatra's life?" he asked.

"Very little," I admitted. "I've read Shakespeare."

"*And you shall see in him, the triple pillar of the world transformed into a strumpet's fool,*" Mr. Hayes quoted, and I blinked at him in shock.

"You've read it?"

He rolled his eyes and continued. "Cleopatra commanded a fleet, battled insurrections, controlled Egypt's vast wealth, and survived famines. All that and history likes to portray her as a mere slip of a woman, a saucy vixen luring men to their downfalls. It's a shame Romans never bothered to understand her. They were guilty of so much worse. Waging war, plundering what they found, and ruling without compromise." Any good humor fled from his face, leaving behind a subtle wary bitterness. "And it's happening all over again in Egypt. Everyone wants something, the French and Dutch, and imperial Britain."

"It was awful to read about," I said, remembering how I used to scour some of the newspapers my parents had brought home with them from their travels. "Even worse to see it in action. Knowing something in theory is nothing compared to the real thing."

Mr. Hayes nodded, his eyes intent on my face, and then they widened in shock. "Did we just agree on something?"

"An anomaly, I'm sure," I said with a little laugh. "As long as we don't speak about your countrymen, I think we'll be safe."

Mr. Hayes twisted his lips into a scowl. I was used to seeing his smirk or smug smile, the mischievous glint barely hidden in his direct gaze. His expression of real distaste took me by surprise. "They are my countrymen in the loosest sense of the word. I'm sure they'd love to kick me out entirely. Not that I'd complain," he added in a whisper.

"And be a man without country? Family?"

He stilled and then fixed me with a flirty grin. "Why, do you want to take me in?"

But I refused to allow him to change the subject with a glib comment. He might think to distract me, but he'd said something that piqued my curiosity. "Why would Britain want to kick you out of the country?"

"Perhaps I was too wild."

I eyed his wrinkled shirt, the unbuttoned collar, and the unpolished leather of his boots. A sharp contrast to a soldier's pressed uniform, trimmed hair, and gleaming shoes. But nothing could detract from his brawny frame, honed by years of activity and training, his face tanned from the outdoors. The gun at his hip, carved with initials that weren't his own. He might have left the army, but the evidence of his time there was certainly present. "So, you disobeyed them?"

"Tell me," he said slowly. "What do I have to do to get you to stop asking me questions?"

"Answer one of them."

He laughed. "Your curiosity has no sense of decency."

I leaned forward and the corners of his mouth deepened at the invasion of his space. He remained motionless, perfectly at ease to see how far I'd go.

"You have no idea, Mr. Hayes. How long were you in the military?"

"Since I was fifteen."

"Do you have siblings?"

"Two; I'm the youngest son."

"Fated to be a soldier."

I struck a nerve. The sharp line of his jaw hardened. "We seem to have strayed off topic," he said. "I was telling you about Cleopatra. Unless you'd like to ask me any more invasive questions?"

I'd learned enough. Mr. Hayes was the spare in his family, probably twice over if the wary bitterness that had crept in his eyes were any indication. He had quit the army—to the displeasure of the people who counted on him to uphold reputation and duty.

"According to the ancient historians Herodotus and Plutarch, she spent most of her time in the palace of Alexandria—"

"I didn't know there was one," I interrupted.

"No one knows where it is," he said. He threw me a sly look. "Cleopatra might very well be buried there. But she claimed a kinship with the Egyptian goddess Isis, wife to Osiris and mistress of the sky. There are a few temples still standing today that venerate her. My point is that Mr. Sterling won't have to search *every* known site."

Realization dawned. "You're saying there is only a handful of places she might be."

He nodded grimly. "He might very well find her, and with the ring he stole, his way was made that much easier. That's *if* the magic latched on to him."

The carriage slowed and I leaned forward to look out the window. The driver pulled up in front of Shepheard's grand entrance, its terrace occupied by several dozens of hotel guests drinking afternoon tea. Plenty of shade from the palms provided respite from the glaring sun.

"On the bright side," Mr. Hayes murmured near my ear, "this is not your problem."

I turned my head, met his eyes. "But it is, and my uncle is doing me a huge disservice by sending me away."

Our faces were close. Sunlight dappled his auburn hair, crisscrossed over his aristocratic nose. The blue in his gaze was the palest shade of cornflower. I couldn't discern the peculiar expression on his face. Our breaths shared the smallest space between his mouth and mine. His smelled like whiskey. I wondered what drove him to keep the liquor on him at all times.

Then he drew away, opened the door, and stepped out. He turned and helped me out of the brougham, his hand holding mine for a beat too long.

"I'll pay the driver and collect your purchases for you. I'll have them sent up to your room."

"Gracias."

"De nada," he said so politely that I blinked.

He released me and I went up to the terrace. The carriage pulled away, and I took a long look at the wide avenue. Assembled in my sight were hundreds of people of all classes and nationalities, in pursuit of amusement, work, something to eat, something to buy. Men dressed in their finest tailored suits and polished leather shoes, wealthy Egyptian women covered in Turkish veils, children chasing dogs, workers on horseback heading toward the stables attached to the hotel used by Napoleon himself.

This might be my last view of Cairo.

The thought made my insides pinch. I had accomplished close to nothing, nothing except finding a magic-touched trinket box.

Mr. Hayes joined me up on the terrace. The palms rustled from the breeze sweeping across the city, a soft song. Overhead, the sky darkened to a bruised purple, and the calls to prayer rose in the dying light. With great reluctance, I turned away from the street. Mr. Hayes stood close to me, his wavy hair tousled, the color a mix of brown and red, as if unsure of what it wanted to be. Much like the man himself.

He stuck out his hand. "Well, Señorita Olivera, it's been a delight to squire your loveliness all around Cairo."

I took his palm, his calluses rough against my skin, but I didn't mind. "Someday, your compliments are going to get you in trouble."

"Not today," he said with a slight smile.

I returned his smile, despite myself. A peculiar expression swept across his face. Impossible to decipher. His eyes darkened, and then he swooped down and brushed his mouth against my cheek. It was over and done with before I could say a word, before I could blink.

Mr. Hayes stepped backward and gestured for me to walk through the hotel's grand entrance.

"Still don't trust me?" I ought to be annoyed, but I had to keep my lips from stretching into a grin.

His own lips twitched and I suspected he, too, was fighting a grin. "Not even a little bit."

We walked inside together with several feet of distance between us. One of the hotel attendants came forward, as if he had been waiting for us. "Sir?"

Mr. Hayes raised his brows. "Yes, what is it?"

"You have another letter," he said with a German accent. "I have it here."

If I hadn't been standing near him I would have missed the slight tightening of his shoulders, his hands almost closing into fists. But he recovered quickly, taking the letter. "Danke schön."

"Bitte schön," the hotel attendant said before striding away.

Mr. Hayes turned to me.

"I hope it's good news," I said.

"It never is," he said. "This is goodbye I believe, Señorita Olivera." He pointed over my shoulder, and I followed the line of his index finger. "Your uncle is just there, across the hall. I would behave, if I were you."

Any feeling of camaraderie for him vanished. I gave him a stiff nod, which he returned with an expression I couldn't easily interpret. It might have been one of regret. He turned and strode after the attendant. My last sight of him was the strong line of his back as it disappeared into the crowd.

My fingers touched the spot he had kissed. I stared at nothing in particular for several astonishing moments, the chatter surrounding me falling into a hush. I shook it off, and returned my focus to my present problem, disappointment clouding my vision. I had come to Egypt hoping to learn more about my parents, about their life here. I'd come hoping to learn more of what had happened to them.

I'd failed. Utterly.

I caught sight of Tío Ricardo standing next to several battered trunks. He looked at his pocket watch with an impatient air, no doubt waiting for Mr. Hayes so they could well and truly be on their way.

Without me.

I contemplated running out of Shepheard's, but reason held me steadfast. Where would I go without money or my things? Stifling a wave of anger, I walked past him, careful not to look in his direction. The grand staircase loomed ahead of me and with every step forward, I felt as if I were taking one backward. My uncle had already wished me goodbye. There was nothing more to be said, no progress to be made—at least for the moment.

I hadn't made it up a few steps before I heard my name being called out. I turned to see Sallam striding toward me. He wore the hotel livery, gold and green colors that made me think of the palm trees lining parts of the Nile.

"I heard you were leaving us already," he said with a sad smile.

It took considerable effort not to shoot a glare in my uncle's direction. Some part of me sensed his forceful gaze cutting through the crowd, focusing on me so fully I actually shifted my feet. But I still wouldn't look at him. I refused to give him the satisfaction.

"Unfortunately, it's true. You can thank my uncle for that."

Sallam frowned. "Well, I wished to bid you a safe journey back to Argentina. I'll send someone up to collect your luggage for you." He reached into his pocket and pulled out a creased note. "You've had a letter, by the way."

Across the front, the message bore my aunt's elegant penmanship. Just what I needed, a lecture that had survived the journey across the ocean. "Oh dear."

"Sorry?" he asked.

"Never mind." I took it from him, thanked him, and then made my way up to my parents' suite. I slumped onto the couch and dragged my hands through my hair, tugging the strands free. The quiet felt oppressive. Wordlessly, I threw one of the pillows across the room. I threw the other for good measure.

This was it. I had no more options before me. My uncle refused to answer my questions, refused to help me learn what had happened to Mamá and Papá, and now he was sending me away.

As if he didn't care.

I clenched my eyes and thought furiously. There must be something I could do. When I opened my eyes, I looked around the room in desperation.

This was where my parents *lived*. I stood and went to the desk and began searching. I didn't know what I was looking for, but I'd settle for anything that told me what my parents had been doing in their last days before leaving for the desert.

This was my final chance.

I rummaged through the drawers, sorting through countless books and loose sheets of writing paper. My parents had stacks of unopened letters, and I read them all, but there was nothing. Greetings from friends back in Argentina, invitations for dinner that were months old. Frustrated, I went inside their bedroom and searched through both of their trunks, tossing their clothes into an enormous heap onto the carpeted floor. I ripped the sheets off the bed and tucked my hand inside both pillows.

Nothing.

Not even a journal or a diary, which I knew both my parents kept.

With a growl of frustration, I dropped down onto my knees and looked under the bed. A letter lay beneath one of Papá's shoes, the corner just visible. I tugged it free and sat back on my haunches, blowing my hair off my face with an impatient huff. My gaze dropped to the back of the closed note.

It was addressed to Monsieur Maspero, but without a stamp.

My uncle's flustered dinner companion. The head of the Antiquities Service. I pulled the letter out.

Dear Monsieur Maspero,

It was wonderful dining with you. Please allow me to beg your pardon for my brother's astonishing behavior. I hope you know that my husband and I respect your efforts and work at the museum, despite what Ricardo might imply. I greatly fear that he's become involved with disreputable individuals associated with illegal activities here in Cairo. Please see the enclosed card.

This is indeed what I fear, correct?

Would it be possible if I might visit you at your office? I must speak with you further about this matter. I'm in desperate need of guidance and assistance.

Yours etc.,
Lourdes Olivera

My attention narrowed to one line. One line that made me feel like I'd been struck down by a fist. The words swam across my vision, each letter a knife to my gut.

... involved with disreputable individuals associated with illegal activities ...

My God, what was my uncle involved in? Who were these disreputable individuals? I slumped to the ground, tears pricking my eyes. I read the letter again and the words blurred together as I pulled out a small square-shaped card, soft to the touch and thick. On one side, an illustration of a gate was debossed on the expensive paper. And on the other, three lines of text printed in black ink.

GEZIRA SPORTING CLUB
24TH OF JULY
3 O'CLOCK IN THE MORNING

Mamá had found this card months ago. I'd not heard of the sporting club, but scheduling an event? a meeting? in the early hours of the morning felt suspicious. I flipped the card again, studying the design intently. My sketchbook was within reach, and I quickly copied the sketch of the gate.

It appeared to be a simple sketch of the entrance of an Egyptian temple. I didn't recognize it, but that didn't mean it didn't exist. My breath rushed out of me again as the implication of what I'd read rattled my bones.

Had Mamá thought Tío Ricardo a criminal?

CAPÍTULO ONCE

*T*o hell with leaving Egypt.

Not until I knew what had happened to Mamá and Papá. My uncle wanted to pack me off, for me to go meekly back to Argentina, to leave my questions unanswered, while he involved himself in criminal activities? Anger blew through my body as if riding a harsh wind. He thought he could make me disappear?

I wouldn't go quietly.

No, I needed to find a way to board the *Elephantine*. Preferably before he dumped me onto a train heading for Alexandria. I thought hard, discarding one idea after another, Mr. Hayes's words swimming in my mind. He'd told me they were heading to the dahabeeyah tonight, leaving the docks at . . . I scrunched my brow. What was the name of the dock?

Bulaq.

That had been it.

I flew into action, my mind racing with thoughts of anything I might possibly need for the journey. Bringing my luggage would most likely slow me down, but I could stuff some clothing and supplies into my bag. I layered my current dress over a spare one, along with a pair of Turkish trousers underneath both skirts. It was hardly comfortable, but I would need a change of clothes eventually.

That done, I cast my eye to my next task.

Colette had certainly worked efficiently. My bed had been made, my trunks stacked neatly on top of one another. I had precious minutes to undo everything she had done. Moving quickly, I threw open the lids and pulled out a medium-sized canvas bag. I'd originally packed it thinking it might be useful for living on-site while my uncle excavated. If anyone were to see me carrying it around along with my purse, I had the perfect excuse lined up. It would serve as my overnight bag in Alexandria.

I rushed to the desk and grabbed a blank sheet, quickly making a list of everything I would need. Papá and I had both been fond of them.

CANVAS BAG:

1. Nightgown
2. Mosquito net
3. Toothbrush, hairbrush, small bottle of perfume. (who knows if there'll be a bathtub at the campsite.)
4. A walking dress to be worn "for the steamship."

TO BE WORN UNDER CURRENT TRAVELING CLOTHES

1. Extra day dress
2. Turkish trousers
3. Leather shoes with the tough soles

PURSE

1. Matches and tinder box
2. Candle
3. Sketchpad and charcoal pencils
4. Handheld mirror
5. Switchblade
6. Canteen

I had much to pack, and I hoped that I could fit everything I needed. When I had looked over my parents' belongings, I had seen several useful items, no doubt meant for living in tents out in the desert. The things I needed were scattered around their bedroom and I rushed to collect all of the items, stuffing everything inside my purse when my fingers brushed against a rough surface.

The echo of magic pulsed, widening in a large, invisible ripple.

My purchase from the bazaar.

I dug farther and pulled out the trinket box, careful not to touch the wood. It swayed in front of me, the whisper of something pulling me forward. I blinked, thought hard, and then looked again in my bag to pull out Papá's switchblade. With extreme care, I cut along the seam, and the encrusted dirt fell away.

The magic inside called to me, and I instinctively understood that it was looking for something. I recalled Mr. Hayes's words, how magic sought out its likeness. I took a fortifying breath and continued to slice through the grime. Another half inch and—

The wooden box split.

A cold hiss rushed around me, grazing against my skin. Goosebumps flared up and down my arms. I instinctively shut my eyes against the freeze. In the flat black, a woman crossed my vision. She wore a long, gauzy dress and her sandals glinted on her feet, bejeweled and elegant. Slowly, pieces from her surroundings came into view. A long chaise set in a gilded chamber ornate with potted flowers. The smell of flowers rose sharply in my mind. The woman walked to her balcony overlooking the long line of a blue coast.

Someone spoke from behind her.

Joy detonated within her. The woman spun away, her face regal and striking, but not beautiful. She wore her hair long and dark and it swung across her shoulders as she ran from the room.

The moment faded and the chill slipped away from me.

The box sat harmlessly in my hands. Nothing had changed; it was still grimy and old. The carvings near faded. But I had seen something. A memory belonging to a woman from the ancient world. Who had I seen?

Perhaps there was more to the trinket.

I eagerly looked inside, but there was nothing. It might have held something long ago, and whatever it was had long fallen out. My shoulders slumped. I brushed my finger inside and jumped. Whatever had been locked inside had held powerful magic. It sang to me, a loud roar that rang in my ears. Beckoned me. Tasted familiar. The flavor made me think of ancient things. Of temples grounded on amber-hued sand. A woman strolling out on her terrace, a falcon trailing after her, watching over her. The lush scent of the garden in bloom. Flowers bursting in lavish color. Her mouth tasted like roses.

The golden ring had made me feel the *same* way.

Cleopatra.

Had I really seen her? My breath came out in a long exhale. I stared down at the wooden box in complete shock, my thoughts racing through my mind. Perhaps the golden ring had once been inside. It made sense why the magic felt so familiar. It seemed highly improbable that I would have found another item that had belonged to the last pharaoh of Egypt. And yet, I had.

I didn't understand *why*.

A loud knock ruptured my thoughts. I blinked, as the shadowy presence evaporated, leaving behind a trace of her like lingering perfume. A woman who preferred roses, who wore pearls in her hair. Quickly, I tucked the wooden box inside my bag. Another sharp knock. It must be the man Sallam had sent up to help with my luggage. But when I opened the door, the person who stood on the other side wasn't a hotel employee.

I clutched the door handle, and my words came out brittle. "Tío Ricardo."

"¿Me permites entrar?"

His shoulders were wide and nearly engulfed the space between the doorframe. He towered over me, and a large part of me wanted to slam the door in his face. I couldn't get my mother's letter to Maspero out of my mind. She didn't trust him. She feared for his safety, for what he might do. I thought of the way he had spoken to Sir Evelyn, arguing about living wages and for Abdullah to have a seat at the table.

Had it all been an act?

I'd never know if I didn't talk to him. "Of course you can come in," I said in a softer tone.

He walked forward, his gaze landing on my packed suitcases. My uncle didn't speak, and I waited for him to reprimand me for disobeying his mandate that I stay inside the hotel room all day. I expected Mr. Hayes had told him every last detail about our excursions. Pressure gathered between my shoulder blades and I braced myself.

"You're displeased with me," he said finally.

I raised my brows.

My uncle sighed, tucked a hand into his trouser pocket. "Regardless of what you may believe, I am thinking about you, Inez. I've never had the opportunity—I don't have—" He broke off, flinching. "What I mean to say is that I'm not a parent. But I do know what Lourdes and Cayo would have wanted, and it would have been for you to be at home, far away from all this."

"But they died," I said, and for the first time, my voice didn't crack. "You're making the decisions now."

He smiled, but it didn't reach his eyes. "I won't change my mind."

"Well, you've said your goodbye," I said. "What are you doing here?"

He appeared to be at a loss, looking down at me with a peculiar expression on his face. It was hard to envision his involvement in illegal activities—whatever they were. What did he do in the small hours of the night? I couldn't imagine him on the other side of the law. Right then, he seemed more like the uncle I remembered. The one with the booming voice and kind smile. Shirt unbuttoned at the collar revealing a bronze throat, and hair scraped back and tucked underneath a leather hat. His pants were well-worn, rolled at the ankle over a pair of scuffed workman's boots.

"I saw you in the lobby." He swiftly glanced at my parents' bedroom. "I want you to know that I'll have Lourdes's and Cayo's things packed away and mailed to you as soon as the season is over. Not long after the new year, I should think."

I licked my lips. "Please change your mind, Tío."

Tío Ricardo rubbed his jaw.

"Inez—" He swallowed. His words came out a sharp plea. "I don't have the time to properly watch over you. I can't do my work while worrying about you. Look what happened to your *parents*. What if something happened to you while I was occupied? I'd never forgive myself." He shook his head and abruptly changed the subject. "Do you have everything you need?"

I thought about the secret supplies I had stashed away and nodded. He looked around and went for my canvas bag. My heart leapt in my chest as he took it in hand. If he were to look through it, he'd find some of my parents' things. Items meant for surviving out in the desert.

"I'll help you bring this down."

"No need," I said quickly. "Sallam already arranged for it."

"Oh." He dropped it back down to the floor, and then cleared his throat. "Do you have money?"

I was about to nod again but then caught myself. It would probably be useful to have some more. I didn't know what I'd come across in my trek across Cairo to the docks. Tío Ricardo dug into his pocket and pulled out several Egyptian piastres. Wordlessly, he handed everything over.

"What time do you sail?" I asked.

"We leave tomorrow morning, but we'll spend the night aboard the *Elephantine* tonight. I want the crew gathered ahead of time to prevent delays in setting off at dawn." He fiddled with the cuff of his shirtsleeve. "I've arranged for your chaperone to meet you downstairs in the lobby in ten minutes. She's an older lady but happy to make the journey with you, and quite literally the only one available on such short notice. Evidently, she has friends in South America and will join them after dropping you off at home. I've also written to your aunt with your arrival details."

"You've thought of everything." I made one last attempt to persuade him. It would be so much easier to spy on him if he'd only let me come as well. "I don't understand why you're doing this."

"You will one day," he said. "And maybe you'll forgive me then."

He inclined his head and walked out. I stared after him, unable to rid my mind of what he said—his sincerity surprised me. I worried my lip, considering.

But no matter how long I dwelled on his words and how he said them, I still couldn't guess what he meant.

---- ✄ ----

I was not an easy child to raise. Constantly hiding myself away when I didn't want to be found, exploring when I ought to have stayed put. Initially, I acted out the most when Mamá and Papá were home. I thought that if they saw how wild I was becoming, they might stay longer. But Papá loved the streak of independence, and he had always encouraged my varied interests. It was Mamá who could rein me in, constantly reminding me of her expectations. And there were a lot of them. And so I learned to behave, but once they left for Egypt . . . my rebellious tendencies flared.

I thanked God for it.

The walk down to the lobby allowed me plenty of time to think through every move and countermove of my hastily formed plan. Outwardly, I schooled my expression, hoping none of my inner turmoil made itself known. By the time I reached the main floor, my hands were slick with sweat.

What if I failed?

Shepheard's brimmed with elegantly dressed guests, waiting to be let into the dining room. They stood in clusters, and the collective chatter echoed in the crammed lobby. The ladies wore elaborate evening gowns; the gentlemen, some of them smoking, wore smart jackets and polished shoes and expertly tied cravats. Egyptian men chatted idly, the tassels on their tarbooshes swinging from their animated conversation. There might have been one hundred to two hundred people socializing, blocking a straight path to the front doors.

In the crowd, standing a foot taller than nearly half the occupants, was Mr. Hayes, dressed more elegantly than I could have thought possible. His black evening wear contrasted with his tanned face, the clothing neat and pressed. Not a wrinkle in sight. He conversed with my uncle, frowning and gesturing wildly. A gasp climbed up my throat, but I hammered it down. Mr. Hayes was probably ratting me out this moment. I honestly wouldn't put it past him. Tío Ricardo bore Mr. Hayes's frustrations with a stony silence.

Then my uncle's wandering gaze found mine from across the room.

Mr. Hayes half turned, following my uncle's line of sight. He straightened at the sight of me, his blue gaze lingering on my face then slowly lowering to my neat traveling gown, the bags I clutched in one arm. The line of his jaw hardened, and he turned away, said something to my uncle, and strode toward the dining room.

For some unaccountable reason, my stomach lurched at the sight of his retreating back. I shrugged my shoulders, as if to shake off the strange feeling. Tío Ricardo strode toward me, eyeing my belongings. "You can give those to Sallam. He'll add them with the rest of your things."

I thought he'd be yelling at me. Furious. "That's all you're going to say?"

"I've said everything I need to," he said.

My brow furrowed. "No, I meant about . . ." I let my voice trail off as I realized Mr. Hayes hadn't told my uncle about our afternoon together.

My assumption had been entirely wrong. Astonishment swept through me. That strange feeling returned, a butterfly fluttering deep in my belly. I deliberately turned away from the direction of the dining room.

"About?"

"I can hold on to my things," I said, answering his previous question. "It's no bother."

"Fine," he said. "Come, I'll introduce you to your traveling companion."

He couldn't wait to hand me over to someone else. He led me through the thinning crowd toward an older lady, who blinked in confusion. She wore an elegant striped silk dress with the customary bustle. I guessed her age to be anywhere in her mid-eighties. The corset accented a narrow waist, and from her wrist dangled a matching parasol. Her face looked friendly, if a little scattered, with a wide gaze and deep wrinkles at the corners of her eyes from years spent laughing.

I liked her on the spot. It was a shame that I was going to have to deceive her.

"Mrs. Acton?" my uncle said, smiling. "I've come to introduce you to your charge."

"My charge? Oh, right. Of course, young Irene, is it?"

My uncle smothered a laugh. "Inez. Do you have everything you need? The money and tickets?"

She blinked at him, her thin lips making a perfect *O* shape. "Young man, it is absolutely *vulgar* to discuss such things in public."

"I beg your pardon," Tío Ricardo said, and this time he couldn't contain his chuckle. "But do you have your tickets? The front desk ought to have handed them to you."

"Yes, yes. Such small slips of paper, I can hardly read the print." She felt around her person, and I pointed to her small silk purse dangling from her wrist.

"It's there," I said as a flash of inspiration struck me. She had a hard time reading the small print. I bit my lip, trying to keep my face neutral. "Thank you for accompanying me."

"And you're ready to depart?" my uncle persisted.

Mrs. Acton nodded, absently searching through her bag. "I'm all packed."

"Excellent." He turned to me. "I really must be off. Safe journey, querida sobrina. I will write, I promise."

Then he left me with a stranger, and didn't look back. Not even once.

"Well, Irina, I think we'll have a grand adventure," Mrs. Acton said. Her voice had a breathy quality to it, as if she was on the verge of laughing. "Shall I introduce you to my friends? They are in the alcove, just there, working on a puzzle. Quite fond of the silly little things. I think we have a few minutes before we must set off, and I'd love a cup of tea."

The moment of my deception came.

I furrowed my brow in mock confusion. "Why, you have all the time in the world, Mrs. Acton. If you'd like, you can sit and join them and even participate in the game."

Befuddlement settled onto her face. It reminded me of a creased silk pillow. "But we must head to the station. The train departs in an hour, I thought."

"Oh! Mrs. Acton, I believe you confused the dates of our journey. We don't leave until tomorrow." I held out my hand. "Here, I'll show you. May I have the tickets, please?"

She fished them out and unfolded them. "But I packed. Your uncle said to meet him down here."

"I think he only wanted to introduce us," I said in a breezy tone. I took the papers from her and pretended to examine them. "See? It says so right here. We leave tomorrow. How fortunate that you're ready to go. I still haven't packed."

"You haven't?" Mrs. Acton gaped. "Well, I like to prepare for my travels well in advance. It's a practice that has served me well. I can send up my maid to you. She's an absolute jewel."

I shook my head. "My uncle has secured the services of a maid, thank you. Well, I'm so glad you'll be able to enjoy that cup of tea. Say hello to your friends from me."

Mrs. Acton regarded me, brow still muffled in perplexity. Gently, I prodded her in the direction of her friends. As soon as her back was turned, I strode out of the hotel lobby and into a night-covered Cairo.

Free, free, free.

I tried not to be smug about it.

WHIT

Ricardo glanced at his pocket watch and scowled. The man we were meeting hadn't arrived for dinner. I kept quiet and my attention wandered, cataloguing the number of people in the room who posed a potential threat to myself and my employer. There were too many of them and my fingers itched for my pistol. The hotel management didn't approve of their guests carrying weapons into the dining parlor. I swirled the whiskey in my glass and took a long sip, hearing my father's disapproving voice as it burned a fiery path down my throat. The man only drank tea and sugary lemonade. Father thought only weak men drank alcohol.

"He's late," Ricardo growled.

"Are you sure we need him?"

"No, but I thought I had everything under control before and clearly I was wrong. I can't afford to make any more mistakes. He's an insurance policy." He glanced at me. "Any trouble today with my niece?"

A waiter came around carrying a tray filled with red and white wine. I grabbed one, hardly caring which, and gulped it down. My thoughts turned to earlier when I'd squired Señorita Olivera about Cairo. Her disobedience was on the tip of my tongue. But the words stayed in my mouth, caught behind my teeth. I remembered, instead, her wary expression as we stood out on the terrace, the sounds of the city rising around us like a billowing crowd. She didn't even come up to my shoulders, and to meet my gaze at all she had to raise her chin and tip her head back almost fully.

Dark curls framed her face, and a smattering of freckles peppered the bridge of her nose, her cheeks, her eyelids. I'd looked down into her changing eyes, green then brown then gold, eyes that held alchemical magic, and had one crystallized thought in mind.

Oh, shit.

It was absurdity that had made me lean down to kiss her. It was annoying to still feel the soft curve of her cheek, to remember her sweet scent swirling in my nose.

Thank God she was leaving.

"Well?"

I blinked, shaking away the memory. I kept my expression blank as I lied to his face. "She's no trouble at all."

Ricardo grunted, and his attention caught somewhere over my shoulder. I followed his gaze to find a burly man with light hair and blue eyes striding toward us, a petite, younger woman at his heels. She wore the latest fashion, her narrow waist cinched, her neck adorned by extravagant lace, reminding me of a territorial hen. Her eyes met mine, coolly amused, a coy smile framing her pink mouth. She looked at me as if I were someone to win over.

Mr. Fincastle and his daughter had arrived.

CAPÍTULO DOCE

*T*he piastres in my purse clinked loudly as I rushed out of Shepheard's, my bag smacking the back of my thigh. I scanned the street below, searching for an attendant who I could convince not to relay my whereabouts should anyone ask. I was prepared to pay whatever they wanted for their silence. A young boy of thirteen or so smiled at my approach, and I reached into my purse.

"Where to?"

"Bulaq, please," I said. "And I'd appreciate it if you kept my outing to yourself."

His brow puckered. "But—"

I pressed two more coins into his palm, and he fell silent. "Please don't worry."

The young attendant secured a driver with great reluctance, pocketing the money, and after he helped me inside the carriage, he gave directions to the docks. During the day, Cairo was fueled by the tourists who walked up and down its streets, buying trinkets and dining in various establishments serving traditional fare. But at night, the city pulsed with life overflowing from live music, the locals smoking on porch steps, eating from carts where vendors served warm bread that was flat and shaped like a disc. Every block we passed was a different scene with its own life and heartbeat. I pressed my fingers on the window frame, hardly able to breathe from wonder. The silver moon rose high over the river, the water sparkling and moving slowly.

I wanted to explore every inch of this version of Cairo.

This was an Egyptian night.

We approached the Nile, dark and expansive in both directions. Like the rest of the city, this area was alive with its own kind of sharp energy. I climbed out of the brougham and stared in amazement at the sight before me. Hundreds of boats and dahabeeyahs were moored, bobbing quietly in the water. Egyptians spread out, chattering in rapid Arabic, dressed in long white tunics and comfortable sandals. Others appeared to be tourists attempting to secure a boat from the local captains. Children ran up and down the street playing with stray dogs, dressed in the same long-sleeved tunics as the adults, the clothing reaching down to their ankles. The strap of the canvas bag dug into my shoulder, and I shifted, trying to find a spot that didn't ache.

Now came the next part of my plan I was less sure about.

Where the *hell* was my uncle's boat?

With a sigh, I approached an older man with a friendly smile. At the sight of me, he lit up, no doubt thinking I'd like to hire him to cart me up and down the Nile. I was sorry to disabuse him of the notion.

"The *Elephantine*?" I asked. "Please?"

He stared at me in confusion and then he pointed to a boat named *Fostat*. I shook my head and said *shokran* under my breath, and continued walking the docks, reading name after name painted on the side of various boats, all the while my ears straining for anyone who might understand English. I approached someone else, asking for my uncle's boat, but with no success. From the corner of my eye, a young boy kept his attention on me as I continued my search. After two more tries, sweat formed at my brow. There were hundreds of boats docked. How would I find the right one? I glanced over my shoulder to find the young boy still trailing after me. I turned away and approached another group, talking low under the moonlight. They eyed me warily.

"I'm looking for the *Elephantine*?"

They shook their heads and shooed me away.

I sighed and pressed on. Then at last I heard it. A scrap of language I understood. I turned toward the source to discover the same young boy behind me.

He saw me looking and approached, his smile flanked by dimples. "You are Inglizeya?"

"No, but I speak English. I am looking for a dahabeeyah."

The young boy nodded. "The *Elephantine*?" When I stiffened, he shrugged and then grinned, his thin shoulders rising up and down in a graceful motion. "I've been following you, sitti."

I furrowed my brow, not recognizing the word.

"Honored lady," the boy translated without a trace of irony. "I heard you ask for the *Elephantine* from the first reis."

Another word I didn't know. "*Reis*?"

"Captain," he explained. His voice reminded me of the softest rustle against the ground, leaves brushed against stone. "I am part of the crew of the *Elephantine*."

At this my jaw dropped. "Truly?"

He nodded, the moonlight making his dark eyes shine. "Come, I'll take you."

I hesitated; the boy seemed sincere, but I had to make sure. "What's your name?"

"Kareem. Will you come?"

I had no better option, but still I stayed put. My bags weighed me down, digging into my flesh. "What is the name of the man you work for? The owner of the boat?"

"Ricardo Marqués," Kareem said promptly.

Any unease vanished at the sound of my uncle's name. Kareem spoke the truth, and perhaps he might be able to assist me with the next step in my plan. "Tío Ricardo doesn't know that I'll be joining him. It's a surprise visit. My uncle would expect to see me in a dress. I'd like to change my clothes into ones that are similar to yours in order to pull off my plan. Will you help me buy some?"

Kareem eyed me, his lips pressed into a line of skepticism.

"I'll pay you for your help." I dug into my purse and pulled out a handful of piastres. Kareem's gaze dropped to the money and before I could blink, he'd snatched it from my hand. They winked in the starlight for only a second before disappearing into the sleeve of his tunic. If I hadn't been watching carefully, I would have sworn they had disappeared into thin air.

"Huh," I said. "Will you teach me how to do that?"

The boy dimpled and then lifted his chin in the direction of a small market in front of the docks. Various items were for sale, including a shop dedicated to spices that warmed my blood as we walked past. Spices I'd never heard of: cardamom and turmeric, cumin and curry. Kareem helped me purchase a long tunic, called a *galabeya,* which partially hid my leather boots. I pointed to his tarboosh, and Kareem managed to find one identical to his.

I dressed behind a woven blanket Kareem held up for me, next to an old building with a crumbling roof, and together we walked to the eastern bank where the *Elephantine* was moored. My traveling dress barely fit in the canvas bag, and I marveled at the bulk of it compared to the light tunic currently gracing my frame. I'd gotten rid of the corset but kept my shift and stockings.

The freedom of movement was *extraordinary.*

Kareem stayed close to me as we boarded the *Elephantine.* It resembled a flat barge, and while it looked sturdy, my stomach clenched regardless. Another boat, another trip over water. I hoped I wouldn't get sick like last time when I hadn't been able to leave my cabin for days. It was the worst I'd ever felt in my life. The rest of the crew rushed around, carrying large baskets filled with food and linens and tools. I kept my face turned downward, my long hair tied in a knot hidden within the fez. By now, the moon hung high overhead, the stars shining brilliantly onto the dark water of the Nile. It stretched on either end for miles, making me feel as tiny as a grain of sand.

"Would you like a tour?" Kareem asked.

I looked around nervously, sure to find my uncle giving orders in his booming voice.

"He isn't here yet. But he will be soon."

"All right," I agreed. "A very quick tour. Is there a place I can put my things?"

He nodded. "You can take the sixth bedroom. We've been using it for storage."

I followed as he showed me around the boat. I'd never been on anything like it before. Long and narrow, with a flat bottom and two masts at the bow and stern. The cabins were situated below deck, the roof forming the upper. Every room had a small window and narrow beds, a fixed washing stand, and a row of hooks to hang up clothing. Additionally, there were two drawers underneath the bed for more storage. Kareem told me which room would serve as mine and I hid my belongings as best I could.

Once we passed the row of cabins, Kareem led me away to show me a grand saloon that measured roughly twenty feet in length, the walls curving at the end. White paneling gave it a classic look, contrasting with the dark velvet curtains hanging on either side of four large windows. A skylight provided additional lighting, and hanging in every available space were wooden shelves holding up dozens of books, hats, and . . . guns.

I raised my brows, confusion flaring. My parents had detested weaponry of any kind and it struck me as odd that they would have permitted them on board.

Kareem pulled at my sleeve and bid me to follow where a charcoal oven in between the prow and bigger mast allotted for the kitchen area. Pots and pans hung on iron hooks above baskets of culinary supplies. I didn't have time to see what was stored within as Kareem moved quickly, pointing out the rest of the crew: the reis, pilot, cook, the steersmen and oarsmen, and a handful of waiters. Kareem himself was an assistant to the head cook.

Taken all together, the *Elephantine* resembled a medium-sized house with a staff of twelve, with plenty of space to spread out.

"Where do the crew sleep?"

"On mats on the upper deck," Kareem said, leading me there. A roof hung above it, and my uncle had furnished the area with a large rug and some chairs. It looked like an idyllic living room, out in the open, the cool breeze touching every piece of furniture with a loving hand. Already, some of the crew were unrolling mats, preparing to wait for my uncle. Everything seemed to be in order. I made myself comfortable on the ground next to several others and listened for the sound of my uncle's arrival. I passed the time by looking outward at the picturesque scene, a hundred boats floating quietly on the grand river, ready for the next adventure.

And then at last, my uncle came, Mr. Hayes in tow, occasionally sipping from his flask as if he were at a dinner party. He looked over the crew with an experienced eye. He'd replaced his dinner jacket and neat shoes with his customary wrinkled shirt, khakis, and scuffed boots that laced up mid-calf. The two men carried their own trunks and bags up the gangplank, where they were immediately greeted by the reis, a man named Hassan. They disappeared down the narrow steps into the long corridor opening to the row of cabins on either side, their voices drifting along with them.

I looked at Kareem and grinned.

He smiled back, the moonlight reflecting in his large, dark eyes.

Having finished their duties, the rest of the crew joined us on the deck, unrolling their mats. I sat among a dozen people, all dressed in similar long-sleeved tunics and hats. The boat gently swayed on the water, a reminder that I'd done the impossible. I only had to remain anonymous, just another member of the crew. My uncle and Mr. Hayes walked toward us, greeting the pilot and cook. I held my breath and kept my face turned away, hunching my shoulders to hide behind the other crew members.

But I heard every word that passed between them.

"All in order?" Tío Ricardo asked.

Someone replied in the affirmative.

"We seem to have acquired a new crew member," Mr. Hayes said slowly. "Weren't there only twelve?"

I tensed, my breath trapped in my chest. I waited for him to recognize me, to hear his insolent voice call out my name. But no such cry of outrage came.

"It's fine. We need the help," Tío Ricardo said impatiently. "Is everyone here? I want to depart at dawn."

"Yes, yes."

My uncle thanked whoever had spoken. The sound of footsteps drew away from the deck. I exhaled slowly, my hands interlaced tightly in my lap. I relaxed a fraction. They all must have moved away, probably to their respective bedrooms. But then a familiar voice, spoken lazily, remarked, "Funny no one talked to you about adding someone to the team."

"Abdullah will hardly quibble about the extra hands," Tío Ricardo said. "You never gave me your report about this afternoon."

I chanced to turn my face halfway in their direction, peering up at them through my lashes. Kareem sat motionless next to me. My uncle and Mr. Hayes leaned against the railing.

"I can confirm Sterling has the ring and is wearing it in public," Mr. Hayes said.

"But you were unable to retrieve it."

My breath caught at the back of my throat as I waited to see what he'd say. Would he inform my uncle of how I'd snuck out of the hotel?

"It was . . . crowded, unfortunately."

"Damn it," Tío Ricardo seethed.

My jaw dropped. Confirmation that Mr. Hayes truly hadn't betrayed me. I still didn't understand why he'd protected me. He barely tolerated my presence, and he could have gotten me in even more trouble with my uncle. But then he might have decided it wasn't worth it since I was well and truly gone. I exhaled slowly, through my nose, like Papá had once taught me. He always knew how to calm me down, especially after an argument with my mother.

Mr. Hayes tilted his head, studying my uncle with a keen eye. "That's not the only thing bothering you, is it?"

My uncle averted his gaze. "I don't know what you mean."

"Yes," Mr. Hayes said smoothly, "you do."

I curled my toes within my boots. After a long beat, my uncle finally responded. "You should have seen the look of loathing on her face."

"I daresay she'll get over it."

"I don't know her well enough to know." Tío Ricardo glared at Mr. Hayes. "Neither do you."

Mr. Hayes's lips pressed tight, as if stifling amusement. "She was certainly . . . plucky."

"Her curiosity is bothersome."

"She was bound to have questions about your tall tale."

"If Cayo hadn't lied to me, he would still be alive," Tío Ricardo said in frustration. "He was a dishonest fool who knew better than to cross me when I want something." He ducked his head, the line of his jaw hard and unforgiving. "This is all his fault."

"You shouldn't speak ill of the dead."

"I can when it's deserved." A sharp gasp climbed up my throat. I ruthlessly tamped it down, biting my lip. He was talking about my father. My eyes burned. What the hell was going on? My mother's letter swam across my vision. Panic edged closer and I fought to keep my breathing even.

It seemed my mother had been right to worry. Tío Ricardo sounded furious, and was clearly after something.

And my father had stood in the way.

PART TWO

UP THE RIVER

CAPÍTULO TRECE

I woke to the clamoring sounds of the Nile coming to life. The taste of
fish and mud and crocodiles in my mouth, pungent and sharp. Kareem
nudged my thigh with his sandaled foot, a bundle of wet rope in his hands.
Gingerly, I sat up, my limbs having fallen asleep during the night. My
knees were wobbly as I stood; I flung out a hand to grip the railing of the
Elephantine. Everyone else had already gotten up, rushing around the deck.
Some carried supplies, others busily rolled up the sleeping mats. Overhead,
the bright blue of an Egyptian morning stretched in every direction.

I couldn't appreciate any of it. I had spent a long and miserable night
agonizing over what I had overheard. My mind held so many pieces of a
puzzle, and none of them seemed to fit together. I'd thought about my uncle, my imagination turning him into the worst kind of villain. A scoundrel
who did . . . *what?* Then I'd thought about Mr. Hayes and his quicksilver
grins and empty flattery and the way his flask was always in easy reach.
In my mind, they had become an untrustworthy pair with shady motives.

Best I stay far away from Mr. Hayes.

And yet.

There had been moments when I'd seen something beyond the implacable mask. The brush of his lips against my cheek. He hadn't revealed my
disobedience to his *employer,* but had kept our outing a secret. He'd stayed
by my side as we explored the city, and I had felt safe, but not crowded.
Looked after, but not controlled. Despite myself, I'd developed a fascination for his easy wit and direct gaze. The hint of softness and loyalty lurking
under the surface. Or I could be hoping to see something nonexistent.

"Allah yesabbahhik bilkheir," Kareem said, jerking me from my thoughts. I recognized the greeting, having heard it many times since arriving in Egypt.

"Same to you," I said.

"When are you planning on revealing yourself to your uncle?"

We were still moored, but I sensed that the general commotion meant we were preparing to depart. Without question, I had to wait until there was no feasible way my uncle could turn back.

"Not until tomorrow at the earliest," I said. "Is there something I can be doing to help?"

Kareem tilted his head, studying me with his wide eyes. "There's plenty to do."

"I'd like to help," I repeated.

"You can assist me in the kitchen, then. I must prep breakfast for the team and crew."

I'd never stepped foot in our kitchen back home, not even to boil water.

"I'm sure I can be useful," I said.

"Your mother once tried to help, too."

I froze. "What?"

"I think she was trying to pass the time. She seemed lonely."

That didn't make sense. Mamá had been with my father; they were inseparable. "My mother was lonely?"

Kareem nodded. "Your father studied his books a lot, or assisted with the planning. He was always off doing one thing or another. Left her by herself most of the time."

"Assisted who? My uncle?"

Kareem nodded.

"Did you ever see my uncle and Papá argue?"

Kareem shook his head, seemingly unsurprised by the question. His face softened, his expressive eyes gazing soulfully into mine. "You look like her," Kareem said. "I'm sorry they passed."

My throat locked up.

"It's good that you're here," he added.

I followed the young boy to the kitchen, surreptitiously wiping my eyes.

Questions filled my mind, near overflowing. I wanted to know what Kareem had thought of Mamá and Papá, if he had spent any time with them and how much. Being in Egypt only reminded me of how much of their lives I had missed. I still didn't understand why they'd forbidden me from ever joining them.

We reached the kitchen, and I looked around the functional space. On a slim, wooden counter, bowls of eggs and fava beans rested alongside jars of various spices. I'd never seen any of the kind before. Lemons and bottles of olive oil lined a shelf barely wider than two feet.

"I'll cook the beans," Kareem said. "You mash them."

"What are we making?"

"Foul with tahini," he said, lighting the stove. Then he pulled down a flat pan from one of the hooks. "Beans mixed with cumin and coriander, lemon, and oil. The team loves it with eggs."

"It sounds delicious. Who taught you to cook?"

Kareem smiled and said, "My older sister."

"How long have you been a part of my uncle's crew?"

"A few years. We all have been trained by Abdullah, your uncle's business partner." The boy glanced at me, his gaze direct, and for a moment, he looked older than I first thought him to be. "Will you cut the lemon in half?"

"That I can do," I said. I took the knife he handed me and sliced the fruit. "This is the first time I've joined my uncle, and I'm curious about his work. He hasn't talked much about Abdullah's latest excavation site. You must have seen so many interesting things."

Kareem spooned ghee into the pan and then cracked several eggs, which immediately sizzled upon contact. My stomach roared to life. I hadn't eaten since the day before at Groppi.

"Your uncle doesn't like us to talk about the site," Kareem said finally.

"Why?"

"Because, sitti," Kareem said, "he and Abdullah never trust anyone with what they've found."

Kareem looked down at my burnt flatbread. His lips pinched and I stifled a laugh. I had warned him. He had showed me all the tools in the kitchen that held on to the magical remnants of some old spell. A bowl that never ran out of salt, a cup that kept clean no matter what was dumped inside of it. Knives that turned food cold, spoons that when stirred, baked whatever was inside the dish. Even so, I'd still managed to mess something up.

"Why don't you go out onto the deck? We're about to depart, I think?"

His tone didn't sound like a suggestion.

I went to the gunwale, careful to keep myself hidden among the barrels of supplies, and away from the observant gaze of Mr. Hayes, who stood on the other end of the dahabeeyah. My uncle was deep in conversation with Reis Hassan and he'd scarcely left the dining room.

I was free to take a last look at Bulaq's bustling scene. Men dressed in their fine, loose robes haggling over cargo, Egyptian sailors sweating under the blistering sun, carrying large trunks on ships bracketing ours. Tourists swarmed in every direction, chattering in a loud babble that carried across the glittering green surface of the Nile.

Two more people joined our party, one with a barrel-shaped chest, broad shoulders, and thinning blond hair, the other a young woman close to my age. She wore a lavish gown with many trims and silk adornments and a wide-brimmed hat. She held herself regally, but her gaze moved restlessly over the whole of the *Elephantine*. The wind teased wisps of honey-blond hair to flutter across her delicate face. If my parents had mentioned the pair, I didn't remember.

The girl suddenly turned in my direction and I ducked behind a barrel. For some inexplicable reason, her presence made me uneasy. Perhaps because she was close to my age, clearly expected and welcomed when I had never been.

Curiosity itched under my skin. I wanted to know who she was, what she was doing on board my uncle's boat.

I stayed hidden until the sails unfurled to capture the north wind and then we were off, leaving behind the pyramids and the city of a thousand minarets. The sharp breeze tore at my hair, loosening my strands from the tight coil stuffed underneath the fez. I clutched the railing, sure that at any moment someone, somewhere would call out my name. But the only sound came from the crew surrounding me, chattering and singing songs as the current yanked us along. The *Elephantine* moved upstream, heading south along with dozens of felucca, small wooden ships with pointed sails in the shape of a large triangle. They peppered the great river, carrying fellow travelers seeking adventure.

I went down to retrieve my sketchbook and then settled back out on the deck, hiding myself among the barrels as I drew the ship from memory.

My burning curiosity regarding the only other female passenger flared again. Her presence remained a mystery—the rest of the crew seemed just as surprised to see her board the *Elephantine* as I was.

My earlier unease returned. She walked around, clearly welcomed and free to do whatever she wished. The girl even made herself useful, unpacking the supplies and carting things into various cabins, while I had to keep myself tucked away, unseen and definitely unwelcomed and useless. While I trusted my disguise, it only worked if I was surrounded with the rest of the crew. People saw what they expected to see, and a teenage girl among the crew would hardly enter their minds—not unless they were specifically *looking* for me.

But my uncle believed me to be on a different ship altogether. As for Mr. Hayes . . . I only needed to steer clear of him for another day. Tension seeped from my skin, loosening my muscles.

I was safe from discovery.

Slowly, I pulled the trinket box from within my purse. The wood stayed warm against my skin, sometimes vibrating, as if the magic held within its small confines wanted to burst free. It only showed that fragile things could survive. The box spoke of a time long past, a name history remembered. Cleopatra.

A new memory swept forward and I gasped, sinking into a moment that was centuries old. The last Queen of the Nile stood over a table, various ingredients scattered before her in shallow bowls and squat ceramic jars. She pored over a single leaf of parchment filled with curious symbols and drawings; I could just make out the sketch of a snake eating itself and an eight-banded star. Her nimble fingers worked to mix, blend, and chop ingredients. I recognized honey and salt, dried rose petals and herbs, along with animal teeth and grease. She wore a long, nearly transparent gown and from head to foot, lapis, garnet, pearls, gold, turquoise, and amethyst jewels adorned her throat, wrists, ankles, and shoes.

Two women stood before her on the opposite side of the table, dressed elegantly but diminished in comparison to Cleopatra's lavish ensemble. They were a reflection of her beauty and grace. I instinctively knew they were her handmaidens.

One of them asked a question, the ancient language whisking over my skin. I wished I understood.

Cleopatra didn't pause in her work but nodded.

The shorter handmaiden asked another question.

Cleopatra replied, her voice distinct. It didn't waver; it wasn't soft. It was the kind of voice that soothed and inspired, that ordered and coaxed.

The scene faded, as if a page had turned. I came back into awareness slowly, the sound of the crew singing helping to usher me into the present. For several seconds, I could only breathe as the horror of what I'd seen resonated in my mind.

Cleopatra was adept at magic. The scene I had witnessed was her creating a spell. I groaned, wishing I knew what she had been doing. Her manner had been confident. She was no stranger to potion making.

A prickle of awareness crept across my skin. Someone was watching me. The hairs on the back of my neck stood on end. I stuffed the trinket box back into my bag, my heart beating rapidly against my ribs. I spun, my gaze darting around the deck. I was hidden behind the mast, surrounded by old barrels, but alarm bells rang loudly in my ears.

There was no one.

Not the crew who worked at their posts, nor the reis or my uncle, who at last had emerged from the saloon. I moved and peered around the strong wood of the mast. Mr. Hayes had settled himself at the front of the daha-beeyah, a lazy grace in the way he leaned against the railing of the *Elephantine*. He stared wistfully in the direction of Cairo.

I wondered if he regretted leaving me behind.

What a *silly* thought. It didn't matter if he did or didn't. I shook my head, forcing the unbidden question from my mind. I snapped around and sank to the ground. The gentle breeze made me drowsy and my eyelids fluttered closed. When I opened them again, a shadow blocked the sun's piercing glare.

Kareem stared down at me, a bowl of food in his hand. "Are you hungry?"

I nodded and he handed me the food, two eggs and the foul—which didn't taste nearly as salty as mine had. The savory taste of cumin and garlic gave me a warm feeling that swept to every corner of my body. I wanted more but refrained from asking. Instead, I followed him back to the kitchen and helped scrub the dishes in a big, soapy bucket.

He kept me busy for the rest of the day, prepping the noon meal of breaded fish topped with charred lemons and a side of roasted eggplants in a thick, savory sauce, and the cleanup afterward. As the hours passed, more tension slipped away as if carried off by the north wind, little by little. With the distance widening between our location and Cairo, it was unlikely my uncle would turn us all around. I still didn't know when or how to reveal myself.

Tío Ricardo would be furious no matter how I did it.

Worry pricked at me. What would he do when he found out? I'd focused so much on getting on board that I neglected to imagine what came after. I had heard his bitter anger when he talked about Papá standing in the way of what he wanted. And here I was, disobeying him.

Without anyone I could trust to help me.

"Do you want to help me serve dinner in the saloon?" Kareem asked, wrenching me from my thoughts.

My instinct was to refuse but curiosity yanked hard on my mind. Everyone would be in the dining room, eating and talking at their leisure. Perhaps I'd catch another glimpse of the mysterious girl who had come aboard. There might be an opportunity to listen to their discussion, which could fill in some of the gaps in my uncle's activities. Presumably, my parents had participated in his excavations, and I might learn something of what they were up to in the days leading to their disappearance.

Kareem looked at me, waiting for my answer. All day, he'd helped me remain unseen and unnoticed by the rest of the crew. Though he never said, I wondered if he had done it because of my parents.

"I'll do it," I said.

---- ✖ ----

Kareem walked ahead of me into the empty saloon, carrying two dishes filled with kushari, a lentil- and pasta-based dish with tomato sauce and rice. In my hands I carried a large pitcher of mint limeade, which I'd already sampled and could confirm was refreshing and delicious. We dropped off the dishes in the center of the table, and I followed Kareem to stand at a discreet distance from the table, where the other servers waited. I kept my head down as another crew member filled the team's glasses.

The party entered, chattering quietly, and sat down at a round table in the lush saloon, all of them men except for the young woman I had seen earlier. There were four of them, only two I knew. My uncle pored over a letter curled in his palm while Mr. Hayes engaged in a tense argument with the brawny gentleman who had accompanied the young woman. Kareem motioned for me to stand behind a particularly tall attendant alongside the wall. I was neatly hidden, and incredibly thankful none of the crew knew who I was. I stared at the tips of my leather boots barely peeking from underneath the long tunic.

"Well, don't keep us waiting," Mr. Hayes said. "What does the letter say?"

"From your foreman?" the brawny man asked in an English accent. He dwarfed everyone else at the table, long limbed and big boned. His posture belied a fondness for sharp lines and rules. His movements were exact and precise as he served himself. The girl's slight frame seemed like a dandelion compared to his stature. One strong wind might uproot her.

And yet her pale gaze seemed to miss nothing. Flickering from the table to the windows lining the curved wall, to her dining companions. She was a fidgety thing.

"No, it's from Abdullah," Tío Ricardo said. "They've managed to discover another entryway leading out from the antechamber. It's heavily blocked by debris, however." He frowned at the message. "Which likely means wherever this entrance leads has already been discovered and looted of anything notable. We can only hope that any reliefs were left undamaged."

"Doubtful," said the larger man. "Thieves have learned how much money they can earn from the carved reliefs. Especially poor Egyptians."

"I'm not paying you for your opinions," Tío Ricardo said, his voice sharp edged.

The man shrugged, his utensils scraping loudly against his plate. The motion made a horrific screech and Mr. Hayes winced as he filled his cup with whiskey from his ever-present flask. I wanted to fill his plate with bread to soak up the liquor sloshing around inside his body.

"That chamber might yield another entryway that is as yet undiscovered," Tío Ricardo said. "But I did tell you, Whit, that we ought to have left days earlier. We might even now be uncovering ground."

"It wasn't possible," Mr. Hayes said mildly. "And you arranged the dinner with Sir Evelyn and Maspero yourself. You can't afford not to line up a license for next season, Ricardo. Think what Abdullah will say if you fail."

My uncle sobered.

"Just to clarify," the brawny British man said, "you *didn't* have an argument with Maspero and Sir Evelyn? Because *my* contract was for the rest of this season and the next."

I looked sharply at the man, whose rigid movements hadn't eased with the progression of the dinner. He glanced pointedly at one of the saloon walls where a long line of rifles were kept. I could almost picture the heavy weight of the weapon in that man's hands. A cold shiver danced down my spine. Mr. Hayes eyed the man with a carefully neutral expression. His behavior was remarkably different than what I'd seen up until now. He didn't acknowledge the girl sitting next to him in the slightest. Not even to ask her for salt. He simply leaned forward and reached across her as if she weren't sitting there.

"Of course he did," Mr. Hayes muttered, sprinkling the salt over his plate. "Ricardo can't help it."

"That conversation was well worth it and you know it," Tío Ricardo said. "There's only so much nonsense I can stomach."

"How, sir?" asked the brawny gentleman. "Not that one, Isadora, it's much too spicy for you."

The girl glanced up, her mouth set in an intractable line. She applied a liberal amount of the red spice over her food. She ate the first bite calmly while the man sighed loudly. I hid my smile. Perhaps there was more to her than I originally thought.

"I'm afraid her mother gives her too much free rein," the brawny man said, as if his daughter sat not two feet away from him. Isadora's light eyes tightened but then her expression smoothed out into one of bland neutrality. I sympathized with her immediately.

My uncle turned his attention back to the brawny man. "To answer your question, I confirmed that neither Monsieur Maspero nor Sir Evelyn know what the hell we're doing here."

"God help us all if they ever do," Mr. Hayes said.

"Which is why you've hired *me*," the large man said.

Mr. Hayes scrutinized the British man. Suspicion was etched into every line of Mr. Hayes's body, from his tense shoulders to the fingers that gripped his fork and knife.

My gaze flickered to my uncle.

He looked just as uneasy as Mr. Hayes, but instead of vocalizing any concern, he said, "I hope we never have to use your services, Mr. Fincastle."

"Here, here," Mr. Hayes said dryly.

"A shame I had to hire you at all," my uncle commented.

"Do you mean because of your lost patrons?"

"Yes, their deaths were a tremendous blow."

"Well, not all is lost," Mr. Fincastle said. "You've certainly become a wealthy man." He flicked his fork around, gesturing to the dahabeeyah.

"That was a vile observation," my uncle said.

Mr. Fincastle smiled coldly. "But true, regardless."

My blood ran cold. Had my inheritance paid for all this? Another thought slammed into me. *Patrons*. My mind spun. They were talking about my parents—who had funded this entire enterprise. Dark spots swam at the corners of my vision. Why hadn't I thought of it before? My knees shook and I used the wall to keep me upright.

Thanks to my parents' deaths, my uncle had all the money in the world.

CAPÍTULO CATORCE

*T*he next morning, the wind continued to push us upstream, much to the relief of the rowing crew. The sails billowed outward, resembling full bellies, propelling us past extraordinary monuments, golden in hue and half torn down. On either side of the *Elephantine* the sandbanks stretched at both ends, a never-ending scroll filled with picturesque scenes of ancient temples and fishermen sitting in their small boats, throwing out nets. Kareem named all the villages we passed.

Some were mud-walled, surrounded by marshes, and others appeared more stately with squat buildings overlooking the sharp green of the water. It spread like a vein to the rest of the land, and I understood why the river was revered in Egypt. It gave life and sustenance, it carried one to adventure and discovery, and it also brought you home. Kareem taught me the names of the gods associated with the Nile: Hapi, the god of flooding; Sobek, the god of the river crocodiles; Anuket, goddess of the Nile's cataracts.

"You know a lot about ancient Egyptian religion," I told him.

"Only because of Abdullah," he said. "He's the scholar among the team."

Kareem led me away from the railing so we could work. I scrubbed the deck, my head lowered, ears straining for any sign of Tío Ricardo or Mr. Hayes. His other companion, Mr. Fincastle, didn't look twice at me, so I didn't bother keeping track of his movements. Around noon, we stopped so the cook and Kareem could go out on land to use one of the public ovens in order to make bread. The main meal, I learned, consisted of a toasted flatbread soaked in olive oil and flavored with salt and pepper, with lentils stirred in until the whole thing turned into a kind of thick soup. For dessert, we munched on dates, and some of the crew enjoyed tobacco and coffee.

After lunch, I continued scrubbing until I reached the very back of the ship, working my way to the mast. My fingers were cramped from curling them around the bristled brush, and my back ached from having spent the majority of the day bent and on my knees. I pushed through the discomfort, liking the immediate improvement to the deck. One good swipe, and the dirt cleared to reveal the handsome wooden planks.

Someone shouted, indiscernible words carried off by the sudden furious wind. I looked up, my hair pulling free in a riot of tangles from out of my hat. Sheets of paper danced across my vision and I jerked back to avoid getting smacked in the face.

"No!" the reis hollered. "Grab them, you fool!"

The captain looked wildly around, pointing in every direction, clearly desperate.

The scene unfolded in a mad rush as several crew members raced around the deck, snatching the loose papers fluttering like wayward snowflakes. I jumped to my feet and pulled two as they rippled over the boards. Another caught my eye, whipping up and over the railing—

I lurched forward, one arm outstretched, fingertips spread wide. The dahabeeyah rocked, the water rippling roughly. My mistake became all too clear. I had no purchase and I'd leaned out too far, and when the boat dipped, I flew forward and flipped down into the river.

No time to scream for help.

Warm water engulfed me, smacking my palms hard. Bubbles erupted in a dizzying dance around me. I blinked, and righted myself, kicking hard. I burst through the surface sputtering.

"Man overboard! We lost one!" someone yelled from above.

I coughed up more water and fought hard to keep myself from going back under. The current pulled, a powerful force, determined to win. Something drifted past my ankle and I let out a horrified shriek. I'd never swum in a river before, and the deep water fueled my imagination to terrifying heights. What lurked below the surface? The water was too dark to see anything clearly and it curled around me in a frightening fist. I tipped my head backward and looked up and met the amused blue gaze of Mr. Hayes. He folded his arms on the railing and his handsome features twisted in laughter, auburn hair gleaming like polished amber in the sunlight. "Did you swim all the way here, Olivera?"

"Hilarious."

"It's a pretty day for it, isn't it?"

"Mr. Hayes," I said, spitting water, "I would greatly appreciate your assistance."

He examined his fingernails. "I don't know. What's in it for me?"

"I thought you had scruples."

Without skipping a beat, he said dryly, "I only know how to spell the word."

That would have made me smile if I weren't splashing loudly, trying to keep my nose above the water. "I'm not a strong swimmer," I said, unable to keep the panic out of my voice.

In an instant, his genial expression turned murderous. "What did you say?"

"I wasn't *planning* on getting in the river."

"Bloody hell." He turned away for an instant and then returned, carrying a long coil of rope. He threw one end down and it spooled a few yards away from me. I hadn't realized the river had taken me outward.

"Can you reach it?"

I struggled forward, slowly but surely propelling myself back to the *Elephantine*. But the current swept me backward; with a muttered curse, I kicked wildly and managed to draw closer to the rope.

"I think I can manage on my own."

"We are going to have words," Mr. Hayes said in a grim voice, preparing to launch himself over the railing. "Several of them."

"Looking forward to it," I said and then spat out more of the river.

"Shit." His eyes widened as he looked at something behind me. "*Inez!*"

I half turned my head to find an obsidian ridge cutting through the surface, a large shadow moving like a bullet under the water line. Horror seized my body and I stopped swimming, paralyzed.

A Nile crocodile. Ten yards away and gaining ground.

There was a loud scuffle overhead, frantic conversation, but it seemed to come from a million miles away; the noise might have been from the moon. I couldn't take my gaze from the predator swimming toward me. I came to my senses and clumsily swam toward the dahabeeyah. A blur of movement came from somewhere next to me, a large body crashing into the river near me. Mr. Hayes came up, shook his head, his hair dark brown and wet, plastered across his face. He reached me in one breath and gripped my hand.

"Oh no, oh no," I babbled.

"I won't let anything happen to you," he said calmly. "Take a big breath."

I'd barely done it before he dragged me below the water.

I couldn't see in front of me, my vision obscured by the murky river. But I knew we went down, down, down, swimming to the bottom. Weeds and long stems of grass reached around us, threatening to ensnare us in the deep. Mr. Hayes's rough palm engulfed mine, his large shape curled around me. An unshakeable tether against the current. Sand billowed out and around as my lungs began to burn. I made to swim up toward the light, but Mr. Hayes held me in place, shaking his head.

He cupped my face in his hands and gently pulled my head forward until our mouths met. Neither of us closed our eyes, and the contact rippled outward, an electrical current I felt in every corner of my body. Bubbles of air passed through his lips and into mine. The pressure in my chest decreased and I turned away, not wanting to take more from him. We waited for three more beats, our fingers interlocked, and then Mr. Hayes kicked off the sandy ground and we shot straight upward, his legs brushing against my own as he propelled us to the light.

We broke through the surface, and I wiped the water from my eyes in time to see Mr. Fincastle take aim and then shoot down into the water from up on the dahabeeyah. Furious bullets rained down ahead of us. His daughter, Isadora, joined him, standing at his side, the dainty wildflower. The wind pulled at her hair as she slowly pulled out a sleek handgun. It looked slim and delicate in her gloved hand.

With utter calm and poise, she pulled the trigger.

My respect for her soared as, together with her father, she shot at the predator.

"Clear?" Mr. Hayes yelled.

"I believe so," Mr. Fincastle yelled back. The *Elephantine* crew surrounded him and his daughter on either side. At his words, they loudly cheered, including Isadora. I could see her smug satisfaction from where I bobbed in the Nile.

"Yes, by all means celebrate what was an entirely preventable situation," Mr. Hayes muttered under his breath. He turned to me, the lines around his eyes tightening with strain. He pulled me into the circle of his arms. His words came out in a half shout. "Are you all right?"

I let out a shaky laugh, trying not to stare at the water droplet high on his cheek. "That wasn't so bad."

"Oh yes, it was a jolly good time," Mr. Hayes said, sounding so much like a British aristocrat that I blinked. His light blue shirt matched his eyes and outlined his muscular shoulders. He kicked back, creating distance between us, and gestured toward the boat. "After you, Olivera."

I swam with him at my side, the wind tearing overhead, rocking the *Elephantine* dangerously. The rope was still hanging off the side. Another was thrown for Mr. Hayes and he wrapped it around his fist once. To me he said, "Tie the other around your waist. They'll pull you up."

After an uncomfortable interval where I was roughly tugged up and over into the boat, I was able to fully breathe for the first time since falling overboard. I recognized the exact moment everyone discovered my gender. The crew surrounded me, gaping at me, the clear curves of my body in full display under the white tunic I wore. I crossed my arms over my chest.

Mr. Fincastle stood before me in his khaki trousers and tall boots, the gun propped over his shoulder. "We have a stowaway it seems. And who might you be?"

The breeze brushed against my wet clothes and my teeth chattered. "I-Inez Emilia O-Olivera. Pl-pleasure to meet you. Thank you for saving us."

Mr. Hayes threw me a disgruntled look. I suppose I ought to have thanked him, too.

With one fluid motion, Mr. Fincastle moved his gun and aimed it at my face. "And why were you on our boat? Here to spy on the excavation?"

I stared down the barrel of the rifle, my heart thumping loudly in my chest. Isadora let out a gasp, and my attention flickered to her.

"What the *hell* are you doing?" Mr. Hayes said, stepping in front of me. "This is Ricardo's niece, you bloody idiot. Put the gun down."

But he didn't. Mr. Fincastle observed me coldly, as if I were a viable threat to everyone on board. His daughter regarded me with a discreet, sympathetic glance. Her father took a step closer. If he pulled the trigger, I wouldn't survive the consequences. I wanted to rail against him, but I instinctively understood that if I moved a muscle, he wouldn't hesitate to shoot me.

"Put the fucking gun down," Mr. Hayes said quietly. He didn't disguise the menace in his voice.

"Are you vouching for her?"

"I am."

Isadora raised her brows and looked between us with an interested air.

Mr. Fincastle tucked the weapon under his arm and held his hands up. "We can't be too careful." And then he strode away, as if he hadn't just threatened my life, moments after saving it.

Isadora stripped off her muslin jacket and handed it to me. "For your modesty."

I blushed, and hastily put it on. "Gracias. I mean, thank you."

She dimpled at me and with one last look at Mr. Hayes, she darted after her father, tucking her handgun within her skirt pocket.

"You can all resume your work," Mr. Hayes said to the remaining spectators.

The crew dispersed. He slicked his dripping hair off his face. With a sudden look of alarm, he began patting down his pants and then muttered a low curse. I almost didn't hear it, my gaze locked on the wet fabric clinging to the sharp lines of muscle delineating the flat plane of his stomach. The wet cotton of his trousers clung to his muscled thighs. He might as well have been naked.

I forced my gaze away, my head oddly swimming. "Did you lose something?"

"My brother's flask. He was very fond of it."

Another crocodile most likely had it now. "Probably for the best."

He glowered at me and then began working the knot at my waist, his warm fingers brushing against me. Warmth pooled in my belly, flushed my cheeks. My mouth went dry, dryer than the golden sands surrounding us. He dipped his chin, focused on the knot, his face inches from mine. His blue eyes were lined with dark lashes, spiky with wet. A warm flush danced across my skin and I shivered. Mr. Hayes paused, raised his eyes to meet mine. It annoyed me that I found him handsome when I couldn't trust him. I bit my lip, and he tracked the movement, his eyelids lowering to half-mast.

Mr. Hayes's expression softened, his gaze warm. "Are you really all right?"

The tender concern in his tone was like sipping something hot. We stared at each other, my breath catching at the back of my throat. Dimly, I was aware that I was dancing too close to the edge. One misstep, and I'd find myself on unfamiliar ground.

Mr. Hayes cleared his throat and glanced down, attention back on the rope. "This is quite an ensemble," he said mildly, voice neutral. "Acquire it recently?"

"I had an extra tunic lying around in my luggage. Seemed a waste not to use it."

He yanked on the rope, and it fell away. A dangerous gleam lurked in his blue gaze. "You're sunburned. Where the hell is your hat?"

"I was wearing one."

"You were wearing a fez before you went over, which doesn't offer even the littlest bit of protection from the rays. The sun can be murderous at this time of day."

"My other one didn't go with my outfit," I said. "I had to have a practical disguise."

"My God, it *was* you," he said in a marveling tone. "Serving us dinner. I thought I smelled vanilla."

"*What?*"

"Your soap," he said, imperturbably. "I ought to have known. But I thought it impossible . . ."

"You really ought to pay better attention to your instincts. They won't lead you astray."

Mr. Hayes flinched as if I'd struck him. He abruptly took a step back. "What is it?"

He shook his head and smiled, but it wasn't one of his real ones. This one was hardened, made of stone. "Come with me, Señorita Olivera."

"No, I'd rather not. Gracias." I gestured to my dripping clothes. "I really ought to change."

He eased one elbow onto the rail and regarded me coolly. "You have to face your uncle at some point."

I bent down and wrung the hem of the long tunic. "I will when I'm ready. What about a few days from now?"

Mr. Hayes gave a short laugh. "What makes you think he won't find you before then?"

Fear skittered down my spine. It wasn't until that moment that I realized how badly I needed an ally. I didn't trust Mr. Hayes in the slightest, but he'd jumped into the Nile after me, even after he spotted the danger. I didn't want to face my uncle alone. "Will you stay with me?"

Mr. Hayes narrowed his gaze. He assessed my face, seeing what I desperately tried to hide. "What are you nervous about?"

"He'll be furious. It would help if you took my side."

He looked appalled. "Absolutely not."

Half-frantic, I thought of something to say that might buy me more time. "After our day together in Cairo, I thought we'd become friends."

"I don't have those anymore," Mr. Hayes said matter-of-factly. "Why on earth would you think so?"

A deep flush burned my cheeks. "You've just saved my life. We've dined together. You kissed me goodbye?"

"It was your mistake to read into my behavior. I treat everyone the same. And if you thought we were *friends,* you might have not lied to me, pretending to be someone else on this damn boat."

Red-hot embarrassment flowed under my skin. I recalled staring stupidly after him as he vanished inside of the hotel, touching the skin his lips had grazed. "So, you kiss every person you meet."

The corners of his mouth deepened. "Is that a question, Olivera?"

"Well, why did you?"

"Why not?" He lifted an indolent shoulder. "Not everything has to mean something. It was just a kiss."

"Be careful. Your cynicism is showing."

"No sense in hiding something you've seen from the beginning." He sighed. Without disturbing his seemingly casual pose, his hand shot forward, ensnaring my wrist in a tight hold. He grinned at my astonishment. "Let's get this over with. Am I dragging you to him, or will you walk with me?"

I lifted my chin, my jaw set, and I fought to ignore how the warmth of his fingers was wreaking havoc on my heartbeat. "Have it your way, then."

"Good girl," he murmured, releasing me.

We strode side by side, Mr. Hayes somehow leading me to the saloon, without actually stepping in front of me or touching me again. He had that kind of presence that commanded obedience. But for some reason, I got the impression that he pushed any form of leadership away with both hands.

He glanced down at me.

I swallowed hard and grimly stared ahead, not wanting to show any of the inner turmoil I felt. Sweat gathered in my palms. I had to make my case to stay.

Mr. Hayes stepped aside at the entrance of the saloon.

I leaned in close, close enough to see every faint line across his brow, the subtle narrowing of his gaze. "If my uncle does decide to turn us around and take me back, then I want you to know something."

He watched me warily. "What is it?"

I knew just how to unbalance him. "Thank you for saving my life. And regardless of what you might think, I do consider you a friend, *Whit*."

He blinked with a quick inhale that was so quiet, I might have missed it had I not been standing less than a pace away from him. The words were true. He'd jumped in after me, just like a friend would have. I didn't trust him, or his involvement with my uncle's schemes.

But Whit had helped save my life.

I strode past him, my heart clamoring against my ribs. My uncle sat at the round table, poring over documents, a cup of black coffee at his elbow. His pen scratched in his journal, and he muttered something to himself in Spanish. He heard our approach but didn't look up.

"What the hell was all the commotion, Whitford? Mr. Fincastle make good on his threat to shoot crocodiles?"

"That he did," I said.

My uncle turned to stone.

I felt, rather than saw, Whit's presence. He stood behind me, lounging against the wall, his ankles crossed. Absolute silence stretched, thickening with tension. Tío Ricardo's fingers flexed around his pen, and then relaxed. Slowly, he lifted his head, his mouth hammered into a thin, pale slash. He regarded me in stunned horror, his attention drifting to the long tunic enshrouding my slight frame, dripping water onto the saloon's carpet.

"Why are you both wet?"

"We had an encounter with the aforementioned crocodile," Whit said.

"Jesucristo." My uncle shut his eyes and then opened them, hazel ones so like mine. "You disobeyed me," he said in marveling tones. "Do you have any idea of what you've done?"

"No, because you won't—"

Tío Ricardo stood abruptly, his chair flying backward. "Did you help her on board, Whitford?"

Whit gave him a pointed look.

My uncle splayed his hands, half-angry, half-exasperated. "Why would you do this?"

I lifted my chin. "It was the only way."

My uncle opened his mouth, and then slowly shut it. He seemed afraid to ask me what I meant, but intuition told me he already knew why I had come. I wanted the truth, I wanted answers. And I would get them any way I could.

I swallowed hard. Sweat beaded at my hairline.

"Get Hassan," Tío Ricardo quietly.

I blinked in confusion—did he want me to . . . no, he'd spoken to Whit, who remained motionless against the wall, his hands tucked deep into his pockets. He might have been posing for a photograph.

"Let her stay," Whit said. "I think she's earned the right to be on the team."

I swung around to face him, my lips parting. He didn't look in my direction. His attention remained focused on my uncle.

"Have you lost all sense?" Tío Ricardo asked.

"We can't turn around, and you know it," Whit said. "She figured out a way on board with no help from either of us; she just survived swimming in the Nile. She's their *daughter*."

"I don't care. Bring Hassan to me."

"We turn around and we'll lose days that we don't have. Are you sure you want to risk it?"

My uncle swiped at the contents on the table. Everything went crashing to the ground. He breathed heavily, his buttons straining against his broad chest. His hands were clenched into tight fists, his knuckles turning white.

I jumped back with a squeak. I'd never seen such violent temper. My father had been a mild-tempered man, his tone soft and approachable. My mother was the yeller, but she didn't throw anything when in a rage. Tío Ricardo paced, tugging at his beard.

Then he stopped and faced Whit with a calculated look.

Swift comprehension crossed Whit's face. "No," he breathed. "I won't do it."

"I pay you a great deal to do what I need," my uncle said. "You'll take her back after we disembark."

Whit pushed off the wall. "You need the crew, and I can't sail the *Elephantine* by myself. Consider that she won't ever give up, and short of going with her to Argentina—"

Tío Ricardo's head snapped back, his mouth going slack. Panic stabbed me in the gut. I didn't like the look on his face at all. Neither did Whit for that matter.

"Absolutely not," Whit snapped. "You've gone too far. I didn't agree to the job only to become a babysitter."

I flinched.

Desperation carved deep grooves along my uncle's brow. "She can't stay here."

I cleared my throat. "I might have to, if only to help you."

My uncle inhaled deeply, clearly fighting to keep calm. "My dear niece—"

But Whit cut him off, his eyes narrowing in my direction. "Explain what you mean."

My attention flickered to my uncle. "When my father sent me the ring, I felt an immediate reaction. It was a spark that I felt everywhere. And then I tasted roses."

Whit shut his eyes and let out a humorless laugh.

"Roses," Tío Ricardo said in a hollow sort of voice. "Are you sure?"

"What is the significance of the rose?" I demanded. Neither of them replied. Annoyance and frustration warred within me. We would get nowhere if they didn't start trusting me. "Without the golden ring, you will need my help to find Cleopatra's tomb."

"You don't know that," Tío Ricardo said, but he didn't seem as adamant. The fight had gone out of him, and he tilted his head to the side.

"Some of the magic latched on to *me*. I can sometimes feel *her*. As if I were in a private memory belonging to her. She's immense, covered in shadow, but I can see a white ribbon in her hair, adorned with pearls. Her feet shimmer from the gems on her golden sandals. That magic reminds me of flowers in bloom." I paused. "The rose."

"Impossible," my uncle said. "*Impossible*. We all feel the remnants of magic whenever we touch an object that's a carrier." He frowned, silently considering for a moment. "The ring must house an incredible amount of magical energy for you to see . . . her. It must not have been handled by too many people since the spell was first cast. And it doesn't necessarily mean it will lead you to her burial site."

Whit let out another short, humorless laugh, and then turned away, his shoulders shaking. I glared at his back, knowing that he understood what I wouldn't say out loud. After all, he was there the day that I had bought the trinket box. The magic in me had led me straight to it.

That he didn't reveal what had happened to his *employer* confused me. It was as if he were protecting me in some way that I didn't understand.

Tío Ricardo wavered, clenching and unclenching his fist.

Whit turned around, his attention solely on my uncle's immovable frame. No one spoke; I hardly dared to breathe. I didn't know why my father had sent me the ring. I didn't know if the ring or the trinket box would really lead me to her. I only knew that the answers were within reach.

"All right," he said quietly. "You're in, Inez."

Elation curled deep in my belly, made my hands shake. But then his words sunk in.

You're in.

What had he meant by that?

But I didn't care. I only wanted to know what had happened to my parents. I couldn't do that from Argentina, or even Cairo. Nothing mattered but discovering the truth.

"Give her the storage cabin," Tío Ricardo said. "Inez, I'll introduce you to the rest of the team. Let me handle everything. Understood?" When I nodded, he relaxed, the tension leaving his shoulders. "I'll find a way to explain your presence to Mr. Fincastle. Appearances must be maintained for the sake of your reputation."

"What reputation?" Whit muttered.

"Inez, why don't you go and get settled?" Tío Ricardo said loudly. "Go straight to the last cabin on the right."

"I can take her," Whit said.

"Actually," my uncle said, "I need a quick word."

Whit straightened, his shoulders tense. He didn't take his eyes off my uncle. I left the saloon, making sure my steps were audible. And then I doubled back on tiptoe, tucking myself in the shadows, my ears straining.

"Do I need to be worried about you?" Tío Ricardo asked.

No response from Whit—unless he'd spoken very softly. I pressed closer to the wall. I kept my breathing steady, but my pulse danced wildly.

"I can't have you distracted. There's too much at stake, and you have a job to do."

"Which I'm handling. I'll find out more in Aswan."

"How?" Tío Ricardo asked.

"My contact assured me they'll stop for supplies. It won't be hard to find out what we need. There are only a few places agents frequent in a city as small as Aswan."

Agents? The only one I knew of was the odious Mr. Sterling. Regardless, it seemed Whit had been tasked with acquiring information for my uncle. I recalled his answer when I had asked him if his errands for Tío Ricardo were legal.

Sometimes.

"You mean the Cataract Bar," my uncle said.

"Perhaps," Whit said coolly. "I know of other places to check. Wherever they are, I assure you I'm on top of it, and there's no need to fear any *distraction*."

"Come now," Tío Ricardo said. "I've seen the way you look at her."

"Well, she has a certain charm," Whit said dryly. "It comes out when she's lying to your face."

"Whitford."

"Her beauty doesn't turn my head, trust me. I have zero intention of courting her."

"Inez is off-limits to you," my uncle pressed. "She's my niece, do you understand? Both of her parents are gone. None of my plans involve any attachment between you and her. Not even in friendship. I don't mean to be rude, but I would *never* allow it."

"Trust me when I tell you," Whit said without a trace of irony, "that she's entirely safe from me."

"Give me your word."

"You have it."

"Good," my uncle said. "She may be more useful than either of us realized."

CAPÍTULO QUINCE

I rushed away from the doorframe, my cheeks burning. Mortification made my blood simmer hot in my veins. When I first met Whit, I had found him an annoying flirt. Since then, I really had thought of him as a friend . . . No. I had to be honest with myself. A small part of me had been fighting against the attraction I had felt for him since our day in the market.

Whit had stood up for me. He hadn't left my side in that saloon. We had faced my uncle together. *Let her stay.* He could never know how much those words meant to me. When everyone always told me no, his defense had felt like a warm welcome.

But he clearly only viewed me as a friend.

Which was for the best. I couldn't forget that. And even our friendship had limits. There was a note from my mother I couldn't bring up to him. A square card with a picture of a gate that I couldn't ask him about. A distrust of his employer that he'd never share.

Whit wasn't a confidant.

He worked for my *uncle.*

By the time I reached my cabin—the storage room, more like—I'd managed to compose myself. From here on out, I needed to remain focused on what lay ahead. I wanted to know what had happened to my parents. If I was going to snoop around the campsite, I couldn't have anyone suspecting my motives or following me around. And ever since the magic had latched on to me, I was curious about Cleopatra. I'd seen her, and now I was heading toward her possible burial site. The desire to find her nearly overwhelmed me.

To do that, I couldn't afford any *distractions* of my own.

I dragged out my canvas bag from underneath the bed and took inventory. I peered at the items scattered around, realizing that most of them were meant for camping. Tents and mosquito nets, rough bedding, and thin pillows. Next to the supplies lay a large leather bag. A quick peek inside showed several bottles of medicinal purpose, along with jars of vinegar and, curiously, cream of tartar.

A sharp rap on the door gave me pause as I wrangled the extra coverlets onto the narrow bed. It was probably my uncle, and my temper spiked as his words ran through me.

He wanted to use me as some sort of pawn in his game.

Tío Ricardo thought he could control me but I would never let that happen.

Another knock jarred me from my thoughts. I sighed and opened the door, scowling.

But it was not my uncle.

Whit regarded me in amusement, hands tucked into his pockets, an easy and familiar smile on his lips. He leaned against the doorframe, his chin dipped down, his face hovering so close to mine. If I hadn't heard him speak the way he had about me to my uncle, I wouldn't have believed it.

He peered over my shoulder. "Settling in, darling?"

And just like that, all good sense deserted me. I stared at him in impotent fury. His words rang loud in my ears. *Her beauty doesn't turn my head.* "I'd advise caution against addressing a lady so familiarly. Some unfortunate girl might read into your words."

He threw his head back and laughed.

"If any one of them mistook it for deeper feelings on my end, well, I'd call them a proper idiot." He regarded me lazily under his half-lidded gaze. "Now, if I were to call a lady by her Christian name that would be an entirely different story."

I stilled, the ground I stood on shifting under my feet. "Care to elaborate?"

"Not really."

I lifted my eyes and met his blue ones. "You called me by my Christian name."

He narrowed his gaze. "When?"

"When I was in mortal peril."

Relief skittered across his face. Loosened those tight lines at the corners of his mouth. "Oh, well, that's different."

"Why?"

"You were in mortal peril."

I rubbed my eyes, suddenly exhausted. My scare in the river had left me shattered. "What do you want, Whit?"

He appeared startled to hear his first name. "Don't call me that."

"Lo siento, do you prefer Whitford?"

"Only your uncle calls me that."

"Whit it is, then. Did you need something?"

He assessed me. "Do you have all the necessities? Toothbrush? Pillow? Blanket?"

"Yes, I managed to sneak some useful things on board."

"A thrilling tale, no doubt."

I recalled changing into the tunic next to the building, worried I'd be seen, terrified I wouldn't make it on board. "It certainly had its moments."

We fell silent, with only the sounds of the Nile disturbing the quiet. The soft light drifting into the cabin from the small window danced across his face. His grave expression stole my breath.

"I'm glad I made it to you in time," he said softly.

"Me too."

He straightened away from the door, a wry smile tugging at his mouth. "Good night, darling."

I examined my wardrobe, considering what to wear. My options were severely limited: two walking dresses, a pair of Turkish trousers and a wrinkled cream blouse, one pair of shoes. I decided against the bicycle costume, and landed on the yellow muslin, warm enough for the cool evenings and ladylike enough for propriety's sake. My hair hadn't been brushed in days and the results were terrifying. Wild curls floated around my face, refusing to be tamed, each strand with a mind of its own. I pulled the upper half away from my face and secured it with a ribbon. The mirror revealed disastrous results: hair barely managed, clothes wrinkled, and new hollows under my cheekbones.

I sighed. The best I could manage on my own.

Morning light poured in from the single window as I splashed cool water on my face before heading out to the saloon. Everyone sat around at the table and stilled at my approach. Isadora smiled over the rim of her mug while her father gave me a less than friendly perusal. Probably searching for weapons hidden in the folds of my skirt. Whit shot him an annoyed look. Kareem poured coffee into waiting cups, and then he gestured to the remaining open seat. My uncle kept his face hidden behind the paper, refusing to meet my eyes.

"Buenos días," I said.

Whit held up his coffee in an ironic salute before taking a long sip. His eyes were bloodshot, tired, and there was a definite droop in the line of his shoulders.

"Up all night?" I asked.

The corners of his lips twitched, and he arched a brow. There was a wicked gleam lurking in the depth of his eyes, and I knew he was barely restraining himself from saying something inappropriate. But he wouldn't, not in present company. "I slept fine," he said in a husky voice.

I blushed and tore my gaze away.

"I fear we haven't been properly introduced," Mr. Fincastle said in the same accent as Whit. I was struck again by his immense frame, all brawn, and the thick mustache that covered a stern mouth.

"I am Señorita Olivera," I said. "That man hiding behind the paper is my uncle."

Damn it, I really had meant to behave.

"Miss Olivera, a pleasure. You're looking a bit more dry," Mr. Fincastle said coolly.

Tío Ricardo lowered his reading material with a dramatic sigh. He set it aside none too gently and regarded me from across the table as I took my seat.

Isadora cleared her throat loudly and threw her a father a pointed look.

"I do apologize for aiming a gun at your face," Mr. Fincastle continued in a begrudging sort of way that spoke volumes. His daughter had clearly given him an earful. She beamed at him and daintily took another sip of coffee.

But the blood drained from Tío Ricardo's face. His mouth opened and closed, and he sputtered several unintelligible words. "You aimed your *weapon* at my niece? She's a child!"

"You paid me for my services." Mr. Fincastle gestured toward me. "She's made a full recovery since. We ought to congratulate you."

"Congratulations," Whit said to me cheerfully.

My uncle threw a murderous glare in the direction of Mr. Fincastle, who nibbled on bread slathered with butter. "I'm afraid I still don't know who you are, and how you've become a member of your uncle's excavation team."

"She is mostly here to keep me company," Tío Ricardo said, and then he gestured to the burly man. "Inez, this is Mr. Robert Fincastle, in charge of our security, and his daughter, Isadora. They recently arrived from England."

That explained Mr. Fincastle's fascination with the weapons lined against the wall. He had probably brought them on board himself. It also explained how Isadora had stood next to him, firing her own pistol. It seemed no matter where I went, I was going to be surrounded by the British. I narrowed my gaze at Mr. Fincastle. Why would my uncle think we would need weaponry at an excavation site? I squirmed in my seat. It seemed highly unusual.

"Mr. Hayes you've met," Tío Ricardo added, almost as an afterthought.

"True, but I still don't know what he does for you," I pressed.

"A little of everything," my uncle said vaguely. "He's an enterprising fellow."

"Thank you," Whit said in mock seriousness.

"Ricardo, this is highly irregular," Mr. Fincastle said. "You ought to send her back. Her delicate constitution cannot handle the demands of the journey."

I bristled. "My delicate constitution?"

Mr. Fincastle gestured dismissively with his hand. "A typical quality found in sheltered females—such as yourself."

His hypocrisy enraged me. "You've brought your own daughter," I said through gritted teeth.

"We agreed I would during my contract negotiations," Mr. Fincastle said. "My daughter isn't delicate. She *also* didn't sneak on board, and she knows how to behave herself."

"That's not to say that I wouldn't have if you'd left me behind," she said with a wink in my direction.

My lips parted in surprise.

"Regardless," Mr. Fincastle said in an icy tone, "I prepared for all eventualities, and suddenly I have a new person to look after. That will cost you, Ricardo, if you insist on bringing her along."

I sat back against the chair and clasped my hands tight in my lap. A vehement protest climbed up my throat. Mr. Fincastle's damning implication of my character grated. He thought me reckless and weak. But my uncle had left me little choice. If he'd been forthright from the beginning, I wouldn't have gone to such extremes looking for information.

"For the moment, it can't be helped," Tío Ricardo said. When Mr. Fincastle made to protest again, my uncle held up his hand, a hard line to his jaw. "I don't see the need to include you in my decision."

Mr. Fincastle kept quiet, but I sensed a deep mistrust toward myself and my uncle. Kareem brought several dishes into the saloon. The scent of sweet and savory food filled the room and my mouth watered.

"Have you been to Egypt before, Miss Olivera?" Mr. Fincastle asked.

"Not once. My parents loved this country, and I thought I'd get to know it for myself." Privately I added, *and to discover what happened to them.* My attention flickered to my uncle, whose presence seemed to fill up the small space of the saloon. The more time I spent with him, the harder it was for me to view him as a criminal. He seemed passionate about his work, and his love for Egypt and its history and culture seemed genuine.

Could my mother have been wrong somehow?

My uncle must have felt my gaze because his own flicked toward mine. Our matching hazel eyes met, his warm and speculative, mine steeped in uncertainty.

Kareem and another waiter brought out the last of the meal. Everything was laid before us. Simple and serviceable plates were piled high with a variety of foods I'd never seen before.

Whit gave me the grand tour around the table. "The pastries are called feteer, and it's delicious slathered in honey. But you can pair it with eggs and salty white cheese." He pointed to a bowl that held round-shaped food, packed tightly into medium-sized balls. "These are called falafels, my personal favorite. Made of fava beans, and quite savory. Have you tried feta cheese? It's also delicious with honey." He paused, throwing me a rueful look. "If you're thinking that I adore honey, you'd be correct. The rest you ought to recognize," he finished in sly amusement.

I did; it was the fava bean stew I'd helped make the day before with disastrous results. To my astonishment, Whit took my plate and served me a little of everything. Isadora watched him with keen interest. Everyone else at the table remained motionless. I could feel the subtle note of disapproval.

"Just how well do you two know each other?" Mr. Fincastle asked.

"We met a few days ago," Whit said with his imperturbable English accent. "So not well."

"I see," Mr. Fincastle said. "Why did you sneak on board the *Elephantine*, Miss Olivera?"

I gestured vaguely with my fork, deciding to be honest. "I don't like being left behind. And I really am excited about all of the sightseeing."

"Sightseeing?" Mr. Fincastle repeated faintly. "My dear, if you wanted to explore the land of the pyramids, might I suggest you pay for the services provided by Thomas Cook? You can join the hundreds of travelers littering the Nile." He shifted his bulky upper body and addressed my uncle. "Or are we adding tourist attractions on our journey, and you didn't tell me?"

"Of course not," Tío Ricardo said. "We are heading directly to Philae."

I perked up at this information. The island was famous for its legendary beauty and history. Excitement pulsed under my skin. "How far away are we, Tío?"

"It's close to Aswan, where we'll be stopping for supplies before arriving."

Since I didn't know where exactly that city was, his explanation didn't help. Ever accommodating, or perhaps picking up on my confusion, Mr. Hayes came to my rescue.

"Aswan is near the first cataract," he said. "And the location of several archaeological sites."

"Cataract?"

"Good God," Mr. Fincastle muttered.

"Inez," my uncle said, exasperated. "I thought you'd been educated on Egypt. What do you know of the Nile?"

"It's my first visit and my *education* didn't extensively cover Egyptian geography," I said in prickly mortification. I calmed myself by finally reveling in a piece of information I hadn't known before. I had been given a destination. Another place where my parents frequented, lived, explored.

Another piece of the puzzle finally revealed.

Was the island the last place they were seen alive?

Once again, it was Mr. Hayes who answered me. "The Nile is divided by six cataracts, the majority of which are found in Egypt. Passing one is very dangerous, as the water level could be too low, the boulders become visible, and the current moves rapidly. In order to get to our destination, we have to successfully cross the first one. Fortunately, we'll stop there and proceed no farther."

"Hidden sandbanks and large, sunken rocks are often an issue," Mr. Fincastle added. "Depending on the current's movement, they might shift. This is what makes navigation tricky by day, and dangerous by night."

No one had ever told me. Until now, our journey upstream had been downright sluggish save for yesterday's near catastrophe. But that had been my fault.

"Last year, we heard the news that a dahabeeyah had been shipwrecked. The passengers had to crawl out through the windows in their night dresses," Isadora said, and I startled. I don't know why I had assumed it was her first time to Egypt, too. It made me feel as if I had even more ground to cover, more catching up to do. "A dangerous undertaking, considering what else fills the Nile."

"I'm aware," I said dryly, recalling my brush with death from the day before.

"Are you still glad you came along?" Tío Ricardo asked wryly.

I lifted my chin. "Of course! It will be an adventure. Just think of the drawings that will fill my sketchbook."

Mr. Fincastle regarded me with keen interest. "You're an artist?"

"I *like* to draw, I'm not sure if that makes me an artist."

"Of course it does," my uncle barked.

My surprise robbed me of speech. It was the nicest thing he'd ever said to me. My cheeks warmed and I hid them behind a long sip of bitter coffee.

"Oh, I see what you're about," Mr. Fincastle said. "I understand you completely, Ricardo. You couldn't secure a photographer after you lost the previous one, and so instead we'll have your niece to keep proper record. Fortunate indeed that she decided to include herself in your plans."

"Actually," Tío Ricardo said, "we did have a photographer. Abdullah's granddaughter, Farida, had been taking pictures for us. But she won't be with us this season. Having Inez render all of the vibrant colors from within the temples would be an asset . . ."

I sat back against my chair. Until he said it, the idea had *never* occurred to me. Until the words were out in the open, I didn't realize how badly I wanted to do it. This would be the perfect ruse. A way to see everything I could on the island. A way to be useful to Abdullah's team.

Before my uncle could say another word, I shifted in my chair to address the burly man head on. "Very clever, Mr. Fincastle. That is the *exact* reason why my uncle ought to invite me to be a member of his team."

My uncle sat in quiet bemusement, as if he couldn't quite believe how I'd forced myself into his plans, and Mr. Hayes laughed under his breath. He'd eaten every bite on his plate and was now helping himself to my pastry. As if there weren't other ones to choose from at the center of the table. Really, his manners were atrocious.

"It will mean practically sleeping in a tent and foregoing the luxuries of the dahabeeyah," Tío Ricardo warned. "Exploring dusty and dark rooms in sweltering heat."

A dreamy expression stole over Isadora's face. Her honey-colored hair was coiled perfectly at the crown of her head, and her dress was the height of European fashion, cinched tight around her narrow waist, a train of fabric curled around her chair. She looked like a damsel from a romance novel, just waiting to be saved. Except I couldn't get the picture of her firing that gun out of my mind.

"Wouldn't you rather sit and draw from the safety of the *Elephantine*?" Mr. Fincastle asked. "A lady such as yourself isn't used to the discomfort of rough travel."

Mr. Hayes snorted.

"I'm up to the task, I assure you."

"She's made up her mind," Tío Ricardo said. "I think she'll manage to surprise us all. Provided she promises to stay out of trouble."

"I can do this." There was no other option. This was the best way to give me freedom on Philae. A way to discover the truth about my uncle, to snoop inside his tent.

I'd do anything to make it work, even help them find Cleopatra's tomb.

My uncle didn't reply, and the rest of our party resumed their breakfast. He kept his eyes trained on mine, so very like my mother's and my hazel ones. He didn't say another word, but I understood him regardless. I heard the words as if he'd spoken them out loud.

Don't make me regret it.

Just wait until he discovered what I could do with a charcoal pencil.

CAPÍTULO DIECISÉIS

After breakfast, Mr. Fincastle and Isadora went out for a stroll on the deck, his rifle propped over his shoulder. She stood in his shadow, her arm looped around his elbow, the affection between them obvious. Pain constricted my breath, trapped in between my ribs. Papá and I took long walks around our estate, rambling and without any clear destination. He was an easy man to love, and he didn't need much to be happy. His books, a strong cup of coffee, his family close by, and Egypt, that was all. I wish I would have asked him more about his parents and what they had been like, and if he had been close to them. I'd never met them, and now I'd lost the chance to learn more about his upbringing.

Every day, I discovered something else their deaths had taken from me.

I blinked the tears away, still staring at the pair. They peered down into the water, no doubt looking for yet another crocodile to shoot. They moved out of view of the window frame, and I turned back to my uncle. Tío Ricardo pulled down a book from one of the saloon shelves, immediately getting lost in its pages.

It struck me then how little time we had spent together. My uncle, a man with so many secrets I doubted I could uncover them all.

But I could start somewhere.

Whit caught my eye, and smiled at me, his expression surprisingly tender. He poured himself another cup of coffee, lifted it in my direction, and then mouthed *good luck* before rising to leave the saloon. I stared after him in disbelief, his intuition profoundly unsettling. Why couldn't he act the scoundrel *all the time*? A brawny rogue who only cared about himself.

It'd be so much easier to forgive.

I shook off the unsettling feeling that I was falling into a pit that I wouldn't be able to climb back out of, and focused on my uncle, hiding behind the hardcover of his book.

"Tío," I said, "will you put down your reading for ten minutes?"

"What do you need, Inez?" he asked absently.

I sat in the chair closest to him. "We've barely spoken since I arrived, aside from you telling me that I needed to leave the country."

"Much good it did," he said with a small smile, putting the book down. He leaned back against his chair, folded his arms across his flat stomach, and studied me, tracking the curve of my cheek, the slope of my jaw. I got the impression that he searched for any sign of his sister.

A sister who believed him to be a criminal.

"I miss my parents," I said softly. "Being here helps me hold on to them."

His face bore every one of his stories; the lines held untold adventures, his scars displayed the perilous moments in his life, the glasses a necessity from long years of being hunched over a book. All put together, he was a study of secrets and academic pursuit, the mark of an explorer.

"What do you wish to know?"

My breath stayed at the back of my throat. Would I have many more moments like this? Only the two of us? When we reached Philae, his attention and time might be pulled in a thousand different directions. "They spent seventeen years in Egypt. Were they happy here?"

Tío Ricardo let out a soft chuckle. "Do you know why I invited them to come?"

"You needed money," I said flatly.

He gave me a rueful smile. "I'd drained all of my personal resources and I refused to accept funding from institutions who demanded artifacts in return. Zazi and I were at our wits' end, and then she had the idea for me to reach out to Cayo and Lourdes. It was the only way she thought the three of us could continue with any integrity. Her brother Abdullah's work had bound us all together . . . but then she died." Acute misery swept across his face, and I wanted to reach forward to take his hand in mine. But I held still, somehow knowing he'd stop talking if shown any pity.

And I didn't want him to stop talking.

"I continued to ask for the money because I believed in Abdullah's mission, and because I knew that Zazi wouldn't have wanted her brother to carry it alone." The line of his mouth relaxed as he fell into a memory. "Your father was happy from the start, but it took time for Lourdes to fall in love with Egypt. But when she did, she fell hard. Soon, she made herself indispensable to the team. She was so organized, and I trusted her to pay everyone on time, keeping track of their hours. She was a favorite among the crew, always making them laugh with some of her pranks. Eventually, she made a life here."

"She played pranks at the excavation site? That doesn't sound like Mamá."

My mother always knew how to behave, knew the right thing to say, and was a favorite in the social circles of Buenos Aires.

"It's who she was as a young girl," he said quietly. "Egypt brought that out of her. Try to remember that she married young, younger than you are now, and to a man much older than her. My parents were rigid people who expected much from their only daughter, and while they had a good name, they didn't have money. Your father made his wealth by working hard, making smart investments, and succeeding in the railroad industry. It was a good match, though, and they both were able to relax here. Become the people they were meant to."

"But still, to play *pranks*..." I let my voice trail off. The idea was as foreign to me as my mother wearing a bright red evening gown. She had never shown any playfulness with me. Hurt pinched my heart and I tried not to think about how we might have laughed harder if she had behaved more like herself around me.

"She has an old silk scarf that can shrink anything it can cover down to the size of a charm." Grief tinged his smile. "I can't tell you how many shoes of mine have gone missing."

I finally found my voice. "Well, I can see her ordering everyone around on the team."

"Much to the dismay of Abdullah. He's the one who likes to keep order, but your mother tried to override his decisions at every turn. I had to come between them many times." He gave a rueful shake of his head. "Between the two of them, I never had a question of who did what, or when. What time everyone would arrive to commence digging, or how long anyone worked. She managed everything and kept records of all the discoveries."

"Records?"

"Yes, she . . ." He hesitated, and then decided against continuing that sentence. "It was important to her that she kept track."

"Where did she keep said records?"

"That's something you don't need to know. But since we're on the subject, I'm going to repeat the need for caution when discussing your time with us here. If you care at all about my life's work, then you'll keep what you see and learn to yourself. Do it for your parents, if not for me."

"You can trust me."

"I wish I could," he said with real regret underscoring each word. "Not for something like this. You might be family, Inez, but you're a stranger to me where it counts and I won't risk everything merely because your feelings might get hurt."

He didn't know me well enough to pass judgment. He hadn't taken the *time* to get to know me. We were strangers by his choice, not mine. "Well, you haven't proven to be trustworthy yourself."

He stilled.

"I know you're keeping something from me," I accused. I hadn't planned on saying any of this to him, but now that I'd started, I couldn't stop. "I heard you talking to Mr. Hayes about Mamá and Papá, so don't bother denying it. What really happened to them? What aren't you telling me, Tío?"

"Listening at doors, Inez? That's beneath a young lady of your upbringing."

I threw my hands up. "Well, I have to if you insist on *lying* to me."

He stood, his guard up.

"You've hired Mr. Fincastle, who brought practically enough guns to outfit a militia. Why must you have security at your excavation site, Tío? My parents wouldn't have approved of having so many weapons."

His words rang out. "You didn't know your parents."

I reared back as if he had struck me across the face. But he hadn't lied, and perhaps that was what hurt the most. In a hundred years, I never would have expected my parents to be so reckless with their lives, and travel across the desert without any precautions. Not unless they had good reason.

"Were they looking for something?" I asked, a sudden idea striking me. "What?"

"Were they," I said slowly, fury lacing each word, "looking for something? Did you send them out there?"

Emotion flickered deep in his hazel eyes. It might have been guilt. But my uncle remained silent, even as my pulse thrashed in my veins. He adjusted his glasses, averting his gaze from mine. My heart sank. That was it, then.

My uncle had sent them on a wild hunt and they'd lost their lives because of him.

"Tell me about their last day, tell me what they were doing." My voice cracked. "Why weren't you with them?"

"*Enough,* Inez," he said, striding away from the table. "It will only give you pain to think of such things. Why don't you rest?"

"We've barely begun—"

"You and I can talk after you've calmed down."

I stared after him, furious at him and at myself for my inability to control my temper. Kareem stepped inside, a fresh pot of coffee in his hands. Silently, he poured me another cup.

"Shokran," I said. Then I glanced toward him. "How much of that did you overhear?"

Kareem smiled. "It's a small boat."

So it was. My uncle couldn't avoid me forever.

———※———

I found Whit journaling on one of the plush chairs out on the deck. Beyond, the Nile swept past a land patterned in greens, browns, and blues. Palm groves dotted the landscape in regular intervals. The beauty surrounding me didn't soothe my frustration. I sank down in the available seat next to him. I blew the hair off my face, my gaze landing on the page he wrote on. I caught a glimpse of confusing numerical scribblings and drawings before he snapped the journal closed.

He looked at me narrowly. "How did your talk with your uncle go, *nosy*?"

I blushed. "I lost my temper."

He *tsk-tsk*ed.

"I think my parents went out in that desert, searching for an artifact, a place, or . . . I don't know. *Something*," I said, watching him carefully. "My uncle is desperate to find it, too. Do you know what it could be?"

Whit lifted an indolent shoulder. "In Egypt? We're all looking for something."

There was note in his tone that gave me pause. Was he looking for what my uncle wanted, too? But the wistful quality in his voice made me think he was looking for something intangible. Nothing that he could hold in his hands or that had a price.

"I don't understand him," I fumed. "I don't understand his decisions, his behavior. His unwillingness to talk to me."

"Your uncle has a reason for everything."

I detected a note of disapproval in his voice. Something that begged a question. "Whit . . . do you trust him?"

He pierced me with a direct look that didn't match his lazy grin. "Why, Señorita Olivera, there are only two people in the world I trust."

"So few?" I eyed him, holding back my hair from flying into my face. The breeze had sharpened considerably. "Your family, I'd guess. Parents?"

The corners of his lips tightened. "My brother and sister."

"But not your mother and father?"

"I wouldn't trust them to save my life if I were on fire," he said with a slight smile.

I couldn't read him. He didn't sound the least bit upset, but his lips had twisted wryly, as if he knew he couldn't quite pull off a cavalier facade. A part of me understood. I was beginning to understand that I didn't trust my own parents. It was hard to when they kept so many secrets. They loved me, but hadn't shared their lives with their only child. It was hard to accept, hard to fathom. Another blast of wind whipped between us, and the boat lurched sharply.

I startled and looked around in alarm.

Whit abruptly sat up in the lounger. "That wasn't—"

The deck of the *Elephantine* groaned as it rocked sharply.

"Is that normal?" I said, my unease rising.

He pulled me up from my seat and to the railing and pointed his finger at the dark river churning as the wind blew around us like a shrill tempest. The water grew tumultuous, rising and falling in between large protruding rocks. "I must find Reis Hassan," he said grimly.

"Will we be all right?" But he wasn't listening to me, his attention was trained on the water. A chill gathered over my skin, making the hair on my arms stand on end.

I gathered the front of his shirt in one hand. "*Whit.*"

He looked down, lips parted in surprise. The full force of his blue gaze met mine. He brought his hand up to my cheek, hesitant and slow, almost touching. Something cold flashed in his eyes, and he dropped his palm. I missed his touch even though I hadn't felt it. Gently, he pried my fingers loose and stepped away from me, his face closing as if it were a doorway he refused to allow anyone through.

The boat dipped again, and something dragged along the underside of the *Elephantine*. "What was that?"

"Go back to your cabin." He left me on the deck. "I mean it, Olivera."

The boat heaved to the right and I stumbled, swinging my arm wide to right my balance. I took a hesitant step forward, and then another, but the boat pitched again, and my stomach dropped to my toes. I doubled back to the saloon. The rest of the crew rushed past me, speaking in rapid Arabic. They all wore expressions of panic.

"Sitti! You must go to your room!" Kareem said, sweeping past me. "It's not safe!"

"As soon as I find my uncle," I said.

But he'd already gone from my sight. I ran into the saloon and found him rolling up a map spread wide across the table. Something battered the windows and I spun around, letting out a gasp.

"Is that *sand*?" I asked.

In two strides Tío Ricardo was in front of me. "It's coming from the desert."

The boat groaned loudly as it struck something hard beneath our feet. His face paled, then he turned me around and pushed me toward my cabin. "Stay in your room until I tell you it's safe to come out, Inez. If we capsize, go out through the window. Leave everything behind. Do you understand?"

Numbly, I nodded and rushed to do what he said, my heart in my throat. I shut the door behind me and sat on the floor, my knees close to my chest. But no, staying inactive during such a time was immeasurably foolish. Suppose we flipped over, what then?

I looked around the room with a critical eye.

What could I stand to lose?

None of my parents' things. They weren't special items to anyone else, but because they had belonged to my parents, they were priceless. The boat rocked, groaning from being thrashed around by the heavy blast of wind. It howled outside my window with murderous intent. I stood on shaky legs, my arms windmilling, and took cautious steps toward the drawers under my bed.

A loud curse brought me up short.

That sounded like my uncle.

I rushed to the door and peered across the short corridor. One of the doors on the opposite side was ajar, swaying in rhythm to the movements of the ship. It creaked loudly. I stepped out into the hallway, my mouth opening—

Through the gap of the door, I caught sight of my uncle. The door swung forward, blocking my view, but then moved back the other way. I moved closer, my steps light against the wood. I thought I'd seen something familiar . . .

Tío Ricardo was rapidly going through his things—not unlike what I had been doing. But in his hands was a notebook, the cover painted with lush peonies. They were my mother's favorite flowers. I'd recognize her diary anywhere.

I was the one who'd painted it, front and back.

My uncle knelt over his trunk and pulled out several loose sheets, reading them quickly and then folding them in half, only to tuck them within my mother's words. Intuition flickered, and an urge to rush inside and demand he hand me my mother's private thoughts nearly overwhelmed me. But I stayed back, for once thinking it through. If I went in now, he'd probably lie to me, and then he'd make damn sure to hide her things from me.

Better to wait until he left the cabin.

Tío Ricardo barreled out of his room, his upper body pitched forward as if he were a charging bull. When he disappeared up the steps, I darted across the narrow hallway, shutting the door behind me.

He'd left the space tidy and organized, the trunk locked. With a muttered curse, I dropped to my knees, pulling a pin from out of my hair. I knew how to pick a lock thanks to my father's fascination with perfecting random talents. He could hold his breath underwater for three minutes, and he knew several different sailors' knots and how to untie them, and for a season, he was fascinated with burglars.

I stuck the pin into the lock and jimmied it one way, and when that didn't work, I tried the other way, thanking my aunt for the times she would lock me in my bedroom whenever I acted out. It opened, and as the boat lurched again, I flipped the lid of the trunk open.

Mamá's journal sat on top of the pile of rolled-up maps.

I would need time to read through every entry, but I didn't have that luxury. I only had tonight while everyone else fought to keep the *Elephantine* hale during the storm. With that thought, I rushed back to my room. I gathered my purse and bag and then sat directly underneath the window as the sand drove in furious bursts against the glass. If the boat were to capsize, I'd want to be closest to an exit.

It was only then that I began to read.

And it was on the last page when I read the entry that changed everything.

My brother and I can never go back. He's gone down a road that I will not follow, but I can't bear to go to the authorities. Oh, but how can I write such a thing? I must! I must! His threats terrify me. The last time we argued, it hurt to pick myself up from the floor. Ricardo said he hadn't meant to hurt me, but he did.

Even now, I carry the bruises. I can't ignore the truth.
I fear for my life. I fear for Cayo's life.
And I don't know what I should do. He is my brother.
But he is a murderer.

At first, I couldn't make sense of the sentences. And then each word crystallized, all sharp edges and harsh lines.

Threats.

Bruises.

Murderer.

My mother had been afraid for her life. I unbuttoned the collar of my dress, gasping, struggling to breathe. She had been living in *terror* of what her brother might do. The despair and desperation etched into every letter brought clarity to my mind. As if the fog had cleared, and I could see what had been hidden from me.

Who had Tío Ricardo killed?

And if he had once, he could again.

All this time, my uncle refused to give me the details surrounding their deaths. And now I finally knew why. The answer had been in front of me all along. Outside the window, the storm raged. A tempest demanding her due. I read the entry again and my vision blurred as I began to listen to what my intuition was frantically trying to tell me. All the clues were there. My uncle hadn't wanted me in Egypt. He engaged Whit in illegal activities. He refused to tell me what had happened to my parents. My mother's note to Monsieur Maspero, begging for help. The curious card with the illustration of a gate, with a time, place, and date on the other side. And now the journal entry where my uncle had laid his hands on her. Hard enough to bruise.

The truth was an iron fist around my heart, clenched tight.

My uncle killed my parents.

I had to get off the *Elephantine*. It took me seconds to pack all of my things. Outside my room, the corridor was empty. The crew, my uncle, Whit, and I'm sure Mr. Fincastle were on the upper deck. No one would notice as I carried my small bag to the railing. No one would notice there was one fewer person on the dahabeeyah. I pulled the door open, looked both ways, and scurried down the narrow hall. Curls of sand slapped my hair, making it gritty and hard. Above, the sounds of people shouting carried over the sharp wind. I made it to the railing, the strap of my bag digging into my palm.

Below, the water churned.

I remembered how the river had swept over my head. Held me in her clutches. With a shaking hand, I reached forward, fear twisting inside me sharply. Indecision hovered close and after one long moment, I let my arm drop.

It was foolish to jump.

My chances of survival were slim. If I stayed on board, my fate was just as murky. I stared into the river deep, fear climbing up my throat. There were crocodiles and snakes, a malevolent current, and blasting winds.

But on the *Elephantine,* a murderer.

I clenched my eyes, breathing fast. I tasted sand between my teeth, and the skirt of my dress whipped around my legs violently. Even if I survived the storm, even if I survived the Nile, what would I do next? How would I continue on to Philae?

My eyes flew open.

The question shocked me. My body wanted to flee the boat, the river, Egypt. And yet there was a part of me that didn't want to give up on my parents. If I left, I'd never know how they had really died. I'd never know why my uncle had killed them. Reason finally took over, beating back my terror. Until now, my uncle had done nothing to threaten or harm me. At turns courteous, and though he had lost his temper the day he discovered I'd stowed away on the *Elephantine,* he hadn't struck me.

As long as he knew that I didn't know the truth, he wouldn't try anything.

I slowly moved away from the railing. Turned and walked back to his cabin, replacing the journal I had taken. Then I went to my cabin in a kind of trance. I would see this through.

Come what may.

WHIT

The rope burned against my palm. Underneath my feet, the deck dipped and rocked, and I bent my knees to keep from tumbling. The rest of the crew worked the sails, trying to use the wind to help us navigate the storm without any damage to the dahabeeyah. Reis Hassan called out orders, the sound drowned out by my rapid heartbeat slamming against my ribs.

The boat shuddered. The wood cracked and groaned, but I held on to the rope. Every gust of wind pushed us onto the banks. Any moment I was sure the rocks would do enough damage to run us aground. I thought about the chemistry books my sister had sent me, the ones I wouldn't have time to save if the water buried us. They had tethered me to her. She had always known about my love of the sciences, my desire to know how the world worked. I pulled harder on the rope, not wanting to lose that connection to her.

The crew rushed around in a dizzying blur wearing tight and worried frowns.

A fleeting thought of Olivera stole across my mind. I'd promised nothing would happen to her. Irritation pulled my mouth into a sharp grimace. I had no business making any promises to her.

The only girl I had a right to think about was the one back in England.

CAPÍTULO DIECISIETE

T he knock on the door came hours later. I'd been pacing through the night, unable to sit or sleep or rest. *My uncle was a murderer.* The thought hadn't left me once, a never-ending chorus to a song I never wanted to hear again. A part of me wished I'd never read my mother's journal at all. My imagination had created a nightmare of my parents' last moments on earth. I couldn't stop thinking about how the two of them might have followed my uncle as he led them deeper into the desert, trusting him with their lives. Never suspecting that he'd leave them out there to burn under the sun.

That was the only way their deaths made sense. Mamá and Papá were too smart to go out there on their own.

The knock came again.

Whit stood on the other side in his customary rumpled state, but perhaps a trifle more so. His whole body seemed to exhale at the sight of me. His perusal was thorough; his gaze raked over me as if he wanted to assure himself I was hale and whole. I knew exactly what he saw: tired eyes, tense jaw, slumped shoulders.

The storm had been awful. But what I learned last night had truly wrecked me.

He bent his knees so he could stare into my eyes. "Are you all right? You look exhausted."

"Estoy bien," I croaked, surprised I could manage to speak at all. I had screamed into my pillow, overwhelmed by my uncle's betrayal.

I cried through the night. When the morning came, I told myself I wouldn't shed another tear until I discovered the truth about their deaths.

And then, somehow, I would ruin Tío Ricardo.

"You've been summoned," Whit said without preamble.

"Is it over?" More croaking. "Is everyone all right?"

"We're all in a right state, but yes."

I sagged against the doorframe. There was that, at least.

"The *Elephantine* survived the winds without any serious issues," he said, his voice curiously gentle. "We're approaching Aswan. While the crew is purchasing supplies, we'll take refreshments at the Old Cataract Hotel. They have the best hibiscus tea in the desert. You'll love it. Abdullah and his granddaughter will be there to meet us. Have I mentioned her before? The photographer? Yes? You'll get along fine with Farida, she has a lot of opinions. The view of the Nile from the terrace will be spectacular, and I highly recommend bringing your sketch pad, Olivera."

He gestured with his hands while he talked, and something caught my attention.

"Whit," I murmured. "Your palms." They were red, a few angry blisters marring his palms.

I reached for them, but he stuffed both into his pockets and leaned back on his heels, creating a wider distance between us. I frowned, not understanding why he suddenly didn't want to breathe the same air, why he suddenly didn't seem to want to be around me.

"Be ready in ten minutes," he said. "Please."

"Are you being polite?" I asked, aghast.

He strode away.

"I guess not," I muttered, blinking after him, watching the long line of his back as he disappeared down the corridor and out of sight. He didn't look back, didn't slow his abrupt departure. I turned away and collected my things, and went off to the deck, encountering the entire staff and crew gathered at the railing in silent contemplation.

I looked beyond and gasped. Without really realizing it, I stepped forward until I stood shoulder to shoulder with Tío Ricardo. The city of Aswan came into view with its tall sandbanks and stately palms, the leaves curled like a finger beckoning me home, and as we drew nearer, the sand gave way to granite. From where I stood, I could easily spot the first cataract sprawled across the river, rocks studding the scenery like mush-rooms rising above a forest floor.

"It's beautiful," I murmured.

My uncle tipped his chin toward me. "There's much more."

Murderer. Murderer. Murderer.

I stiffened at his proximity, and a second later, I forced myself to relax my shoulders. The smile on my face didn't feel natural.

"How much more could there be?" I asked.

He met my gaze. "More."

"There is the island of Elephantine," Tío Ricardo pointed out to me as we waited for an empty carriage to take us to the Old Cataract Hotel. "I've always loved it."

I made a noncommittal noise and shifted away from him. Every word out of his mouth unnerved me. My eyes found Whit. He stood off to the side next to everyone's trunks, and while he remained helpful and polite, he still wouldn't look in my direction. I must have done or said something wrong. But what? Our interactions had been normal. Well—normal for us, anyway. I fought down my unease, reminding myself that he had a job to do and I was merely an item to be checked off on a long list of respon-sibilities.

"If you'll excuse us for the rest of the evening," Mr. Fincastle said as a brougham came to a stop, "my daughter and I have a previous engagement that we can't miss."

"But I wanted you to meet Abdullah," my uncle protested. "He's wait-ing for us on the hotel terrace with his granddaughter. Won't you cancel?"

Mr. Fincastle's lips tightened. I got the impression he didn't appreciate being put on the spot. "I'm afraid meeting your foreman—"

"Business partner," my uncle corrected with a narrowed gaze. "Which you already knew."

"Will have to wait for the introductions until tomorrow," Mr. Fincastle said, as if my uncle hadn't spoken.

"But surely we can take a few moments to say hello, Papa." Isadora brushed dust off her skirt.

"We're already late," Mr. Fincastle said, his tone brooking no argument.

She fell silent, her fingers gripping her handbag tightly. I suddenly wished I'd made more of an effort in getting to know her on the *Elephantine*. Except she was never far from her father. He was constantly at her elbow, or directing her to their shared cabin, or in deep conversation. She never seemed to have a free moment.

"The *Elephantine* will depart for Philae in the morning," Tío Ricardo said. "We'll meet in the lobby of the Old Cataract. Please take care to be punctual."

Mr. Fincastle's lips tightened, but he nodded and led his daughter into a waiting carriage.

We climbed into our own, and the two drivers wove us through the crowded street until we reached a picturesque building in the Victorian style, painted the color of a sunset. It stood on a granite cliff that faced Elephantine Island. The lush greenery surrounding the establishment gave a feeling of refinement. Whit hopped out of the brougham first, and then turned to assist me, his hand stretched toward me.

I debated ignoring it, decided it would be childish, and accepted his help. His calloused fingers closed over mine for a brief moment, and a tingle radiated outward from the touch, climbed up my arm, and stole my breath.

He dropped my hand the second my booted foot touched the ground.

"Gracias." I dropped my voice. "What's wrong, Whit?"

He raised his brows. "Why, nothing, Olivera." He smiled, but it looked forced. The kind of smile I used with my uncle.

Whit walked over to the driver to assist with the luggage. Hotel attendants rushed forward to greet us, and they led our party through the grand entrance decorated in gold and maroon with arched doorways and beautifully carved wooden furniture, the elegance rivaling Shepheard's. I barely had time to take in every detail before we were led straight out to the terrace overlooking the Nile River.

"Abdullah!" my uncle called out to an older man dressed in a casual suit, well-made but without any pretension. His rich brown skin contrasted with the pale cream of his linen shirt, and a young woman leaned forward to adjust one of the buttons at the collar. She was dressed in a comfortable walking dress, serviceable, and without any frills. A light shawl around her shoulders fluttered in the cool breeze and on her feet were strong leather boots. She was pretty, with luminous skin and warm brown eyes that sparkled with intelligence.

Abdullah and Farida.

Whit immediately strode toward her with a wide grin, and she stood to greet him with a matching smile. Abdullah clasped hands with my uncle and he motioned for the rest of us to gather around the wooden table. Before I took my seat, I approached Abdullah.

"Sir," I said, "it's a pleasure to finally meet you. I'm the daughter of Cayo and Lourdes Olivera—"

"But I know exactly who you are," he cut in. "I'm truly sorry for your loss, Señorita Olivera."

I swallowed hard, blinking back the sudden moisture filling my eyes, and I blindly took a seat next to the young woman, who inclined her head.

"You're the photographer," I said.

Farida laughed. "How wonderful that sounds. I'm learning photography, but I'm not a professional. Yet." Her voice was warm and sweet, and she motioned toward a wooden box that sat on the table with a circular lens, a leather carrying case next to it. "I was just taking a photo of my grandfather."

My mouth dropped open. "Is that a *Kodak*?"

Farida nodded. "My grandfather bought me one during his travels. It can take up to one hundred pictures with a click of a button."

"One *hundred*? Marvelous," I exclaimed, reaching to brush my finger against the frame. An invisible spark jumped, reaching toward me, as if I'd found a hidden current. My eyes flew to hers and she winked at me.

I stared down at the portable camera in astonishment. It had been made with a magic-touched object. Farida lifted it off the table and snapped a photo, and for the next half hour, we took pictures of my uncle and Abdullah, of a laughing Whit as he struck silly poses, and of the glimmering Nile River curling around the rocky bluff. We ate a delicious meal of falafel, hummus, and a creamy tahini dip, and drank hibiscus tea loaded with sugar. Whit had been right, I adored it.

Abdullah wiped his mouth with a linen napkin. "I hate to bring up business, but where is your new hire, Ricardo?"

"He had plans, evidently," Tío Ricardo said with a roll of his eyes. "But he and his daughter will meet us in the lobby tomorrow morning."

"And the pair have been sworn to secrecy?"

I swung my head in Abdullah's direction. Despite the cool drink I'd been enjoying, my mouth went dry. The square card tucked within my bag swam across my vision. "Secrecy?"

"She doesn't yet know what we do," Ricardo said.

"You haven't told her?" Abdullah asked in surprise.

I clutched the edge of the table, my attention swerving from one man to the other. Were they all involved with my uncle's illegal activities? And were they about to share what exactly they did? Out here, in the middle of the terrace, the sun shining, and fellow diners surrounding us? Farida taking pictures?

Ricardo took a sip of his espresso. "I didn't originally factor her into our plans, and besides, it's your kingdom, Abdullah. I merely work in it. I thought it prudent to speak with you first. Inez has a certain talent that might be useful." They shared a look, loaded with meaning, but one I couldn't interpret. Farida raised the Kodak and clicked the button.

"What kind of talent?" Abdullah asked.

"I am an artist," I said, my brow furrowing. "I can copy the architecture of Philae with relative ease, I think."

Farida nodded in approval. "It will be a nice complement to the photographs I've taken."

"Exactly," Tío Ricardo said. "What do you think, Abdullah?"

"Given her parents' deaths, she deserves to know," he replied.

"I quite agree." Whit pushed his empty plate aside. He stood, his expression apologetic. "Forgive me, but I have a few errands I must run before we set out tomorrow morning. It was a wonderful meal."

With a small wave, he ventured off, even as I sat reeling in my chair. He was a part of the secret. The nefarious secret. The confirmation left me feeling unaccountably sad.

"Then I advise that you tell her only what she needs to know," my uncle said, picking up the thread of conversation. "I can't promise that she'll be here overly long."

My mouth flattened. I understood my uncle's implication all too well. He ruled my life, and any moment, he could decide to send me back to Argentina. There was no sense in telling me everything, even if I had a right to know what they were up to. My parents only funded their whole enterprise, after all.

"For over a decade, I have been leading an excavation team in various locations with the hope of understanding the heritage of my countrymen," Abdullah began. "Over the years, we have made astounding discoveries."

I frowned. "But I never heard of any."

"You wouldn't have," Abdullah replied. "Because after every single one, I've given the directive to cover our tracks. It was actually my sister Zazi's idea, and before she passed, she asked Ricardo and I to continue the practice. No one on my team is allowed to take anything, or reveal what they have seen. We have kept the same loyal crew since the beginning, and our goal is to record what we've found so that future generations can learn about our history."

Farida reached over and took his hand. The affection between the two shone between them like starlight.

This was the nefarious secret? I had been expecting . . . I shook my head, aware that they were all waiting for my reaction. "I think it's a tremendous undertaking," I said slowly. "And I'm happy to be a part of it, however small."

"Welcome to Egypt, Inez," Abdullah said, smiling broadly.

I clenched my hands in my lap, hardly hearing the words. My uncle worked for Abdullah because it was what his wife would have wanted. He dealt with the awful bureaucrats in Cairo, endured countless hours digging under a hot sun, and worked alongside his brother-in-law—all for the love of his departed wife.

I wish I'd never learned that information.

Because when I looked up, Tío Ricardo met my eyes and smiled at me, and I knew the truth.

No one at this table knew my uncle was a killer.

No one except, perhaps, Whit.

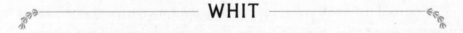

WHIT

The brothel was smoky and crowded. I lounged against the bar, and swirled the whiskey in my glass once, twice. Incense wafted in the air, clinging to my clothes. My informant told me Sterling's agents would be here. They had a fondness for this particular establishment.

I put the glass down without drinking from it. I needed to be clear-headed for this.

Finally, two men parted the velvet curtain to the room's entrance and I straightened, alert. They were exactly as described: pale-skinned and light-eyed, and English. Their shirts were starchy, their collars were pressed. And they were already inebriated.

Brilliant.

They marched right up to the bar, standing less than a foot away from me. One of them ordered drinks while the other glanced around in an assessing way. Looking for any signs of trouble. The bartender set to work, saying over his shoulder, "No Basil tonight?"

The shorter agent shook his head. "Stuck in Cairo on some nasty business."

"Blanche will be disappointed," the bartender said, his voice edged in sarcasm.

I glanced down into my glass. I recognized the name of the famous French dove. Auburn hair and brown eyes the color of whiskey, freckles on her shoulders, across her collarbone. I ought to have known Basil was her patron.

"Did you not like it?" the bartender asked in a gruff voice. He was new, a foreigner judging by his accent. German, I'd guess.

I shook my head absently, my attention already on the madame. She stood off to the side, surveying her kingdom with a dispassionate eye. Her silk gown glinted in the pale candlelight, a softness that contrasted to the strong line of her spine.

If I had any chance of seeing Blanche, I'd need to win over the madame.

I pushed the drink across the bar, paid the bartender, and slowly made my way over to her. She spotted me the minute she sensed my intention, tracking my slow movement through the crowd. The madame smiled, sharp and with interest. She was baiting me, luring me closer.

But I wanted to be caught.

"Evening," I said to her with a careless smile.

"I've seen you here before," she murmured in a throaty voice.

"I need Blanche."

Her dark brow furrowed. "You've had her before?"

"Is she available tonight?" I asked, my expression carefully neutral.

"She is not," the madame said, her tone contrite. I didn't believe it for one second. "But if you come back tomorrow, perhaps—"

"It has to be tonight," I said, and pressed a wad of Egyptian piastres into her hand. "I'm willing to make it worth your while."

The madame stared down at the money, visibly weighing her decision. With obvious reluctance, she handed it back to me. "I'm afraid it's impossible."

Her perfume curled around me in a tight fist. Deliberately, I pressed the money back into her palm, and then added more bills. "Half hour."

The madame glanced around her, lingering on someone in the crowd. Tension gathered across my shoulders as I waited, my hand hovering close to the pocket in my jacket. I'd hand over every note I had to see Blanche. But then she nodded to herself and gestured toward the staircase. "Half hour," she agreed. "Don't make me come looking for you."

"I can work fast when extremely motivated," I said with a wink, already moving away, dizzy with triumph and thinking of Blanche. When I reached her door, I gave it a sharp rap and it swung open, revealing the slight woman known to bring men to the brothel in droves. Her nightgown slipped low on her shoulder, revealing the constellation of freckles dusting her pale skin. For some unaccountable reason, another set of shoulders

swam across my vision. Ones that were narrow and straightened in defi-
ance.

I pushed the unwelcome thought away. It had no place in this room.

Blanche opened the door wider, her warm eyes lingering on my face,
a smile blossoming. She liked what she saw. With a coquettish smirk, she
motioned for me to follow her inside. Anticipation pulsed in my blood,
made my head spin. Lavender swirled in her wake, the scent intoxicating,
but it made me think of another, something sweeter.

I shut the door behind me, my gaze latching on to Blanche. She stood
by the narrow bed, her hip cocked, and she untied the knot of her nightgown, revealing the swell of her breasts. Below, the mood was riotous and
consuming. Conversation loud and obnoxious, the music deafening. None
of it came through the door. The bedroom was ripe with tension, and quiet
with anticipation.

Blanche walked toward me, her robe parted, revealing long legs. She
reached up, her small hand curving around the back of my neck. Her chin
lifted; she stood close enough I could see every single one of her sooty
eyelashes. Slowly, Blanche pulled my face down, her lips inches from my
mouth, her blue eyes pinning mine.

The potent hit of desire never came, even as I waited for it. I ought to be
drowning in this woman, but instead . . . Frustration curled tight around
my edges as I firmly clasped her hands and set them away from my face.
"No need to go any further, Mademoiselle."

She paused, delicate brows pulling together. I stepped away from her
and approached the bed, feeling like I could breathe again. I dropped the
last of my money onto the bed, and then turned to face her. Deliberately,
I swept her robe back over her shoulders, covering every inch of skin, and
said, "I need something else from you."

PART
THREE

JEWEL OF THE NILE

CAPÍTULO DIECIOCHO

The water lapped gently against the *Elephantine*, and I leaned over the railing, staring into the deep green of the Nile. Whit reached forward and clasped a warm hand around my arm, gently pulling me back. I shot him a questioning look. His shoulders were drawn tight, and there were deep hollows under his eyes.

"I'm not in the mood to save you if you fall in."

I raised my brows at the curt tone. "Are you hungry or just tired? Or perhaps drunk?"

His bemused expression made me laugh. "I am not drunk. If I were, you would know. I am, however, hungry and tired and hot and, generally, annoyed."

"You are not having a good morning," I observed.

He gave me a flat look.

I narrowed my gaze. "What were you doing last night?"

"That," he said softly, "is *none* of your business."

"Inez," Tío Ricardo called out. "Don't miss it."

I turned away from Whit in time to see Philae come into view, backlit against the morning light, soft and far reaching. Stately palms rose up from the water, the leaves softly swaying in the gentle breeze gliding over the river. Tall and imposing colonnades made of golden-hued stones towered over the *Elephantine*, an immense gate that welcomed travelers into another world, another life. Piled rocks framed either side, ancient and formidable, solid in strength, and set against a backdrop of bruised purple hills. Surrounding the island were other smaller ones, rocky and formidable guards to the jewel of the Nile. The temple pylons grew taller as we made our slow approach. I'd never seen anything so beautiful in my life.

Isadora and her father stood on my other side, and they were animatedly talking as they examined Philae from a security standpoint. "There are too many places for boats to come and dock," Mr. Fincastle said.

"Perhaps we can ask some of the crew to stand guard," Isadora suggested.

I turned to face them. "Guard against what, exactly?"

"Why, unwanted visitors, of course," Mr. Fincastle said.

"I figured that much on my own." I gritted my teeth. "Who is my uncle expecting?"

"Nosy tourists," he said. "It's merely a precaution."

Then with a cold smile he strode away. Isadora remained behind, her delicate features awash in the golden light of the early morning. "He can be quite infuriating, I know. But he means well. He takes his job very seriously."

"I wish I knew why my uncle hired him," I admitted.

Isadora threw a swift glance over her shoulder and then her gaze swung around to meet mine. Her eyes were very blue, the same color as her father's. "I believe he was hired because of what happened to your parents."

Well, well. Her father's leash on her wasn't as tight as I'd thought. "I thought as much, but *why*?"

"Because their deaths caused quite a stir in Cairo society."

I inched closer. "What do you mean?"

She arched a brow. "Your uncle doesn't share much with you, does he?"

"Unfortunately not."

Isadora let out a thoughtful hum. "He's not the sort of man you can ask directly, I suppose."

"None of my tactics have worked thus far."

"Then I would reevaluate your strategy."

She had a direct manner, honest and unapologetic. Despite her youth, I got the impression she viewed her circumstances with a world-weary and jaded perspective. I wondered what her life was like, where she had traveled, the people she had met. I wondered why she'd have to come up with strategies in the first place.

"This is an odd conversation," I said with a laugh. "What would you recommend?"

She gave a dainty shrug, her lips twitching. "There are ways to get what you want, but it requires a subtlety one has to learn."

I couldn't quite keep the disapproval out of my voice. "You mean manipulation."

"When the occasion calls for it." Isadora let out a delighted laugh. "I see I might have offended you. Well, no matter. I enjoy *your* company, Señorita Olivera."

"Thank you." I scrunched my brow. "I think I feel the same?"

Another twinkling laugh. "I'll tell you what your uncle won't. Señor Marqués felt pressure from the Antiquities Service to provide stricter protection for the excavation team. Your parents were the darlings in Egypt and their tragic demise caused much speculation. None of which painted your uncle in a favorable light. His reputation suffered greatly, and I heard he almost lost his position and good standing with Monsieur Maspero. Are you familiar with the gentleman?"

I nodded. The dinner I shared with them felt years ago, but I recalled the strained tension between the three men. Isadora's information tracked.

"Do you mean to tell me your father was hired for appearance's sake? Not because of any real reason?"

She gave a dainty shrug. "Losing all respect seems reason enough for me, Señorita Olivera. I would fight to keep my name out of the mud. A good name is immeasurably useful."

What a pragmatic way to view one's need for a good character. "Where did you hear about my uncle almost losing his position?"

Isadora tucked a wayward strand of gold hair behind her ear. "My father often hosts museum and government employees in our hotel suite. He likes to maintain open avenues of communication, and people talk. Sometimes, they talk in front of me as if I'm not there. Quite shortsighted of them."

My lips flattened. The more I learned about her father, the less I liked. In fact, my opinion of him had swerved into sharp dislike. He sounded like a mercenary. She must have seen my expression because she laughed again.

"Trust me, Señorita Olivera. My father is his own person. He never does anything without good reason or benefit to himself."

"You're trying to tell me Mr. Fincastle isn't under anyone's thumb."

"*Well*," she said slowly, drawing out the word, "he's working for your uncle, isn't he? My father must not have paid any attention to the gossip." She paused, visibly musing, and then with a slight shake of her head she seemed to discard whatever thought had struck her.

"What?" I asked. "You were thinking of something."

"Oh," she said. "Nothing of import."

Isadora turned away from the railing, but I reached out and took hold of her arm. She raised her brows inquiringly.

The question bubbled to the surface, without my meaning it to. "Would you teach me how to shoot?"

"You'd like to learn? It will take hours and hours of practice and work to become competent."

"I don't mind the effort or the challenge."

She dimpled. "I'll teach you, if I can call you Inez."

I knew I liked her. "It's nice to have a friend, Isadora."

"Likewise," she said with a smile before walking away to join her father on the other side of the boat.

I turned my attention back to the temple. This building was thousands of years old and it made me feel my mortality. It would be here long after I left. I wasn't frightened but humbled by my realization. When I was finally able to tear away my gaze, it was to find my uncle gauging my reaction. He'd come to join me, and I hadn't heard his quiet approach. He sent a small smile my way. My reaction must have passed a test. I'd been suitably awed.

"Welcome, Inez, to the birthplace of ancient Egypt." He gestured to the calm stretch of the river. "This is the southern Nile Valley, the cradle of their civilization. Here you'll find their earliest art carved on the rocks, their first city, and temple. On the island, you'll see the last time anyone wrote in Egyptian hieroglyphics, the last breath of Egypt's pagan religion before Philae became a Christian shrine."

I shielded my eyes from the hot sun. "When was that?"

"Almost four hundred years after the death of Christ." I glanced back at the island, so tiny and remote amid the long ribbon of the Nile. "There used to be an obelisk, smaller and deemed portable by a Mr. Bankes," my uncle continued. "He sent it on to England where it decorates a country estate."

Imagine looking at a centuries-old monument and thinking it would make a handsome *lawn ornament.* "That's appalling."

"In this case, it helped immeasurably to decipher the hieroglyphs," he said.

I set my mouth to a stubborn line. "It doesn't make it right."

"No, it doesn't." He glanced at me, hazel eyes piercing. "Don't forget your promise to me. You must never speak of your time here."

"I won't, Tío." I glanced at the towers of Philae. "Are we staying on the island?"

Tío Ricardo nodded. "We have a campsite on the eastern side. You're welcome to stay on the *Elephantine* if you'd prefer to bypass the experience of sleeping in a makeshift tent of sorts."

My hands curled tight over the railing. We had already gone over this. "Whatever accommodations you've constructed will be fine for me."

My uncle merely shrugged before drawing the other men away to make preparations for disembarking. One of them inquired after Whit, but Tío Ricardo said, "He had a long night. Leave him be."

I turned away from the railing and found him resting on one of the deck loungers. I only had a view of his profile, his eyelashes casting a shadow against his angled cheekbones.

He was a handsome young man.

Who could not be trusted. The fact that I wanted to appalled me. I had too much to lose to place my faith in the wrong person. Mr. Hayes reported to my uncle, but there was a small part of me that wished he were on *my* team. That he would move heaven and earth to help see me through the mess I was in. Perhaps it was only loneliness that made me feel that way, but I suspected it was actually because I liked Whit, and I wanted him to like me back.

I pushed away from my spot on the deck and went below to pack my purse and canvas bag, determined to be ready to leave when it was time.

I wouldn't be left behind again.

I stared at my home for the duration of the excavation season. The crumbling structure was rectangular shaped with no ceiling or doors to speak of. It was partitioned into five narrow rooms, the width of each amounting to no more than four or five feet. Looking at it from the front, it resembled a wide-toothed comb, with the bedrooms fitted between each spindle.

"We're sleeping in there?"

"That's right," Whit said.

I took inventory: no washroom or lavatory. No kitchen or main living space to rest after a long day, presumably spent digging. No place to store clothing.

"Having regrets?" he asked, smirking.

I met his gaze head on. "Do you have an extra chamber pot?"

His grin faded. He turned away, but not before I caught the faintest blush staining his cheeks. I'd embarrassed him. I never thought such a thing would be possible. I studied him more carefully, noting how his eyes looked surprisingly clear. Less red-rimmed and more alert. He'd lost his flask in the Nile, but there was plenty of drink on board the *Elephantine*. He must not have been partaking.

The realization was like an arrow to my heart. To me, it didn't seem like he was drinking to enjoy it, but rather to forget. This felt like the first step in a new direction.

I couldn't help wondering what he ran from.

"This building is all that remains from the dormitories belonging to the priests who lived on Philae," Whit said after a beat. "The walls are made of limestone without any embellishment or decoration, and so your uncle thought we might use them as the priests once did." He pointed to the top. "We've stretched out a long tarp above and, as you can see, curtains have been placed in front of each division to act as doors. Your uncle, Abdullah, and I each have a room while Mr. Fincastle and his daughter will share one."

"Plenty of space for me," I concluded, picking one of the empty rooms. "Without it, I suspect I would have been left behind on the *Elephantine*. Who else slept here?"

"Your parents," he said, watching me closely. "They slept in the same exact quarters."

It still happened. That feeling of having been dropped a hundred feet at the mention of Mamá and Papá. The feeling that I couldn't get enough air into my lungs fast enough. It would always feel this way. The pain was a forever fixture in my life. Much like having arms and legs and ears. Their death was a truth that was both strange, and yet profoundly ordinary. People died every day. Well-meaning distant relations told me that one day I'd be able to move past it. But I'd traveled thousands of miles only to discover that I couldn't leave this new weight I carried behind me.

My parents were gone forever, but I brought them with me wherever I went. This was why I would fight to find out what my uncle had done. I wouldn't be able to move on if I didn't. And there was a part of me that wanted to finish what they began, and to help find Cleopatra. They might not have wanted me to be involved, but now that I was here . . . I wanted to make them proud.

"Do you want to see the headquarters?" Whit asked, jarring me from my thoughts.

I blinked. "Sure."

He spun around and took two enormous steps to the left of our campsite, spreading his arms wide.

Another structure stood close by, a partial wall made of golden stone. Somehow, I'd missed it entirely, too preoccupied by where I was supposed to sleep. Pressed against the wall was a long wooden table covered by various supplies: brushes and scalpels, candles, handheld mirrors, and bundles of rope. Several crates littered the floor, overflowing with what appeared to be junk. Broken handheld mirrors, mismatched and worn shoes, fraying ribbons. Nothing worth saving at first glance, but something told me that each item held the remnants of old magic. Energy pulsed through the air, like someone drawing a finger across still water, making ripples. I felt the soft vibrations against my skin.

"We try to find objects that haven't been handled much. Forgotten items stored away in attics and the like," Whit said. "That's why you can feel the old magic in the air. It will fade in time the longer the items are used around the campsite."

The *Elephantine* crew also served as the digging crew, and they situated themselves in a cluster some fifty feet away from the dormitories, surrounding a large fire pit. The campsite was an easy distance from the archaeological site, only a fifteen-minute walk or thereabouts, and nestled in a palm grove.

Whit rummaged through several large maps littering the table, and then he handed one to me. "Here, this is a map of Philae, if you wanted to see it."

I studied it, noting the size of the island. It appeared to be on the smaller side and I decided to include it in my journal. I went back to my room, Whit trailing behind me.

"What are you doing?"

"I wanted to copy the map for my sketchbook," I explained. "It won't take but a moment."

He waited as I quickly gathered my things together and then as I sat on one of the campsite's mats to draw the island. After I finished, he came to stand behind me, observing my work.

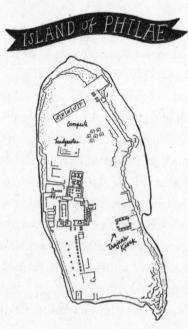

I walked inside my room, surprised to find it was more spacious than I first realized. I could comfortably stand at my full height and stretch both of my arms wide and still not reach either end.

Whit poked his head in. "Well?"

I glanced over my shoulder. "I have an idea."

He eyed me warily. "Have I told you how much I live in terror of your ideas?"

"That's rude."

But the errand turned out to be successful. Whit carried back one rolled-up rug for my room, a handful of books that would serve as a small nightstand, and a single bowl for washing.

"After you're done decorating, I'll show you around the temple," Whit said as he balanced all of the items across the sandy terrain.

Decorating meant unrolling the rug; it covered the entire floor of my room, one end curling up the wall because it was wider than the space allowed. I'd already brought over the extra bedroll and linens, and one of the crew had carried my belongings inside. Whit handed me the stack of books, his hand brushing against mine, and I startled from the electrifying zip that ran up my arm. He flexed his fingers as I placed the books next to the bedding. The bowl went on top of the literature. While the space felt dark, I had plenty of candles and matches should I need them.

All put together, the effect turned out to be cozy.

I stepped outside to where Whit waited. "Where are you sleeping?"

He pointed at the room directly next to mine.

My body flooded with heat. "Oh."

Whit grinned. "I hope you don't snore."

"I wouldn't know," I muttered.

He took mercy on me. "Are you ready to see the temple?"

I set off after him, mimicking every step as he crossed the packed dirt of the island. The temple looked large and solid to the left of us, casting us in cool shadow. We were mere ants to its size and grandeur. On the right stood a roofless structure on a platform. Fourteen massive columns resembling palm trees created a rectangular shape.

"Trajan's Kiosk; he was a Roman emperor. Probably constructed two thousand years ago," Whit said. "The locals call it Pharaoh's Bed."

"It's beautiful."

"It was never finished."

I stopped walking, the back of my throat tickling. "But why?"

"Remains a mystery," Whit said, squinting in the sunlight. "Are you all right? You're a bit peaky."

I nodded, but I felt uncomfortable. A sharp prickling surrounded me, pressing into my edges. I wanted to push back against it, as if it were a wall closing in on me. "Let's keep going."

Whit obliged and led me to the front of the temple where a wide and open courtyard sprawled before it. Covered colonnades enclosed the irregular shape, and crude stones set in a honeycombed pattern stretched from one end to the other. The first pylon, a kind of gate, stood high, blocking parts of the blue sky. The lines of the structure were sharp and unforgiving; I supposed they'd have to be, to survive the ravages of time. Beyond the first pylon was another court, and yet another enormous gate. Reliefs of Egyptian gods and goddesses were carved on the walls, detailed and magnificent.

We were not the first to have come here. Several depictions and hieroglyphics had been destroyed, whole sections ruined. It was hard to fathom, hard to look at without feeling a keen sense of loss.

Whit followed my gaze, his mouth set at a grim line. "The work of the Romans when they converted the temple to a Christian church. If you look closely, you can see the excavation team who carved the wall the year they were here in 1841."

"Excavators *carved* the wall?" I tilted my head back to scan the imposing wall, and sure enough, several explorers had left their mark. The crude etchings were several stories high from the ground. "I don't understand how they reached the top? Why not scrawl their name and date closer to the ground, at eye level?"

"Because when they did so, it *was* at eye level," Whit explained. "The bottom part of the structure was covered entirely in sand. Years of erosion revealed the whole temple, but until then the ground was higher up, which is why travelers were able to scratch the limestone near the top."

"They weren't the only ones. Napoleon noted his arrival in 1799," said a voice from behind me.

I startled and whirled around; I hadn't heard my uncle's quiet approach. He stood with his hands on his hips, a leather bag slung over his shoulder. Rolls of maps poked up from within. "Tío Ricardo. Mr. Hayes was giving me a tour of the temple."

"Was he?" My uncle shifted his attention to Mr. Hayes. "Well?"

Whit shook his head. "Nothing yet."

I looked at the pair of them as some silent communication passed between them. "Tío?"

"Have you felt any magic?" my uncle asked.

I shifted on my feet. There had been something, but it wasn't exactly the same magic as the trinket box and golden ring. "Not yet."

"Keep trying, Inez."

"I will." I thought hard. My parents had excavated here, their last known digging site. Papá *could* have found the ring here. If that were true, then there could be a connection between the ring and the wooden box to the island of Philae—something that pointed to Cleopatra. "But we haven't explored the interior of the temple."

My uncle stepped aside. "By all means."

We passed through the second pylon and straight into a portico. I gaped at the painted ceiling. The column burst with color reaching up to the capitals, carved to resemble lotuses, palms, and papyruses. The paint appeared soft in hue, a rainbow of pastels in shades of coral and green. As a traveler, I was in awe; as an artist, I was inspired. The space opened at the center, allowing a square of light to pass through, casting the rest of the room in a golden glow. My fingers itched to capture every detail, every line and curve made thousands of years ago by intrepid artists.

But as much as there was beauty, there was also ruin, too. Sections of the pavement had been pulled up, the ground strewn with broken fragments of shattered cornice. A constant reminder that for more than a millennia, treasure hunters from within and without stole from sites up and down Egypt.

"Anything?" my uncle asked.

I shook my head, staring at a particularly demolished corner of the portico. All I tasted was the bitter tang of regret. We moved into the interior of the temple, a large room that opened into various halls. Whit stood next to me, and for the first time, I noticed the smallest freckle above his lips. A long shadow scored the line of his jaw. I might draw blood if I let my finger trail it. His blue gaze shifted to mine, as if sensing how keenly I studied every curve of his face.

He abruptly turned away.

Mortified, I forced myself to study my surroundings. The walls were covered in black smoke, the remnants of some careless traveler lighting a torch. The chamber opened to a hallway but when I went to explore that section, my uncle held me back.

"Try to see if you feel magic here." He kept me in the main room, carefully watching as I walked around the dimly lit space.

"It's hard to see anything," I commented.

Tío Ricardo reached into his leather sack and pulled out an old sandal. He buckled the straps together and the pointed toe of the shoe lit up in a blue flame.

I gaped.

I had seen ordinary objects with the remnants of magic give up a smattering of sparks. But the shoe stayed lit, and the room was washed in its azure light.

"Quite a collector's item," I said.

"We have a few like it," Tío Ricardo said. "Your mother packed whatever she could find in Buenos Aires. She found all sorts of things most people would have thrown away. The campsite is littered with them, some of it helpful, some of it not."

"Do you remember when she shrank your spectacles?" Whit asked, laughing. "She placed them on your notebook, and you thought they were a spider?"

"Oh no," I said, smiling despite the ache in my heart. "What happened?"

"What normally happens to spiders around Ricardo," Whit said. "He screams at them for existing and then they are subject to the heel of his boot."

"That damn handkerchief," Tío Ricardo muttered. "That was my favorite pair."

I waited, hoping they'd say more about her. I had many memories I wanted to live again, too. Every crumb felt like a feast to me.

"Still nothing?" Whit asked.

He leaned against the wall, his arms folded tight across the flat of his stomach, his ankles crossed. They both waited for me to tell them if I felt any magical energy.

I thought about lying. I wanted to be useful. If my uncle didn't think so, I wondered how quickly he'd suggest I return to Argentina. But telling a fib wasn't an option. They'd find out the truth regardless. Instead, I peered at the walls, the reliefs carved into the stone. In here, it was hard to make out the detail of the hieroglyphs.

"Who is this temple dedicated to?"

Whit opened his mouth, but my uncle beat him to it. "We believe Isis. Though, Hathor is also represented. Do you see the woman with a cow's head? That's her, sometimes known as the goddess of love and music."

My shoulders slumped. "I feel nothing. But there are other places to explore."

My uncle put his hands on his hips, and glared at the toes of his boots. His shoulders were tense and rigid. Then he jerked his chin up, hazel eyes meeting mine. "I need you to do better, Inez. You're here for a reason. Don't forget it."

"Tío," I began, half-confused, half-alarmed by the quiet anger controlling his voice.

"She's been here for half an hour," Whit said. "Give it time."

"We don't *have* time. You *know* why!" Tío Ricardo exclaimed. Sweat beaded at his hairline as he tugged at the sleeves of his cotton shirt. Rough, frantic movements. "I would never have agreed to you being here if I knew you wouldn't come through, Inez."

A shiver scored down my back.

"Why not?" I asked. "What aren't you telling me?"

My uncle ignored me, and glanced at Whit, raising a brow. Another one of their silent conversations. Mr. Hayes nodded once. Almost instinctively, his hands reached for his pockets, and then he seemed to remember they were empty. His jaw clenched, as if fighting off an invisible demon. He noticed me staring and his expression cleared.

My uncle stormed out of the enclosed space. I waited for Whit to explain what had just passed between them. But he merely gestured toward the entrance. We left the temple of Isis or Hathor, worry sticking to me like sap.

My uncle's desperation unsettled me. His rebuke had felt like a slap to the face.

It made me think of Mamá and how she worried for him. For herself.

Desperation made people dangerous.

CAPÍTULO DIECINUEVE

_W_e stepped out into the sunlit courtyard, Whit walking ahead. Usually, he matched his pace to mine. Not today, evidently. He had a strong curve to his back, a proud line to his shoulders. I remembered the moment when he'd breathed into my mouth, saving my life in the deep of the Nile River. My stomach flipped as my mind revisited the kiss in Cairo, the slight brush of his lips against my skin. How he'd lingered for one long beat, hovering close, his warm scent enveloping me, faintly smelling like our library back home, old books and whiskey and leather.

Sometimes, I caught him staring when he thought I wasn't looking.

I couldn't help wondering if he was as confused as I was. Attracted and fighting it. Charmed, but trying not to be. I wondered if he was as inconvenienced as I was. Maybe that was the reason for his determined aloofness? A question was out of my mouth before I thought it through. "Suppose my uncle succeeded. Would you have been sorry to see me go?"

"Desolated," he said cheerily, without turning around. "I don't know what I'd do without you."

"Can you take nothing seriously?"

He turned his head halfway in my direction. "Was that a serious question?"

It had been, but now I regretted asking. "The moment has passed."

Whit faced forward. "Probably for the best."

There he went, using my words against me. How unspeakably annoying.

We said nothing until I pulled out an easy question as we walked through the pylons. "What are you going to do for the rest of the day?"

"Assist Abdullah. What did you think of him?"

"I like him," I said. I couldn't quite keep a twinge of bitterness out of my tone. Had my parents wished it, I could have met him years ago. "I wish I knew him better. I barely know the story of how my uncle and Abdullah met."

"They infuriated each other from the first." Whit slowed down, shortening his strides. "Ricardo was a young excavator, utilizing tools and practices he'd learned in Argentina. Abdullah took one look at his methods and proceeded to correct every single one."

I laughed. "I can imagine how much my uncle appreciated that."

"Oh, he hated it. But digging in the desert is entirely different than moving around rocks. He's learned a lot from Abdullah regarding excavating in Egypt. Then he married Abdullah's sister, Zazi. Did you ever meet her?" Whit fell silent. "They rarely speak of her, but she loved Egyptian ancient history. It makes sense she and your uncle got married, and why he's still here, doing what she would have wanted. Your uncle is very loyal."

"My mother said her death hit him hard." I frowned, recalling a long-ago conversation I'd overheard during his last—and only—visit to Buenos Aires. "She said he could be reckless at times, moody."

Whit nodded, thoughtful. "That is certainly true. Abdullah keeps him in line, though."

I tried to keep my tone nonchalant. "Can you?"

His gaze flickered to mine. "That's not my job."

"What *is* your job?"

"I told you, I assist—"

I shook my head. "No, I'm talking about your other duties."

His expression turned stony. "I'm his secretary—"

"His secretary who carries a gun? Who follows people out of dining rooms? Who stays out all hours of the night?"

Whit stopped, his eyes hard. "You won't stop, will you?"

I shook my head again.

"I get him things," he said shortly. "Sometimes it's information. Sometimes it's something he's lost."

The stern line of his mouth forbade any more questions. But I'd learned enough. Whit did things my uncle wouldn't dare to. It didn't sound legal, and the hard edge to his voice made me think it was sometimes unsafe. I wished I could ask him more questions. I wanted to know if he liked his job, I wanted to know why he would risk his life for my uncle—a man who was involved with criminals.

Like Mr. Whitford Hayes.

He turned and began walking, his tone friendly and engaging, as if he were a host at a dinner party. He talked as if the last few minutes hadn't happened. It was his way of diverting me. As if I could ever forget the real reason why I was there in the first place. But I knew enough about him to know that pushing him now would be pointless.

"Most of the excavation team have been with us for ten years or so," he said. "As a result, the crew is highly sought after but they refuse to work with anyone else. Your uncle pays very well, thanks to your family's generous contributions, and he also works alongside everyone. You'd be surprised at how many archaeologists here don't want to get their hands dirty."

My mood soured.

Now my uncle had unrestrained and unchecked access to my fortune. Frustration stole over me. Everything inside me screamed that my parents' deaths had something to do with their fortune.

Terror gripped me in an icy hold.

"What are you thinking about?"

I blinked.

"You had the most peculiar expression on your face," Whit explained.

For a moment, I was seized with a desire to tell him. To work through my suspicions, to not be alone anymore. But that would be reckless. I had no one I could turn to. I dodged the question by turning his attention somewhere else. "What does the team do in the off-season?"

"They go back to their families, work on their farms, and so on. You're full of questions. Shocking," he muttered under his breath.

I ignored the dig. "So, how do you assist Abdullah?"

"By keeping track of who does what, making sure everyone is paid accordingly and on time. I help with moving earth around, wield a pickaxe, and so on. In addition, I detail our findings. Your mother used to keep a perfect record, and most of her tasks have fallen to me."

I let the despairing feeling run its course. The dread pooled in my belly, robbed me of breath. And then I exhaled, and the moment somehow became bearable. Not fine exactly, but livable.

Whit frowned. "Would you rather I not mention either of them?"

That intuition of his. I swore it was going to get me in trouble one day. I didn't want to discover things I liked about him.

"It's all right," I said, after clearing my throat. "Seeing where they slept and learning how they worked makes me feel closer to them in a way that wasn't possible in Buenos Aires."

We rounded the corner and ran straight into my uncle. He looked harassed, as if wanting to be at work but having to do a million things before then. He strode forward in a hurry, carrying a bundle of something in his arms.

"Tío?" I asked.

"Whitford, I'd like a moment with my niece," my uncle said. He waited until Whit stepped away before he shifted to give me his full attention. "I wanted to apologize. For earlier. I lost my composure, and I didn't mean to sound harsh. Forgive me."

I glanced down at the art supplies in his arms.

"I thought you'd like to begin sketching and painting."

He went looking through my things? I swallowed the angry tangle of emotions rising up my throat. My uncle had no right to poke around my room. As if he owned that, too. I'd hidden my mother's damning letter in the sleeves of one of my starchy, button-down shirts. The card with the illustration of a gate had gone into the pockets of my bicycle pants.

Had he found them?

His expression was closed off and remote, back to its stoic lines. The sun bore down over me, but it didn't stop a chill from skipping down my spine.

"I want you to draw the paintings in the temple, por favor. Here are your pencils and a set of paints." Tío Ricardo handed them over as he called out, "Whitford, watch over her." He reached into the deep pockets of his vest and pulled out the half-chewed-up sandal. Carefully, he buckled the strap and the tip of the shoe ignited in a sharp blue flame.

Whit took the shoe turned candle. "I will."

Tío Ricardo shot Whit a look filled with meaning, fiddling with the light scarf around his neck. A plaid pattern featured in the design and it looked incongruous with the rest of my uncle's rough wear. "And I need to be briefed, don't forget."

"I haven't." Whit gave him a nod and then Tío Ricardo left.

"Briefed about *what*?" I asked.

"Where do you want to start?" Whit asked, taking my things from me.

His refusal to share anything was really starting to annoy. But I let the matter drop; it was a small island, I'd get it out of him eventually. For now, it seemed as if I had some work to do. I never expected my uncle to allow me to record any of the superb Egyptian reliefs or paintings. It was surprising and . . . curious. He'd gone out of his way to make me feel unwelcome, but now he brought my supplies to me? It felt off, in a way that I didn't understand . . . except if he'd gone inside my room with the sole purpose of snooping through my things.

Which might mean that he was suspicious of me. For all I knew, he could be wondering if my parents had shared more about their time here than he originally thought.

All the more reason to sneak into *his* room.

"I want to paint the portico," I said.

We returned to the temple, and I found a comfortable place to settle. I propped up my large sketchbook across my knees and began to do a loose drawing of the columns topped with what looked like palm leaves. The colors, while muted, gave me enough of an impression to know what they would have been when freshly painted. The bold reds and greens and blues reduced to pastels. Whit sat beside me, his long legs stretched out before him and crossed at the ankles, his back against a low screening wall. He watched my progress as I worked.

"That's really something," he said after I'd completed the initial drawing. "Can you draw?"

"Not even a little bit," he said lazily. "My sister is the artist."

He fell silent and I looked up from my drawing. His voice had turned soft, and almost protective. As if he'd do anything to keep her safe.

"This is where you tell me all about her," I said, mixing paints on a spare sheet.

"Is it?"

I waited, quite used to his diversionary tactics, and arched a brow.

He laughed. "Her name is Arabella, you curious fiend."

My brow remained exactly in place.

"She's a wonderful person. Endlessly curious, like you," Whit said, rolling his eyes. "And we're very close. She loves her watercolors. I suspect she'd rather remain in the country to paint than have a season in London."

"I've heard of those." I paused. "The dancing sounds fun."

"They're absolutely not. Starchy clothing, deplorable small talk, and determined mothers foisting their equally determined offspring onto every known eligible bachelor in the country. And there is nothing interesting about the quadrille."

I wrinkled my nose. "That sounds like a section of meat." At his confused expression, I added, "In Argentina, my favorite cut of meat is the cuadril."

"Oh, well in England, a quadrille is a horrifyingly boring dance."

"I wouldn't know, I've never danced it."

"I'd rather have the steak. You can trust my word."

That brought me up short. "No, I can't."

He lowered his lashes and gave me an inscrutable look. "Smart girl."

The air between us caught, as if on an electrical current that zipped between our breaths. His eyes lowered to my mouth. Warmth spread to my cheeks. I was seized with a desire to tip my chin upward, my lips closer to his. But I stayed rooted, the blood roaring in my ears. Whit wrenched his face away, the line of his jaw tightening.

The moment passed, disappointment crashing against me like a battering ram. Whitford Hayes was a terrible, preposterous idea. He worked for my uncle. He knew more about my parents, truths he wouldn't share. He drank too much and probably flirted with every woman he met. It was hard to feel special if I was just a drop in the bucket.

But he had saved my life. Cared to make sure if I was comfortable. Took my side in arguments with my uncle.

Whit shifted away, closing himself off.

"I suppose," I began, wanting to draw him into conversation. I lifted my brush and began painting the top of one of the columns a lush, soft green that reminded me of the sea. "You are such a *bachelor* English mothers are constantly throwing their daughters at, hoping for an engagement."

Whit regarded me for a beat without speaking. Then he twisted his mouth in distaste. "I used the word *eligible*, remember? You are confusing my oldest brother with me."

"You also have a brother."

"Correct." His expression twisted into one of exasperation. "Porter."

"So, no young ladies for you?" I pressed.

"Has anyone told you that you're unspeakably irritating?"

"They've said I'm unspeakably curious."

He laughed. "All right, Olivera. I was a cadet by the age of fifteen, my commission purchased practically when I was still in the nursery. I haven't seen an Englishwoman in years." He lifted his gaze from my work in order to meet mine. "And you? Do you have a beau courting you?"

"Not really, but I suppose there *is* someone if I want there to be."

Whit stiffened, and his lips pinched slightly. An interesting reaction that both thrilled and terrified me.

His voice was nonchalant, but I didn't believe it. "Oh?"

"My parents had picked out the son of a consul. Ernesto Rodriguez. He's exactly the sort of person my mother would approve of. Polite and well-mannered, connected, and from an old Argentine familia."

"How wonderful for him."

"I can't tell if you're being sarcastic," I said.

"I'm not," he said, predictably.

"Liar."

"I keep telling you, Olivera. Don't believe anything I say." Then he wrenched his gaze away. I resumed my work, squinting at one of the columns, trying to discern the hieroglyphs, but the reliefs were too far away. I stood and handed him my sketchbook, careful not to smear the paint. I dusted myself off, and walked closer to the reliefs carved into the stone, brow furrowed. There were hundreds of symbols I didn't know, drawings of various people in different kinds of clothing.

"Olivera."

"Hmmm?"

"Will you please come over here?"

"In a moment."

"Now."

Well, now I wouldn't go over there for another ten minutes. "I'm busy, Whit."

"That's six times now," he said. He stood and walked to me, my sketch-book open. For some reason he appeared to brace himself, as if preparing for something he didn't want to hear.

"You're counting how many times I call you by name?"

"I notice because I haven't given you permission to address me so informally."

I let my gaze travel from the buttons undone at the collar, his wrinkled and untucked shirt, and the windswept, untidy hair. "You can't be serious."

"I thought you said I was never serious."

"So you *are* paying attention to me. I wasn't sure how much of that was because my uncle is paying you to do so. I notice the way you stare."

"I *stare* at many pretty ladies, Olivera. Don't make anything of it," he said, but the words came out stern, without their usual teasing lilt.

"You've certainly warned me enough."

His blue gaze narrowed. "I don't like your tone. Just what are you implying?"

"Methinks the gentleman doth protest too much."

"Bloody hell," he said. "Shakespeare again."

"What did you want, Whit?"

A muscle in his jaw ticked. "I want you to explain *this*." He pointed to an illustration in my sketchbook.

An illustration of the gate.

I crossed my arms. "It's a temple gate."

"Right." Whit narrowed his gaze. "Where did you see this?"

I waved my hand airily. "In a travel brochure, I think. I can't be sure."

The parenthetical lines bracketing his mouth deepened. Late afternoon light cast his features in a softened haze. His hair appeared burnished copper in the cozy dimness. "Try."

"Honestly, I don't remember." I was incredibly proud of my nonchalant tone. "If you haven't noticed, my sketchbook is filled with such illustrations.

I ought to do a better job of taking notes, but I forget. Why the sudden interest in the gate?"

"It's not something I've seen around too much."

His carefully worded reply didn't escape my notice.

"But you have seen it. Somewhere."

"I didn't say that."

"You certainly did," I countered.

"Well, I can't stop you from thinking that," he snapped. "Inez, this is important. Tell me where you've seen this *particular* gate."

"Only if you tell me the significance."

Whit clenched his jaw. "I can't."

"Because my uncle wouldn't wish it."

"You think so?" he asked, his chestnut brows climbing to his hairline. "That's quite an assumption."

We stared at each other, a line drawn between us. I had stumbled onto something, I knew it. What I couldn't decide was how Whit truly felt about it. If he wanted me to figure out something that my uncle was deliberately keeping from me.

Then it hit me.

"I understand," I said in a hush. "You won't outwardly disobey my uncle."

"Did it ever occur to you that he might want to protect your feelings? Maybe the details would upset you." He tugged at his wayward hair, clearly torn over what to say to me. "The essentials are the same, Olivera. Your parents are both gone, and nothing you discover will change any of that."

"So the gate has something to do with my parents." I ground my teeth in frustration. Annoyance built inside me, one brick at a time. I understood Whit had a job to do, but right now, he stood in the way of the answers I desperately wanted—*no*, the ones I needed. This was about my family, information on what had happened to them.

How they *died*.

"Are you always so good at following orders?" I asked bitterly.

He straightened away from me, his blue eyes lit with an anger I'd never seen. "As a matter of fact, I am not."

"I find that very hard to believe."

"You don't know anything about me. I've *kept* it that way."

"I know enough," I countered.

"Listen, you fool—"

"Not five minutes ago you said I was smart."

"You don't know me," he repeated, furious, raising his voice to speak over me. "You don't know the things I've done. You asked me once if I was in the British military—I'm not." He leaned forward, his face inches away from mine. "Would you care to know why?"

I stubbornly remained silent.

"I was dishonorably discharged," he said in a frigid voice I didn't recognize. I'd seen him exasperated and impatient, furious and aloof. But he'd never sounded so coldly detached. Not even once. "You know your way back to the campsite, don't you?"

"Whit—"

"Mr. Hayes, if you don't mind," he said with some of his former asperity. "Let's observe proper etiquette."

"If that's what you really want."

"It is."

"Fine."

"*Fine*," he said.

"By the way," I said, lifting my chin. "We're basically even."

Whit stiffened.

"You've said my name twice."

"That doesn't make us even. It makes us idiots!" Whit shouted. He pinched the bridge of his nose and inhaled deeply, fighting for control. His next words came out measured. "Well, it won't be happening again, that I can promise you." He strode away in a huff, his posture rigid, his back ruler straight.

Ugh, ugh, *ugh*. I pressed my fingers to my temple, trying to unravel the knots in my mind. But nothing made sense anymore.

What did the gate have to do with my parents' deaths?

WHIT

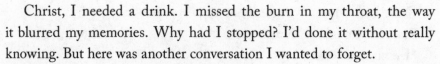

Christ, I needed a drink. I missed the burn in my throat, the way it blurred my memories. Why had I stopped? I'd done it without really knowing. But here was another conversation I wanted to forget.

The silly chit knew *nothing* about me.

I was tired of her assumptions. Tired of the hurt that bloomed in her changing eyes whenever my voice went sharp. What the hell did I care anyway? I strode quickly, wanting as much distance from her as possible. Ricardo could deal with her for the rest of the day. I signed up for a lot of things when he offered me the job. I was to protect his interests. Putting my life at risk was a given. It meant late nights, and countless hours of waiting and watching in shadowy corners. It meant pulling the trigger of my pistol.

What I didn't sign up for was his niece.

I was starting to hate the way she saw through me. The military had shaken my faith in humanity, but it gave me a way to protect myself. I learned how to bury my emotions, to never allow myself to feel. I stopped making friends when I began losing them. With my own eyes, I had witnessed the horror that men wasted on the earth. I remembered more than I wished to, remembered, too, the long days afterward, minutes filled with whiskey on my breath and bloody fists and hazy nights. Before Ricardo found me in a Cairo alley, battered and bruised from another senseless bar fight, holding on to a gun that didn't belong to me.

"You ought to put your brawn to better use," he'd said. He cleaned me up until my head cleared long enough to realize I had another option available. I had more days spent sober, and with time, I passed Ricardo's test and became a part of his team.

I didn't want to ruin my last days in Egypt.

All too soon, I would have to leave if I didn't find what I was looking for. Funny how my fate came down to a single sheet of paper.

I found Ricardo at headquarters, bent over the map, his index finger pressing hard on the paper as if he wanted to smudge away any imperfections. He glanced up at my approach. I wasn't trying to be quiet. Frustration still churned in my gut.

"Why aren't you with Inez?"

"I needed a break," I muttered.

Ricardo's expression turned sympathetic. "Understandable."

He misunderstood, but I didn't bother correcting him. He wouldn't appreciate what I really meant, anyway. "I know why Basil Sterling hunts for Cleopatra."

Ricardo slowly straightened, his shoulders tightening as if bracing himself for the worst.

"Why?" he asked through clenched teeth. "Glory? Money?"

I nodded. "Yes, but it's more than that."

"Mierda," he snarled. "What the fuck else does he need her for?"

I curled my lip, hardly wanting to say the words. "Her body—her mummy. He believes it holds magical properties. Cleopatra is said to have been adept at magic," I reminded him. "We don't have concrete proof she cast spells, but it's an educated guess based on written accounts."

The blood drained from Ricardo's face. "And?"

I sighed. "He's going to cut up the body and pulverize it. The magic is rumored to heal any sickness." I paused. "There's a rumor he's ill with consumption."

Ricardo's eyelids drifted shut. "Damn."

"What do you want to do?"

His eyes opened, blazing and intense. "We find her first, and then make sure that he *never* does."

CAPÍTULO VEINTE

*W*ith a sigh, I sat back down and finished painting until my back was sore, my fingers cramped. I worked until the moon rose high overhead, silvery light streaming inside from the rectangular hole in the ceiling. When I finally finished, I stood, stretching my stiff limbs. I desperately wanted to search through my uncle's room, but it'd be foolish to attempt such a thing during my first day here. I'd have to be strategic, and do it when Whit wasn't hovering near me.

With a last look around to make sure I wasn't forgetting anything, I made my way past the two pylons and then outside to the large courtyard. There was no one in sight, quiet save for the gentle hum of the Nile flowing on either side of the small island. The song of the river kept me company on the way back to camp.

As I walked past Trajan's Kiosk, I felt a peculiar tingle in my fingers. The same one I'd felt earlier. The feeling grew as I drew closer to the immense structure. I was alone, my path illuminated by a million twinkling stars guiding every step. The scene felt ancient and immortal. Magic pulsed in my blood. I took another step, and then another, until I was close enough to touch the platform of Pharaoh's Bed. My fingers brushed along the limestone.

I tasted roses.

The memory rushed from all sides, looming large in my mind. Cleopatra sailed in extravagant finery, floating on a sharp blue river on a barge fashioned with a gilded stern and immense purple sails. In her hand, she read a letter. A summons from Marcus Antonius to account for her misbehaving. She was meeting the great general for the first time—frustrated, nervous, and annoyed.

A shiver ran across my skin as her feelings invaded my body.

I pulled away with a sharp gasp. The magic thrummed in my blood, reached every corner of my body, and thundered in my ears. I'd never heard it so loud, never felt it so strongly. Recognition blazed, a triumphant roar ringing in my ears. How did the magic pull me in so quickly? More important, *why* did it? I tossed out one idea after another. Cleopatra had clearly created a spell to preserve her memories, tasting sharp and sweet like roses, and the effects of the magic had anchored it to the golden ring, and once I'd touched the ring, traces of the magic latched on to me, as magic was known to do. And whatever magic stayed with me recognized the magic in Trajan's Kiosk. Maybe in this entire island? It was as if Cleopatra had left an imprint of herself behind, a woman who had lived over two millennia ago. I could feel her presence and her emotions. She was alluring and earthy, a woman who knew how to provoke, a woman who knew how to lead.

History also remembered her as a woman adept in the occult.

I stepped away from the platform, my heart beating erratically against my ribs. The awareness dimmed and I could breathe again. I wanted to run inside, but I held myself back. Behind me, the sound of everyone gathering for the evening meal filled the darkening night: low murmured conversation, a crackling fire, and soft laughter.

"Inez?" Tío Ricardo called.

My feet refused to move. Trajan's Kiosk loomed large, a dark silhouette against the moonstruck sky. For some reason, the touch against the stone made me think of my father. He'd stood here, like I did. Touched by the same lure of the magic. The picture in my mind was tangled and messy but I was beginning to see how it was all connected.

My parents' deaths.

Mamá scared for her safety.

Cleopatra's tomb.

Papá and the golden ring, touched by the same magic that had clung to my skin.

"Inez!" The edge of impatience in his voice dispatched a flutter of nerves deep in my belly.

I turned away reluctantly and walked across the sandy expanse between the ancient buildings and our campsite. The air had turned cool and I hunched my shoulders against the night breeze. My uncle waited, limned in the firelight blazing behind him. He watched me narrowly as I approached, a severe line to his shoulders.

"What were you doing?"

Sweat dampened my palms. I kept my voice neutral. Instinct told me to keep my discovery quiet until I knew the rules of his game. One misstep, and he'd sweep me off the board. "I only wanted a closer look. It's a magnificent structure."

Tío Ricardo drew closer, and I stiffened. He leaned forward, peering intently into my face. I held myself still and fought to keep my expression neutral. "Did you feel anything?"

"Nothing." I licked my lips. "Can the feeling of magic fade?"

Tío Ricardo was silent, still intently studying my expression, and then finally straightened. "I don't know. Perhaps? Come, it's time to eat with the others."

I breathed a sigh of relief.

He led me to where everyone gathered, sitting on jutting stones or mats and narrow blankets. I perched myself next to my uncle, the warmth of the blaze combating the chill air settling around us like a thick coat. Whit sat across from me, our argument hovering between us like an unwanted houseguest. His fingers were absently moving over the handle of his gun. A nervous twitch I'd seen him do before, his thumb brushing over the initials engraved in the steel. He turned his head in my direction, blue eyes glittering like sapphires, and my stomach swooped sharply. Then he deliberately looked away, engaging in conversation with a crew member on his left.

Tío Ricardo handed me a mug. "You'll need something warm to drink."

With a murmured thanks, I took a long sip. The weight of everyone's stares settled on my shoulders. I was the newcomer, a stranger. Even Mr.

Fincastle seemed at ease, reclining on a mat, one of his guns within hand's reach. Isadora sat primly, her back straight, balancing a plate on a bended knee. She threw me a smile and then continued her quiet conversation with her father.

I wrestled with this strange night.

Magic thrummed near me from Trajan's Kiosk, a constant lure, but I concentrated on the strangers surrounding me. It struck me all over again. In a land so far from home, where the people I wanted to be with the most in the world would never join the circle around the fire. I sensed the team's sympathy, but I was alone, without even my uncle to keep me from feeling adrift. I'd been foolish to think of Whit as a friend. His loyalty to my uncle was as immovable as one of the great pyramids, and Whit would guard his secrets and interests as fiercely as a sphinx. I sipped my tea as a way to have something to do with my hands.

Abdullah sat on the other side of me, an affable smile on his face. "Your father was a marvelous storyteller. He knew how to make people laugh. Is that not a nice thing? Here, I see that you've finished your tea. Would you like more?" He talked fast, his hands wildly moving. I nodded in bemusement, and he reached around me and untied my uncle's necktie from around his neck, and then he held it up for me to see. "My favorite magic."

"What is it?" I'd seen Tío Ricardo wearing the garment earlier, the pattern an unexpected fashion choice. It was a Scottish plaid in bold reds and greens.

Abdullah motioned for me to hold up my empty mug. I did so, and watched in amazement as he wrung the necktie over it. Hot water poured into the cup, steam curling up into my face.

"That's extraordinary," I said.

Kareem ran over with a tea bag, and I thanked him. My uncle's lips twitched in amusement as Abdullah shook out the necktie, aiming away from everyone. When he returned the square-shaped fabric to my uncle, it was completely dry. Tío Ricardo tied the ends into a knot around his neck.

"There's more magic in a crate over by headquarters," Abdullah said. "Useful things for digging and researching. Feel free to explore it."

"Oh yes, I will. Shokran, I'm eager for you to put me to work."

"You'd like to dig alongside the rest of us?" Abdullah asked with a wry smile.

My uncle peered at me. "It's a hard day's work, Inez. I've been doing it for over a decade and it never gets easier."

"It's not the same thing," I said. "But I've always liked to search for things, Tío. I'm afraid I'm much too like my parents and you, for that matter. If you teach me how to excavate, I'm sure I can do the job properly."

My uncle shook his head. "I'd prefer that you sketch and paint what you can."

I sipped my tea in lieu of responding. He could tell me how to spend my days, but he had no say in what I did at night. I thought back to that frantic moment on the dahabeeyah, the instant I saw him tuck my mother's journal into his trunk. What else of hers did he want to keep safe? I wanted to discover everything he hid from me.

I wanted to know about the mysterious gate.

But first, I needed leverage.

---※---

I stepped gingerly out into the night, my eyes slowly adjusting to the darkness, and found a softly treaded path toward Trajan's Kiosk. The Nile lapped against the rocky coast of the island, a push and pull that soothed my fluttering heart. I carried some of my parents' supplies: matches and a candle, Papá's switchblade, a canteen of water, my sketch pad and charcoal pencils. The night whispered against my skin, and I wished for my uncle's enchanted shoe. It would make observing my surroundings much easier.

From what I could see, the path behind me remained empty. I scrambled across the sand, reaching Pharaoh's Bed as quickly and as quietly as I could. The call of the magic flared to life, roaring as fiercely as a proud lion. I took a step forward but the hair on the back of my neck rose, and goosebumps flared up and down my arms. My knees shook as I halfway turned around, waiting with my breath trapped between my ribs, expecting to see someone following me.

But only the stretch of sand greeted me.

I kept still for several seconds longer before whirling to face the kiosk.

But the sensation of someone watching shook me, and my hands were not altogether steady as I stepped inside.

Only then did I strike the match and light the candle.

The small flame barely illuminated the grandeur of the enclosed space. The upper half of the structure displayed enormous columns, reaching three stories or more, while the bottom half were walls covered in bas-reliefs. I stepped closer, examining each carved area, looking for any signs of the goddess Isis. The magic thrummed, as consistent as my own heartbeat.

"Find anything interesting?"

I jumped and somehow managed to cut off the scream at the back of my throat. "*Whit!* Por el amor de Dios!"

As was his usual manner, he lounged against the entrance, ankles crossed. He regarded me in bemused stupefaction. "I can't find any reason why you should be out of bed at this hour, Olivera. Are you perhaps lost?"

I glared at him.

"No? I didn't think so."

"Surely my uncle doesn't expect you to keep an eye on me day and night."

"That would certainly be scandalous," he said, smiling faintly.

"I thought you were mad at me."

"I don't care enough to feel anything, one way or another," he tossed back. "Now why don't you tell me what you're doing out here?"

Dios, he was such a liar. I saw the furious gleam in his eyes before he had stomped away, the sharp, tense line of his jaw as he clenched his teeth. He had felt something, even if he didn't want to admit it.

"Does it look like I'm in mortal peril?"

He narrowed his gaze. "I'm still determining if you're a danger to yourself."

"That's rude."

"I repeat. What are you doing here?"

"I'm exploring this building without my uncle's watchful eye." I held up my sketch pad. "Haven't you heard? My time here is extremely limited. I thought I might draw the interior."

He bent forward, laughing.

"*Sssshhh!* You'll wake them!"

Whit stifled his amusement and stepped inside. "Good Lord, you are such a terrible liar."

I stiffened. "I'm not."

His lips twitched. "You mean you don't feel magic's pull right now? You're not trying to discover the link?"

I turned away in disgust. There was no point in lying. "Of course I am."

I expected him to drag me away from Trajan's Kiosk, hollering at me to go to bed, but he did none of those things. He merely went and sat in the corner, his long legs stretched out before him.

"You don't have to stay here," I said after a moment.

"Don't I?"

I glared at him, and his expression softened. "I'm going to make sure no one bothers you."

"You're not going to make me go?"

"I've been trying to get you to leave since the moment I met you." Whit shrugged. "I've learned that any attempt is futile."

"Oh. Well, do you know what it is I'm supposed to be looking for?"

He smiled. "I said I would guard you, I didn't say I'd help you, Olivera. Your uncle wouldn't appreciate it. I have my *marching orders,* after all." A hint of anger punctuated his words. Enough for me to glance over. His face held all of its usual charm, the laughing lines bracketing his mouth, his blue eyes crinkling at the corners. The only thing that gave away his frustration was his clenched jaw.

"It was unfair of me to suggest—"

"That I don't have a mind of my own?" he asked, and this time he let me see his anger. "That I can't make decisions independently, irrespective of what I've been told to do?"

"Yes. Um, that. I'm sorry." I paused. "So you were dishonorably discharged. Do you want to talk about it?"

He looked faintly outraged. "Absolutely not."

I turned away and continued examining the walls. "So your plan is just to sit there and watch me—wait a minute." The magic jumped, a sensation that made my stomach lurch. I peered more closely at the wall, found nothing of note, but then my gaze dropped to the floor. Parts of the pavement were dusty and covered with smaller pebbles and packed sand. But there was something that called to the magic moving restlessly inside me. I dropped to my knees, the warmth coming from the lit candle and my nerves making my skin dampen with sweat, despite the cool night. Gingerly, I brushed my fingers against the stone, moving things around, feeling for something I knew to be there, even if I didn't know what that something was.

My fingers glided over a bumpy stretch of stone. I moved away more sand and pebbles until a small cartouche that spelled out *Isis* stared up at me. A thrill of discovery fluttered to my limbs. It was intoxicating, a sensation I wanted to feel again and again. "Whit."

He was next to me in an instant. "I knew you'd find it," he said, grinning.

"You couldn't have helped me?"

"Actually, no."

"What? Why not?"

He sat back on his haunches. "Ever since your parents' deaths, your uncle has only allowed Abdullah with him at the start of each day. He only lets everyone else inside after the tunnel has been opened."

"But not you. Doesn't he trust you?"

"Problem with authority, remember?" he said wryly.

"What about Mr. Fincastle?"

"To a certain degree, I would think. Imagine not trusting the man hired to protect the team," he replied. "It's unlikely he'll involve him unless it's absolutely necessary."

"Speaking of security, where is it? Shouldn't this place be guarded? I expected it to be so."

"And you still came out here alone?"

"Just answer my question, Whit."

"Mr. Hayes."

"No. I've earned the right to call you by your name."

His brow quirked. "You think so?"

I ticked off the reasons using my fingers. "I've outsmarted you at least twice. You showed me around Cairo, I know about your family and your secret—"

"Hardly a secret," he muttered.

"You saved my life in the river. We survived the near sinking of the *Elephantine*—"

"That's an exaggeration."

"And now we're defying my uncle. It's nice to have a companion on that score."

"Happy to be here to suit your needs," he said with some degree of sarcasm, but I read the humor in his gaze regardless. "It's not guarded because that would immediately telegraph the kiosk's importance."

"Oh, I suppose that makes sense." Some of what he'd mentioned earlier finally registered. I looked down. "Wait, there's a tunnel?"

"Yes. Which we'll find presently." Whit looked down and ran his hands across the stone. "I wonder if you press down . . ." He did, but nothing happened.

I placed a light hand on his arm. "Can you lift it? There's a significant gap around the stone in comparison to the ones surrounding it."

He complied, lifting and tugging, until the stone cleared the others fully.

I looked underneath. "Well, what do you know?"

Whit gently placed the top stone on the ground and joined in on my examination. A raised circle rose up from the ground, no more than a few inches. I reached forward and tried turning it, but the cylinder remained firmly in place. At the top, there was an inscription faintly carved into the surface.

"How's your knowledge of hieroglyphs?"

"Fair," Whit said, squinting. "Careful not to drip the wax."

I righted the candle. "Can you read it?"

"Some," he muttered. "Not nearly as well as Abdullah or your uncle, however. I think it's another cartouche of Isis, but she's surrounded by other figures I don't recognize."

"Interesting. Her guardians perhaps?"

Whit made a noncommittal grunt.

"How large is the tunnel opening?"

"Not very, I have to go in sideways to enter."

The magic inside was near bursting, threatening release. I had no idea how that kind of energy moved, how it chose where to go. But I felt it moving like a strong current in my bloodstream. Desperate, I brushed my fingers alongside the corners, and I felt an area of bumpy stone.

"There," I murmured. "Found it."

I pressed hard, and a small rectangular space gave way, moving inward with the sound of stone scraping against stone. The floor in front of us dropped about five inches, a depression that formed another rectangular shape.

"There it is, Olivera," Whit said, grinning. He got onto his knees and carefully slid the pavement backward where it tucked neatly underneath, revealing narrow stone steps descending into a flat darkness.

"Do you want to go first, or shall I?"

My body thrummed with barely contained excitement. "Me."

Whit smiled and held out his hand. "After you, then."

CAPÍTULO VEINTIUNO

I inhaled deeply before scooting forward to place my feet inside the narrow opening. Then I slowly, and with much care, moved down, the flame of my candle giving enough illumination so I could make out the next step, and then the next. My pulse raced, and the magic in my blood sang in tune to my heartbeat. The walls were dusty and appeared to be made of packed dirt. Whit followed after me, staying close behind. His breath was a soothing presence, like the steady rise and fall of the ocean lapping against the Argentinian coast.

"Are you all right?" he whispered.

"Of course," I said.

"Most people are afraid of dark, enclosed spaces."

"Oh, I'm afraid of dark, enclosed places," I admitted. "But I wouldn't miss this. Not for anything."

I reached the last step and found myself in what appeared to be a small, square room. I moved the candle around until I found a narrow opening with a jagged edge, as if someone had blown through it.

"Dynamite?" I guessed.

Whit shook his head. "Too risky, it might cause structural damage. No, it was a tiny amount of gunpowder, targeting specific areas."

I let out a whistle. "Isn't that *still* risky?"

Whit smiled slightly. "Not if you know what you're doing."

I looked at him quickly. "Was it *you*?"

He bowed, an irreverent grin stretching his mouth.

I could only stare at him, gaping.

Whit cleared his throat, his gaze dropping. If I didn't know better, I'd say he was embarrassed. "It's a simple chemical explosion. A child could do it."

This man was made of nothing but self-deprecation and peril and cynicism. He knew how to handle explosives. "No, I don't think a *child*—"

"Let's move on, shall we?" Whit said, his eyes snapping to mine. "Ricardo found this place with your parents and Abdullah, and not long after, we blew through to the next room. You can imagine their disappointment when they discovered the rather plain presentation."

So I was right. My father *had* been here.

I kept my attention on the opening, itching to dart ahead. "I'm sensing there's more you're not telling me."

"Your senses are to be admired," he said wryly. "Ancient Egyptians used to create labyrinths at the burial sites in order to confuse or waylay tomb robbers. Therefore, this room is a ruse."

I gestured to the ragged opening. "Shall we go through?"

"As you wish."

I led the way, stepping over a pile of rocks, Whit at my heels. Within seconds, we were standing in yet another plain room. This one smelled even mustier and more damp, but it, too, opened into another room. Whit gestured for me to continue until we stood in a third room, just as plain and ordinary as the previous ones. I stepped closer to the walls, but there was no ornamentation, or hint that there had ever been, of any kind. The steady presence of the magic was my only guide.

It sensed something beyond the walls.

"Another ruse," I murmured. "But what about . . ." My voice trailed off. From the little I could see, my uncle and his team were working on the right side of the room. There were half a dozen round and square pointed shovels, pickaxes, and helmets propped against the stone.

"What about *what*?" Whit said, watching me closely. "Feeling any tingles? Vibrations? An annoying buzz much like a pesky mosquito?"

"I wouldn't say *annoying*—wait a minute." Those were the exact ways I felt the magic pulse through me. I narrowed my gaze, struck by a new possibility I hadn't considered. "Have you felt it before?"

"Not *me* personally, no."

"Then who?"

"Your father."

I stepped closer, desperate to know more. "Tell me everything."

"It isn't much," he said. "He was curiously private about certain things, your father. But he'd picked up something—"

"What was it?"

"Well, I didn't know at the time, but *now* I think it might have been the ring he sent you. Your father said he also tasted the magic, but he never said it was roses."

I thought hard, trying to connect all the pieces in my cluttered mind. I remembered what I'd overheard the night I had snuck aboard the *Elephantine*. "Did my uncle know about Papá?"

Whit paused. "He did."

I opened my mouth, but Whit held up his hand. "No more questions. It's late, and we have more to explore. I don't fancy having your uncle find us down here."

I blinked. I'd completely forgotten about the world above, and the people who slept unaware of what we were doing dozens of feet underground. The knowing of it sent a delicious thrill to my fingers. Was this how every archaeologist felt?

Whit dug his hands into his pockets. "Well? Anything?"

But I still had one more question. "Does my uncle believe he's found Cleopatra's tomb?"

Whit hesitated, his brows puckering. Every muscle along his jawline jumped. I waited, but he remained stubbornly silent, his moral compass refusing to point anywhere but due north.

Except for when it was inconvenient for *him*.

"You can't answer, can you?"

He smiled ruefully. "I can't talk about *any* of your uncle's excavations. Do you feel anything in this room?"

Trust didn't come easily, but I sensed that we'd circle around each other, getting nowhere, if one of us didn't bend a little. I could do this on my own, come back while he slept, but I was tired of carrying the foreign magic by myself. It was too big, too powerful of a notion to shoulder. Aid was within reach; I only needed to ask for it. I pointed to the left side, and gave him one truth. "Yes, and I'm sorry to say that my uncle is looking in the wrong spot. There's something on the other side of this wall. That's where he ought to excavate."

"Are you sure?"

I nodded.

Whit grinned approvingly. "Good work, Olivera."

* * *

I stared up at the tarp gently rustling against the ruined stone walls of my makeshift bedroom. Everything confirmed my suspicions about my uncle's bizarre behavior: they were incredibly close to finding Cleopatra's final resting place.

My mind reeled. Such a find would rock the Cairo community, and scores of foreigners would travel to Egypt wanting a piece of history. The Antiquities Service would hasten to Philae and take over the excavation, the last thing my uncle would want. What I still didn't know was what his discovery had to do with my parents. Why had he deliberately led them out into the desert?

Maybe he had brought them to a temple with that particular gate, left them to die?

I sat up in the bedroll, the mosquito net surrounding me like a bridal veil. Hot tears pricked my eyes and I angrily wiped them away. Part of me wished I'd never come to Egypt. Then I would never have discovered such a horrifying betrayal. I would never have known how families could turn on one another in unforgiveable cruelty.

I had been naive and stubborn.

But I finally knew the truth.

What I needed was a plan. I'd have to conduct thorough searches of his cabin on the dahabeeyah *and* his room here in the camp. He might have taken his most important valuables off the boat, so I'd start with the easiest target first. Getting inside his room ought to be no problem. I knew how my uncle worked. He liked to get his hands dirty, and he wouldn't lounge while the others dug. Which gave me plenty of opportunity to search his room, thanks to my job sketching and painting the ruins.

But I'd made a foolish mistake tonight.

I'd revealed far too much to Whit and I wasn't certain that he wouldn't tell Tío Ricardo what we'd done tonight the first chance he had. I couldn't allow him to do that.

With a sigh, I shoved away the netting and stood.

The curtains weren't thick, and moonlight poured into the small space through the loose weave. I pulled them open and crept outside. Cool air settled around me, teasing loose strands from my braid. The stretch of makeshift rooms stood before me. Whit had ducked into the one next to mine after we'd walked back from Trajan's Kiosk. I stood in front of his quarters, suddenly seized with the full awareness of what I was about to do.

I'd never, in my whole life, spent so much time with a man without the presence of a family member. But since arriving in Egypt, I'd spent an incredible amount of time with Whit. I'd had more freedom than I'd ever been allowed. It was the first few sips of delicious, cold water and I found that I was thirsty for more.

But sneaking into a man's room in the dead of night?

I'd gone to bed wearing the loose Turkish trousers and oversized cotton shirt that buttoned up to my chin. I was covered from head to foot but it still didn't matter. This was a definite boundary I'd never have dreamed of crossing.

It had to be done.

I couldn't allow Whit to tell my uncle what I'd discovered. It might secure my stay for the time being, but it also meant my uncle would be aware that I knew about all of his lying. I needed more time. One more day to conduct my searches.

With a steadying breath, I swept aside the curtain and walked inside Whit's room. Darkness enclosed the narrow space—

A strong hand clapped hard against my mouth. I squirmed against the brute strength, but I might as well have been grappling against one of the pyramids. The arm around my waist tightened and then I was flipped, landing on my back against the bedroll. My breath whooshed out of me in a fast current. A heavy weight settled at an angle over my chest. Warm breath brushed across my face.

"Who are you?" someone snarled in my ear. With a start, I realized it was

Whit. His voice sounded rough and gravelly, nothing like his usual drawling charm.

"It's me," I whispered. "Inez."

He stiffened.

A long torturous beat stretched between us, neither of us moving, hardly daring to breathe. It might have only been the two of us alone on Philae. His arms bracketed my head, the long line of his chest pinning me down. Innocent terror overwhelmed me. Not of *him*, but of the intimacy flaring between us. His furious breaths brushed against my face. Whit pushed up and sprang backward. The curtain remained open and moonbeams flooded his room. He kneeled on the ground beside the bedroll, his face twisted in fury. Silently, he went to an upended crate and struck a match. Without ceremony he lit a candle, and the flame illuminated his room.

It was neatly arranged, far tidier than mine. He didn't have many worldly possessions: a few tins of tooth powder, one comb and razor, and a small square of mint-hued soap near the washbasin. A leather journal rested atop a stack of books, the gold foil on the spines revealing each title: *Elemental Manual of Chemistry, Lessons in Elemental Chemistry: Inorganic and Organic,* and *Handbook of Chemistry.*

Whit moved, stepping in front of the stack, effectively blocking my view. "What the bloody hell are you doing?" he whisper-shouted. "I could have hurt you."

Silver light cut across his face, the sharp lines of his cheekbones and jaw, the furious set to his shoulders. I had no idea he had any interest in the sciences. It seemed incongruous with the Whit I knew, the former soldier, a roguish brawler who drank too much. This was a side of himself he kept hidden away—but then I remembered how he'd spoken of gunpowder. *A simple chemical explosion.* Curiosity burned in my gut, questions rose in my throat. I swallowed hard, forcing myself to remember the reason I had come.

"I have to talk to you."

"It couldn't have waited until morning?"

"No, I couldn't risk you talking to my uncle about tonight. You're oddly honorable when you want to be."

"The hell I am."

I brushed aside his comment with an impatient flick of my hand. "Who did you think I was? Why the extreme reaction?"

"That was extreme?" He let out a low, harsh laugh. "You're absolutely right. I should have invited a stranger in disguise for a spot of tea in the middle of the night. How dare I defend myself?"

It was more than that. I felt the tension racking his brawny frame. He'd been half-furious, half-afraid. Something had put him on edge. He'd been expecting an attack, for someone to creep into his room at this ungodly hour.

"What happened?" I asked quietly.

Whit stiffened.

"It's obvious *something* did."

"Why don't you want your uncle to find out?" he asked abruptly.

"What makes you think he can be trusted?"

"Because he saved my life, Olivera."

"What?" I asked, forgetting to whisper.

Whit threw me a furious look and quickly stood and went to the entrance. He shifted the curtain aside an inch and peered outside. After a moment he let the fabric drop and then sat on the ground, staring at me warily.

"I'm not leaving until you explain what happened."

"I can make you leave."

"You won't touch me again."

Whit wrenched his gaze from mine, his lips pressed flat. Finally, he spoke in a low volume, every word yanked out of him as if without his permission. "It was right after I was kicked out of the military. The things I saw . . ." His voice trailed off and he shuddered. After a beat he began again. "I'd sunk low, spent more time drunk than sober, and I'd backed myself into a corner. Ricardo got me out and has stood with me ever since. Satisfied?"

It wasn't the whole picture, but I'd learned enough to understand the reason behind Whit's unwavering loyalty to my uncle. He was in Tío Ricardo's debt. Instead of answering his question I said, "Swear to me that you won't tell my uncle."

"I can't do that."

"Dame un día más."

"Why do you want one more day?"

"Whit."

"Mr. Hayes," he corrected. "I told you to observe proper etiquette. I'm not used to being the one who has to remember the rules, and it's really starting to annoy me."

I scrambled forward, onto my hands and knees, and crawled toward him. He remained motionless, alert and wary. Our faces were inches apart. "You can't just pretend that you don't feel it. What exists between us."

"Listen, there's *nothing*—"

I leaned forward and pressed my lips against his. Shock reverberated through me. Whit didn't kiss me back, but he didn't pull away either. We froze, and for a fleeting moment I wondered if it was because he didn't want to break the connection. Slowly, I brushed my mouth against his, and I felt him soften imperceptibly. A subtle shift in his weight, his lips relaxing under mine, moving with infinite care against my mouth for one single breath. His tongue touched mine, gentle. I pressed harder—Whit stiffened and then moved away.

His breathing was harsh, his words hoarse. "Like I've said, Señorita Olivera." He kept his expression flat and guarded. "There's nothing be-tween us. There can never be."

I sat back on my heels, breathing hard. The taste of him still in my mouth.

"I'm getting married."

I blinked. "*What?*"

"I have a betrothed," he said in a cool voice, his fists clenched tight against his thighs.

The word landed in a thud between us. *Betrothed.*

My cheeks warmed as I stood, turning and scrambling toward the open-ing, desperate to create distance between us. Miles would been preferable, but I'd settle for my room. I'd made a terrible mistake, how could I have been so silly as to—

"Señorita Olivera," he whispered.

I stopped, my hand curled around the itchy fabric of the curtain.

"I'll keep your secret for one more day," he said. "After that, if you don't tell him you know exactly where he ought to dig, then I will."

WHIT

Bloody hell.

CAPÍTULO VEINTIDÓS

I fled into my room, my heart beating erratically against my chest. I frowned into the darkness. The flame from the candle had gone out, the moonlight barely illuminating the small rectangular space. I stepped inside, my blood rioting from what had just happened. Whit had a betrothed. He was getting married. I couldn't believe it, didn't *want* to believe or imagine the woman he would one day call *wife*.

A dark shape moved in the corner of the room.

I froze, my scream trapped at the back of my throat. A voice whispered, soft and familiar. A voice I thought I'd never hear again. The sound reached me in a murmured hush, urgent, a subtle note of panic puncturing every word. Goosebumps flared up and down my arms.

"Sit down, Inez."

My knees gave out.

I slumped onto the worn rug, the rough fabric scratching my skin. The shape moved forward, and the outline of a body covered in dark clothing became clearer as my eyes adjusted to the darkness. There was the sound of a match being struck and then a flame appeared, flickering and unsure.

She calmly lit the candle, but her hand shook, and then she closed the curtain and sat down beside me. I couldn't make sense of who I was seeing, even as hope bloomed deep in my chest. Slowly, she reached forward and touched my damp cheek. I hadn't known I was crying. Silent tears dripped onto my clothing. I moved forward, and her arms wrapped around me in a tight embrace. My body trembled uncontrollably, and she made a low hum, trying to soothe me.

"Mamá." I pulled away, impatiently wiping my face with my sleeve. "*Mamita.*"

Her scent enveloped me, and it was so familiar, a sob climbed up my throat.

"*Sssshh,*" she said. "It's all right. I'm here."

I could barely speak. "Am I dreaming?"

She raised an index finger to her lips. I could barely hear her words. "Softer. Whitford is a light sleeper."

I blinked at her in confusion, and then I looked over her shoulder, expecting to see my father. But she had come alone. I gripped her arms, hard, my heart understanding before my mind did.

My mother was alive.

Alive.

It was as if I were back in the Nile, swimming against the current, and disoriented. Not trusting my ability to know which way was up. I rubbed my eyes, my eyelashes were wet. It'd been nearly a year since I'd last seen her. Time had left its mark on her youthful face. New lines marred the smooth skin of her brow. I'd forgotten how much I resembled her. The same hazel eyes, the same tanned skin and freckles. I was her mirror image.

"I can't believe—" My throat locked and I swallowed back a painful lump. "You're here. *Alive.* All this time . . ." My voice cracked. A second chance with my family; I could hardly believe it. I don't know what I had done to deserve such an extraordinary miracle. "Where is Papá? Is he coming, too?"

"Inez." She clenched her eyes and used her hem to wipe her sodden cheeks. "He's gone."

I brought my knuckles to my mouth. The ground seemed to tilt under my knees. I cried harder, even as I heard my mother make more shushing noises. For a moment, I thought my world had been made right again.

"I've been destroyed by grief," I said in between hiccups. "I never thought I'd see you again. How is this possible?"

Mamá caressed my cheek, her touch soft. "I never thought I'd see you again, either. I've dreamed of this moment even though it was impossible. You've grown so much, hijita."

Her words sank into me, one by one. She hadn't expected to see her only daughter again? Was she trying to tell me that she'd chosen to stay in Egypt forever? Is that why she let me think she'd *died*?

"I've missed you so much," she whispered. "You will never know how much."

My grief evaporated, and something fiery burned under my skin. "Where have you been?"

"Inez," Mamá said again, trying to reach for me, but I shifted away.

"Where were you?" I whisper-yelled. "All this time, *where were you?*"

"Inez—"

My blood simmered, roiling hot in my veins. "Why didn't you write? Why didn't you come *home?*"

"I couldn't," she said. "It was too risky. There are very few people I trust, and I couldn't guarantee that any letter would reach you untouched." She smoothed the hair off my face. "I've been so worried about you. It killed me to have to stay away from you."

"Too risky," I repeated. "To write to your own daughter? I *mourned* you. I'm still mourning you."

Mamá shut her eyes in resignation. "I'm begging you to keep your voice down." She sighed and when her eyes opened again, they were haunted and terrified. "We don't have much time, tesora. When I saw you arrive, I thought it was a mirage. What are you doing in Egypt?"

"What do you mean? I came to find out what happened."

"I should have expected that." Her face crumpled. "Lo siento. I don't know how you'll ever be able to forgive me. But I wouldn't have done it if it weren't important."

Her words finally registered. "Wait a minute. You *saw* me arrive?"

"I've made camp on Philae in a secluded area, far from the temple." She hesitated. "I've had help from the women in staying out of sight."

"I don't understand," I said slowly. "You've been on this island the whole time?"

"Not the whole time." She hesitated. "I've been in hiding."

My hold on her tightened. "Hiding? From . . . from Tío Ricardo?"

Her mouth dropped open. "How did you know?"

"Know what?"

She leaned forward and cupped my cheeks. "Has he hurt you, Inez?"

I shook my head. "I found your letter."

"My letter?" She furrowed her brow. "What letter?"

"The one you never sent to Monsieur Maspero. I found it in the hotel suite and read it. Mamá, why are you afraid of your own brother?"

Her face turned white in the dimness of my room. "Inez, you must go back to Argentina, *por favor*. The situation here is too perilous."

"Yes, we'll go together and—"

"No, you have to go without me. I can't—I *won't* leave until I finish what I started."

"What is it? Tell me what's going on. I've been frightened ever since coming to Egypt. Did Tío Ricardo hurt you? Did he hurt Papá?"

She brushed more of my tears away with the back of her hand. "Inez, your uncle has involved himself with an illegal smuggling trade of Egyptian artifacts. I've been trying to stop him, but he's too well connected. He's different, more desperate and—" Her voice cracked. "He's not the brother I've known all my life. He's changed, and I watched it happen." Her face twisted. "I *let* it happen. This is my fault."

My mind reeled. I recalled Maspero's fear of the return of illicit auctions. But it sounded like they had not only returned, but the buying and selling of artifacts had been running rampant. My mother made a small noise at the back of her throat, and she looked so guilty my heart cracked.

"How could you say that?" I asked gently. "He's a grown man."

She turned her face away, her chest rising and falling with agitated breaths. I'd never seen her so discomposed, rattled, and nervous. My mother never let her emotions run away from her, at least in parenting me.

"Inez, when I come to Egypt, I—" She squeezed her eyes shut. "I act a little differently, and I've allowed myself more freedoms than I normally would while in Buenos Aires."

I knew, instantly, what she meant. I remembered the more youthful clothes I'd found in the hotel room. I had wondered about them, at the different side of my mother I had never seen before.

"Go on," I said softly.

"Your father and I let ourselves become distracted, and I was swept up in the grand adventure," she said, her lips turning downward. "I knew my brother was toeing a fine line, but he assured me that he had everything under control, that he would never become involved with the set of people rumored to be involved in illegal activities. I ought to have paid better attention. I ought to have talked to him more, asked for help. Your father and I didn't know what to do, so we did nothing." She lifted her gaze, turned toward me. Her hair hung in dirty strands, framing a tight and narrow face. "I don't know if I can protect you. I need you to go home, Inez."

"I'm not leaving you. I won't do it."

Mamá shut her eyes, resigned. "Why I haven't been able to curb your stubbornness, I'll never know. Inez, this isn't Argentina. I allowed you some freedom, but I won't here."

I took her hand. "I thought I lost you. Let me help you."

She opened her eyes, visibly weighing what to say. "Do you know who your uncle hopes to find on Philae?"

I nodded. "Cleopatra. He thinks she might be buried under Trajan's Kiosk; that's where they've been tunneling."

"And do you understand the enormity of such a discovery? Finding the last pharaoh of Egypt is akin to finding the Holy Grail. It's every archaeologist's dream. One of the most important discoveries, second, maybe, to that of Alexander the Great or Nefertiti. The artifacts found in her tomb will be worth millions on the black market. Your uncle can't be allowed to sell such priceless art at Tradesman's Gate."

"Gate? What gate? *Oh!* You mean the card," I breathed. "I found it in your hotel room. There's an illustration of a gate on one side."

"It's an illegal exchange of artifacts," she said in a hushed voice. "Most times, the Curators—who are known as the tradesmen—run an auction with buyers. But the metaphorical *gate* always changes location, and it's very hard to attend unless you have an invitation."

"And this is what you've been doing," I said. "Trying to track down the moving gate, trying to stop Tío Ricardo from participating."

Mamá nodded. She tucked a strand of my hair behind my ear. "This situation is too much for you. If anything were to happen to you . . ."

"But you can't stop him on your own," I whispered-yelled. "He's close to finding her, I think. I felt the magic myself."

Mamá furrowed her brow. "Magia? Qué magia?"

"From the golden ring Papá sent."

She remained silent, staring at me with a confused expression on her face. Her bafflement turned to profound shock. "A ring?" she repeated dumbly.

"The one he mailed me," I prompted. "The one belonging to Cleopatra?"

"Of course." Her brow cleared, and she nodded. "That one. I'd forgotten he'd sent that to you for safekeeping. That was months ago, shortly before he . . . He must have known . . ." Her words trailed off. She shook her head, as if to clear her thoughts. "What about it?"

"Well, when I first put it on my finger, I felt the magic seep into my skin. Some of the energy transferred to *me*. I've put together that Cleopatra herself had performed a spell to preserve her memories. The leftover magic recognizes anything connected to her and the spell she performed. I think the most powerful object to have traces of the magic is attached to the golden ring."

"That makes sense," she mused. "If it had remained undiscovered for thousands of years, the magic had nowhere else to go until very recently. Very few people would have had the opportunity to handle the ring."

Her expression turned thoughtful.

"What is it?"

"There might be a way to stop him," she whispered so softly, as if talking only to herself. "But it would mean putting you in harm's way. Your uncle will be watching you and I'm not sure if it's wise for you to get involved."

"It's too late," I said. "I'm already involved."

My mother sounded terribly sad. "I know."

"I was planning on rummaging through his room, seeing if I could find any clues to what happened to you. But maybe there's something else I could find? Something that might help us?" A sudden thought struck me. "Did you know he has your journals?"

A muscle in her jaw jumped. "I didn't, but it doesn't surprise me. He'd be looking for anything that might paint him in an unfavorable light. He can't afford to lose his firman."

"All the more reason why I should snoop inside his room."

She shook her head. "You mustn't draw attention to yourself. Promise me that you won't go looking. There's too much at stake."

"But—"

This time, she sounded more like herself. Stern and uncompromising. "Promise me."

I gave her a jerky nod.

Satisfied, she leaned over and kissed my cheek, and then wrapped her arms around me tightly, and I felt how much she didn't want to let me go. "As much as it terrifies me that you're here, I'm happy to see you, querida. I've missed you."

"Me, too," I said, fighting tears. "I'm so heartbroken about Papá. I can't believe I'll never see him again."

She wiped my tears. "Yo tambien, hijita. I loved him so much, and I know you were his whole world. Nothing would have made him happier than to have you here with us, and if things had been different, we would have brought you with us. I hope you know that. Your uncle has been slowly going down this road for a long time." She shrugged helplessly. "We haven't been getting along for years, constantly fighting, every day another argument. It was no place for you."

"All the same, I wish you would have brought me."

"Maybe it was a mistake not to." Her eyes tracked over every line and curve of my face. "You've grown up, Inez. I see so much of your father in you."

"But everyone says I look like you."

She smiled, and it was almost wistful. "It's the wisdom in your glance, the stubborn jaw, and unruly hair. You're more like him than me. Always wanting to learn, and so *curious*. Every year on your birthday you wanted a new book, another sketch pad, bottles of ink, or a train ticket to another country. You're here because you are your father's daughter, Inez."

My mother stood and wrapped a thick, dark scarf around her head. "I'll come back to you when it's safe, and when I've finalized a plan. Be careful until then and speak of this to no one."

"I won't," I promised.

"And you mustn't tell Whitford you've seen me."

"Perhaps if you told him what you know about Tío Ricardo? He might believe you."

She hesitated, unsure, her movement frozen. Reluctantly, she slowly shook her head. "No, Inez. Swear to me that you'll keep my secret."

I nodded.

She went to the entrance, her fingers gripping the fluttering curtain. Her voice dropped even lower, and I strained to hear her. "There's one more thing you have to do for me."

"What is it?"

"You must pretend to love your uncle."

I recoiled, unable to disguise a full-body shudder. "But—"

"Love him, Inez," she said. "Work to earn his approval. Strive to get to know him without revealing anything of yourself to him. He'll use whatever weakness he finds against you. Treat him like family. He must never suspect you know the truth."

———— ✖ ————

The morning came with extraordinary splendor to the Nile. Lavender stripes reached from one end of the river, heralding the fiery burn of the sun's rising. Egrets dotted the banks as the fishermen set off for the day's catch. I yawned hugely, wiping the grit from my eyes. Sleep evaded me all through the night. I pulled the curtain shut and stretched, enjoying the cool touch of morning.

Everyone else had risen early.

Half the crew prayed with the rising sun, a sight familiar to me since my first morning in Cairo where the sound of hundreds of mosques signaled the time for prayer, the Azan, five times a day. The other half of the crew were Coptic Christians, and they moved quietly, preparing for the long work ahead.

I made my way to the roaring fire, rubbing my arms to fight off the chill. One of the crew took an elegant fountain pen and shook the ink into the fire pit. Flames erupted from the splatters of dark liquid, embers dancing in the air from the ink droplets. Tío Ricardo nursed his drink, watching the others, and avoiding looking in my direction. One of the women serving our party placed a warm cup of coffee into my hands. I sipped the strong brew, my sketch pad tucked under my arm. Whit stepped out of his room, his blue gaze unerringly finding mine. His face was remote and closed off. I recognized it for what it was. His armor was back in place, a knight defending a vulnerable fortress.

His engagement was the moat surrounding it.

I couldn't pin the moment when I wanted more than a friendship with Whit. I'd have to forget what I had begun to feel for him, and instead focus on what annoyed me the most. He was high-handed and exasperating, secretive and closed off. He'd made his feelings clear last night.

But I remembered the way his mouth had felt against mine.

I looked away, remembering my mother's plea. The distance was for the best. I only wished my heart felt the same way. He couldn't be trusted, I reminded myself for the hundredth time. He'd retreat behind the orders given to him by my uncle, and keep me at arm's length with his meaningless flirting and roguish winks.

He was my uncle's man, through and through.

Tío Ricardo pointed to the empty seat beside him, and I settled onto the mat. "Buenos días, Tío," I said. My pulse jumped in my throat; I was sure that he'd see through my nonchalant behavior. Disgust mixed with my fear. He wasn't honorable or decent. He was a liar and a thief.

"Did you sleep well?" Tío Ricardo asked.

"I did." I'd brought out my sketch pad and flipped to what I'd completed the day before instead, telling myself that I had a mission.

"Is this what you were hoping for?"

Tío Ricardo looked down, the lower half of his face near covered by his thick, grizzly beard. His hazel eyes widened as he took my painting into his weathered hands. I'd captured the massive columns, the ghosts of the vibrant colors decorating the capitals, the hieroglyphics etched into the stone. Hours had passed as I painted, but I barely noticed.

"These are lovely," he said, beaming.

A compliment at last—I ought to note the date on the pages. My uncle noticed the rest of the crew and team eyeing the journal curiously, and to my astonishment, he passed it around. Isadora held it first and she pored over the drawings.

"Why, these are extraordinary! I couldn't draw a straight line even if someone offered me a kingdom. You'll have to teach me, Inez."

"It only takes practice," I said.

"Nonsense," she said. "If that were true, I would be able to sew and I'm afraid I still can't."

I smiled and she handed the journal to her father. Mr. Fincastle barely glanced at it, but Abdullah marveled at the detail and I felt a swell of pride in my chest. I sat up straighter and fought a blush. When the notebook reached Whit, he handed it to someone on the digging crew without looking, sipping from his cup.

"I observed the making of it," Whit explained to Abdullah's astonishment.

"Speaking of which," Tío Ricardo said. "Inez, I'd like you to sketch and draw the interior of the temple of Isis this time."

"I look forward to it."

"Whitford will be with you."

"He'll only distract me," I said, keeping my voice nonchalant and calm. I couldn't handle another encounter with Whit. "I work faster without someone hovering over my shoulder, anyway. I promise I'll be safe and won't come out until I've finished."

"Still, I'd feel better if Whitford were with you," my uncle said, frowning.

I couldn't keep my eyes from flicking in his direction. He stared mutely into his mug, the corners of his mouth crimped. His distaste of being in my company was all too clear.

"I'll join you," Isadora said suddenly, looking between us.

I threw her a grateful smile.

"You'll get dusty," Mr. Fincastle said.

Isadora gave a dainty shrug. "I daresay no one will mind my dirty hem."

"I certainly won't," I said. "I'm *incredibly* happy to have *your* company."

If I hadn't been looking in his direction, I would have missed his quick eye roll. But he tightened his hold on the cup, his fingers turning white.

My uncle glanced at me pointedly. "You'll let me know of any developments?"

I fought hard to keep my expression bland as I lied straight to his face. "Of course, Tío."

Isadora assessed us with a speculative gleam in her eyes. Intuition flickered sharply. I might have fooled my uncle, but possibly not her. She had observed the tension between me and Whit, coming to my rescue. She had somehow known I had lied to my uncle. Isadora collected information while she remained a mystery to me. It suddenly dawned on me that I was making myself vulnerable.

If I weren't more careful, she could discover the biggest secret I kept.

CAPÍTULO VEINTITRÉS

*W*hit stayed outside with the digging crew, working alongside them, while Abdullah and Tío Ricardo shouted instructions, their hands as dirty as everyone else's. They all worked in cohesion, speaking to the long years between them, seeming to understand one another without talking. Gunpowder disappeared down into the tunnels under Trajan's Kiosk, along with shovels and pickaxes. Isadora and I cleaned up after the morning meal, washing plates and cups in a big luggage trunk brimming with soapy water. Once the dishes were done, we flipped the lid closed. When I opened it again, the old water was replaced by fresh, clean water. A marvel out here in the desert.

I wished I could fit inside for baths.

Isadora must have felt the same because I caught her looking longingly at the trunk, too. But she looked prim and neat, her hair perfectly braided and coiled high over her head. You'd never know she'd spent the night in a makeshift tent with crumbling walls and a tarp stretched over her head.

"Shall we?" she asked, gesturing toward the temple of Isis.

We carried the sketch pad and pencils and paints, along with my canvas bag, stuffed full with a canteen of water and a small meal put together by Kareem. We settled inside the interior of the temple, surrounded by columns and bas-reliefs, and I worked for a couple of hours while Isadora explored. She seemed on edge, restless, as if there was something on her mind and she was only waiting for the right moment to bring it up. I *felt* that she knew I had been lying.

When Isadora returned, she sat down beside me with her knees tucked demurely beneath her, her ankles covered by the volume of her linen skirt. She had the kind of manners and modesty my mother approved of. My clothing had already acquired a fair bit of dust and the tips of my fingers were stained from my pencils.

"Any progress?" Isadora asked.

I flipped my sketchbook around to show her.

"Mr. Marqués will be pleased, I'm sure. At least, I hope he will be. He seems like a man who is hard to please." She nudged my shoulder. "But easy to deceive."

My lips parted in surprise. "An interesting observation. What made you think of it?"

Isadora arched a brow. "Next time you lie, don't clasp your hands tight."

I snapped my mouth closed and glared at her as she let out a peal of laughter.

"Don't worry. He believed you," she said, wiping her eyes, still chuckling. "But now I'm very curious. What developments are you supposed to report?"

"My progress," I said, taking care to keep my hands light on my knees. "He wants me to move quickly and worries I'll cause delays."

"Hmmm." She tilted her head. "Why is he in such a rush, do you think?"

"He doesn't tell me such things. Remember?"

"Very annoying," Isadora said, nodding. "Your relationship with him isn't what I expected."

"What do you mean?" I asked, continuing my drawing.

Her brow furrowed. "I was told your family was close."

She regarded me with frank interest, and I realized how lonely I'd been for female companionship. I missed Elvira, who knew how to make me laugh. What would she think about what my mother had done? Would she forgive her?

I wasn't sure I did.

But I wanted to. Desperately. A second chance had been granted, and it seemed childish to squander the opportunity to spend more time with Mamá.

Isadora remained silent, waiting for me to reply. I liked that about her. Not many people were patient enough with silences.

"My parents spent a lot of time here," I explained. "So they knew him better. I'm still finding my way, as it were. He's a hard man to get to know."

"How are you liking it here?"

"More than I expected," I admitted. "It's so different experiencing it than reading about it. For years, all I wanted was to come along with my parents, but I was never allowed. I think a small part of me resented the whole country."

"And now?"

I looked around at the immense pillars, the hieroglyphs surrounding us, journal entries and records on the walls that survived generations. "Now I understand what the fuss was about."

"Tell me about your mother," she said suddenly. "I hardly get to see mine. She doesn't care to travel with my father."

"My mother was . . . dutiful," I said. "Loyal to us, I think, and very determined to raise me to be well brought up and dignified. I don't always live up to the standard she set for me, clearly. Why doesn't your mother like to travel with your father?"

"He likes to tell her what to do and how to behave," Isadora said with a tired smile. "They argue constantly, and sometimes I think my mother likes to have her own space without the constant headache that is my father."

"He seems like a handful."

"I can manage him," she said, grinning. "I'm here in Egypt, aren't I?"

I returned her smile. I understood her completely. So much of my life had been learning how to manage the people responsible for me.

I returned to my sketching and the drawings came to life as the minutes went by, detail by detail. I worked with a confident hand, my lines coming out straight, thanks to the efforts of my drawing instructor.

This moment always enraptured me, the slow creation of something that hadn't existed before. It was part of the reason why I felt such an affinity to the temple, to the art plastered on ancient walls. Art should outlive its creator. As I painted, I tried to imagine the artists who had labored in the heat, painstakingly painting every flower petal and face.

I admired their dedication. I was in awe of their talent. I didn't want the artifacts to cross Egypt's borders, never to be seen again.

My reproduction paled in comparison, but I was reasonably proud that I could capture something so beautiful at all. When I completed the first painting, I stood, stretching my sore limbs.

"I think it's lovely," Isadora offered. She must have noticed my critical eye lingering over every detail. "Much better than I would have done. In my hands it would have looked like an infant had somehow found a paintbrush." She stood up, stretching. "I think I'll return to camp if you're all right here on your own?"

She turned away but then paused and glanced over her shoulder. "Inez."

"Hmm?"

"I can find out why your uncle is in a rush. Perhaps he thinks the crew is about to make a big discovery."

My mouth went dry as I silently cursed my foolishness. The search for Cleopatra wasn't common knowledge among the team. It was why I didn't want to tell her about the magic that had latched on to me. "Maybe."

She gave a little wave and set out.

I returned to my work, though every time I heard the slightest sound I expected to see my mother emerge from out of the darkness. But no one came as I painted the rest of the portico. I guessed they were all hard at work unearthing another entrance. Or what they *hoped* would be another entrance into a new chamber under Trajan's Kiosk.

If Whit kept his word, then they were looking in the wrong place. The thought sparked an idea. Maybe there was a way to keep my uncle from finding Cleopatra's tomb. I could lead them in the wrong direction—

"There you are."

I startled, and barely caught my brush from splattering all over the page.

Whit prowled closer, carrying the lit sandal engulfed in his rough hands.

"Some warning would have been courteous," I said dryly.

He stopped in front of me, his toes brushing up against my boots. "We need to talk, Olivera."

His tone was gravelly and impatient, a layer of frustration building up every word until it loomed like a fortress.

"About?"

He glared at me. "Last night."

"Last night," I echoed. He folded his arms across his chest. I stood, thinking it was perhaps better I had the conversation on my feet. "What about last night?"

Had he heard my mother in my room? Or did he want to yell at me for kissing him?

I hoped it was the latter. That, at least, I could talk about.

He glowered at me. "You know what about. Quit being evasive, I don't like it."

"I don't need any more clarification on your marital status," I said.

"That's wonderful," he said. "But that's not what I was referring to."

"Oh." I swallowed hard. "It wasn't?"

He slowly shook his head, a dangerous gleam shining back at me from the depth of his cold eyes. "Who the hell was in your room last night?"

The blood drained from my face. We'd been careful, talking so low that even I had had trouble hearing her, despite being less than a foot away from her.

Mamá was right. Whit was a light sleeper. I frowned. How would she know that?

"I'll wait while you come up with a plausible explanation." He scowled. "A lie, most likely."

I backed up another step. Whit remained motionless, coldly furious. His arms were still folded tight across his broad chest. I always forgot how he towered over me, his presence taking up so much space I could see nothing else but him.

"There was no one in my room last night."

He pressed his lips together into a flat line. "Bullshit."

"Even if there were, it would be none of your business."

His fingers dug into his arms. "Why are you here, Olivera?"

Whit's question caught me off guard. My mind scrambled in a million directions, and my palms began to sweat. I couldn't figure out why he'd ask me that question. He sounded suspicious—as if I had something to hide, and not the other way around.

I fought to keep my voice calm. "I'm here to learn what happened to my parents. I'm here because I want to find Cleopatra."

"That so?"

I nodded.

Whit took a step forward. "I think you're hiding something from all of us."

Anger pulsed in my throat. How dare he try to corner me like this when he kept secrets *professionally*? He knew that my parents hadn't gotten lost in the desert, just like he knew that my uncle was just as corrupt as the antiquity officers he supposedly hated. The hypocrisy galled me. I threaded my hands through my hair. It chafed against me, to remain silent when I wanted to scream. The words sat on my tongue, burning. I gave in to the flames, the insistent roar that demanded I *do* something, and skirted around Whit.

He followed after me. "Damn it, Olivera! We are not finished with this conversation."

Nimbly, I rounded a column, intent on losing him, and ducked into a small room that opened to another even smaller room. The minute I stepped foot inside, the taste of roses burst in my mouth. I stopped and Whit crashed into me. I fell forward, but he wrapped a strong arm around my waist.

"Are you all right?" He released me and gently placed his hands on my shoulders, turning me around to face him. He peered down at me. "What's happened? What is it? You've gone pale."

I couldn't even pretend to hide it from him. The thrumming under my skin felt faint, as if it were a magic from a distant land, beckoning me home. I shifted under the weight of his gaze and walked slowly around the chamber, tilting my head, sensitive to every subtle shift in the magical current flooding my veins.

"I thought you didn't feel anything in the temple," Whit said. "You're shaking. What the *hell* is happening?"

"I didn't walk this far inside. Never made it to this room the first time. It's very faint." He blinked. I wasn't making sense. I let out an impatient sigh. "Whit, I *feel* magic."

His lips parted. "There must be something here, then."

In unison, we began a search, examining every corner, studying each of the stones. But I came up with nothing. No sign of Isis's cartouche carved into the walls.

"Holy shit, Olivera. Come look at this."

I was arrested by an intricate painting of a banquet. I wished I understood more hieroglyphs. "Just to be clear, you addressing me by my family name is observing proper decorum? And cursing?"

"Will you just walk over to me, please? Preferably with less cheek. Thank you," he added at my approach.

"This way is much better."

He blinked. "What way, exactly?"

"This version of yourself, which I suspect is closer to who you were before."

"Before *what?*"

"Before you were dishonorably discharged."

He stared down at me with dawning outrage. There was an exasperated curve to his mouth. "You're so . . ."

"Forthright?" I supplied helpfully.

"Aggravating."

Aggravating was much better than indifferent. But then, I wasn't supposed to care because of his marital status and all. "What did you want to show me?"

He pointed to the single column in the small room, three feet thick and reaching up to the ceiling.

I nodded, immediately understanding his thoughts. It had stood out to me, too. "It's the only room in the temple that has one like it."

"Exactly." He lightly tapped his finger against the column. "This is the hieroglyph for *sun*, and right next to it is the hieroglyph for *moon*."

"Hardly unusual. Those symbols must be all over various walls across Egypt."

"True," he conceded. "But taken with the knowledge that Cleopatra named her twins—by Marcus Antonius—Helios and Selene, Greek for *sun* and *moon*, I think the finding is interesting. Especially inside a temple of Isis, a known identifier for Cleopatra."

"You don't need to convince me further. I know the column is important. I *feel* it," I said quietly. "You search the upper half of the column and I'll take the bottom."

"Do you enjoy ordering me around?" he asked, faintly amused.

"Does it look like I do?" I tossed back. Question for question, just how he liked it.

His response only proved my point. "You don't think it actually works, do you?"

Without missing a beat I said, "You're here, aren't you?"

"How is it that a moment ago, I wanted to strangle you, but now I feel like laughing?"

"It's part of my charm."

"We aren't done with our earlier conversation."

"I can hardly wait. I love it when you interrogate me," I said sarcastically.

Whit chuckled through his teeth as he began his careful examination of the column. My portion consisted of dozens of bas-reliefs, a variety of letters in the ancient Egyptian alphabet carved forever into the stone. While I studied each one, I couldn't help hoping that I would paint something that might be worth saving, something that would outlive me. My fingers brushed along the lower half, searching for any unusual creases or divots, while I also paid close attention to the sudden flare of the magic swimming in my veins.

"Whit," I whispered.

He knelt beside me. "I see it."

Together we pushed down on a small section of the bottom lip of the column. The front of it scraped forward, a thick door that followed the curve of the column. The stone had moved forward only an inch, but it was enough purchase to pull from. We stood. His rapid breathing filled the small space. I was in the same state. As if I'd run for miles.

Excitement propelled me forward and I reached for the door. The magic rose within me like a strong current, and I could do nothing but ride it. I was helpless against its strength. "Together, Whit."

As one, we pulled at the door and the scraping noise reverberated in the plain room. It wouldn't budge easily, and it took our combined efforts to widen the entry enough for us to pass through. Within the column, narrow steps appeared, descending downward in a curve. I stepped forward, but Whit caught hold of my shoulder.

"Absolutely not," Whit said. "I go first."

The magic in me roared in protest. "But—"

"Go get your candle, and a canteen of water."

"Don't you dare take another step without me," I said. "You won't be happy if you do, I promise you."

"I haven't been happy for quite some time, Olivera."

I whirled around to face him. "Can we talk about that?"

"*No.*" Whit rolled his eyes. "Now go and retrieve your things."

The items were by the rest of my art supplies, abandoned next to the sketch I'd done earlier that day. When I returned to the back room, I found Whit exactly where he said he'd be. A part of me had really believed he would have gone on without me, especially after his flippant remark about his happiness. Or unhappiness, rather. He hadn't sounded desolated, exactly, but wearily resigned.

But he'd kept his word.

He lit a candle and led the way down. I placed a light hand on his shoulder as we went, the space above us growing darker the farther we progressed underground. The staircase was narrow, and several times I had to resist the urge to suck in my stomach. It wouldn't have made a difference. It was a tight squeeze regardless. Whit had to slide down sideways in order to fit his brawny frame. I don't know how he stood it. It felt as if I were in a tight fist. The only sound came from our sharp breaths mingling together in the cramped space.

At last we reached the bottom after the sixteen never-ending steps, but a thick wall deterred any forward movement. Whit shoved against it using his not-so-inconsiderable brawn.

"Well?"

He grunted.

"Any movement?"

He glowered at me. "I think we're going to have to push together."

I joined him on the last step, our shoulders pressed tight together, the long line of his leg hard against mine. There was no room to create any kind of distance between us.

"Why are we always finding ourselves in dark, enclosed places, Olivera?" Whit muttered.

"The thrill of adventure?"

He snorted and placed one hand on the wall and I followed suit. "Ready?"

"Yes," I said. We heaved, grunting and panting, but the wall wouldn't budge. We couldn't put down the candle and lit sandal and use both of our hands, not without blowing them out. After a second we stopped, and inhaled air that tasted centuries old, filling our lungs and bellies. "I have an idea," I said in between huffs.

"I'm listening."

"Lean against the wall, and use our feet to push. The space is small enough—"

Whit was already moving. He propped up both legs, his feet flat against the opposite wall, and I did the same. Together we pushed and the wall gave, little by little. We didn't stop until the door pushed forward enough for both of us to squeeze through. A gust of warm air slapped our faces, whistling up the round staircase. The hair on my arms stood on end. Our lighting illuminated only a few feet ahead, but it didn't matter. We saw enough. We'd found something.

Surrounding us were untold treasures that had been hidden away two thousand years earlier.

CAPÍTULO VEINTICUATRO

*W*hit tugged me close to his side, the pair of us laughing like idiots. His powerful frame engulfed mine, the long line of his body pressed against my slighter one. Tears streamed down my face, and I blinked them away, not wanting to miss even a moment. Cleopatra's essence swirled around me, and I understood that there were more objects tied to her, matching the spell caught up in the golden ring.

"We need more light," Whit said hoarsely.

"How *incredible* that my uncle's sandal isn't enough," I said between gasping breaths.

We laughed harder, tears dripping down our faces.

He lifted the lit shoe, and I did the same with the single-wick candle, and together we gazed into what the tiny flames revealed. They cast the chamber in a soft golden glow, touching countless objects decorating the space. They were organized by likeness and size. A large chest stood pressed against the left side of the room, and on the opposite was what looked to be a wooden *chariot*.

The walls were covered in gorgeous paintings, faded from the long years since the original painters brushed color over stone. Scenes of Cleopatra dining at an elaborate table with golden plates, of her in a long procession surrounded by attendants. A gorgeous couch sat in the middle of the room, sculpted in bronze and inlaid with ivory and mother-of-pearl. The entire room shimmered from turquoise tiles lining the walls, glinting in the candlelight. Plush rugs, rolled up tightly, were propped in both corners, and even from where I stood, I saw the intricate weaving of roses. My fingers itched to draw every detail.

"This looks like the treasury," Whit murmured. "The room before the actual burial chamber, and it's definitely been looted."

I glanced at him in surprise. "How can you tell?"

"It's like organized chaos in here," he said. "Her chamber wouldn't have initially been left like this. More likely . . ." He walked back to the staircase, lifting the candle to examine the curve of the entrance. After a moment, he let out a noise of satisfaction. "You can see here where the door was reinforced at least once."

I followed him as he drew the candle close to the various statues, some tiny enough to fit in my palm, others large enough that they met my hip in height. My gaze snagged on an entryway that opened to another space. The magic sang under my skin. My pulse jumped in my throat as I stepped through, Whit directly behind me. The firelight created monsters on the elaborately adorned walls.

The next chamber was smaller, and at first sight I thought painted entirely in gold.

"Holy *shit*," Whit said.

My eyes were assaulted by the stately beauty. Thousands of objects sparkled back at me: golden shrines topped with statuettes of deities, models of boats and barges, and several chariots. Whit's attention snagged on rolls of parchment piled high. He stared hungrily, but when he noticed me looking, he turned away and motioned toward an enormous statue greeting us, topped by the figure of a jackal reposed, and decorated with gold leaf accents.

"Anubis," he said.

We stared in awed silence until Whit spoke, destroying the moment.

"I have to get Abdullah and Ricardo."

Any elation I felt vanished in the next breath. Dios, what had I done? The room seemed to press close around me, squeezing me like an iron fist. The word ripped out of me, vehement and loud. It reverberated in the small space. "*No!*"

He gaped at me. "No? What do you mean *no*?"

I had made a terrible mistake. This shouldn't be happening, least of all with Whitford Hayes. The enormity of what I'd done crawled against my skin. My mother would be horrified by this development. The sense of failure tasted sour in my mouth. "Please, can we pretend we never found her?"

"Have you lost your senses? They've been searching for Cleopatra for years, Olivera. Do you really want to take that from them?"

"Fine, but only Abdullah. I don't trust my uncle."

His jaw slackened. "You don't trust *Ricardo*?"

I shook my head.

"What the bloody hell is going on? Is this because of who you had in your room last night?"

"No."

Whit glared at me. "I'm not going to let it go."

Panic pricked my body from my head down to my feet. I'd ruined my mother's plans, her wish to keep Ricardo from dismantling and destroying Cleopatra's final resting place.

"I can't explain," I whispered. "Please give me more time—"

"To do *what*, exactly?"

Footsteps sounded from the staircase hidden within the column. We both froze. "Whit," I said in a panicked whisper. "Someone's coming."

Whit rushed back to the entrance of the antechamber with me at his heels. He stopped so abruptly I crashed into him, and he reached out to steady me. When I tried to step around him, he swung an arm to block me. He kept us inside the treasury, but still within sight of the staircase. Whit pulled out his revolver, keeping it trained on the last step. I moved the candle farther into the adjoining room. Darkness engulfed the antechamber.

"Smart," he said in a hushed voice.

Someone descended, the sound of harsh breathing growing louder and louder. I locked my breath inside my chest, afraid to make any noise. A small glow of blue light appeared, slowly crawling forward, corresponding with the soft scuffle of shoes against stone. Scuffed leather boots appeared first. Then long legs encased in loose trousers, stained with dirt and grime, and then a slim waist, and at last a grizzled, weathered face, at once familiar and dangerous, followed.

Tío Ricardo.

I'd led him straight to Cleopatra. My mother would be devastated, horrified. His knees bent and he staggered backward as he gazed into the antechamber. He barely held on to the guttering torch in his hand.

"Dios," he murmured. But then he straightened and in a panicked voice said, "*Inez!*"

I stepped around Whit, the light following my movement. I was shaking, remembering that I had a role to play. "I'm here, Tío."

My uncle swerved in the direction of my voice, squinting. Whit's arm brushed against mine as he holstered his revolver. Upon seeing me, my uncle stepped forward, and then abruptly stopped at the sight of Whit at my elbow. Tío Ricardo's dark brows slammed together.

"Explain," he said in a hard voice.

Whit inhaled, opened his mouth—but I was faster, immediately turning the tables on him.

"Were you spying on us?" I demanded.

Whit slapped his hand over his eyes, groaning.

"Spying on you?" Tío Ricardo asked in a voice edged in ice. "No, I was not spying on you. What the hell is going on here? How long have you been down here?"

"We only just found her," I cut in. Whit exhaled, an exasperated huff that sounded like the loud clamor of an alarm bell. Tío Ricardo stiffened, but at least his attention was on *me*.

"When I went deeper inside the temple, I felt the magic. It was overwhelming. I followed that magical pulse and Mr. Hayes had no choice but to assist me."

"No choice," my uncle said faintly.

I threw my hands wide. "It wasn't his fault."

"I don't need you to defend me," Whit drawled.

"That's what *friends* do."

Tío Ricardo fixed his attention solely on me. He inhaled so deeply, his shirt strained at the buttons. "Don't ever go down into a tunnel or a tomb or a dark cavern without me, Inez. Understand?"

"Fine."

"Whitford, will you go and bring Abdullah? Be discreet, please."

I glanced at Whit as he left but he didn't meet my eye. He disappeared up the hidden staircase, taking my candle. My uncle and I stood several feet apart, a small stretch of light dancing between us. There was only a handful of times in which we'd ever really been alone. Goosebumps flared up and down my arms. Not for the first time, I wondered how treacherous he really was.

But . . . he'd sounded relieved to see me.

"You found her," he murmured.

"The magic from the golden ring did." I shifted on my feet, glancing around the antechamber, half covered in gloom. The antechamber didn't have the same amount of artifacts as the other, smaller room Whit had named the treasury, but there were still a fair number of priceless objects. Figurines and furniture, pots of honey, and jewelry boxes. The truth swept over me in a towering wave and I couldn't breathe once the thought took hold.

My uncle eyed me shrewdly. "You've come to the same realization, then."

My voice came out breathless. "Papá found this room before he . . . died. He must have, because Papá took something of Cleopatra's from here and then mailed it to me."

"The golden ring. Which is how you were able to find this place at all. He ought to have given it to me."

Tension seeped in between us, poisoning the air. A whisper of fear pressed close. I was alone, underground, and without resources, facing a man I barely knew at all.

A soft thudding noise drifted down from the direction of the hidden stairs. More light married with ours, and Abdullah appeared, an excited smile on his face. He squeezed through the opening, followed by Whit, both of them holding slim torches.

Abdullah's jaw dropped and tears gathered in his dark eyes. My uncle strode toward him and they embraced, laughing and chattering quickly in Arabic.

It disconcerted me, seeing my uncle fool his brother-in-law so completely. My uncle was a snake, lying in wait for the perfect opportunity to strike. He would double-cross Abdullah just like he did my poor parents.

Whit sidled up next to me. "Are you all right? I ran the whole way."

I glanced at him, noticed how the tuft of hair that laid at an angle across his brow was damp with sweat. The tension I'd felt earlier lifted.

"You ran the whole way?" I murmured.

He shrugged. "It's what a friend would do."

Abdullah and Tío Ricardo explored the antechamber, marveling over every little thing. They touched nothing, and stood in stunned awe as they examined every detail, every carving, every statue. I itched for my sketchbook. I wanted to capture the paintings on the wall, wanted to draw all of the various objects strewn about the room. A part of me wanted to sit in the luxurious couch, but I followed Abdullah's example. They were careful to keep their distance, not wanting to disturb anything.

"It's been looted," Abdullah said.

"Most certainly," my uncle agreed.

I didn't need to look in Whit's direction to see his smug smile.

"Look at this," my uncle exclaimed as he studied a stretch of the wall. We all gathered around him and peered up. It was an interesting scene depicting soldiers with weapons.

"The battle of Actium," Whit said.

Abdullah clapped a hand on Whit's shoulder. "So you do pay attention when I talk. You're correct. This is when Cleopatra lost everything—family, rank, her throne, lover, and life."

"When they lost the fight for Alexandria to Octavian, Marcus's ward and Caesar's heir," Tío Ricardo explained, "Marcus Antonius fell on his sword, and Cleopatra followed days later."

Abdullah pointed to the wall. "They are both portrayed here, side by side, along with their children: the twins Cleopatra Selene and Alexander Helios, and then their youngest, Ptolemy Philadelphus. Selene was married off, her twin murdered, and their younger brother was never heard about again, consigned to obscurity."

"After the battle," Tío Ricardo said, "Octavian, now named Augustus, forbade anyone in Rome to use the names Marcus and Antonius together. All traces of his accomplishments, any merit or recognition, were scratched from Roman history. He went down as infamous—a traitor."

"Marcus Antonius is commemorated here, though," Whit whispered.

There was a note in his voice that made me look at his face. He wore a peculiar expression, one I couldn't interpret. I stepped closer to the wall, enraptured by the sight of the doomed family. From behind me, Abdullah made a loud noise of astonishment. He'd walked into the adjoining room, the treasury. Whit continued to stare at the wall, transfixed.

"*The evil that men do lives after them. The good is oft interred with their bones,*" he quoted.

"Why is Shakespeare a constant in our conversation?"

He tore his gaze away from Marcus Antonius. It occurred to me then how much Whit might identify with this soldier who had lived and fought and loved two thousand years earlier. A man who had turned against the land of his birth. Erased from his country's memory and history, his accomplishments willfully forgotten.

I didn't want to feel any sympathy toward him, but I did. No matter how many times I told myself that he was getting married, that he was loyal to my uncle, that nothing I said to him was safe, I *still* felt the annoying pull of attraction.

I turned away from him and went to join my uncle and Abdullah in the next room. I felt, rather than heard, Whit follow me. A silent presence that somehow managed to soothe and unsettle.

The paradox that was Whitford Hayes.

I expected to find the two men in the same state of awe as before, but instead they both were staring at a painted wall, adorned by hundreds of glittering mosaic tiles in vivid lapis lazuli, rose quartz, and turquoise. It pained me to have to stand so close to Tío Ricardo, when all I wanted to do was to take myself far away from the man who had torn my family apart. His words were a constant refrain in my mind, and I turned them over as if they were a riddle to be solved.

He certainly knew how to play a part.

"Look at this beautiful scene," Abdullah said, gesturing to the carved reliefs of people carrying bowls filled with fruit. "Picking grapes. And here they are sealing all the jars."

"Do you think we'll find them in here?" I asked, surprised. "Two-thousand-year-old grapes?"

"Possibly turned into wine by now," Whit said, grinning, leaning close to the wall. "Yes, look, here they are recording the vintage."

"Fascinating," my uncle breathed. "This tomb looks and feels Greek and Egyptian. There's even a bilingual quality to the text on the walls." He followed the line of the wall, musing and muttering under his breath in marveling tones. "Look here, Abdullah, paintings of the death of Osiris *and* the abduction of Persephone."

"Plenty of scarabs, too," Whit commented, studying the carvings.

"What is their significance?" I asked. "I've seen them everywhere. On amulets, walls, pillars, as figurines, and on clothing."

"They are symbols of rebirth and regeneration and serve to protect those who have gone on to the afterlife," Tío Ricardo answered. "Beetles are also associated with the Egyptian sun god, who, of course, died and was reborn again every day. He—"

"Ricardo, don't get distracted. There must be a door here somewhere," Abdullah said, placing his torch in a cast-iron holder near the treasury's entrance.

"I agree—why else would they not place any of the treasures against the wall?" Tío Ricardo said.

"They didn't want to block the way through," Abdullah replied. "But curious—wouldn't they want to dissuade tomb robbers?"

"Unless they were caught," Whit said. "Suppose they came in and were discovered as they attempted to haul everything out. The ancient Egyptians might have reinforced the staircase door, and punished the robbers. Since then, the tomb remained undiscovered. It might not have been easy to sneak onto Philae when it used to be a holy place for centuries afterward."

"A plausible theory," Abdullah said.

We all studied the door and the answer came to me in an instant. It might have been the magic swirling under my skin, or the picture of Cleopatra's children in the foreground of my mind.

"Some of these tiles are stamped with the moon or the sun," I said.

My uncle and Abdullah said at the same time: "Selene and Helios."

"Others have Cleopatra's cartouche. Here's another for Marcus Antonius," Whit pointed out. "Curious how Julius Caesar was left out."

"Perhaps not *that* curious," Abdullah mused. "Ricardo, what do you think is on the other side of this wall?"

"Her burial chamber," Tío Ricardo said. "I see where you're going with this, sahbi. You're wondering if Caesar was left out on purpose because he wouldn't have been buried with Cleopatra."

"Who else would have been?" I asked, my mind reeling. It never occurred to me that she might have been buried with anyone else. Could the tiles be hinting at who else was with her?

"She begged Octavian not to be parted from Antonius," Whit said. "Would he have honored her request?"

"Unlikely," Tío Ricardo said slowly. "Cleopatra was a thorn in his side. Why would he have relented?"

"To appease Egyptians," Abdullah said. "Their pharaoh had just been conquered. She was beloved by her people, and was the only Greek ruler to have bothered to learn Egyptian. They would have wanted her last wish to have been respected."

I stepped forward and instinctively pushed down on a turquoise tile etched with a drawing of the sun. It depressed fully, becoming flush with the wall. The same thrill of discovery roared in my fingertips. We were becoming good friends. Then I tried the other marked tiles. Each of them worked like buttons also.

Whit snapped his fingers. "Just like the column."

"We found Selene and Helios upstairs in the room. It's how we knew to examine the pillar," I told Abdullah. I was still having a hard time looking in my uncle's direction. Every time I did, I saw traces of my mother. The sister he'd betrayed.

I shouldn't be helping them but I couldn't leave either. My mother would want to know everything that happened, and I wouldn't fail her again.

"I think we ought to try pressing the stamped tiles in different orders," Whit said. "There are only eight such tiles, excluding Marcus Antonius. He wasn't represented on the column."

We all agreed, each of us taking two tiles.

"On the count of three," Tío Ricardo said. "Starting with you, Whitford."

"WaaHid, itnein, talaata," Abdullah said.

Whit pressed his tiles, I followed, then Tío Ricardo, and last, Abdullah.

Nothing happened. We exhausted every sequence we could think of until one last obvious one remained.

"Dios mío," Tío Ricardo said. "Perhaps Marcus *is* buried with her."

We included the soldier's tiles in our sequence but it still yielded no results. My uncle growled in frustration.

Abdullah made a sound of surprise and bent down, pointing to a small tile near the ground stamped with an image of a falcon. "It's *Horus*."

"The son of Caesar and Cleopatra—Caesarion!" said Tío Ricardo. "He was sometimes associated with Isis's own child."

"Cleopatra, Caesarion, and Marcus Antonius," Abdullah said. "That's who is on the other side of this wall. We only press those tiles."

My uncle nodded, resigned. But after pressing them in various orders, the wall still didn't budge.

"What about pressing the tiles all at once?" I suggested. "Because they're buried together?"

Abdullah nodded his approval, and my heart warmed. "All together. At the count of three."

"WaaHid, itnein, talaata," Whit said.

We pressed the tiles and a loud click followed the long groan of undisturbed stone moving for the first time in two millennia. The outline of a door appeared, the edges following the square shape of the tiles. Abdullah gave a final push and the panel swung forward. Air burst forth, swirling around us in a warm embrace. The candles flickered but held through the onslaught.

I looked at Abdullah, but he wasn't fazed by what had happened. He seemed to have expected it. Perhaps it was a typical occurrence when opening a room for the first time in over two thousand years.

Tío Ricardo went and retrieved the torch and handed it to Abdullah, who went through first, followed by my uncle. Whit gestured for me to go next.

With a deep inhale, I walked into the tomb.

CAPÍTULO VEINTICINCO

$\mathcal{W}$e were met by another barrier. I bit my lip in frustration, eager to see what lay in wait but terrified of advancing any farther. Neither Abdullah or Tío Ricardo appeared to be concerned by the thick wall. It was massive, centered by two shrine doors carved with more hieroglyphs. Each one had a copper handle, and the handles were tied together with a thick rope spiraling from left to right.

"Made of papyrus fiber," Abdullah commented.

"We'll have to break the seal in order to confirm who's on the other side," Tío Ricardo said, sounding more boyishly excited than I'd ever heard him. He pulled out his pocket knife, intending to cut through the rope, but he hesitated. With a rueful shake of his head, he stepped away from the barred entrance and handed Abdullah the knife.

"You've come to your senses, then?" Abdullah said archly. "I thought I taught you better than that."

Ricardo rolled his eyes. "You ought to do the honors."

"Use your head, Ricardo," Abdullah said. "Always rushing around without thinking." He was silent for several long beats, considering. "We have Inez draw the seal first. Then after it's been recorded, I'll break the seal. But we *do not* open the sarcophagus, nor remove it from the chamber."

I let out a soft sigh of relief. My mother and I had enough time to come up with a plan. "My supplies are just upstairs. I can start drawing the other rooms, if you'd like."

Abdullah nodded. "And the crew?"

"Do you wish them down here?" Tío Ricardo asked.

Abdullah considered the question and then shook his head. "Not yet. I suggest they continue working on the rooms under Trajan's Kiosk." A gleam of excitement lurked in his warm brown eyes. "Now that we know what's underneath the Temple of Isis, I wonder if the two might connect underground."

Excitement pulsed in my blood. That must have been the magic I felt underneath the kiosk.

"Agreed," Tío Ricardo said. "Whit, while Inez is drawing, we'll record our findings of everything inside both rooms." He turned to me. "Can you handle the responsibility?"

"Of course," I said.

"Bien, bien," Tío Ricardo said. "I think we ought to invite Mr. Fincastle to keep watch at the staircase entrance."

"I will help record the artifacts," Abdullah said.

My uncle inclined his head, and one by one, we walked back through the two chambers and up the hidden staircase, each of us with our marching orders.

---※---

My mother came to me that night while the rest of the camp slept. I sat on my bedroll, anxiously fiddling with the sheets until her outline appeared on the other side of the curtain, lit by the soft light of the moon. She tugged the fabric away and stepped inside. She was dressed in dark clothing again, a long black gown and double-breasted jacket obscuring her slight frame. She'd wrapped a scarf around her head, covering her hair and most of her face.

I stood and raised my index finger. Then I pointed in the direction of Whit's room. She understood immediately, and beckoned for me to follow her outside. Wordlessly, Mamá led me toward the edge of Philae. The moon hung high above us, illuminating our path. Several times she paused to look around us, watching for danger. It was Mr. Fincastle who stood guard but even he'd gone to bed. Finally, she slowed down once we reached the riverbank.

Then she turned and wrapped her arms around me in a fierce embrace. She smelled different, not like her usual floral perfume that always reminded me of her. Here in Egypt, her scent was earthier. I still couldn't believe she was alive and that she'd found me. I was immeasurably lucky. I'd gotten a second chance, when I had no hope for one.

"Something happened today," she murmured. "All of you were inside the temple for a long time. Why?"

I licked my dry lips. "Mamá, it was my fault. I felt magic, and it was overwhelming, intense. I led them straight to her tomb."

Every part of my mother went still. "Cleopatra has been found."

I nodded miserably.

She faced the Nile, watching the slow current sweep past us. Millions of stars glimmered in the pitch-black night, reflecting off the watery surface. "Did you know ancient Egyptians used to throw their valuables into the river?"

I nodded. "During the annual flood, in worship of Anuket."

Mamá bent and dipped her palm into the water. "Imagine everything she's seen through the centuries."

It was a sobering thought. The Nile knew everything, had seen the best and worst of Egypt.

"Cleopatra would have been brought to Philae all the way from Alexandria, over water, in a procession unlike any other." She stood, her face pale. "Your uncle will destroy her final resting place. He'll make millions illegally trading the artifacts at Tradesman's Gate."

"Mamá, how could we stop him? What could we possibly do?" I let the question permeate the cold night before continuing. "We ought to leave for Cairo, tonight. We can book passage back to Argentina, and leave all of this behind us."

"How would we do that? Two people can't man the *Elephantine*, and we certainly can't swim back to Cairo. We're on an island, surrounded by a river filled with crocodiles."

"But you made it here on your own," I pointed out.

"Hardly," she said at the tail end of a scoff. "I joined a party of tourists. We could do the same, but it'll be weeks until my friend arrives. And I'm here for a reason, Inez. My brother has done me wrong, has done *us* wrong."

"Then we ought to write to the authorities," I pressed. "It's the right thing to do."

She shook her head. "We have to act *now*, Inez. I don't know how long I'll be able to stay dead. This is the time to move against Ricardo; he'll never suspect it."

"But he does, otherwise he wouldn't have hired Mr. Fincastle."

She waved a breezy hand. "He did that to ensure his protection against his competitors."

Miércoles. There were *more* people to fear?

Suddenly, I wanted to leave the damned island. To put this whole miserable business behind us. "Why can't you leave all this? You gave Egypt seventeen years of your life." I thought about the six lonely months every year without my parents, back in Argentina, hurt that they never took me with them. Missed birthdays and holidays, countless hours I'd never get back. Now my father was gone, and all I wanted was to hold on to Mamá. Terror gripped me. I didn't want to lose her to Egypt. "Hasn't it taken enough?"

Mamá let out a shuddering breath. A quiet sob that fractured my heart. "I *can't*. I thought you understood."

"What? What don't I understand?"

"*Ricardo murdered your father.*" She gasped in between each word. "He died in my arms."

A loud ringing roared in my ears. My breath was trapped in my lungs, a tight pressure that made my head spin. Despair carved itself on my skin, and I rubbed my arms, feeling suddenly cold. "What?"

"Your uncle got rid of him."

I flinched, and covered my face with both hands. Mamá moved closer and hugged me, holding on tight.

Her voice became fierce against my ear. "I won't let him get away with it. I want him to know it was *me* that ruined him. The person he underestimated, the sister he believed insignificant and not smart enough to understand his work."

A prickle of unease settled onto my skin. In my life, I'd never seen her give so much of herself away, even to me. She was always so poised, so contained. I wiped at my eyes with my sleeve, overwhelmed with grief and heartache. I hated seeing my mother this way, but I understood her anger, her rage.

She pulled far enough away to stare into my face. "Will you help me, Inez?"

There was no question. She was alive, and I would do anything to keep it that way. Whatever happened next, we'd do it together. I prayed it would be enough to keep us both alive. My uncle was a cannon that could obliterate us, Abdullah, the entire digging crew. He had much to gain from this monumental discovery. I nodded and she smoothed down my curly hair, so like my father's. He didn't deserve what had happened to him.

"Yes," I said. "But I think we should warn Abdullah. He needs to know the truth about the man he's in business with."

All the blood leached from her face. "Didn't you hear me?" She reached for my arm and held on tight, her nails digging into my skin. Panic laced her words. "Your uncle is a killer. What will happen to Abdullah if he gets in my brother's way?"

"I don't—"

"He'll kill him," Mamá whispered. "Inez, I can't— I can't—"

"What, Mamita?"

"I can't lose anyone else. Abdullah is my friend, and I won't let you put him at risk. Inez, you must swear to me that you will keep him safe and *say nothing.*"

"I swear it," I breathed.

She held on to me for several more beats, as if to assure herself that I truly wouldn't put Abdullah in harm's way, that I would keep my word and not turn my uncle's murderous eye toward him. I held her stare unflinchingly, and she slowly nodded.

Mamá released my arm and I exhaled, fighting the urge to rub the tender skin. "How can I help?"

"I have an idea that might work." She bit her lip. "It will take courage, Inez."

I made a face at her. "Have I not told you the story of how I got to Egypt?"

She smiled, the first real one I'd seen since the moment I learned that she was alive. Mamá pulled out a long silk kerchief from her pocket and handed it to me. It was soft to the touch, embroidered in a delicate floral pattern.

"You and your flowers," I mused. "Do you ever miss your garden?"

"I've spent the last decade living half my life in Egypt," she said. "After so much desert, of course I miss the green. I miss a lot of things whenever I leave Argentina. Té de maté, empanadas. The way I could smell the ocean from the balcony of my bedroom." She lifted her eyes, identical to my own. Eyes that changed color, eyes that wouldn't settle. "You."

My body flooded with warmth. I hadn't known how much I'd wanted to hear her words. How they would feed me.

"What do you need me to do?" I asked.

"The magic is old; whoever cast the original spell must have been very powerful. This will shrink anything it can fully cover—"

"Like your brother's spectacles."

She shrugged, the hint of a mischievous smirk curling her mouth. "It's possible. I've only tried to use it on very special occasions."

"I bet," I said. "While teasing your brother?"

"He makes it so easy," she said, smiling. Slowly, the warmth bled from her face, and I knew she was remembering what he'd done to us. The life he stole from our family.

I cleared my throat, wanting to distract her from her thoughts. "So you would like for me to . . ."

"Shrink as many artifacts as you can while you're working," she said, her voice serious and grim, "without anyone knowing."

My mouth went dry.

"At night, you'll give them to me for safekeeping."

"Tío Ricardo will notice if anything goes missing," I protested.

"Keep your voice down," she said, with a nervous look up the bank. "Be strategic with what you take. Look for redundancies, every tomb has them. Repeats of jewelry, statues, trinket boxes. I sincerely doubt my brother will have memorized every item. We won't be able to keep everything safe, but if you work fast, I think we can keep plenty from his greedy hands."

Mamá leaned forward and placed her palms on my shoulders. "Now listen to me, Inez, this is very important." She waited for me to nod. "You must shrink any papyrus you find, any scrolls, rolls of parchment, first."

I frowned. "Why? Surely my uncle would go after the jewelry first? They'd fetch a higher price?"

My mother shook her head. "Not this particular sheet."

"*What* sheet?" I asked. "If you tell me what it looks like, perhaps I can search for it specifically."

Mamá considered, but then shook her head reluctantly. "No, it might look more suspicious if it looked like you were on the hunt for the sheet itself."

Another question bubbled to the surface. We were still surrounded by the Nile, far enough away from Aswan to be an issue. "But even if I succeed, we are still stuck on this island."

"No, I have a friend who's coming to assist me. He said he'd be here sometime before Navidad. He'll help us load everything onto his dahabeeyah. From there, we sail to Cairo."

My mind reeled. "But what about Tío Ricardo's criminal associates? I'm assuming he will have told them of the discovery."

She nodded, her expression turning thoughtful. "They're predominately in Thebes, so if we make it to Cairo before they can come to Philae, we should be safe. It will be harder for them to snatch the artifacts from the Egyptian Museum, and from under Monsieur Maspero's watchful eye."

"How do you know all this?"

"I spent a lot of time spying on my brother and going through his correspondence." She wrapped her scarf tighter around her hair. "I'll come to you, Inez. Please don't try to find me. It's too risky—for both of us."

"Will this work?"

She inhaled deeply and then let out a long, calming exhale. "It has to. Your father would have wanted us to help, in any way that we could. I imagine he's pleased we're working together for something he had loved so much."

The task before me wouldn't be easy, but it helped knowing that I was working against the man who had taken my father from me.

Mamá cupped my cheek. "Be careful. Remember what I said—behave like a doting niece toward your uncle."

Then she went up the bank and disappeared into the night.

———— ✄ ————

The quiet of the antechamber pressed into me from all sides. Sweat gathered at the base of my neck as I drew one figurine after another, a parade of Egyptian gods and goddesses filling up my sketchbook. Abdullah or my uncle continually passed through, Whit on their heels, cataloguing every single item. It was tedious work.

It also prevented me from using my mother's silk kerchief. I wiped my brow and threw a look over my shoulder. The three men were huddled by the entrance to the treasury, bent over the thick leather journal in Whit's hands. They whispered among them, Abdullah gesturing wildly toward the artifacts.

Dread pooled deep in my belly.

A part of me hated the plan, but the other didn't want my uncle to succeed. He had murdered my father, and he thought he'd gotten away with it. My eyes flickered to Abdullah.

And now he was going to betray his brother-in-law.

I inhaled and then slowly reached inside my bag propped up against my knee. No one was looking in my direction. I pulled out the kerchief, and dropped it into my lap. Then I scooted closer to the grouping of artifacts at eye level. Their hushed voices drifted as they walked into the treasury.

I exhaled and draped the square-shaped fabric over a statue of Anubis. There was a light *popping* noise and the kerchief fluttered to the ground. The statue had shrunk to the size of a small charm. I glanced over my shoulder again. They were still in the other room.

I did three more statues, one right after another. Carefully I tucked them into my bag, sweat gliding down my cheeks. I was at war with myself, hating the necessity of moving the art from its original resting place, but knowing my uncle would do far worse. At least these items would be safe from his grasp, and my mother would be proud of my efforts. My gaze flickered over the hundreds of glittering artifacts situated in every corner and surface of the chamber, until it snagged on a blue figurine of an asp, roughly the size of my palm. I peered closely at the intricate carving, recognizing the unique azure shade as ancient Egyptian faience.

Shakespeare came to mind as I studied the poisonous viper. "*Come, thou mortal wretch / With thy sharp teeth this knot intrinsicate / Of life at once untie: poor venomous fool / Be angry, and dispatch,*" I murmured. Goosebumps marred my arms. According to legend and Roman historians, Cleopatra died by the bite of a snake. It seemed appropriate that such a figurine would be included in her burial chamber. Quickly, I drew the figurine into my sketch pad.

When I finished, I closed the book. My attention returned to the statuette and with measured care, I ran my index finger lightly over its head. Magic pulsed around me and I drew my hand away quickly.

Too late. The memory came unbidden, and I knew I'd found another object Cleopatra's spell had touched. She stood hunched over, tears streaming down her cheeks as she cried out in horror, in pain.

In despair.

She sobbed as if someone had died.

Goosebumps flared up and down my arms. Was I witnessing the moment she learned of Antonius's death? Cleopatra collapsed onto the ground and beat her chest.

The weight of her sorrow crushed me. I gasped, struggling to pull free, and a second later, I came back to myself. The quiet of the antechamber, the weight of my sketch pad on my lap. My fingers were stained, and my breath huffed out of me in sharp pants that tore at my lungs.

Without really thinking about it, I dropped the kerchief on top of the serpent, needing distance from it. I didn't want to feel her pain again. It hurt like a knife to the gut.

"How's the work coming along?"

A loud gasp escaped me, and my hand flew to my heart as if by its own accord. I looked up to find Whit towering above me, gently carrying a mountain of scrolls in a small wooden crate. His gaze flickered to the sketchbook in my lap, the kerchief spread on the ground before my bent knees.

"Has anyone ever told you that it's abominably rude to sneak up on someone?"

He eyed me quizzically. "The military encouraged it."

"Are we at war? I had no idea."

"Britain is at war with everyone." He started to walk away but paused. "Nice scarf."

I swallowed painfully. "Gracias."

Whit walked off, joining my uncle and Abdullah in the other chamber. My pulse jumped in my throat. Did he suspect? Would he remember that it had belonged to my mother? I shook my head, clearing my mind of suspicious thoughts. He wouldn't have complimented it if he'd recognized it. I let out a slow exhale. Carefully, I plucked the kerchief off the shrunken asp and placed it within my bag. Then, I let my gaze rove over the hundreds of objects in the antechamber.

I had a lot of work to do.

That night, I handed twenty-nine priceless figurines to my mother. She took each one and wrapped it carefully in another scarf, and then placed the artifacts in her large leather bag.

I licked my dry lips. "There's hundreds more. I barely made a dent."

"Every little bit helps, Inez," she murmured. "We're doing the right thing." She twisted her lips. "Even if it feels wrong. I'd much rather leave the historical objects where they are. I hate what I've asked you to do."

"Me too," I said, hope fluttering now in my chest. Perhaps she'd change her mind. There had to be another way to stop my uncle from—

"Remember, you only have until Navidad to save whatever we can. Have you been able to shrink any rolls of parchment?"

I nodded and then she kissed my cheek, returning the way she came, taking a narrow path that led somewhere past the temple.

Her words ought to have given me comfort. She didn't want to disturb the tomb any more than I did. It ought to have helped, knowing we felt the same way, that we were on the same side. But as I watched her disappear into the darkness, I couldn't help the nagging sense that I was making things far worse.

For all of us.

CAPÍTULO VEINTISÉIS

*T*wo weeks went by and we still hadn't opened the tomb. After another conversation at headquarters, Abdullah and Tío Ricardo both decided to record and draw everything prior to breaking the seal. The digging crew continued to work under Trajan's Kiosk, slowly but surely moving underneath the Temple of Isis. There was a veritable labyrinth under our feet, and Whit was down there more often than not, helping to blow through each room. When he didn't have a bag filled with gunpowder in his hands, he could be found standing near me in the antechamber, meticulously recording artifact after artifact in a thick leather-bound journal, not unlike the one I used for my sketches. He seemed as interested in the artifacts as Abdullah and my uncle, constantly looking through the room as if he searched for something in particular. If he did, he never told me what he hoped to find.

Even Isadora had been roped in to the tedious work, but she never complained of the monotony. Sometimes she was there before me, bent over a notebook and painstakingly taking note of every artifact in her section.

The days were long. Whit worked alongside me, but the moment he ducked out of the antechamber, I pulled out the kerchief and shrunk anything that shimmered or was made of gold.

This was, by far, the worst part of my day.

But every time Ricardo walked through the chambers, eyeing everything appreciatively, my guilt subsided. He picked up several pieces of jewelry, studded with precious gems, and my stomach would clench, wondering if he was setting a price. Thankfully, Abdullah caught him, and yelled at him for his foolishness.

Meal times were filled with lively conversation, Abdullah keeping us entertained with stories of his children and grandchildren. Afterward, my mother and I met on the riverbank, hidden behind tall papyrus plants. Over the course of two weeks, I'd managed to shrink close to two hundred artifacts. I tried to pick through items that weren't recorded, or were easily overlooked due to their placement in the chamber or size.

But I worried all the same and I was unable to hide my unease from Mamá. I gave her the day's stash, hating myself, and she caught my hand in hers.

"What is it?" she asked.

I forgot how easily she could read me.

"I just wish there was a better way," I murmured. "Tío Ricardo is overseeing the recording of all the artifacts. Why would he do that if he was planning on stealing them?"

"Inez, consider this carefully," she said. "Anything noted down could be scratched out, rewritten, or the page might even be torn out. Who keeps the records at the end of the day? Is it your uncle?"

I thought about the leather journal, often in the hands of Whit or Isadora. But when the day was finished, the book went to my uncle, and not Abdullah. Where it stayed until the next morning, when my uncle would return it to Whit for the day's work. My uncle could easily tamper with the records—but wouldn't Whit notice? Isadora seemed too observant not to notice any unusual changes.

Except . . . there were literally *hundreds* of limestone statues and boats and pieces of jewelry. I wouldn't notice if a few were erased or scratched out.

Mamá made a good point.

"My friend will be here tomorrow, Inez," my mother whispered, squeezing my hand. "Are you ready to go?"

I shook my head. "I'll pack tonight."

———✖———

By next morning, everything I owned was once again inside my bag. I looked around my narrow room, cataloguing the worn rug, the empty crate that served as a nightstand, my thin bedroll. I'd spent nearly a month on this island, working along with the crew—if not one of them. I knew everyone by name.

And every day, it destroyed me that my uncle would betray them. I wanted to warn them, but as my mother had wisely pointed out: we didn't know who we could trust. Some of the crew might be working for the same criminals as my uncle. Grave robbing was a centuries-old profession in Egypt.

I stepped out of my room, wearing my linen skirt and jacket, and while clean, it bore the story of the long hours I had spent underground. I approached the camp, rubbing my arms to fight against the chill. Whit saluted me by lifting his tin cup. I could smell his coffee from across the fire. I settled onto an available mat, aware of my uncle's watchful gaze.

I gratefully accepted a mug filled with tea from Kareem. My mind refused to dwell on anything other than it being my last day on Philae.

Long-held emotions threatened to bubble to the surface. I lowered my gaze, careful to hide my watery eyes. I was relieved to leave behind my wretched uncle. Relieved, too, for the artifacts I was able to snatch under his nose. Monsieur Maspero would ensure they had a home in the new museum in Cairo. Then he'd send antiquities officers to Philae, which would further disrupt my uncle's plans.

But a small and quieter part of me rebelled at the idea of leaving Whit.

For the hundredth time, I reminded myself that he was getting married. The wisest and least painful course was to move on. Nothing good could come from pining after someone unavailable.

Isadora came to sit next to me, dropping gracefully to her knees while balancing a mug filled with hot tea. She didn't spill a single drop.

"You look remarkably refreshed for someone sleeping in a tent."

"I've had lots of practice." She dimpled at me. "You know, you're a sly one. So many secrets."

"Oh?"

"You never say his name."

The chatter among us seemed to dim. I took care to keep my face neutral, despite the betraying flush that bloomed in my cheeks. "Whose?"

She arched a honey brow. "Mr. Hayes, of course."

"He just doesn't come up in conversation all that much," I said after a beat. "I don't think that's it."

I shifted to face her fully, bringing my legs around so they were inches from her voluminous skirt. She took an idle sip from her mug, laughter lurking in her pale eyes. Her amusement grated me. I didn't like to think my feelings were that obvious, especially because they irked me to begin with. "What do you think it is?"

"Have you seen the way he looks at you? So . . . so possessive."

"He's getting married," I said in a flat voice. "Nothing can come from his looking."

"A pity," she said. "He isn't boring when so many men are."

"And you are more than what you seem, Isadora," I said, purposefully letting my gaze drift to her neat appearance. But I knew she hid a weapon somewhere on her.

"So are you," she said.

A loud commotion came from the direction of the boat docked on the far side of Philae.

"Dios, what now?" Tío Ricardo snarled, yanking me from my reverie.

Whit sat across from me, looking over the records in his journal. At my uncle's outburst, he glanced up and met my gaze, a small grin tugging at his mouth.

I looked in the direction my uncle was presently glaring to find a group of people rowing up to the sandbank. One of the men looked vaguely familiar. My uncle routinely despaired of the tourists crowding the river. The island of Philae, though more out of the way than other attractions found in Thebes, was a prime destination. There was a reason it was called the Jewel of the Nile.

"A group of women travelers." Mr. Fincastle shielded his eyes from the sun's glare with one hand, while the other hovered above his revolver. "And several gentlemen. Definitely American."

"Definitely not welcome," my uncle muttered.

My ears perked up. Could one of them be my mother's confidant?

The tourists were unaware of their unwelcome, and gaily approached us, talking loudly among themselves. Tío Ricardo sent a pleading look in the direction of Whit, who grinned hugely, snapping his journal closed and then bounding to his feet. He met the group before they reached our campsite.

Whit paraded his charm and several young ladies in their party glowed with pleasure. I shook my head ruefully. The *Mr. Hayes* mask he wore for everyone else was on full display. When I glanced over again, it was to find Whit watching me. My gaze flickered pointedly to one of the pretty ladies and I raised my brows.

He lifted an insouciant shoulder and I laughed, if only to hide the ache tearing at my heart. Whit still wouldn't talk about the years he spent in the military, nor would he say much else about his family, but an easy camaraderie existed between us. He sought my company whenever there was any free time. I counted on him to bring me dinner when the hour grew late and I still hadn't finished a particular sketch, and I always made sure his coffee was hot in the morning. It wasn't everything, but at least we had a few smalls things between us that felt real.

I stood, brushing the sand off my linen skirt, and walked toward the temple as was my usual habit after breakfast. As I walked past, Tío Ricardo lifted his head in my direction.

"Inez, are you almost done?"

I fought to keep my tone pleasant. Every day, it had been harder and harder to do. I lived in terror of him discovering my secret. I barely checked my grief, my anger, around him. "The painting of the antechamber is complete, and I've finished the detailed sketch of the treasury and have already laid down the base paint. From here, it's adding in details."

"Good," he said.

"Ricardo!" Whit called.

My uncle groaned into his teacup. With an exasperated sigh, he stood and dragged himself to the group of tourists. They eyed him in awed fascination, the archaeologist in his element: thick hair tousled, serviceable trousers, and knee-high scuffed boots, his face lined, tanned, and weathered from the hot sun. He made quite a picture, surrounded by ancient monuments, and I understood why more than one lady began fanning herself.

I was about to continue my way to the temple when my uncle suddenly turned around from the party and stomped back to us, his face set in a pronounced scowl. He threw himself back onto the bit of rock he'd been using as a makeshift chair. Two letters poked out of his tanned fist.

Curiosity kept me in place. "What is it?"

Abdullah grinned. "An invitation?"

Tío Ricardo visibly weighed his response, his frown becoming more pronounced as the seconds ticked by. If someone were to carve him, this would be the expression. My uncle in his most natural state.

"I deplore it when you're smug," my uncle grumbled back.

I sat down on a rock. "Who is the invitation from?"

"The New Year's Eve ball held at Shepheard's every year," Abdullah said cheerfully. "Your uncle never goes."

"Why don't you want to go?" I interrupted.

My uncle shuddered. "Because, Inez, it means tearing myself away from here, when there's so much work to be done. I won't announce our findings *ever*, and while I trust the majority of our team, I know it's naive to believe our discovery won't go unnoticed for long. It's imperative that we record everything we've found with proper and distant objectivity *before* the incompetent gentlemen who call themselves archaeologists descend onto Philae. Idiots, all of them."

He had almost convinced me. But I remembered the harsh lines of his face when he talked about Papá, remembered how he'd led me to believe that both my parents had died, lost in the desert.

My uncle ought to be on stage. He'd make a fortune.

"No one will come looking here during the ball," Abdullah said mildly, picking up the thread of conversation. "Don't forget that I'll be here to maintain order, as I haven't been invited."

"Like I said. Idiots," Tío Ricardo said. "Most are glorified treasure hunters, stealing anything that can be moved. And I do mean anything—coffins and mummies, obelisks, sphinxes. Literally *thousands* of artifacts. There are a very few," my uncle said, "who care about keeping proper records, who understand the necessity of knowledge and safeguarding Egypt's past."

"But as they are Egyptian, they are often excluded like I am," Abdullah said with quiet fury. "And until I'm not at a disadvantage from the field of study, none of what we excavate will be shared with the Antiquities Service."

My heart broke for him. My uncle's deception would shatter him.

"Ricardo." Abdullah held out his hand. "Give it to me, please."

Wordlessly, my uncle handed the second letter to Abdullah, who read it once, then twice.

"I don't understand," Abdullah said. "Maspero revoked your firman? But why?"

Anger etched itself onto my uncle's face. "I suspect Sir Evelyn had something to do with it, the bastard."

"You *must* go to the party," Abdullah said. "And make it right. You know what's at stake."

"Zazi hated the Cairo set," Ricardo protested.

"She did," Abdullah agreed.

"But she came with me."

Abdullah was already shaking his head. "My coming would make things worse. You know this."

"But—"

"I know my sister, and she'd tell you to go."

Ricardo groaned. "We can cover—"

"It won't be enough to fool a seasoned archaeologist." Abdullah leaned forward, brows furrowed. "Think of what Zazi would want, Ricardo."

My uncle stared mutinously at his brother-in-law. But in slow degrees, he softened under the weight of Abdullah's quiet firmness. "Fine, I'll go. The day after Navidad."

Somehow, I'd forgotten all about Christmas fast approaching. We never celebrated as a family on the actual day. My parents were in Egypt every year, and so we exchanged gifts when they returned. This past exchange had been my last with my father. I wish I had known. I had been closed off and surly, annoyed that I was given a consolation holiday during *winter* when everyone *else* in Buenos Aires celebrated properly during our summer in December.

When Papá had asked to play a game of chess, I had said no.

I gathered my supplies, and stood, preparing to finally head back to work. Whit remained ensconced in conversation with the attractive tourists, and I carefully kept my gaze from flitting back to where he stood.

"Inez," Tío Ricardo said as I brushed past. I paused, and raised an eyebrow. My uncle kept his attention on his mug, his fingers gripping tight around the handle. "Tomorrow, we break the seal at first light."

Somehow, I managed to keep my face utterly neutral, as if his including me hadn't sent a tremor through my body. My uncle eyed me curiously and I shifted under his attentive gaze. A sharp line appeared between his brows. It occurred to me that my lack of reaction confused him, given how long and how hard I'd persuaded him to join the excavation team.

I forced a smile, trying to hide the truth.

I would be long gone by the time they opened the tomb.

Whit found me hours later, hunched over the painting, painstakingly capturing the detail of a jewelry box inlaid with pearls and turquoise. He hovered behind me, watching me work.

"You've made it too big," he said.

I turned and glared up at him. "No, I haven't."

"Why are you scowling?"

"I'm not," I said, hating the catch in my voice. "Why aren't you with your new friends?"

"They've left, alas," he said. "But they did give me a letter for you. A certain gentleman brought it over and he seemed quite annoyed with me when I wouldn't tell him where you'd gone."

My brows rose. "I don't know any gentlemen here."

Whit eyed me severely. "He said to tell you that he still wanted to have that dinner whenever you return to Cairo."

I thought back, and then widened my eyes. "It must be Mr. Burton; he was staying at Shepheard's."

"Hmmm. How did you meet him?"

I watched him keenly. "He escorted me to dinner."

"To dinner," he said. "How kind of him."

"Does that bother you?"

He shrugged. "No, Olivera. Why would it?"

His words might have sounded nonchalant, but I detected a faint tightening at the corners of his mouth. My jaw dropped. "You're jealous."

He let out a crack of laughter. "Not bloody likely."

"I have to admit I'm surprised by your behavior," I said. "Or did you think I wouldn't notice how you can't keep your eyes off me?"

"Your uncle has asked me to keep an eye on you," Whit snapped. "If I'm looking, it's only to make sure you're not getting into trouble."

"I know how to behave," I said, mildly offended.

"Ha," he muttered under his breath.

We stared at each other for several minutes, his frustration rolling off him in waves. I lifted a brow and dared him to explain himself. But he stayed stubbornly silent for one long intolerable beat. Then, in a much calmer voice, he asked, "Do you want your letter, or don't you?"

I held out my hand.

There were only two people who knew where to find me in Egypt and I could guess how they felt about my leaving without saying goodbye. I had left a note, but I could just imagine what my aunt would have thought about that. Guilt needled me, and while I didn't feel bad about tricking my aunt, I did regret leaving my cousin. But if I told Elvira my plans, then she would have wanted to come. If she came, then my aunt would have done anything and everything to get her back. I couldn't risk it. "Give it to me, then."

Whit dug into his pocket and pulled out two envelopes he'd tucked inside. He gave them both a cursory glance and then handed me mine, the other he stuffed back into his pocket with a slight frown. My aunt's neat and prim handwriting stared up at me. I never read her first letter, and frankly didn't know where I'd put it. I hadn't seen it in weeks, not since we'd left Cairo. With a shudder, I placed the envelope inside the pages of my sketch pad.

Whit raised his brows. "Who's it from?"

"How did Mr. Burton know where to find me?"

"The staff at Shepheard's must have assumed you'd be with Ricardo. Who's it from?"

"I'll read it later."

"Not what I asked."

"It's none of your business, Whit."

"What if it's important?" he pressed.

"Trust me, it's not." I narrowed my gaze at him. "I thought we didn't discuss personal matters."

He rolled his eyes and sat next to me, folding his long legs close to his body so as not to knock anything over. "We don't unless they make you upset."

"I'm not upset."

"I know when you are, Olivera," Whit said. "You wear everything on your face."

"Then stop looking at my face," I said pointedly.

Whit opened his mouth, and then snapped it shut.

"What were you going to say?"

"Absolutely nothing helpful," he muttered.

"I'll tell you who it's from if you tell me who sent yours," I said. "Nosy."

His eyes flicked down to his pocket. "It's from my father."

"Oh." He rarely talked of his family. A small part of me wished I hadn't pressed, but he'd annoyed me with his questions. Whit didn't say anything else, and so I cleared my throat and said, "Mine is from my aunt. She must be furious."

"She probably wants you to come home."

"I bet your family wants the same for you."

His hands flexed, tension rising around him like steam over boiling water. We sat in silence and when it became clear he wouldn't say more, I resumed working.

"We're opening her tomb tomorrow," Whit said suddenly. "Did your uncle tell you?"

I pressed my lips into a thin line and nodded.

"Why aren't you more excited?"

I would have been. My time in Egypt had softened my resentment, had seduced me with its sweeping expanse of desert filled with temples and a million secrets hidden beneath its golden sand. The people here were warm and kind and incredibly hospitable. I'd become part of the team, and the feeling of all of us working toward the same goal was intoxicating, heady in a way I hadn't expected. I wanted to be there with them as they opened Cleopatra's tomb.

Impossible, because I wouldn't be there. I cleared my throat and tried for a nonchalant tone. It had just occurred to me that this would probably be the last time I'd be alone with Mr. Whitford Hayes. I met his gaze, knowing that I wouldn't answer his question because I didn't want to tell another lie. I was sick of the secrecy, the sneaking around, the heavy weight pressing on my shoulders.

I wanted to deal in truth—as much as I could stomach, and I wanted to start right then.

Then it could be over.

Over before it ever began.

"Whit, I'm going to tell you something, and I need you not to say anything. I don't want to know what you think or what you would have said. I just want to tell you something true. All right?"

He narrowed his eyes. "I'm not going to like it, am I?"

"Probably not," I admitted.

"Then don't tell me."

"I'll regret it if I don't."

Whit flattened his mouth, his shoulders tensing as if preparing for a mortal blow.

I took a deep breath, and forced myself to meet his eyes. They were formidable and cold. I shivered.

"I'm attracted to you, Whit. More than I'd ever expected." *More than a friend,* but I bit down on the words. I still had my pride, and she governed me ruthlessly. "There's no tomorrow for us, we don't even have today. But I wanted you to know how I felt. Even if you don't feel the same way."

He regarded me without saying a word. He kept quiet while I stood, and quiet while I gathered my things. It was only when I went to walk away, my legs trembling, that he finally spoke.

"Inez," he whispered, his voice hoarse, "it goes both ways."

I paused, shoulders stiff, wanting to throw myself in his arms. To give in to what we both wanted. But we were impossible. He was going to be *married.* I clenched my jaw and walked out of the chamber and then up the stairs, my heart pounding the whole way back to my room.

In a matter of hours, I would be leaving with my mother, carrying hundreds of priceless artifacts to Cairo where they'd be safe from Tío Ricardo's clutches.

I ought to feel relief. But I couldn't stop thinking how I might have made a mistake in telling him how I felt.

WHIT

The devil damn me.

The light from the torch cast flickering shadows against the wall as Inez walked away, her sweet scent trailing after her, slowly driving me insane. She held her shoulders straight, the weight of the world on them. It would have been easier if she hadn't spoken, and I was a *fool* for saying what I did. No better than a lie. With shaking hands, I pulled my father's missive and read each line, my heart in my throat.

> *Whitford,*
> *I tire of writing the same thing over and over. Your mother is at her wit's end. I don't know how much more she can take. This will be my last before I come myself.*
> *You will not thank me for the visit, I promise you.*
> *Come home.*
>
> *—A*

A yawning pit opened inside me, threatening to devour me whole. I hadn't found the parchment despite searching for weeks. It had been a futile, desperate wish. Nothing could keep me here any longer. I stood, a calm reserve settling over me, and walked to the guttering torch.

And set the letter on fire.

CAPÍTULO VEINTISIETE

The moon's reflection rippled over the water as the song of the Nile swirled around me. Frogs croaked, birds trilled, and every so often a sudden splash punctuated the still night. I stood on the bank, arms folded tight across my shaking chest, my large bag by my feet. Cold seeped under my linen clothing, and a chill skittered down my spine.

Mamá materialized from out of the darkness, her slight form taking shape high up on the bank. She waved, and I returned the gesture. My hand fell awkwardly to my side when I spotted a taller figure coming down with her. It was a man, dressed in a casual suit, his dark hair windblown. He had kind blue eyes, and a tentative smile.

"Inez, this is my friend I was telling you about."

He held out his hand. "It's nice to meet you. Your mother has told me all about you."

I pulled back my palm. There was an easy familiarity between them, and his relaxed manner loosened the knot of tension between my shoulder blades. But my mind burned with questions. When did they meet? How was he involved in our situation? Why did she trust him? Did he know about Cleopatra, my uncle, or Papá?

Mamá gestured to my bag before I could ask my questions. I held my tongue, knowing I had plenty of time during the ride back to Cairo. For now, we had to move quickly.

"Any more artifacts in there?" Mamá asked.

I nodded with a quick look at her friend. He seemed unsurprised by the question. "I managed to get six more." I bent and rummaged through my neatly packed things and procured the jewelry, wrapped carefully in one of my shirts. I gave the bundle to my mother.

"My boat is just over there," he said, using his chin to point. I followed his line of sight to a narrow boat, tucked within tall shrubs. I picked up my bag and trudged after them, my heart racing.

This was it.

On Christmas morning, Tío Ricardo and Whit, along with the rest of the crew, wouldn't find me anywhere on Philae. As if I'd disappeared, vanished into another world like in a fairy tale. I had thought about leaving a note for Whit, but decided against it. I'd already said everything I wanted to say. I couldn't tell him where I was going, and who with, nor what my plans were. There didn't seem a point in leaving behind a message.

This chapter of my life would soon be over.

Mamá's friend reached the boat first and he gently took my mother's things and placed them within. Mamá patted her clothing, frowning. She turned around, her chin dipped, searching the ground.

"Have you lost something?" I asked.

"Yes, my small silk purse. It has my headache medicine," she said. "I never travel without it."

We all got onto our knees, searching the rocky beach. I came up empty, and then decided to retrace my steps. I glanced nervously in the direction of the campsite. Any minute, I expected to hear my uncle shouting at us. To see Whit running toward me, disappointment carved into his features.

"I might have dropped it higher up on the bank?" Mamá whispered, walking a few steps behind me.

"I'll go look," I said. "I'll meet you by the boat."

Mamá nodded and turned around, moving silently back to her friend. I raced up the bank, crouched low, and began the search. Thick groupings of prickly plants obstructed my view, but I picked my way carefully. Finally, a glittering bag shown like silver in the moonlight. I grabbed it and went down the way I came, slipping on a rock. I managed to keep my balance, and by the time I reached the shore, my breath was coming out in panting gasps. I looked for my mother, but found no one.

The area was eerily quiet.

I strode to the stretch of sand where I'd last seen Mamá and her friend, but saw neither. At first, I couldn't comprehend what I saw. The shore stood empty; only their footprints gave any indication they'd been there. Panic pulsed in the air around me. Had my uncle discovered them? Or Mr. Fincastle? But I would have heard some commotion, surely. I walked up and down the shore, my dread mounting. My breath burst from my mouth in loud huffs.

Realization crept over me.

The boat was gone. Well and truly gone.

I looked out over the Nile, and a lump caught at the back of my throat. The blurry outline of the boat was in view, far enough in the distance I had to squint to make out the shape. It moved noiselessly over the water.

Carrying my mother where only the river knew.

———— ✖ ————

It was Noche Buena.

Christmas Eve. And my mother had left me behind.

I don't know how long I stood before the Nile, hoping that it had been a mistake, that they'd lost control of the boat somehow. I would have believed a crocodile had carried them off.

Anything but the truth.

An ache between my eyes grew, pressure that widened in painful ripples. My eyes burned. I slumped onto the sand, sharp rocks digging into my flesh. I barely noticed. The last two weeks flashed through my mind, one horrifying scene after another. I couldn't make sense of it. Why had she left me here? Did she not want me to help her with the artifacts?

I was so cold, and terrified, and riddled with guilt. A nagging sense that I'd behaved like a fool permeated my senses. I reached for my mother's silk purse and rustled through it, hoping to find—

My fingers found a small, folded note. It was much too dark to read, and so I stumbled onto my feet and made my way back to camp. Shame curled deep in my belly, a physical ache as if I'd drunk poison. When I reached the camp, I made sure to walk as quietly as I could, remembering that Whit slept lightly.

I struck a match and lit a candle once inside my cleared-out room. The rug and the crate were the only items I'd chosen to leave behind. With shaking fingers, I unfolded the note.

Dear Inez,

This is goodbye. I know it would have been kinder to let you think I'd died, but once you arrived in Philae, I had to factor you into my plans. I urge you to leave Egypt. Forget what you've seen and heard, and move on with your life. You have so much ahead of you. Marry the son of the consul, have your own family, and begin again.

Don't come looking for me. You won't like what you find, Inez.

Mamita

A loud cry escaped me. I slapped my hand over my mouth, trying to quiet my sobs. Confusion and grief warred within me. I didn't understand why she'd left me, why she had made me believe that we were going together.

"Olivera?"

I froze, tears still streaming down my face. Whit stood on the other side of the rustling curtain, his bare feet visible. I bit down on my lip, trying to remain silent.

"Olivera, I can hear you," he said quietly. "Are you all right?"

I fought to keep my voice steady, but failed. "Go away, Whit."

He dragged the fabric to one side and stepped inside, blinking in the dim light. His gaze dropped to the ground where I sat huddled on the rug. Whit sank to his knees beside me and reached for me, pulling me close to his side. The strong line of his leg pressed against mine.

"Inez," he whispered. "I'll go if you want me to, but I need to know if you're all right. Are you hurt?"

"I think my heart is broken," I whispered.

He wrapped his arms around me, his thumb drawing circles at the small of my back. The caress loosened the awful knot in my chest, unraveling it slowly. I breathed easier, and my tears slowed. Whit had never been this gentle with me. This patient. He waited without pushing for more. It was a side of him I'd never seen but knew existed. His breath was free of whiskey, his eyes were clear. I hadn't seen him drink in weeks, not since losing his flask in the river.

Whit's confession lingered between us.

It goes both ways.

Energy like the oldest kind of magic zipped through my body. I let myself sink into the moment. Because the minute I opened my mouth, I knew everything would be different. The truth had a way of changing things. Slowly, I slid my hand across his chest, felt his steady heartbeat under my palm.

I would allow one more breath before I pulled away. But then he used his index finger to tip my chin up, and our eyes met in the soft light. His blue eyes dropped to my mouth and I shivered. He was going to kiss me, and I wouldn't do a thing to stop it, even though I should. He was going to hate me afterward, but at least I'd have one memory of a perfect moment. He shut his eyes and exhaled, and when he opened them again, his hands gently moved me farther away, creating a slither of space.

"Will you tell me what's upset you?"

"I want to," I said. "But I'm afraid to."

"You don't have to be afraid of me," he said. "Not ever."

Whit waited, his expression open and guileless.

"I've made a terrible mistake," I said. "I don't know how much you know, how involved you are with . . . everything, but I'm tired of keeping secrets. Of lying." I licked my dry lips, keeping my gaze focused on my lap. "Two weeks ago, that night you heard someone in my room, I found out my mother was alive."

Whit tensed.

"She told me Tío Ricardo was involved in an illegal smuggling trade of Egyptian artifacts. His active participation with Tradesman's Gate."

"That's a lie," he whispered fiercely.

"How do you know?" I demanded.

He hesitated and I plunged on. "I believed her," I said, shrugging helplessly. "She's my *mother*. Why would she say that if it weren't true?"

Whit averted his gaze, jaw clenched. "What else did she tell you?"

"She asked for my help. My mother, who I thought had died, asked me to help her." I licked my lips. "So, I did."

Whit's words were hushed, laced with dread and foreboding. "What did you do, Inez?"

I squeezed my eyes, scared to meet his gaze. "I shrunk many artifacts inside Cleopatra's tomb these past couple of weeks, and gave them to her. The plan was to take everything into Cairo, and entrust it to the Egyptian

Museum. We were going to involve the Antiquities Service, and I was hoping they'd come to put a stop to my uncle's treachery."

Whit clenched his fists.

"I packed my things," I whispered, "and met her down by the river earlier tonight. And then she left me here, taking all of the artifacts with her. My mother left me a letter"—I gave it to him—"but now . . . you're telling me that she lied to me."

"She absolutely did," he said through clenched teeth.

He read the letter, his other hand still clenched in a fist and pressed tight against his thigh. When he finished, he folded the note and handed it back to me.

"Is that all?" His voice sounded strained, as if he were trying to rein in his temper.

I shook my head. "She told me Tío Ricardo murdered my father."

"*What?*"

I flinched. "I overheard him talking about Papá, that first night I stole onto the dahabeeyah. It sounded like they'd argued."

"They did, but your uncle did not kill your father."

"Then *who* did?" I exclaimed. "It became very clear that my uncle was lying to me from the start. Making up some harebrained story about my parents getting lost in the desert. I didn't know what to think, who to believe. I still don't know if I can trust *you*. In Cairo, I found a letter my mother had written addressed to Monsieur Maspero, asking for help because she believed her brother had turned into a criminal."

He positioned himself so that he was sitting cross-legged in front of me. "Your uncle isn't involved in the smuggling trade, Inez." He took a deep breath. "There's an organization named The Company, and members are called Curators. They are the ones who run Tradesman's Gate, and your mother procures goods for their auctions."

I fought to make sense of his words, putting the pieces together and trying to understand what he told me. "My mother is a Curator," I repeated.

Whit nodded. "Ricardo suspected the truth, but he also thought that your father was involved." He met my eyes, careful and guarded. "Are you saying he isn't?"

"Not according to my mother," I whispered. "She says *he's dead*."

Whit paled, and tugged at his hair. "You have to know something, Inez. She was . . . having an affair. I found out by accident, and she made me swear not to say anything. Promised me that it was a mistake, that she was ending it. But afterward, I noticed she was gone for long stretches of time. Barely writing to your father. I thought then she might still be."

Thunder boomed in my ears.

I couldn't believe what Whit had told me. It was wrong, like a moonless night or a dry riverbed. I shook my head, the ringing in my mind growing louder.

When I spoke again, my voice was hoarse. "She seemed so glad to see me."

"That could have been real." He hesitated. "How much was she able to take?"

I let out a bitter laugh. "Close to three hundred artifacts in the form of jewelry, funerary boats, and limestone statues."

A peculiar expression crossed his face, as if he'd had a thought that devastated him. "What about any parchment rolls? A single sheet?"

I raised my brows. "Mamá asked about a single sheet, too. I *knew* you've been looking for something. What is it?"

"It would have had a drawing of a snake eating itself. An ouroboros. Does that sound familiar?"

I shook my head.

"The sheet would also have had writing in Greek, more drawings and diagrams," Whit pressed. "It would have looked like instructions."

"*No,*" I said. "I didn't find anything like that. What is it?"

"Alchemy," he said.

"Alchemy?" I repeated.

"It's not important now. What matters is Lourdes."

Right. My mother, the thief.

"There's still something I don't understand. What about the letter to Maspero?"

"The one you found in their hotel room? She could have easily planted that. Think about it—why wouldn't she have sent it?"

The envelope came vividly to mind. The weight and feel of it, the creased letter within. It hadn't even been stamped. I wanted to argue, to defend her, but words failed me. Every moment with her was tainted, ruined by her deceit. And like a foolish child, I'd helped her steal priceless works of art with monumental historical significance. My uncle would be devastated when he learned of the truth.

Mamá had thought of everything.

"She wanted that letter to be found, wanted the suspicion to fall on her brother. I've been such an idiot," I said. "The whole time, she was manipulating me."

Whit placed a soft hand on my arm. "She used your affection for her against you. It's despicable. I would have believed my mother, too."

Shame sucked me down like quicksand. I didn't deserve any compassion, any grace. What I'd done was unpardonably foolish. "You don't have to be kind to me."

"And you," Whit said sternly, "don't get to be hard on yourself. Not over this."

I heard the words, but couldn't accept them. I'd made a terrible mistake, and everything in me wanted to make things right. "What do I do now?"

"Go to bed," he said, his voice gentle. "In the morning, we'll talk to Ricardo."

My heart leapt. "You don't have to do that with me."

"I know. But I will." Whit removed his hand, and I immediately missed the warmth of his palm against my skin. "Try to sleep, Inez."

He turned to go.

"Whit," I said.

He waited by the entrance. "What is it?"

"You're terribly decent," I said. "Despite pretending to be otherwise."

"Just as long as you don't tell anyone," he said with a slight smile. Then he ducked out of my room.

I flung myself backward onto my bedroll, my mind whirring. The only way to make things right was to stop my mother somehow.

But I had no idea how to do it.

CAPÍTULO VEINTIOCHO

I opened my eyes on Christmas morning filled with dread. I sank farther beneath the blanket, grief hovering in the room like fog in the industrial part of Buenos Aires. In a matter of minutes, I'd be facing my uncle and telling him I'd betrayed all of them, right under their noses. After washing my face and getting dressed, I stepped out of the room, palms clammy with sweat. Whit stood leaning on the stone frame, a cup of tea already in his hands.

Wordlessly, he handed it to me and I took it with a meek smile.

"He's by the fire," he murmured. "With Abdullah."

I flinched. Of course. I couldn't have the conversation with only my uncle—what I'd done impacted Abdullah, too, even more so. Most of the crew were already at work, my uncle and Abdullah examining a journal laid out before them. They were probably discussing the opening of the tomb. My stomach clenched.

I'd utterly ruined the moment for them.

We walked side by side and then sat in front of them on the available mats, our bodies close. He was a good friend, one of the best I had.

Tío Ricardo didn't glance up from the journal. "Shouldn't you be heading into the treasury to work on the sketches?"

I clasped my hands tightly in my lap. "I have to tell you both something."

In unison, they lifted their faces and focused on mine. I'd barely slept, exhaustion making my shoulders droop, my voice low.

"What is it?" Tío Ricardo said impatiently. Abdullah dropped a careful hand on my uncle's arm, as if signaling for him to remember his manners.

He knew how to do that well. A useful skill to have as a business partner, not to mention family.

Whit gave me a sidelong glance. The silence stretched. I was stalling, the words trapped in a tangle at the back of my throat. From the corner of my eye, I spotted his slight movement. His warm palm engulfed mine. Squeezed, and then released it.

I took a fortifying breath, and spoke in halting words. I fought to keep myself from crying, to keep my tone measured. Neither of them interrupted, but their expressions became more horrified as I continued. Tío Ricardo seemed to have turned to stone. He barely breathed. Whit stayed by me, silently supporting me. When I finished, the quiet felt heavy and oppressive.

"If it's the last thing I do," I said, my voice hoarse, "I'm going to stop her."

My uncle stood, swaying, and stumbled away. I heard his low roar but it wasn't entirely made of fury. He sounded anguished. The urge to go to him overwhelmed me. He wouldn't want my comfort, but I had to try. I prepared to stand but Whit flung out his arm, stopping me.

"Give him a minute."

"But—"

My uncle kicked the sand. If he were a kettle, he'd be steaming. He wasn't a flame, he was a blaze razing everything to the ground.

"Maybe more than one minute," Abdullah said, his face turned away in my uncle's direction. "Let him feel his anger. It doesn't last long anyway. He'll return when he's ready."

He came back after ten minutes, his color high, graying hair disorderly. I'd seen him tugging on it and I was worried he'd hurt himself. My uncle resumed his seat, breathing hard. Then he met my gaze squarely.

"She set out to ruin me," he said in a barely controlled voice.

I nodded.

"Paint me as a thief. A *murderer*."

I nodded again.

"And you believed her," he said.

"Ricardo," Abdullah said sharply. "We need to focus on the lost arti-facts."

"They're gone by now," Tío Ricardo said bleakly. "There's no getting them back. Lourdes is well on her way to Cairo, and from there she'll hand the artifacts over to her lover. He'll make sure they're never seen again until the items come up for sale at Tradesman's Gate."

"And once they're in the hands of collectors," Abdullah said slowly, "in museums or with historians, someone will discern their origins. It will only be a matter of time before people discover who we've found."

"But it will take days for Mamá to reach the city," I argued. "We have time to catch up to her, we have time to involve the proper authorities. We have names, we have a location. We ought to pack up and go, right this minute."

"We're opening the tomb today," Abdullah said. "We can't leave Cleopatra unattended, and we've come too far to cover our tracks. Too many people come and go from Philae."

My uncle visibly weighed the situation, clearly torn. I could tell he wanted to rush off and find my mother, and take back what was stolen, but Abdullah's words made sense. I tried to catch his eye, but now he refused to look at me. Whatever ground I'd gained, I'd lost. His trust in me had been misplaced and the betrayal drew him away, creating distance.

There might have been a vast desert between us.

"I agree with you," my uncle said at last.

"We open the tomb, and we record what we can," Abdullah said.

"And then Whit and I will go and find out what I can about the lost artifacts," Tío Ricardo said.

"Too much time will be lost," I said. "Let's go and—"

"We're in this mess because of your foolishness," my uncle snapped. "And there's no *we*. Once the tomb is opened, you'll stay behind to complete the drawings."

My temper flared. "Maybe if you had been honest from the start—"

Tío Ricardo glared, the muscles in his jaw ticking.

Whit tugged on the sleeve of my dress, wordlessly communicating for me to stop talking. Mamá was getting away because of me. I couldn't sit and do nothing. I couldn't draw. "Tío Ricardo, por favor—"

"Not another word," Tío Ricardo said, jumping to his feet again. "I don't have time to hear any more of your idiocy."

Whit glared at my uncle. "It's her *mother*."

Tío Ricardo made a noise of disgust and stormed off. He hadn't taken twenty steps before he was accosted by Mr. Fincastle and Isadora. They had huddled close by, watching our interaction with keen interest. My uncle gestured toward me and then walked out of sight. Isadora walked up to our little group as her father followed my uncle wherever he had gone. She wore a neat blue gown, her narrow waist cinched tight by wide ribbon. Her golden hair swung around her shoulders.

"Good morning." She smiled. "I trust you all slept well?"

No one replied.

"We'll open the tomb after lunch," Abdullah said. "All of you be ready by then." He stood, his grief tugging the corners of his mouth downward. "It's a holiday, isn't it? Feliz Navidad."

He walked away and my heart shattered.

I'd ruined everything. I ought to have known, I should have suspected. Abdullah's quiet grief cut me deeply. I would have preferred that he yelled at me like my uncle had done. His disappointment hurt worse, but wasn't he as much to blame? His lying and determined secrecy had worked against *all* of us. I wished to heaven I had—

Whit nudged my knee with his. "Stop it."

I startled. "What?"

He leaned forward, and spoke quietly so that Isadora couldn't hear. "I know what you're doing. You can't change what happened, or what you did. Try not to destroy yourself over it. Your mother betrayed you. If there's anyone you can't forgive, let it be her."

Tears pricked my eyes. "I don't know if I can do that."

"Try," he said gently. He stood up and held out his hand. "Come on, Olivera. I have something I want to show you."

"Did you still want to learn how to shoot?" Isadora cut in. I'd almost forgotten she was there. "I can teach you now, if you'd like. It's my gift to you."

Whit's brow creased. "I can teach you how to shoot."

I jumped to my feet. Suddenly the idea of blowing something to smithereens sounded wonderful. "Let's go."

"Olivera—" Whit began. Isadora raised her brows at his familiar use of my name.

"If you want to learn, I can teach you right now," she said.

"I'm in good hands," I said to Whit. "You've seen Isadora fire her pistol, haven't you?"

"Come find me when you're done, then. Trajan's Kiosk. And for God's sake, don't hurt yourself."

Isadora pulled me away and led me far from the others, close to the water, an expanse of space surrounded by trees and large rocks. I followed her down to the bank, my shoes filled with hot sand. Something slithered across my vision and I let out a shriek.

She turned around, her gaze landing over my shoulder. "A scorpion. Good thing it didn't sting you."

I shuddered as the insect meandered up the hill. It stopped and perched itself on a smooth rock. I turned away and met Isadora down by the water.

"I think it best we aim out to the river, for now. Then, I'll set up proper targets once you've gotten used to the feel of the gun going off."

"Gracias," I murmured, my head still full of Tío Ricardo's disappointment. His furious expression was carved in my mind. I'd never forget it, not as long as I lived.

"Are you all right?" Isadora asked. "You look pale."

"My uncle and I had an argument," I said, because if I could escape telling another lie, I would. I was sick of them. "I was at fault. Well, *mostly* at fault."

"Did you apologize?"

I let out a bleak laugh. "It didn't do much good."

Isadora pulled at her lip. "Everyone makes mistakes."

"While true, it doesn't exactly make me feel better." I hesitated. "I trusted the wrong person."

"You are trusting," she agreed. "Far too much."

I blinked, surprised. Anger sparked, lacing my blood. "You don't know me at all."

Isadora pulled out her gun, sleek and shiny in the sunlight. She raised it and aimed at my heart. Something flickered in her eyes. I couldn't define the emotion. The world dimmed, narrowed to the barrel of her weapon. "I know you're the type of person who would leave the safety of the camp with a near stranger, even knowing they carried a weapon."

I backed away a step. "What are you playing at? Lower it."

Isadora rolled her eyes. "Now you're scared. A little too late, Inez." She swung away, aiming for the scorpion up the bank. She inhaled and pulled the trigger.

The bullet blew the insect apart, sand kicking up from the shot.

Wordlessly, she handed me the gun. "Your turn."

CAPÍTULO VEINTINUEVE

I approached Trajan's Kiosk, the sun high in the blue sky. In ancient Egypt, the god Ra reigned over the sun and sky, giving warmth and life. And on the island of Philae, cut off from most modern conveniences, it was easy to imagine him guiding my steps as I descended into the belly of Pharaoh's Bed. My lesson with Isadora had gone well, and while I wouldn't win any awards for my shooting, I was reasonably proud of my aim.

Isadora and her reckless streak. After she'd pointed the gun at me, she behaved as she normally did. Observant and thoughtful, cheerful and competent, flashing her dimpled cheeks. She acted as if she hadn't threatened me with a weapon. But maybe that had been the point.

Was she telling me to be more careful?

"Olivera?"

I returned my attention to the present. Footsteps sounded close by, and a flickering light appeared on the stairwell, followed by Whit's brawny frame.

"Still in one piece, I see." He said it in a teasing voice, but I detected a note of relief in his tone.

"She's a good teacher."

"What do you think of her?" he asked.

I considered the question. "I enjoy her," I said slowly. "She doesn't quite fit the mold of an English rose, well-mannered and buttoned-up, but I think that's her appeal. She's crafty and strategic and charming—when she wants to be. I've never met anyone quite like her. What about you?"

"She's hard to read, harder to pin down."

"Isadora is like . . . you."

I thought he'd be offended, but to my surprise, he nodded. "Exactly."

"So that's why you don't like her. Or trust her."

"Olivera, I can't trust myself."

He led the way through the tunnels, until we ducked into a new room, recently found given the taste of dust and smoke from the blast of a dynamite stick. Above, the roof stretched high above us, dark and foreboding. Large boulders were piled along the craggy wall. The chamber was narrow and I coughed, clearing my throat of smoky air. He propped the candle securely between two rocks, and threw his sport coat over a tall boulder, and then turned to face me.

Dirt smudged his cheeks, and the glow from the candle cast his features in shadowed hollows. Only the blue of his gaze shone brightly in the dimness.

"What are we doing here?"

"Let's call it my Christmas present to you," he said with a slight smile. He motioned for me to stand next to a long spool of coiled rope on the ground, the other end reaching high upward and disappearing into the darkness of the tall ceiling.

"My Christmas present," I repeated as he tied the other end of the rope around my waist. His breath brushed my cheek as he worked silently. I lifted my chin and stared at his downturned face, his attention solely on the knot.

Whit pulled out my uncle's enchanted sandal from his vest pocket and handed it to me.

"Buckle the strap," he said.

I did so and the tip of the shoe immediately caught fire, a fiery blue. Then without ceremony, he climbed the boulders, up and up, until I lost sight of him in the flat black of the chamber.

"Whit?" I called up.

"I'm here," he said. His voice echoed down. "Are you ready?"

"If I must be."

His faint chuckle reached my ears. "Hold on to the rope with your free hand, Olivera. Don't scream."

"Don't—*oh*!" A sharp tug propelled me off my feet and I was launched upward. Whit passed me on his way down, and I barely caught his flash of a smile before I flew up toward the ceiling, buoyed by his weight as he nearly landed on the ground. The blue flame illuminated the ragged walls of the cave, and the higher I went, the smoother the walls became. Whit slowed my ascent.

"See it?" he called up.

I squinted, using my legs to turn myself around. "No. What am I supposed to— Miércoles!"

I was staring at a stretch of ancient paintings in blues and greens and reds. A woman made of stars, having just swallowed the sun and moon, where they'd travel through her body to be reborn at dawn.

"It's the goddess Nuit," I whispered. Sweat dripped down my face from the heat of the fire, and my palms grew slick, but I didn't care. I was staring at something so incredible it stole my sadness for a breath. I was weightless, seemingly floating with only the rope a reminder that I wasn't alone.

Whit tugged and I looked down. He was barely visible. I whistled and he lowered me down, slowly and carefully. When my feet touched the ground, he loosened the knot around my waist. His hands were steady and sure, and I wanted them to explore my body.

"That was beautiful." I cleared my throat, overcome. "Gracias."

He smiled. It was one of his real ones. "Feliz Navidad, Inez."

I cleared my throat. "I have something for you, too."

"Do you?"

Without meeting his eye, I bent and retrieved my bag and rummaged through it. I pulled out the sketchbook and flipped through to the middle. A single sheet had been neatly torn away and on it was a sketch of Whitford Hayes. But not the one I had done in Groppi, all those weeks ago. This drawing showed Whit in the way I'd always remember him. His direct stare, his emotion hidden just beneath the surface.

Wordlessly, I handed the drawing to him.

He wiped his hands on his trouser pants and carefully took it from me. He lifted his eyes. His mouth opened, but then just as quickly shut. As if he couldn't bring himself to lay bare his thoughts.

"Thank you," he muttered hoarsely. "But you didn't sign it."

"Oh," I said. "I thought I had, do you have a pen? Pencil?"

He nodded absently, attention still riveted on the drawing. "In my jacket pocket."

I walked to where he'd discarded it and rummaged through the pockets. He had all manner of things tucked within. Pen nibs, a handkerchief, loose Egyptian coins, a switchblade. Whitford Hayes was prepared for everything.

I kept rummaging. "Why do you have matches?"

"In case I need to blow something up."

Chuckling, I continued my search. My fingers grazed something small and smooth. Curious, I pulled it out, astonished to recognize the button I thought I'd lost. It had been missing since the day at the docks.

When I'd first met Whit.

Wordlessly, I held it out for him to see. "Why do you have this?"

He glanced up, and immediately went still. Twin flags of deepest red raced across his cheeks.

"I've been looking for it," I said, filling the silence when it became clear his reply wasn't coming. "Why did you take it?"

"It was loose," he said, a bit defensively.

I waited, sensing there was more.

He threaded his hands through his hair and gave me a slightly peeved look. "I don't know," he said finally. "Your mother talked a lot about you, the books you've read, the pranks you pulled on your aunt and cousins. What you loved to eat, how much you loved coffee. That day on the dock, I thought I was meeting someone I already knew, but you still surprised me. I wanted to laugh when you fled from me, that cheeky smile on your face."

A warm glow spread through me.

"I couldn't bring myself to throw the button away . . ." He sighed, and then added softly, "Or give it back."

I blushed, knowing how much it cost him to be that vulnerable with me. To reveal any feeling toward me. Without thinking, I went to tuck the button in my own pocket, but Whit held out his hand, palm facing up.

I let out a disbelieving laugh. "You'd like to keep it?"

Wordlessly, he nodded.

I gave it to him. Then he carefully rolled his gift and placed it and the button into his jacket pocket, his hands trembling a little.

"Happy Christmas to you, too, Whit."

My feelings for him had shifted, grown deeper, despite my efforts. I was sickened that I hadn't told him the truth about how I felt when I had the chance. It took everything in me not to kiss him again. Disappointment crashed around me. Now it was too late. He had a betrothed. Someone waiting for him back home. And while my feelings went deeper for him, he only felt attraction for me.

Attraction was nowhere near love.

I cleared my throat, my eyes burning and cheeks aflame. "We ought to go."

But neither of us moved. The quiet pressed close around us. We might have been the only two people on Philae. In the whole world.

"I've been engaged since I was ten years old," he said quietly. "My family arranged it. We've met exactly twice."

"Why are you telling me this?"

He ducked his head, his attention fixed on the toes of his worn boots. Then he sighed and met my gaze. "You're right. It doesn't matter, it never did."

My breath whooshed out of me in a long exhale. Should I feel relief? Perhaps so.

"We'll always be friends, Olivera."

With deliberate precision, he reached for my hand. His calloused palm was rough against mine. He laced his fingers through mine and I shivered. His eyes warmed as he slowly, so slowly, drew my hand toward his mouth.

He placed a soft, lingering kiss on the back of my wrist.

I felt it in every hidden corner of my body. Whit released my hand, and then he led me out of the tunnels and back into the sunlight.

His gift to me had only made me feel worse.

---- ✄ ----

I joined everyone after they had said their prayers for the noon meal, and for once, conversation was scarce and awkward. The crew seemed to sense the tension between my uncle and myself, more so than usual. The heat clung to my linen traveling dress, wrinkled and stained with paint splatters and dirt. This was my official working dress, which meant that I was wearing it nearly every day. I tried my best to clean the worst of the stains at night but the desert's mark couldn't easily be wiped away.

Elvira would be *horrified*.

I missed her with a sharp ache, my thoughts turning toward her more often than I expected. I knew what her days were like, even though I was a world away. Breakfast in the early morning—but no coffee—followed by lessons. A break for a light lunch, and then social calls around the neighborhood. A late dinner, and then bed. But I always managed to break free from the routine in some small way, and Elvira followed.

Little adventures with a laughing shadow at my heels.

I wish I'd thought to bring something of hers, if only so I could feel her near. Conjure her smile and the sound of her voice in my mind.

When lunch ended, my uncle and Abdullah conferred quietly with Mr. Fincastle and Isadora, and after another moment, they beckoned Whit and me over to join them a little ways from camp.

"Do you have your things?" my uncle asked in a flat voice as I joined them. I gestured to my bag, filled with my sketch pad, charcoal pencils, and paints.

"Does the crew suspect what we're doing?" Whit asked.

"It was meant to be a secret," Abdullah said. "So naturally everyone knows."

"Send them away," came a gruff voice. Mr. Fincastle stood between the columns lining the courtyard, half-hidden in shadows. He came forward, a rifle in his hands, and looked uneasily toward the temple entrance. "You ought not to trust them."

Abdullah's usually smiling face tightened. Tension coiled in his shoulders. "And why is that, Mr. Fincastle?"

"Don't answer that," Tío Ricardo snapped. "As I've repeatedly said, I don't care for your opinions. I've hired you to do a job and I won't have you disrespecting any of the crew. Is that clear?"

Isadora stiffened at my uncle's sharp tone. Her hand crept toward her pocket. I knew what she kept hidden.

"You're making my job harder," Mr. Fincastle said and then he strode toward the first pylon, the line of his back unbending and rigid. He could having been marching toward the front lines, prepared to give his life for God and country.

His devotion unsettled me.

"He's never failed at anything," Isadora said. "And he's good at what he does. You ought to let him do it." She moved away with deliberate steps after her father. As if she wanted to make it clear that she wasn't running away from us.

"I never should have allowed you to hire him, Ricardo," Abdullah said when Isadora was out of earshot.

My uncle stared after Mr. Fincastle's retreating form. "You know why I pushed for it."

Whit's gaze flickered to mine. Because of my mother, the criminal and smuggler, and her unfortunate involvement with The Company.

Hot shame bubbled up my throat, tasting like acid.

I felt, rather than saw, Tío Ricardo's pointed frown, his disapproval coming off of him in waves. Without a word, my uncle strode forward and disappeared inside the temple, fastening the strap of the sandal as he went. A spark rose and caught fire, and flames engulfed the tip of the shoe. We followed after him and then he motioned for Abdullah to go down the stairs first. We were all of us quiet and focused, walking single file through the antechamber and treasury.

A young voice let out a sharp yell.

I turned around to find Mr. Fincastle holding Kareem by the scruff of his long, pale tunic. He kicked his legs, aiming for Mr. Fincastle's shins, but his short height gave him no advantages.

"Release him," Abdullah barked.

"He was following the lot of you—"

"He's hardly dangerous. Let him go." My uncle stepped forward, and pointed his index finger toward Kareem, who squirmed violently to get out of Mr. Fincastle's iron grasp.

"Where there's one, the others will follow," Mr. Fincastle said, but then roughly released Kareem. He aimed a furious glare toward my uncle, and then disappeared up the stairs.

"He's a menace," Abdullah said disgustedly. "Come, Kareem, you may join us."

"But behave," Tío Ricardo warned. "And for God's sake, don't break anything."

Kareem nodded, his warm brown eyes lighting up. He wiped his hands on his long galabeya, and then shot a smile my way. Whit struggled to hide his grin, and then he gestured for Kareem to go ahead of him. Together, we all pressed down on the tiles, and the hidden door swung open with a loud groan that ruined the deep quiet. Ahead, the thick wall blocked our path, the tall doors locked and sealed by a heavy rope spiraling through both copper handles. A heavy feeling of intrusion settled onto my shoulders. We were disturbing something that had remained hidden, kept safe from prying eyes.

We ought to leave them undisturbed and in peace.

I glanced at Abdullah, and he wore a similar expression of unease and disquiet.

"What are you thinking?" Ricardo asked, watching his brother-in-law carefully. "Have you changed your mind?"

"We've already talked about this," Abdullah said with a trace of annoyance. "I would prefer we leave her untouched, but I know there will be others who won't share the same intent. I fear I will regret turning back, without writing down and studying what we've seen before this sacred place is destroyed." Abdullah took a deep breath. "Don't ask me again. We press on."

Ricardo stepped aside. "Then unwrap the rope."

Abdullah stepped forward and began working. Whit nudged my arm and pointed to the two statues standing on either end of the double doors. I hadn't noticed them before. They were tall women, dressed in long robes that looked more Greek than Egyptian, at least to my untrained eye, and carved in extraordinary detail. At once, I thought of Shakespeare.

"Iras and Charmian?" I guessed. "The handmaidens of Cleopatra?"

Tío Ricardo nodded. "Guarding her even now, in the afterlife."

"*In time we hate that which we often fear*," I quoted. "Charmian has the best lines."

"Not true," Whit said. "*Finish, good lady; the bright day is done, and we are for the dark*. I felt bad for them both."

I understood why he would. Two young women doomed to die with their queen, their loyalty leading them to the underworld, a future with no more bright days and only the lasting darkness.

Whit regarded me thoughtfully. "Do you think the three died by asp or poison?"

I considered everything I knew about Cleopatra, gathered from what I'd read by the historian Plutarch and the memories that had seeped under my skin. "She was a renowned strategist and a meticulous planner, and it seems inconceivable to me that she'd trust her fate to a wild animal. Aren't asps famously sluggish creatures?" I shook my head. "No, I think she came to her death prepared."

"Hemlock, then," Whit said. "I quite agree, but you have to admit the asp makes for a more dramatic tale, being the royal emblem of Egypt."

The room had gone curiously quiet and I turned around, expecting to find the wall breached. But instead, Abdullah and Tío Ricardo stared between me and Whit, the pair of them wearing bemused expressions.

"Are you quite finished with your morbid discussion?" Tío Ricardo asked in a dry voice.

I blushed and looked away from Whit. Abdullah finished untying the rope, and handed it to Whit. Then he looked at my uncle and together they each pushed one side of the door, and it swung forward, revealing another room pitched in smothering gloom. Warm air pulsed and whooshed

around my face, tugging at my hair. It tasted ancient, of long-buried secrets and shadowed rooms enclosed by stone.

All the candles flickered wildly and were snuffed out. Flat black smothered us in darkness. Kareem gasped, and I reached for him, finding his
narrow shoulders. I squeezed him, letting him know he wasn't alone. Even
if it felt like it. Someone shuffled closer to me, a large presence smelling of
sweat and leather.

Whit.

He brushed my fingers with his, and I unlocked my clenched jaw.

"No one panic," Abdullah said. "Ricardo, the sandal?"

There was a muffled sound as my uncle hurried to obey. A blue flame
blazed to life, and I let out a sigh of relief. The men struck matches and
relit the candles. I leaned forward to look at Kareem.

"Are you all right?"

He nodded, and shot me an embarrassed smile. I gave his thin shoulders
another squeeze. We all stepped through, carrying our various forms of light.
My breath lodged itself at the back of my throat, and my heart slammed hard
against my ribs. For two thousand years this room had lain quiet in obscurity.
Its magnificence hidden away under rock and sand.

Not anymore.

I stood where ancient Egyptians had once stood. Breathed the same
tight air, felt the press of the four walls enclosing us. I blinked to adjust my
eyes and slowly the room settled in front of me, the edges becoming crisp
and clear. Before me stood a raised dais where a sarcophagus rested above
the other two flanking it. The taste of roses burst in my mouth, and I knew,
without having to look more closely, who was interred in the center.

The last pharaoh of Egypt.

Cleopatra.

"Plutarch was wrong. He wasn't cremated—Marcus Antonius is on the
left," Tío Ricardo said hoarsely.

"Caesarion on the right," Abdullah said. The sarcophagus of Cleopatra's first child with Caesar bore several markings, and behind him stood an
immense statue. Above the head of the statue was Horus, in the form of a
falcon, the wings spread wide as if he were midflight.

"How kind of Augustus to allow them to be buried together," Whit said dryly.

"Not kind," Tío Ricardo scoffed. "Strategic. He didn't want civil unrest to sweep through Egypt, and Cleopatra was considered a goddess in her own time. Don't forget, Augustus still had her children to contend with."

"They are depicted with her on the walls," Abdullah said. "Extraordinary."

I felt as if I couldn't take in all the details in the room fast enough. Beautiful scarabs decorated the walls, their wings spread wide. Hundreds of statues surrounded the three sarcophagi, many of strange animals, and there were eleven long paddles propped against one of the walls.

"For the solar boat," Whit said, following my line of sight. "It would have taken her and her family to the underworld."

"Look at this!" Kareem exclaimed.

As one, we all looked in his direction. My uncle's face twisted in horror. Kareem stood by a jar, one skinny hand holding the lid, and with the other, he'd used his finger to scoop up whatever was stored within. Dark, thick liquid coated his index finger.

Kareem brought it to his lips.

"*No!*" Abdullah yelled.

Too late, Kareem licked the sticky mass. His expression turned thoughtful, and then he grinned, and replaced the lid. "It's honey."

"That honey is over *two thousand years old*," said Tío Ricardo. "I can't believe you'd put something like that in your mouth."

Kareem shrugged. "It smelled good."

Whit shifted his feet, half turning toward me, his eyes crinkling at the corners. I couldn't help it, I burst out laughing. Abdullah ruffled Kareem's hair, chuckling.

"No more honey for you," Abdullah said fondly. "Go and assist the crew."

Kareem took off, his sandals slapping against the stone.

Tío Ricardo shook his head, muttering to himself. Then he focused his attention back to more pressing matters. I listened as Abdullah and Tío Ricardo pointed out various depictions on the walls. On the north wall, Cleopatra with the goddess Nuit. Depicted on the west wall, the twelve hours of Amduat, and on the east, the first spell from the Book of the Dead. Finally, the south wall displayed Cleopatra with various ancient Egyptian deities: Anubis, the god of the dead, his jackal head turned sideways; Isis; and Hathor.

And last, wrapped around her sarcophagus, was a Hellenistic carving of the Battle of Actium, the day the Queen of Kings lost everything. Cleopatra stood on the prow of a hexareme warship while her soldiers rowed her toward her last stand against Octavian. After his victory, he christened himself Augustus.

Everything inside the chamber was touched by gold. My mother would want to lay her hands on everything and steal what she could. Time was moving too fast, the distance between us growing steadily. I wanted to run out of the room and race after her.

"Inez, you have your work cut out for you," Tío Ricardo said, watching me shrewdly, guessing my thoughts. "Best to start immediately."

By the end of the day, I could hardly flex the fingers on my right hand. They were too cramped and sore, but I was reasonably proud of my progress in capturing the burial chamber. I stumbled into my room, dusty, dirty, and bleary-eyed, too tired even to eat. I set my lit candle on the stack of books next to my bedroll and immediately went to the washbasin. I cleaned my face, neck, and hands, and dropped onto the blankets, vowing not to move for hours.

It lasted for only a moment.

Worry knotted tightly, deep in my belly. I paced the room, flapping my hands in agitation. I couldn't believe my uncle wanted to leave me behind when it was my fault. The desperation to make things right between us nearly suffocated me. I needed to do something, anything, to distract myself. I thought about going to Whit, but I forced myself to remain in my room.

I couldn't go to him anymore.

I cast my eye around the chamber and my gaze landed on Tía Lorena's letter, stacked on top of the crate. I really ought not to be such a coward about it. What could she possibly have written that could rival what I'd felt today?

With a groan, I pulled out the note. I expected to find several sheets, but there were only two pages, folded haphazardly. Frowning, I sat up, squinting in the dim lighting, and read the first missive.

> *Dear Inez,*
> *I hardly know where to begin. You haven't replied to my last, which makes me think it must have gotten lost in transit. There's no easy way to write this.*
> *Elvira has gone missing.*
> *I am at my wit's end. There's been no word, and the authorities have been no help. Come home. I beg you.*
> *Come home.*
>
> *Lorena*

The next few seconds were a blur, the words swimming in front of me nonsensical and wrong. How could Elvira have gone missing? My aunt was mistaken, she—I blinked back tears, remembering the first letter she'd written, shortly after I had arrived in Egypt. I launched myself into a search of my room, throwing around books, rummaging through my canvas bag, cursing all the while. The letter remained stubbornly hidden from me. How could I have been so careless?

Then I remembered the second sheet tucked inside the envelope. With shaking hands, I pulled it from within and read to the last line.

> *Inez,*
> *My sister would never have been so reckless, if it wasn't for your influence. I warned you that sneaking out into Buenos Aires would only bring trouble. Now, she hasn't come home and it's your fault for showing her the way. We fear she's been kidnapped—or worse.*
> *If anything happens to Elvira, I will never forgive you.*
> *And you can count on me making you miserable for the rest of your life.*
>
> *Amaranta*

"Damn it," I cried.

"Good gad!" Whit exclaimed from behind me. "What the bloody hell is the matter now?"

I whirled around, frantic. He yanked the curtain aside, his features pulled tight into a frown. "Whit! I must find my uncle."

He stepped into my room. "What's happened? You've gone white."

"Where is my uncle?"

He gently pulled me into the circle of his arms and I squirmed against him, desperate to find Tío Ricardo. They'd just had the evening meal, he would surely still be up. "I must go!"

"Easy, Inez," he murmured against my hair. "Go where?"

"Buenos Aires!"

He stiffened and pulled far enough away to look down at me, concern written across his handsome face. "You're—" He broke off, his lips parted. "You're leaving Egypt?"

I exhaled and fought the terror pecking at me like ravenous vultures. "My cousin Elvira has gone missing. My aunt tried to tell me twice, and fool that I was, I ignored her letters."

"Hold on. Is it possible this is a ruse?"

I blinked. "A what?"

"Would your aunt lie to you? Perhaps this is a strategy to get you to return home."

The thought hadn't occurred to me, but as soon as his words registered, I was already shaking my head. "She wouldn't do something like this. Not after what I went through when I learned about my parents. She wouldn't make something like this up concerning Elvira." I squeezed my eyes shut. Even though I'd said the words, I hardly believed them.

Whit gently led me out of my narrow bedroom. By the time we found my uncle—reading atop his bedroll—I was shaking once more, tears streaking down my face.

He flung his book aside and jumped to his feet. "Qué pasó? What's happened?"

"It's Elvira," I began. The lines around his mouth tightened as I finished giving him all the details and then handed him the crumpled letter.

My uncle stared at me gravely, a deep crease between his dark brows, and then read the letter once, then twice. Terror gripped me. What if he didn't believe this was from my aunt? What if he didn't believe *me*?

I'd lied to him. Betrayed him.

Tío Ricardo could refuse to let me go with him. He could call me a liar, a fool. Both those things would be true.

Tension twisted between us as I held my breath and waited.

"I'll take you back to Cairo," he said quietly. "Pack your things."

 # WHIT

Inez left the room, her skirt twirling around her ankles. I turned my focus to Ricardo. With Inez and him leaving for Cairo, it was the perfect time to broach a subject festering in my mind. I didn't want to bring it up, but I had to. It was long past time.

Ricardo dragged a tired hand across his face. "What a mess."

"I know."

Ricardo hunched over the book where I'd been keeping careful track of all the artifacts. He scowled down at the heavily marked page. His belongings were strewn everywhere in his narrow room, creating a mess. He liked to throw things when he couldn't shout.

"It was right here all along," he said.

"What was?"

"Inez's deceit," he said. He jabbed his index finger onto the sheet. "She was careful to take copies, but not always. The blue serpent is missing. It'll be worth a fortune, a perfect model of the asp that killed Cleopatra. The only snake in her entire tomb."

"You're still angry at her."

"There will never be a day when I won't be," he said tiredly. "Why aren't you furious?"

I leaned against the wall, crossed my ankles, and shrugged. "How well do you think she knew her mother?"

"Not an excuse."

"I think it is," I said quietly. "Lourdes made herself a stranger to her own daughter. She didn't know she was leading another life here; she didn't know how good of a liar her mother is. And don't forget, Inez believed her mother dead. We thought the same when we couldn't find her for weeks and weeks. You would have done anything for her; remember when you thought other Curators had murdered her?"

"That was before I knew how she had betrayed me," Ricardo said, slamming the book closed. "What do you want?"

"It's time for me to go home," I said.

He turned to face me, his jaw dropping. "*Now?*"

I had looked for the parchment again earlier, but there had been no trace of it. I couldn't ignore my family anymore—not without a reason, and I had none. "There are too many letters from home. I can't overlook them."

He was silent, considering. "This has nothing to do with Inez leaving Egypt?"

"Nothing," I said. I was always going to leave, one way or another. Even if I had found what I'd been looking for.

"You still have time on your contract with me."

I nodded. I had expected him to bring it up. "You brought me back to the living, Ricardo. I'll always owe you. But I can't stay any longer. My sister needs me."

"All right," he said, his tone cold. "Then I'll look for your replacement when we reach Cairo."

I gritted my teeth. He knew I'd prefer to stay. "Fine."

"Fine."

I turned to go, my back straight, that yawning pit deepening in my belly. I wasn't ready for my time here to be over. I wasn't ready for what came next. I would be a husband to a stranger. I would have to have *children* with her.

"Whitford."

I paused and half turned. Ricardo approached, and he settled his hand on my shoulder. "You've done good work for me. I'm glad you turned your life around."

"It's not really my life, though, is it?"

Ricardo gave me a pitying smile. "You still have a choice."

"No, I don't."

He sighed, and squeezed my arm. "I know you've come to care for Inez. Thanks for leaving her alone."

I left before I had to tell another lie.

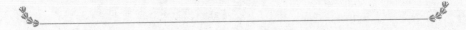

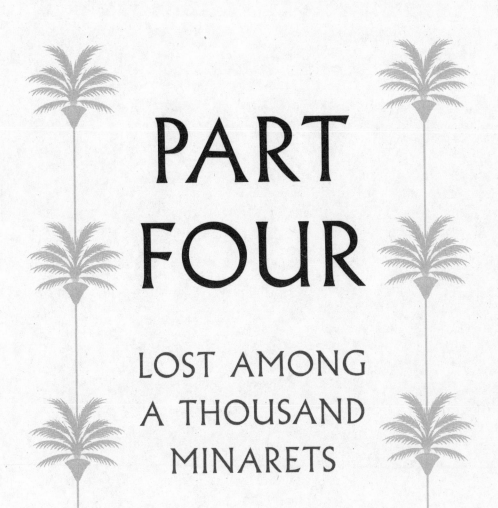

PART FOUR

LOST AMONG A THOUSAND MINARETS

CAPÍTULO TREINTA

*T*rue to his word, my uncle prepared for us to leave with the first streaks of dawn the next morning. I'd spent a miserable night, tossing and turning, praying that Elvira had been found. At some point, Whit had appeared at my door, as if I'd summoned him. Wordlessly, he'd held out a tin cup filled with brandy.

I took it from him, conscious of my thin nightgown fluttering softly around my body. He never once looked down past my eyes. I took a sip, and the liquid burned a path down deep in my belly.

"I heard you," he'd said softly. "Restless. I thought it might help."

I took another sip and then handed the cup back to him. "I don't have a taste for it."

He'd stared at it in wonder, the tin small against his large hand. "Me neither. Not anymore."

"You don't miss it?"

"I only needed it to forget," he'd said after a beat. "But I can't run anymore. Keep it, and drink. It'll help you fall asleep, Olivera." He'd turned away before I could say anything else. There was so much I wished I could say. But I bit my tongue and fell back into bed. The brandy had calmed me down enough to think through the situation logically. It took several weeks for mail to make the journey from South America to Africa. She must have written both letters back to back. For all I knew, Elvira was already home and safe.

But then, why hadn't Tía Lorena written another letter?

It was possible that it just hadn't arrived yet. Perhaps by the time we sailed back and arrived at Shepheard's, there would be another letter waiting for me.

The thought brightened me up considerably.

Kareem came to help me with my belongings, and as I stepped out of my room—possibly for the last time—I spotted Whit assisting my uncle with his luggage. He glanced over, looking as disheveled as I felt, and studied my face. His gaze flicked from my tired eyes to the downward curve of my mouth, and then he frowned. My uncle called for him from where he stood by Trajan's Kiosk, and Whit turned away to continue helping him.

I said goodbye to the crew, and then to Abdullah and even Mr. Fincastle, whose gruff goodbye confirmed my initial dislike of the man. Isadora surprised me by giving me a tight hug.

"Remember to not be so trusting," she whispered. "I won't always be there to teach you how to shoot. You do remember how, don't you?"

"I'll hardly forget the lesson," I said dryly.

"Write to me," she said. "You know where to find me."

I promised her I would. Before anyone could call me away, I ran to the Temple of Isis, my boots kicking up the hot sand in my wake. Inside the temple, everything looked the same, while I felt my insides were being wrung out to dry. This would be my last chance to see Cleopatra's final resting place, before it was discovered by the rest of the world. This moment was for just her and me, the taste of roses in my mouth, the magic rioting under my skin.

When I finally made it to the burial chamber, tears pricked the corners of my eyes. The objects and artifacts glinted gold from the light of the soft flame of my candle. I didn't want to forget any of the details, but more important, I didn't want to forget what it felt like to have found her.

I'm glad she rested with her family. Glad, too, that everything that had been provided for her journey through the underworld was accounted for and recorded. Years from now, Abdullah's careful recordings would be a guide for those studying the last gasp of her life on Earth. Time slipped by and I forced myself to turn away from Cleopatra's sarcophagus. My gaze lingered in the treasury, wishing I could place the ring back where it belonged.

The ring had started everything.

Papá had sent it to me for a reason. I might never know it, and the thought nearly killed me. I felt as if I were saying goodbye to him all over again. What had happened to him?

I wished I had the answer.

My thoughts returned to Elvira, and I knew it was time to go. I passed Kareem on the way back to the campsite. I called him over with a quick wave.

"I'm leaving, and I wanted to say goodbye. It was wonderful meeting you."

He smiled. "Don't be sad, sitti. You'll be back."

I blinked away tears. I hoped that was true, but that depended on what had happened to Elvira. It also depended on my uncle.

"Ma' es-salama," he said.

I made my way down to the water, where the *Elephantine* waited. All of our belongings were grouped together on the bank, and Tío Ricardo and Whit were in deep conversation. The former appeared stern, the latter frustrated. Then my uncle boarded the dahabeeyah as I joined Whit on the sandbank. He looked as rumpled as ever, wrinkled shirt untucked, boots worn and scuffed beyond the help of polishing, and his hair windswept, falling at an angle across his brow.

We stared at each other, Whit's hands deep in his pockets, and my own nervously clasped behind my back.

"What were you two discussing?" I asked finally. It hadn't looked like a friendly conversation.

He stared down at me. "I never wanted you to feel anything for me," he said. "I'm sorry that you do."

"I'm not," I said.

"I'm coming with you to Cairo."

My heart lifted, practically soaring upward like a bird with outstretched wings. But Whit read the apparent joy in my face, and he shook his head. "I have to go back to England."

I crashed back onto solid ground. "You're going back?"

"After the military, I was a mess. Maybe parts of me still are. But Ricardo gave me a job, purpose. Direction. It helped to straighten me out a bit. But I can't continue ignoring my responsibilities. My parents expected me to return a year ago. I can't keep putting *it* off any longer."

It being his marriage. We were going to be a world away from each other, me in Argentina, him in England. And he would have a *wife*. His days in Egypt had always been numbered. Regret filled me slowly as I thought of our time on this island together. The way we had worked together, cataloguing every discovery, no matter how small. We had been a team and now we would be nothing at all. Not even friends.

"I'm sorry you didn't find what you were looking for," I said softly. "What was it?"

He remained quiet for a long beat and then shrugged. "Cleopatra had an ancestor—*also* named Cleopatra—who was a renowned alchemist and Spellcaster. I was looking for a single sheet of parchment she'd written on before she died."

A memory flickered in my mind. Elusive and hazy. "What did it say?"

He laughed humorlessly. "I was chasing a rumor, Olivera. It probably doesn't exist, or if it did, it was destroyed a long time ago."

"What did it say?" I repeated, the memory becoming sharper. Cleopatra had been preparing something, reading a . . . had it been a scroll? Or a sheet? I couldn't remember.

"It's time to go," Tío Ricardo shouted down at us from the dahabeeyah.

All thoughts of Cleopatra and her ancestor scattered. Neither of us reached for the other. I didn't think I could, disappointment clouding my vision. Whit remained silent, too, as if he couldn't bring himself to say anything else.

I joined him on the deck, the distance between us stretching, as if he'd already gone.

———— ✖ ————

We arrived in Cairo on a sunny afternoon, the last day in December. The rest of the journey had been slow, and there had been trouble with the *Elephantine* that kept us from sailing for a few extra days. The hours were filled with long evenings spent alone. My uncle had kept to himself, writing letters and sending them off when we stopped in Thebes for food and other supplies. Whit was friendly when we had to be around each other, but he never sought me out for conversation and he often retreated to his room after dinner. I knew it was for the best. But my heart was still broken and my emotions swung wildly. I was anxious to be on my way, to help find Elvira. I was desperate to stay and help them find my traitorous mother. I promised myself I'd make things right, but now I was leaving.

Back and forth the pendulum swung, leaving my nerves raw and wrung out.

"I'm going to book your passage to Buenos Aires," Tío Ricardo said as we walked up the steps leading to the front door of Shepheard's. The front terrace was as crowded as on the day I'd first left it. Travelers enjoyed tea and catching up with old friends. The street below bustled with its usual familiar activity, hackney cabs clamoring up and down the main avenue.

I'd miss Cairo, and grief gripped me like a too-tight dress clenched around my ribs.

I was making the right choice. Elvira needed me. But I couldn't seem to forget how badly I'd failed—*everyone*.

"Would you like to send a telegram?" Tío Ricardo asked, jarring me from my thoughts. "It's faster than regular post."

"Sí, por favor," I said in Spanish. I'd gotten in the habit of conversing with my uncle in English, but now that I was leaving for Argentina, my mind had already made the switch. "How early do you think I can depart for Alexandria?"

"That depends on you," he said. "Would you like to hear word from your aunt? It's possible that Elvira might have already been found."

"I thought of that as well," I said, waiting for my eyes to adjust to the dim lighting of Shepheard's lobby. People milled around in small groups, chatting gaily, while others were seated in the various couches along the walls. The granite pillars stood tall and imposing, reminding me of the ones found in Philae. I missed the small island, an ache that tore at my skin, my breath, my heart. I had no way of knowing when I'd ever see her again. "There might be a letter waiting for me."

We hurried to the front desk and Sallam's familiar smile greeted us. "Hello, Señor Marqués, Señorita Olivera, and Mr. Hayes. It's wonderful to see you again, and in time for the New Year's Eve ball, too."

He gestured to several hotel attendants carrying vases of beautiful blooms to the ballroom. They were a riot of colors, bold reds and pinks and purples. I would most likely be missing the night's festivities, but I returned his grin with a faint smile of my own. "Sallam, is there a letter here for me?"

He immediately began checking the drawers, and rummaging through stacks of paper and letters. After he looked though everything, he checked again and then looked up at me. "There's nothing for you. Were you expecting something?"

My uncle placed a tentative hand on my shoulder. Whit shot me a look filled with sympathy. Worry seeped under my skin. I had really hoped that there would have been word about my cousin's welfare. The silence spoke volumes; Elvira still hadn't been found.

"Is it possible for Inez to send a telegram?" Whit asked.

"Of course," Sallam said, frowning slightly. "Señorita Olivera, would you like to sit? You look pale."

"No, I'm fine, please, let's just send word—"

"Inez!" a voice called from behind me.

The floor tilted under my feet and I clutched the front desk, my knees wobbling. I whirled around in time to receive the hug thrusted on me. Blue feathers tickled my nose, and I stepped back, my eyes watering. "*Elvira!* You're *here*—"

My voice broke. She wasn't missing, she wasn't in danger.

I hadn't lost someone else.

Hot pressure built behind my eyes. Elvira laughed and went for another hug, smelling like orchids, like the garden back home. "I arrived a few days ago."

I squeezed her back, and then I pulled away, halfway between relief and exasperation. "I received a note from your *mother,* who thinks you've gone missing! She sent two letters, Elvira, terrified out of her mind. What were you thinking?"

"I left her a letter!" she exclaimed. "The same way *you* did. She must not have found it." Her face scrunched in bewilderment. "At least, I *thought* I left her one."

"Por el amor de Dios," Tío Ricardo muttered. He stepped forward, looking harassed and annoyed. "Your cousin, I take it?"

Elvira immediately turned toward Tío Ricardo. "We've met once before, Señor. Don't you remember?"

The lines fanning from the corners of his hazel eyes tightened. "Dios save me from wayward females. I'll be booking a passage for the both of you—"

"No, you can't," I cried, thinking fast. "I could stay and help—"

"Your cousin can hardly travel back on her own," Tío Ricardo said. "You'll have to accompany her for the return voyage."

The noise in the lobby rose to a deafening roar, but all I could hear were my uncle's words repeating themselves in a horrifying manner. "You're still sending me away. Even after . . . everything."

"Because of your prima," my uncle said slowly, as if he were speaking to a willful toddler. "You can thank her for that."

Elvira had the good sense to appear sheepish. "I'm afraid I didn't think beyond meeting you in Cairo. Surely, we don't have to leave so soon."

"I must return to my work," Tío Ricardo said coolly. "I haven't the time to manage you both."

Frustration loomed over me, and I fought to keep myself from shaking. While I'd been worried and distraught, he had been kind and thoughtful, intent on helping me. But now, his earlier anger toward me had returned. I still wasn't forgiven. In one sentence, my uncle had reduced everything I'd done—all of the careful artwork and sketching—down to nothing.

But then, this served as the ultimate punishment. I met Tío Ricardo's gaze to find him watching me. A hint of a challenge lurked in his hazel eyes, confirming my suspicion.

Elvira's attention had flickered to the brawny man attached to our group. She studied Whit, and her green eyes gleamed with appreciation. He sketched an ironic bow, his roguish attitude so like the one I'd first encountered on the docks of Alexandria all those weeks ago. It was the mask he wore, and I doubted he'd show me what lay beneath it ever again.

"I must find a chaperone for you two," my uncle continued. "It's perfectly clear that I can't trust either of you to behave as young ladies should."

My right eye twitched. As if he cared about the rules of propriety. Anger bubbled to the surface and I fought hard to keep myself from glaring at my cousin. If it hadn't been for her, I'd at least still be on Philae.

"I'm going to send a telegram to your aunt," my uncle continued gruffly. "Meet me down here at half past eight. I'll escort you both to dinner. Whit, I'd like a word."

He led him away as if he couldn't escape fast enough.

Elvira tugged impatiently at my sleeve. "There's so much I have to tell you."

But I didn't want to hear any of it. "Why are you here, Elvira?"

Her smile dimmed at my expression. "I came to be with you," she said. "I would have gone with you, had you asked me." There was a faint note of accusation in her voice. "It's clear you need me. Look at the state of your clothes!"

I glanced down in surprise. My ensemble was rather worse for wear, the Turkish trousers stained with stubborn dirt, but at last clean enough to wear, and my once-white shirt no longer truly white. My leather boots were as scuffed as my uncle's, and I didn't need to look in the mirror to see that the sun had tanned my complexion to a rosy hue.

In comparison, Elvira looked every inch the young lady in a resplendent day dress that complemented her dark hair and eyes. All her bows were tied prettily and not a hair was out of place from its elaborate updo.

"You made all of us worry," I said finally.

"I made *you* worry?" She laughed. When I didn't join in, it died on her painted lips. "What about what you did?" she said, anger threading her voice. "How many times did I sit by your side as you cried about being left behind? Your parents died and then you were gone, without a word to anyone. Without telling *me*."

She was right. I'd behaved abominably. It was unfair to be angry with her—she didn't know how her arrival had upended my life. "Elvira, I'm so sorry. Perdóname."

"Of course I forgive you. I came all this way so you wouldn't be alone." She reached out to hold my hand. "And I had to sneak away, because my mother would never have allowed it otherwise."

For a second, I sympathized with my uncle. He must have felt the same way I did when I had first seen her, all alone in a city she didn't know.

"I just can't believe you sailed all the way out here on your own—"

"I had help," she said. "Your maid arranged everything the same way she did for you. She even dressed me in black for the voyage. Really, it was quite easy when I pretended to be you. I kept asking myself, what would Inez do in this situation?" Her lips pulled into a sly smile. "Turns out, quite a lot."

"You need to write Amaranta," I said. "She's furious, and threatened me with a life of misery should anything happen to you."

Elvira paled. "Dios, she's terrifying when she's angry."

"Oh, I know. I used to hide from her underneath my bed."

She laughed. "You did not."

"No," I admitted. "But I thought about it." I hugged her again. "So you have a room here?"

"Well, sort of," she said, and for the first time since seeing her, she looked anxious. "I arrived and told the kind gentleman at the front desk that I was family, and waiting for you to arrive. He put me in your room—in your parents' room, I suppose. Do you mind?"

I shook my head.

Elvira sagged against me in relief. "Oh, I'm so glad. I worried that it would have bothered you." She linked her arm through mine. "Well, come upstairs. I have something I think you need to see."

"What is it?"

She bit her lip. "A letter from your papá."

CAPÍTULO TREINTA Y UNO

*E*lvira had her own brass key, and she used it to open the door. I stepped through, half-anxious to read the letter, and half-terrified. These words would be my father's last to me. They would wreck me, no matter what they were. My cousin seemed to sense my inner turmoil because she quietly and efficiently lit the candles about the room, leaving everything touched in a soft, golden glow.

She opened the door to my parents' former room and I gasped. Elvira had organized the entire suite; no longer were my parents' things strewn everywhere. Their luggage was stacked side by side on the sofa, all of their clothes folded neatly. Their journals and letters were stacked atop each other on the coffee table. She had made up the bed in their room, and had put piles of various things on the bedspread in like categories.

My cousin watched me, wringing her hands. "I wanted to be helpful." It was far more than I had done.

"Elvira," I breathed, overcome. "Gracias."

She daintily sat down on one of the chairs facing the sofa and smiled in relief. Then she reached forward and plucked the top letter off the pile, and held it out to me. I sat in the armchair next to hers, eyeing it warily, and then I took it out of her hands.

"It's dated from July." She hesitated. "Would you like to be alone?"

I considered her question, but her presence felt familiar, like a return voyage home. "No, gracias."

With a deep inhale, I opened the envelope and pulled out the note and began to read.

My darling girl,

If you've found this letter, then you are more my daughter than I could have ever dreamed, and I need you to know how incredibly proud I am of you. By now, you must have discovered your mother's deception. If you have not, I beg you to keep asking questions, keep searching for the truth. Your curiosity and stubbornness will assist you on your quest.

Your mother is many awful things, but worst of all, she is disloyal. Please take care that she never lures you into her trap, like she did to me. I pray that you are smarter than me in that regard.

Lourdes and I have reached our inevitable end. I wish I would have seen what she was earlier. Perhaps we both could have been spared. But now I must protect everything I hold dear from her vile hands. Which is one of the reasons I sent you the golden ring, querida. Because of it, I was able to make a discovery on Philae that I've tried to keep from everyone else—especially your mother. But I might have failed. Finding people to trust has been supremely difficult, thanks to your mother.

I must end this letter, but I beg you to do one more thing for me.

Please, never stop looking for me.

Your loving papá

Here, the letter ended abruptly, my father's handwriting cutting off in a discordant loop. It was that final squiggle that terrified me the most.

"Where did you see this?"

"It was sealed and tucked in with the rest of their correspondence. It must have gotten mixed up with everything else and was never sent out. Or he might have forgotten to add it to one of his packages he sent to you? I know he was terribly absent-minded."

My mind raced. Clearly, Papá had found Cleopatra's tomb because of the magic pulsing between the two objects—the ring and . . . the *trinket box*. The same thing had happened to me. He'd taken the ring from the antechamber, knowing that if anyone found the wooden box in the bazaar, it could potentially lead them to the same magnificent discovery. And knowing who and what my mother was by then, he tried to keep Cleopatra safe from her clutches. But my mother found a way to Philae and had used me to access the artifacts.

A feeling of profound bitterness stole over me. I shook my head to get myself clear of it, holding on to the rest of the letter, and what my father was trying to tell me.

What had happened to him afterward? Dread piled high on my shoulders as realization dawned. My mother might have found him, and was holding him captive somewhere, or worse, she might have killed him. But maybe he was hiding, and even now, hoping I'd find him. I curled the letter in my palm, the last line searing itself into my mind like a scorching brand against my skin.

I would never stop looking for him.

"Inez?" Elvira asked. "Are you all right?"

I handed her the letter and jumped to my feet, thinking hard. I began pacing, waiting impatiently for her to read.

When she finished, she glanced up at me, a puzzled expression on her face. "I'm very confused."

Quickly, I explained to her what had happened since my first day in Cairo. The golden ring stolen by the wretched Mr. Sterling, the finding of the trinket box in old Cairo, and my having to sneak on board the *Elephantine*. I told her about my uncle, and how the magic had led me to the underground tunnels underneath Trajan's Kiosk, and then to the hidden staircase in the Temple of Isis. Last, I told her about my mother and what she'd done. Shame burned down my throat. The only person I didn't mention was Whit.

I was still too raw to even think about him, let alone speak of him.

She listened to everything without saying a word and when I finished, she leaned back against the chair and gnawed her lip. "So there's been a fair bit that's happened since leaving Buenos Aires."

A watery chuckle escaped me. "A bit."

"We need to go to the authorities," Elvira said. "Right now. Let's skip dinner and—"

I shook my head and her voice died down. "It's not an option. Remember Mr. Sterling? He's a prominent member of society and has connections in every level of government. I don't trust him. I can't trust anyone except for you and perhaps Whit—" I broke off, forgetting that I wasn't going to bring him up.

Elvira, of course, noticed my slipup. "Whit? Who is Whit? What kind of name *is* Whit?"

"His name is Whitford Hayes, and he works for Tío Ricardo," I said. "The brawny one you couldn't stop staring at who arrived with us."

"And you're on a first-name basis with him? My mother would be scandalized." She grinned. "I love this. Tell me more."

"We worked together." I had to wrangle the conversation back to sensible matters. "We've become friends, so please don't let your wild imagination run away from you. You're not Emma Woodhouse, despite what you may believe."

She waved her hand dismissively. "I'm telling you, were she real, we'd be the best of friends. It's my goal in life to romantically pair off at least one couple. Speaking of, what about my mother and your uncle?"

I made a face. "That's appalling."

"They are not related." She pulled at her lip, blinking fast. "I think my mother is terribly lonely."

It was hard to picture my aunt that way. She always seemed so impenetrable, a stronghold that would never crumble. "I think you should write your own love stories. You're a talented writer, Elvira."

Her eyes widened. "How would you know?"

I winked at her. "I know where the manuscript is hidden, darling." She pivoted, reaching for a throw pillow, and threw it at my head. It missed me by several feet. "As if you haven't read my diary!"

"I can't *believe* you read—" She broke off, panting. "Do you really think I'm talented?"

"Yes," I said, crossing the room to give her a tight hug. "The most talented. You need to finish the story, Elvira. Promise me."

Her eyes lost focus, as if she had wandered into a dream. "Would there be anything better than seeing one of my stories, bound up in leather, and sitting on a shelf in a bookshop?"

"I can think of nothing better," I whispered. "You *will* finish it."

"I promise." She stepped away. "Will *Whit* be at the ball?"

I nodded. "Please wipe that smug smile off your face. He has a fiancée."

"But he's not married yet," she said with a smile. "Maybe there's a kiss at midnight in your future."

I rolled my eyes. Whit would certainly never do that again. "I wouldn't get too excited; we haven't been invited. My uncle is permitting us to join him for dinner. Last I checked, dinner didn't mean dancing."

She blinked innocently at me. "Are you sure? Because if you are, then you're going to have to explain the invitation that I have in my possession." With a fluid motion, she revealed a small card on thick cover stock from the pocket of her day dress. Elvira presented it to me with a flourish.

I barely glanced at it. "You already know what you're going to wear, don't you?"

"Of course," she said. "I am my mother's daughter. I've also picked out something for you."

I stared at my cousin in helpless fascination as she rummaged through the trunk I'd left behind and then through hers. At last she produced a gown wrapped in tissue paper, which she laid out carefully on my bed.

"I didn't know what to pack, so I brought two of everything," she said. "I think this will look lovely on you."

I didn't disagree. Gold florals were stitched on the ivory silk, and cream lace covered the hem in delicate vines, as if rising from a forest floor. The shoulders were accentuated by soft pink tulle, creating a kind of cap sleeve that would gently flutter against my arms.

"Are you sure you don't want to wear this?"

Elvira smiled mischievously, and carefully unwrapped her own gown. I let out a laugh. Her gown was identical to mine, but instead of ivory, her silk looked the lightest shade of spun gold.

"We're going to look like twins," I said, laughing.

"You need a bath," she said, eyeing me critically. "I'll order one for you. And I recommended washing your hair twice."

The bathtub was in a small room adjoining my parents' former room, and once it was filled with hot water, I sank into it, sighing deeply. I loved every minute of living on Philae, but I wouldn't lie and say I hadn't missed modern conveniences. As my cousin recommended, I washed my hair twice with the rose-scented soap she'd brought from Argentina and then climbed out with clean hair and glowing skin—if a little sunburnt.

We got ready slowly, each of us helping the other with the infernal corsets and bustles, and the long trains of our dresses. My hair had finally dried by then and Elvira braided it and wrapped it high on my head, pinning it with pearl-studded clips. I helped pin her thick hair up using a lace ribbon.

Elvira lit a match and outlined her eyes, and I followed suit. We applied cream of roses to our skin, rendering it soft and dewy, and tinted beeswax on our lips. The routine settled me, reminding me of the countless balls we'd readied ourselves for together. We looked at ourselves in the mirror, and I turned to my cousin.

"Would Tía Lorena be ashamed of me?"

"Not even a little bit."

She linked her arm through mine and together we made our way down to meet my uncle.

My last night in Egypt.

WHIT

I snapped my leather trunk closed as a loud rap on my hotel door broke the solemn quiet, interrupting the running list in my mind in preparation for my departure. My ticket back to England had already been sent for, and I'd left instructions to burn my uniform the moment I left Shepheard's. I don't know why I hadn't done it yet. No, that was a lie.

It had everything to do with the general.

Another knock came. "Whit, I know you're there. Drowning in bourbon, most likely."

I opened the door to reveal Ricardo. "I haven't drunk anything in an age."

He grunted and pushed his way inside, turning to study the made-up room. Other than my uniform, I was leaving nothing of myself behind.

"I need you to do one more thing before you go," Ricardo said. "When do you leave?"

"Not for a couple of days," I said, shutting the door. "I have a few things to tie up."

Namely, the assurance that no one would follow me back to England. I'd made enemies in Cairo, and while their arms might not reach England, I still had scores to settle. Debts to pay.

Ricardo pulled out an envelope and handed it to me. "This should cover it, and then some."

Payment for services rendered. "What do you need me to do?"

"My sister absconded with hundreds of artifacts, and if she's smart—which we both know she is—then she'll want to sell quickly. The longer she has that kind of baggage, the riskier it is for her. I need you to find out if my sister is in Cairo."

"Jolly," I said dryly. "She will have gone underground—but I can ask around."

"Yes, I'm sure your Curator friends in The Company will be pleased to see you," he said, moving to the door.

"The ones who don't want to kill me, sure," I muttered. "My questions might arise notice in your direction."

"See that they don't. Whatever means necessary." He grabbed the doorknob and then half turned in my direction. "Don't lose yourself again, Whit."

I didn't have the heart to tell him that I was already lost. The minute I stepped foot back in England, Whitford would virtually disappear, to be replaced by my title. Then he left, shutting the door behind him with a measured click.

I sighed. One last hurrah.

I'd always loved Cairo's crowded streets. They offered an easy way to become invisible. An effective trait I needed in order to sneak into a certain building surrounded by opium dens and brothels. This part of town offered myriad forms of entertainment for tourists wanting something besides temples and tombs. My taste had run along similar pursuits before Ricardo found me, up to my ears in debt.

I crept up the crumbling side, digging my fingers into the grooves, and then heaved myself up and through an open window. If I knew Peter, he was holed up in the back room smoking hashish, delegating his duties to others while he enjoyed a long break from divvying up stolen artifacts.

The hallway stank of sweat and stale air, but it didn't slow me down as I peered into the rooms lining the corridor. A plume of smoke revealed the man I searched for. He sat, reposed and comfortable on a low banquette, surrounded by dusty pillows, his feet crossed on a worn and dirty Turkish rug. Tall stacks of crates were piled around the room, some labeled for Bulaq, but most weren't. I'd bet good money they were filled with trinkets, waiting to be fenced.

Egypt attracted all manner of opportunists. Peter Yardley, a fellow Englishman, worked as an antiquities officer and secretary to the consul general. But before he came to Egypt, he had worked as a mercenary, trading in secrets, drugs, and antiquities.

"Who goes there?"

I stepped into the room, and kicked the door shut. "Hello, Peter."

A soft chuckle reached my ears. "No one calls me that but you."

The smoke cleared, revealing Peter's slight frame. Deep hollows in his cheeks and bloodshot eyes displayed his exhaustion. His clothing hadn't seen a bar of soap in some time, reeking of sweat and hard liquor. An uncomfortable feeling bubbled under my skin. I hadn't looked so different not too long ago.

"You look terrible."

He grinned, and motioned for me to have a seat on a low chair across from him. I remained on my feet, conscious of the noise coming from the floor below. I counted three, perhaps four, different men working.

Peter's smile dimmed and his hand dropped. "I take it this isn't a strictly social call?"

I shook my head. There are Curators who provided illicit goods for

Tradesman's Gate. Peter ran one of the auctions, and when we used to play cards, he once told me he knew someone who knew someone who had inroads with a lady who often fenced stolen artifacts. I had relayed the information to Ricardo, and at the time, we'd wondered if it had been Lourdes. "Have you heard of any large shipments coming into Cairo recently?"

He sat back against a cushion, dark eyes narrowing. "There are always shipments coming in. Are you going to sit?"

"No."

"Then why don't you tell me where you've been these last few months. I never see you at the table anymore, Whit."

Because I couldn't stand playing cards, even if it was the best way to hear things.

"My luck ran out." I pulled out the envelope tucked deep in my jacket pocket and placed it on a round table that stood close to his elbow. "Speaking of, I believe this makes us square."

Peter fingered the corner of the envelope. "Here's an idea—why don't you keep this and come work for me? I never understood why you didn't before."

"I'm leaving Egypt."

"Shame."

"Everything comes to an end, eventually." I turned to go, and as I reached the door, I said half over my shoulder, "Careful at the warehouse in Bulaq, Peter."

"*Stop.*"

I froze underneath the frame. Slowly turned to face Peter, who had jumped to his feet, his hand gripping a pistol. "How did you know about the warehouses?"

"Lower your gun."

"Hayes," Peter said, cocking the gun. "*How?*"

I kicked the stack of crates closest to me. Bottles of whiskey and rum were perched on the top one, and they clanked loudly, but I pointed to the bottom two. Written on its side was the location of a warehouse close to the docks. "It's written right here, idiot."

"Aw, shit." Peter kept his weapon aimed at my chest. "I think you're going to have to sit down after all. We need to have a chat, you and me."

Without meaning to, I'd stumbled onto something I shouldn't have seen. "You're not going to shoot me, are you, Peter?" I asked softly.

"Not if you do what you're told. You really only have two options. It looks like you'll be working for me from now on. Unless you'd prefer the alternative, more dead option."

I laughed and shook my head. "Not bloody likely."

"Sit the hell do—"

I launched one of the bottles of whiskey straight at him. It spun and Peter instinctively fired. Glass shattered and the liquor splattered on the walls, soaking into the rug. The rich smell made my head spin. Peter was reloading his weapon, loudly yelling, but my revolver was already in my hand, thumb brushing against the initials that weren't mine.

Point, aim, shoot.

The force of the bullet snapped his head backward. Blood dripped from the hole between his brows, flanking his open mouth. He had been calling for the others, and there was no chance of my leaving alive. What was one more dead body?

I'd seen dozens.

I left without looking at the mess, the sounds of shouting from the ground floor in my wake.

CAPÍTULO TREINTA Y DOS

*E*verywhere I looked, something shimmered. Golden curtains that shone brightly in candlelight, paper flags with long ribbons that fluttered from the cool breeze wafting in from the open windows. The hotel was dressed in its holiday finest in preparation of the New Year. My uncle led us through the entrance to the decorated dining hall, where a waiter led us to our seats at a silver-clothed table. Persian carpets adorned the tiled floor, while the table displayed the finest china and cutlery and enormous bouquets of flowers. Elvira inspected everything with a well-trained eye, and it was only the slight widening of her gaze that betrayed her favorable impression.

We were joined by several other couples, the ladies in resplendent evening silk and satin gowns that glittered in the soft lighting, while the men wore fine pressed suits and tailored jackets, their formal dress dark and elegant.

My uncle showed up in a plain gray suit, stone-faced and thin-lipped. He hadn't bothered to comb his hair. If I weren't half-afraid of him, I would say the look suited him. He stood out in a sea of overly starched men, their hair slicked back from too much pomade. The stagnant air filled with a blend of expensive perfume and champagne and sweet blooms.

"That is a House of Worth gown," Elvira whispered as one lady sat across from me. "I would bet all of my money on it."

"You don't gamble, and you certainly don't have money," I whispered back.

"I've sent word to your mother," Tío Ricardo cut in, pouring acid on our conversation. "You're welcome."

Elvira colored slightly and managed a low *gracias*. She recovered quickly and changed the subject. "Señor Marqués, tell me all about your time in Philae."

I kicked my cousin underneath the table while my uncle looked coldly furious.

"Oh dear, what have I done now?" Elvira asked, wincing. "Are questions forbidden?"

"Don't bring up my uncle's work—" I hissed.

"You've been in Philae all this time?" one of the men asked from down the table. His accent was French. "But there's nothing there. It's an old holy site that's been thoroughly excavated by now, surely."

My uncle shrugged. "Everywhere else was taken."

The man nodded sagely, completely buying Tío Ricardo's nonchalance. "It's a pity my countrymen don't regard you more highly, I think."

"I've managed well under Monsieur Maspero," my uncle replied faintly. Then he turned toward me and said, "How do you find the menu, Inez?"

I glanced down and read a few lines, translating the French in my mind, my mouth watering. To start, a mushroom and onion soup, followed by a fresh salad featuring a medley of roasted vegetables. I particularly looked forward to the main dish, roasted lamb with a mint jelly sauce, accompanied by buttered asparagus and whipped, creamy potatoes.

"It looks wonderful," I said, knowing full well he'd only asked the question in order to turn the subject of conversation away from him. When the waiter came by, my uncle ordered wine for the three of us, and then proceeded to have a conversation with the gentleman on his right.

That was the last he spoke to either of us for the rest of the meal.

I didn't blame him for his anger, his frustration that I had believed so little in him. To think him capable of murder. I was disappointed in myself for having been taken in by my mother's lies.

If I couldn't forgive myself, then I certainly understood why my uncle couldn't forgive me.

But I regretted that he still wanted to send me back to Argentina, taking away my chance to make things right. A part of me knew that I'd carry that regret with me for the rest of my life.

---※---

The dancing began shortly after dinner, and incredibly, my cousin and I were never short on partners. As the clock drew closer to midnight, I was whisked off onto the dance floor, and twirled around in time with the band playing modern songs. Elvira danced with a tall blond gentleman who looked vaguely familiar. I lost sight of her several times, but we eventually found each other by the refreshment table, laden with bowls of lemonade and chilled white wine.

"That last one was a bore," Elvira said, limping toward me through the tight knit of ladies hovering by the dance floor. "He stepped on my toes. Twice."

"My last dance partner only spoke Dutch," I offered in commiseration. "He thought you were my twin."

Elvira laughed in between sips of lemonade. "We've heard that before." Her gaze flickered through the crowd. "There are so many foreigners here. I've had at least one American talk down at me."

I watched her closely, a smile already waiting on my mouth. "What did you do?"

She shrugged. "I insulted him sweetly in Spanish, and he thought I was complimenting him."

I laughed. "That's my girl."

Elvira's gaze widened. "Well, he's finally arrived."

Curious, I pivoted and searched the crowd for my uncle's familiar tall form and disheveled dark hair. I found him immediately, next to a broad-shouldered man with auburn hair and brawny arms. He wore black from head to toe, and it suited him. A dark knight with a heart of gold.

Whit.

"Doesn't he look as if he'd win a fistfight?" Her voice had taken on a dreamlike quality.

"I don't encourage violence," I said, my words coming out high-pitched.

Elvira raised her eyebrow.

Across the ballroom, Whit turned away from my uncle, his brows pulled into a tight frown. His blue gaze scanned the room until it landed on mine. We might have been the only two people in the room. With determined ease, he parted the crowd, his eyes never leaving my face.

"You are in so much trouble," Elvira whispered-yelled.

The man in question reached us, and inclined his head toward me, and then my cousin.

"Hello, Whit. Allow me to properly introduce my prima, Señorita Elvira Montenegro. Elvira, this is Whitford Hayes."

"Lord," he said with a slight smile. "Lord Whitford Hayes."

"You're a *lord*?" I asked, dumbfounded.

He inclined his head and then addressed my cousin. "You've been found. I meant to congratulate you earlier."

"Accepted," she said. "It's wonderful to meet you, *Lord* Hayes."

Whit's blue eyes flickered to mine, crinkling in amusement. I folded my arms across my chest, furious that he'd failed to mention that he was a *peer of the realm*. No wonder he had to rush home. His future wife was probably a duchess or a princess.

"And how do you know my cousin?" Elvira asked. "Why is she addressing you by your first name? Why haven't I heard anything about you?"

Whit regarded my cousin with a peculiar expression that was at turns amused, annoyed, and insulted. "We worked together," he began dryly. "She addresses me by my first name because she's earned it, *and*"—he slanted the annoyed look my way—"I don't know why she hasn't said anything about me. We're colleagues, so to speak."

I was not, under any circumstances, imagining the slight emphasis he'd placed on the word *colleague*.

"What game are you playing now, Whit?" I asked, unable to keep the anger from my voice.

"No game," Whit countered. "Only clearing the air. Dance with me."

"Was that a question?" Elvira asked. "I really don't think it was. Inez, would you mind clarifying if we're rooting for Mr. Hayes's pursuit?"

Before I could reply, Whit replied, "I'm here as a friend. I thought, at the very least, that's what we were."

"We are," I said quietly.

"How dull," Elvira added. "But I've just seen your uncle heading this way, and he doesn't look pleased. I suppose I'll have to ask *him* to dance now. You can thank me later with punch."

She disappeared in a wisp of tulle and lace, heading off my uncle's determined stride.

Whit ducked his head to look into my face. "Would you like to dance, Olivera?"

He held out his hand and I took it. In no world would I be able to refuse dancing with Whit. He pulled me close, and for the first time, I noticed that his eyes were ringed in a deep blue. His sun-drenched skin glowed golden in the candlelight. The music swelled, and Whit slid his hand down to the small of my back. I lifted my chin to look up into his face, and his warm breath danced across my cheeks.

"So, you're a lord."

Whit visibly weighed his response before coming to a decision. "My father is a marquess."

I frowned as he turned us round and round across the ballroom, nimbly guiding us through the other dancing couples. I didn't care that he had a title or that he came from money. I cared because it was another part of him he didn't want to share. He had so many secrets, and it pained me to know that I'd never uncover all of them. "Why have you never told me? I thought I would have *earned* that much."

"What would it have mattered?"

"I've made my life a mess," I said. "I've been vulnerable, and embarrassed and ashamed. My mother is a criminal, my father is probably dead. You've seen me at my worst. And I still don't know your name."

His arms tightened around me. "Yes, you do."

I shook my head. "Not the one that comes with your title."

"It's Somerset," he said softly, his breath brushing against my cheek. "But I never want you to call me that."

I forced myself not to loosen, not to melt into his hold. I didn't want to soften. I didn't want to break any more than I had already. I'd given him so much, and there were still parts of him that he held out of reach.

"Inez," he said. "I was trying to stay away from you, and I didn't want you to know me, or I you."

I narrowed my gaze to hide my disappointment. "So what's changed?"

He placed my hand on his heart. I felt its steady force under my fingers and I shivered. "Because I want one memory with you dancing. One thing that's mine before we part ways . . ."

Tension seeped out of my shoulders. His blues eyes were locked on mine, and I felt myself give a little. He stared at me with infinite tenderness, and it nearly broke me to know that he'd never have the chance to look at me that way again.

"One thing I can carry with me back home," he continued in a hush.

I swallowed hard, my resistance disappearing, and I drew closer.

His lips brushed against my temple. "I know it's selfish, and I hope you can forgive me for it."

This was one memory I wanted, too.

"Forgiven," I breathed.

Whit twirled me around the dance floor, holding me close, his minty and clean scent making my head spin. Couples swirled around us, whispering and gossiping, and counting down the minutes until the New Year. He released the tight hold around my waist, and backed a step away from me. "Thank you for the dance."

A familiar face came into my line of sight. The blood drained from my face. It'd been a month since I'd seen him, but I'd know him anywhere.

"Olivera? Inez, what's the matter?"

Whit's face swam in my vision, but I couldn't tear my attention away from the man coldly staring at my uncle dancing with Elvira. He clutched a flute of champagne, and Cleopatra's golden ring glinted from his littlest finger.

"It's Mr. Sterling," I whispered. "He's here and staring at my uncle. He looks furious."

Whit half turned his head, a casual gesture that didn't hide the sudden tension locking his jaw.

"Do you think he's part of The Company? The one that deals at Tradesman's Gate?"

"We suspect that he is," he whispered against my ear. "We've been trying to figure out a plan to track down your mother, but your uncle also wants me to steal the ring back."

At the front of the ballroom, the band changed songs, alerting everyone the countdown to midnight had begun.

"Why did my uncle send for you when we've already found Cleo—" I broke off when Whit aimed a pointed look in my direction. I quickly amended my statement, and in a more moderate tone continued with, "Why does my uncle want the ring back? He doesn't need it to find her."

He didn't, because he'd had *me*.

Whit remained silent, his arms folded tight across his chest. "Can you truly think of no reason why your uncle would want the ring back?"

It was the way he said it that made me realize what had been so obvious to my uncle. Mr. Sterling could use the ring to find Cleopatra's tomb himself. If he was part of The Company, then he had a way to find Cleopatra. If he ever found her tomb, what would become of her? Would she be allowed to stay in Egypt? Would her possessions adorn exhibits in foreign countries?

I didn't like to think of the probable outcome.

"It may not matter," I said slowly. "The magic might have transferred to him regardless. He wouldn't need the ring in order to find her tomb."

He shook his head. "I don't think so, because he would have gone to Philae by now. The magic makes that kind of transfer depending on the strength of the spell, or if it bloody wants to. Think of how many people might have handled the ring since the spell was cast. There could have been dozens before it was eventually put inside her tomb."

"And then my father, me, and, finally, Mr. Sterling," I listed. "So, how are you going to steal it? That piece of jewelry is jammed onto his finger."

"I have my methods."

My uncle would make sure my cousin and I were on the next available train to Alexandria, but before then, I wanted to do something to aid my uncle after everything I'd done. Papá had entrusted that ring to me, and Mr. Sterling had stolen it right off my finger. "Let me help you."

Whit shook his head. "I have contacts in the city who can assist me. You'd only get in the way, Inez. And besides . . . you're leaving."

"I can do something before then," I said desperately. "I made a mess and it's killing me that you both are having to clean it up and I won't even be *here*."

It was killing me that I would never know Papá's fate. I did not want to stop looking for him. How would I continue the search from another continent?

He stared at me steadily, and it struck me how tired he looked. Deep shadows marred the skin under his blue eyes. "There's nothing you can do. Think about Elvira. Would it be fair to spend your last couple of days here ignoring her? This isn't your problem anymore, Inez."

My gaze skittered to the ornate clock at the front of the ballroom. "Two minutes until midnight."

"So it is," he said. "This is goodbye."

The hand moved forward on the clock.

"One more minute," I breathed.

Whit was grim and serious as everyone around us clapped and cheered, the gentlemen throwing their hats, the ladies twirling their handkerchiefs in the air. I remained utterly motionless, trapped by Whit's incendiary stare. He slowly leaned forward and whispered, "Happy New Year, Inez."

"Feliz año nuevo, Whit."

The noise around us rose to a deafening crescendo as he softly brushed his lips against my cheek. Then he straightened, and melted into the riotous crowd.

CAPÍTULO TREINTA Y TRES

*E*lvira and I walked back up to our room, filled with the taste of champagne and the music lingering in our ears. With every step, the cracks in my heart deepened. One day, I'd have to put all the pieces back together.

But tonight there was no escaping my misery.

I was never going to see Whitford Hayes again.

"Did you kiss him?"

I blinked at her. "Surely you're not going to interrogate me after I've had too much to drink?"

"You look so sad," she said. "I thought he might be the reason why."

"Like I told you earlier, he's getting married." I cleared my dry throat. "I might ask if you kissed any of the men you danced with."

Her cheeks warmed. "I'm having morning tea out on the terrace with one of them."

My brows rose. "You'll need a chaperone."

"You're not serious," she said.

"Elvira."

She shrugged delicately. "Will I really need one? I'm in a different country—"

"Primarily filled with British people who have very similar rules regarding etiquette—just like Buenos Aires society. Many of whom travel to Argentina on business and leisure, I might add."

Elvira set her mouth at a mulish line. "You sound just like your mother." I froze, and she immediately slapped her palm against her mouth. "My mother. I meant to say *my mother*. Oh, Inez, I'm so sorry. Lo siento!" She reached for my hand and squeezed. "Forgive me?"

"It's all right," I said, despite the sudden drop in my stomach. Her words were like a slap to the face. I knew she hadn't meant it, but it still stung. "I'm ready for this night to be over."

We swept inside, our dresses wrinkled, hair disheveled, a pair of wilted flowers. Elvira dropped onto the couch, yawning hugely. I cast her an amused glanced as I took out my pins, freeing my wild hair, and strove for a light tone. "Elvira, at the risk of sounding like *your* mother, promise me that you'll wake me before your rendezvous. I'll accompany you . . . no, don't make that face. It *is* the proper, and safe, thing to do."

"All right, *all right*."

"Why is this so important to you?"

Elvira shifted in her seat, her eyes wide and pleading. "Inez, I've never been on my own before. I just want time to do something that's not on a schedule or approved by my mother. One day, I'll be married to a perfect stranger, very likely. Someone chosen for me. But tomorrow, I'll be spending time with someone I picked. Can't you understand?"

It was incredible how quickly we fell into similar patterns. Elvira would follow me anywhere, trust me to lead her on the grand adventure. And it was my responsibility to look out for her. To protect her from whatever scrape I'd landed us in. Like the time we got stuck in a tree when we were six years old, or the time I'd gotten us lost in the heart of downtown Buenos Aires. She trusted me to get us home in one piece.

But the minute we docked, our lives would be scheduled, and shepherded into a future my aunt approved of. These were the last moments of unencumbered freedom.

"I understand," I said. "Have your morning with the fellow." Then I swooped down and gave her a kiss on the cheek. "But I'm still going to be there. Don't forget to wash the soot off your face before bed."

Elvira rolled her eyes and then stood, helping me out of the tight confines of my evening dress. She pulled a little too tightly on the stays of my corset and I yelped. When I stood in my chemise, I returned the favor and then we both went into our separate rooms. Without my parents' things, the bedroom could have been anyone's.

I wasn't sure if that made me feel better or not.

⊱—✖—⊰

I awoke to the sound of loud knocking. I rubbed my eyes, gingerly sitting up in bed as the noise grew louder. With an incoherent sound of protest, I pushed aside the mosquito netting and climbed out of the bed and drew on my white dressing gown, stumbling out into the main room of our suite. The sharp knocking continued and I yanked open the door.

I hadn't expected to see Whit again.

He stood on the other side, his fist raised. He dropped his arm abruptly and sagged against the doorframe. "You're here."

I made a show of looking around. "Where else would I be?"

"I need to come in," Whit said.

I stepped aside to let him through and he closed the door behind him. He looked uncharacteristically frazzled, dressed in his usual button-down and khaki trousers, his worn boots laced up to mid calf, and yet there was a frantic pull to his expression. Eyes wild, breath coming out in short gasps, as if he'd run the whole way to my room. And then it hit me. What if he changed his mind about us? I licked my lips. "What are you doing here?"

"Is Elvira here?"

At first, I didn't understand the question. Then his words cut through the mental fog of fitful sleep. Dread pooled deep in my belly. "She *ought* to be."

Whit stood in the middle of the room, his hands deep in his pockets, a grim line to his mouth. "Go look, Inez."

I was already heading to the adjacent room, and when I opened the door, the empty bed stared back at me cheekily. A groan of exasperation escaped me. I had told her to wake me, to not go down without me. I spun around, my hands flying onto my hips.

"Where did you see her?" I demanded. "No doubt enjoying a pastry out on the terrace with her morning date—"

"Who?" Whit interrupted.

"The man she danced with. I didn't learn his name." My lips parted; I hadn't thought to ask. I had assumed I'd be with her for the rendezvous.

Whit was making a commendable effort to keep his attention trained on my face, but when I moved, the slide of my robe revealed the frilled hem of my nightgown. He turned away abruptly and sat down on the available chair, unoccupied by my parents' trunks.

"I didn't see her personally," he said, his voice grave and serious. "I went down to the lobby for coffee and the hotel clerk remarked that he saw someone who looked like you get into a carriage around eleven in the morning."

"She wouldn't have," I said. "She isn't stupid. There must be some mistake."

"Fine," Whit said. "Where is she?"

"I told you, taking tea out on the terrace."

"I didn't see her out there," Whit said gently.

A roar sounded off in my ears. "Let me get dressed."

"Please," Whit muttered.

I went to my room and shut the door behind, and quickly decided on a day dress in a light green and cream stripe, and realized that I had a problem. The dress would only fit with a corset and bustle, and while I could put on the latter, I couldn't do the former without assistance. I groaned. This day was already off to a terrible start. I opened the door and stuck my head out.

"Whit, you're my friend, aren't you?"

"Yes," came Whit's impatient reply. "What in God's name is taking you so long?"

No one felt the urgency of the moment more than I did. My mind raced with possibilities of where Elvira might be—because I *knew* she would never get in a stranger's carriage. "So you wouldn't mind cinching my corset for me?"

Whit dropped his head into his hands. "Damn it, Olivera."

I remained silent.

"I'll go find someone to help you," he said rather desperately, standing.

I shook my head. "That will take longer. Will you please just tie up my laces? It won't take a moment and then we'll never speak of it again."

Whit glared at me, and I waited patiently for him to see there was only one course of action available. He muttered a distinctly foul word under his breath and walked toward me, his blue eyes icy and fixed solely on my face. "Turn around," he said through gritted teeth.

I obeyed quietly, sensing that if I antagonized him further, he'd probably start bellowing. I was worried for Elvira, but for half a moment, I let myself smirk.

Whit's tone was deadly. "Stop smiling."

"I wasn't."

He tugged at the stays fiercely and my breath whooshed out of me. "You're a rotten liar." He worked quickly, his fingers accidentally brushing against my upper back.

"You've done this before," I remarked casually. "It's not an easy thing to figure out. Judging by how effectively—"

"Quiet," Whit snapped.

My grin returned.

"I'm done," he said, his breath tickling the back of my neck. "Go put on your gown—"

I turned around with an apologetic smile. "The dress has two dozen tiny buttons on the back. I'll need your help."

Whit's expression turned murderous. I quickly went and put on the bustle and then stepped into the dress, putting my arms through the sleeves. I came back out, wisely checking my amusement. Whit's expression hadn't changed. He walked around me and began buttoning me up.

"This dress is absolutely ridiculous."

"I agree with you. I'd much rather be wearing what you're dressed in."

Whit let out a snort. "Society would never let you be so progressive."

"Maybe not now," I said lightly, a delicious thrill skimming down my spine from the heat of his fingers I felt through the fabric. "But someday."

I had to remind myself that he had a betrothed.

Whit stepped away from me as if I were an open flame. "I've finished. Unless you'd also like me to brush your bloody hair and braid it for you?"

"Do you know how to—"

"*No.*"

I quickly braided it and followed him out of the room, trying to catch up to his long stride. We reached the lobby and briskly walked around, looking outside on the terrace and then the several alcoves in the adjacent rooms. Elvira wasn't in the dining hall, nor was she in the ballroom. The clock read close to noon.

"Whit," I said slowly, panic rising in a smothering wave. "Where is she?"

"Let's go speak with Sallam again," he said. "Try not to worry. She might have linked up with an old acquaintance."

"She knows no one here," I protested as he led me to the front desk. The lobby teemed with people and we had to skirt around them.

"Don't forget that Cairo has an extraordinary number of visitors this time of year," he said. "Look around, she might have seen an old friend."

Sallam greeted us with a smile. "Good afternoon, Mr. Hayes and Señorita Olivera. It's nice to see the two of you together. You've just missed Señor Marqués—he was off to a business meeting. I believe you're expected to join him? Shall I acquire a hackney cab for you?"

"Not at this moment," Whit said. "Can you tell us if you've seen Señorita Montenegro this morning?"

He blinked and stoked his graying beard. "Come to think of it, I thought I saw you, Señorita Olivera, getting into a carriage this morning, but wearing a different dress. It must have been your cousin, then."

I stood motionless, refusing to believe my cousin could have been so silly. "What kind of carriage? Did you see who she was with?"

Sallam shook his head. "It was only a quick glance, I'm afraid, but he bore the look of your uncle. Tall and broad shouldered. In fact, I assumed it was Ricardo."

"My uncle? Tío Ricardo took her somewhere?" I repeated, fear pricking my heart. Now I understood why she'd gotten into the carriage in the first place. She had known her companion. I turned to Whit. "What do we do? How do we find her?"

Whit placed a gentle hand on my arm, about to lead me away from the front desk, when Sallam said, "A message arrived for you this morning, Señorita Olivera." He rummaged through the cubbies and produced a small, square-shaped envelope. The handwriting looked vaguely familiar.

I took the note and thanked him, and followed Whit as I tore it open. There was a single sheet of paper inside, along with two tickets: one for a seat on the train leaving for Alexandria the next morning, and another for a steamship heading to Argentina. I impatiently yanked out the note and read the scant few lines.

Then I read it again, my heart beating wildly against my ribs as if it were a wild animal locked in a cage. I barely noticed Whit stopping and taking hold of the note.

He read it quickly and the strong line of his jaw locked. It might have been made of iron. "*Shit.*"

My pulse thundered, making me strangely light-headed. I barely recognized my surroundings as Whit took me back up the stairs, down the long corridor, and inside the room I shared with my cousin.

Elvira.

Elvira, who had been kidnapped.

"Give me the note," I demanded, rounding on Whit. "There's been some mistake."

He handed it back to me wordlessly, his eyes blazing as I lowered my gaze and read the lines again, written in a messy scrawl.

Dear Inez,

I'm afraid I had to take very drastic measures to ensure your safety. Elvira is lost to you, and while I'm sure you will never be able to forgive me, I do hope you'll understand in time. Perhaps when you have a daughter of your own.

You must leave Cairo tonight.

It will only be a matter of time before they've realized they've taken the wrong girl to the docks and come after you.

Lourdes

My hands shook as the note fell to the floor. My mother had sacrificed Elvira. The sister I never had. Her selfishness staggered me. Mamá only cared that they never find *what was most vulnerable.* Someone her associates could use against her. A weakness to exploit.

Me.

Whit bent and scooped it up, a thoughtful expression on his face.

"What is it?" I asked.

He shook his head. "Nothing, I—"

"Tell me." Panic clawed its talons into me. I couldn't imagine where my cousin could be in a town I barely knew. Some of my terror must have shown on my face because Whit bent his knees, his blue gaze now level with mine. I didn't try to hide my fear.

He was silent, clearly worrying about something.

"Tell me," I demanded again.

"I wondered if they meant the warehouses by the docks," he said slowly. "I know there's been smuggling activities there from when Ricardo had me snooping around to see what your mother was up to."

"Whit, I have to find a carriage. I'm going after her."

Whit rarely shouted but when he did, it made my ears ring. "Absolutely not!"

"They want *me*," I said. "Don't you understand? Read my mother's note again. She must have had one of her associates mark Elvira in some way. Last night, we wore nearly identical dresses. Anyone could have confused us." A horrifying thought struck me. "The man she was dancing with . . . he might be working with my mother . . ." My voice trailed off. I gripped the lapel of Whit's jacket. "She's in danger, but it ought to be me."

"So you're going to take her place?" Whit asked. "You could die."

I shook my head. "I don't think so. My mother will hear of what's happened, and she'll come for me. I'm her weakness. Look how far she went to warn me."

"Your *mother*? Don't be naive!" Whit shouted again. "Lourdes would allow your cousin to die. She probably killed your father and then lied to you about it. She's heartless and conniving and manipulative. Why do you think her enemies had to resort to kidnapping? She must have done something unforgivable, and they want whatever she *stole* in exchange for your life."

"You're talking about the artifacts."

His jaw locked. "I'd bet you every pound I have that she double-crossed them."

"My mother might let Elvira die for me, but I can't do that. I'm not my mother."

Whit gripped my arms, his face wild and desperate. "I won't let you do this."

"I don't answer to you."

"You don't answer to anyone, which is part of the issue," Whit snapped.

"I wasn't aware I had issues."

"Of course you do, everyone does."

"Well, then what are yours?" I asked. "Actually, don't bother. I know them."

"I'm sure that you do," he growled. "I haven't hidden them from you." He released me in frustration, and threaded his hand through his tousled hair. "We need to involve your uncle. He has to know about this."

"Fine," I said with a heavy sigh. "Go and leave a note for him at the front desk."

Relief loosened the fear etched across his face. He nodded and took my hand. "I promise we'll do everything we can to get her back."

I forced a smile. "I believe you."

Whit squeezed my hand and left, the door closing behind him with a quiet click. I counted to ten, and then followed him out, careful to keep my distance. My uncle would no doubt try to help my cousin, but it was *me* my mother's associates wanted. There was no way around that.

Out of the corner of my eye, I saw Whit stride to the front desk. I quickly darted across the lobby and then raced down the front terrace steps, my hand already high up in the air, summoning a cab.

Whit was wrong. My mother had bought me tickets to help me out of the country. She wouldn't want me to die, and no amount of money would change that. In my heart, I knew she cared enough about me to be a liability against her enemies.

I would bet my life on it.

CAPÍTULO TREINTA Y CUATRO

I arrived at the docks, the outline of the pyramids a dark smudge against the blackening sky. The hundreds of feluccas and dahabeeyahs gently swayed with the rhythm of the river. Behind me stood a stone-fronted building with a painted sign that had faded years before. Rats scrambled across the path as I drew closer to the lapping water. Locals chatted with tourists, advertising their services as pilots and navigators of the Nile.

I looked around uneasily. The warehouses lined the docks, a familiar stretch of buildings I remembered seeing from the last time I was in Bulaq. I had no way of knowing which one held my cousin. All of them appeared to be abandoned. Some even had broken windows. I walked toward the first in the line, nibbling on my lower lip. Because of the crowd, I felt relatively safe. Who was going to hurt me in front of all these people?

I tried not to imagine what Whit would say to that.

The door in front of the first warehouse was locked. I looked to the next entrance, and that one, too, had a long chain barring entry. I walked past three more entrances, rounding the corner and searching for a hint that my cousin might be hidden inside. Large stacks of empty crates and barrels littered my path, towering over me. The noise of the crowd by the docks fell to a soft hush as I drew farther away from the water. Each door I passed didn't permit entry.

Then, from the corner of my eye, I spotted movement. There were two men dressed in trousers and double-breasted jackets roaming a stretch of ground in front of one of the buildings. They were brawny, and talking quietly, standing several feet away from me, but routinely looking around.

I was about to call out to them when a stranger's hand clapped over my mouth. A strong hand wrapped around my waist and pulled me backward against a hard surface. I struggled, and aimed a kick backward. It connected to the man's shin.

"For fuck's sake, Inez," Whit hissed in my ear.

I immediately stopped struggling as he ducked us both behind a large stack of shipping crates.

"You are the most annoying human being I've ever had the displeasure to meet," Whit snarled. "I could strangle you myself."

"I have to do this," I said fiercely. "You didn't have to follow me."

"The hell I didn't." Whit took my hand, and attempted to drag me back the way I came, but I resisted.

"I'm not going!"

"What if I can't save you?" Whit asked, his eyes wild and in full-blown panic. "Please don't do this to me."

"I can't leave—"

"Let's go before they see us. They have men patrolling—"

The click of a loaded pistol sounded like a cannon blast.

"Whit!"

An assailant had crept behind us and aimed the barrel of a gun at the back of Whit's head. He smiled, blue eyes blazing, his teeth gleaming in the moonlight. Whit released me, and crouched, swinging his leg wide. The man tumbled to the ground and his gun went off, the sound reverberating in my ear. From far away, people screamed.

Whit leapt onto the man and threw a punch. The gun flew out of his hand, skittering against the floor. It landed with a loud clatter by my feet. I instinctively dropped to the soiled ground and grabbed it.

"Inez, run!" Whit yelled as the two men I'd seen earlier encircled him, their fists raised high. Whit ducked beneath the first jab, and blocked another with his forearm. He swung hard, hitting the side of one man's head, rattling teeth. "Inez," he shouted as he landed a kick at the second man, "I thought I told you"—Whit narrowly avoided the third man's right hook—"to run!"

"Watch out!" I yelled in terror, and without thinking, I swung up my arm and fired the pistol straight into the air. Whit didn't flinch but the other attacker did and he took advantage of the distraction by throwing another punch.

The third man jumped to his feet and pulled out a dagger and flung it at Whit, who narrowly stepped aside. The momentum sent the knife somersaulting through the air, sinking into one of the barrels.

Whit whipped his revolver from out of the holster and shot at the third man, who narrowly missed a shot to his stomach. The sound of a loaded pistol echoed in my ear. From the corner of my eye, I caught sight of a tiny hole and the sharp glint of silver metal aimed at my temple.

"Drop it," a man growled.

I dropped the weapon.

"Kick it away from you."

I did as he demanded.

Then, in a louder voice, my attacker yelled, "Stand up and stop fighting my men or your lady dies."

Whit stood, his face pale, chest heaving. Two of the men he'd fought were unconscious by his feet. "Take me instead."

"Whit! *No.*"

But he ignored me, staring fiercely at my attacker.

"Toss your gun to me," my attacker said.

Whit didn't hesitate. He tossed it, and it clattered at our feet, initials facing up. Tears burned in my eyes. He never told me who that gun belonged to, but I knew how much it meant to him.

"I'm here for Elvira. Please release her," I said quickly. "I'll come quietly but don't hurt her or my friend."

From behind me, a voice cut the air, sharp and familiar. "Bring them both on board."

The man holding the gun lunged at me, covering my nose and mouth with a dirty rag. The chemical scent made me gag, and my eyes watered. Dimly, I heard Whit let out a furious roar. I struggled against the viselike bands across my ribs but the edges of my vision blurred.

I blinked, and the world turned darker.

I shut my eyes and saw no more.

They had put me in a tomb.

The walls were jagged, the color of a tawny mountain cliff. The space was narrow and crowded by crates and barrels. A single candle illuminated a small stretch of space. I struggled, but my hands wouldn't move; something rough scraped the delicate skin around my wrists. My arms were pulled behind me, tight and uncomfortable.

"Whit?" I called.

"Here," he said, walking around the pile of crates stacked one on top of the other. His hands were bound behind him, too, and there was a bruise forming on his right cheek. Blood oozed from his lip.

"You're hurt," I said.

He dropped on his knees in front of me. "You've been out for hours," he said, his voice rough and urgent. "How do you feel?"

"Dizzy. Thirsty. But I think I'm all right. What did they do to me?"

"That rag was soaked in chloroform," he said, anger making his voice vibrate. "It was *dripping*. I was scared they'd given you too much."

"I'm fine," I said, inching forward so our knees could touch. "Do you have anything we can use in your pockets?"

"They took everything," he said bleakly. "The gun. Even the button."

I groaned. "Please tell me you have a knife hidden somewhere."

Whit grimly shook his head. "They found the one in my boot."

"Intrepid criminals," I said. "Have you seen Elvira?"

Again he shook his head. "It's the first thing I did after they placed us in here. I checked every part of this wretched tomb. No Elvira, or signs that she'd ever been in here."

A hard lump settled in my stomach. "Dios, I hope she's—" I broke off at the sound of footsteps approaching.

Four men appeared at the head of the tomb, still dressed in dark clothing and wearing black masks. The one in the middle looked familiar to me, but I couldn't place him. He was tall and narrow hipped. The other three might have fought Whit at the docks, because they were both limping slightly.

"Get up," the tall man said.

Shaking, I awkwardly got to my feet. Whit did the same, but the three men immediately gripped his arms, hauling him away from me.

Whit kicked and struggled, and was rewarded with a fist to the face. He doubled over, gasping. They rounded him, kicked his stomach, his ribs. His grunts of pain roared in my ears. One of them flashed a dagger and swiped at his arm bent over his face to protect his head. Blood gushed from the long, deep scratch.

"Stop," I yelled. "Stop it!"

"In order to avoid any further confusion, I'd like to know your name," the tall man said quietly. His voice sounded so familiar, the hair at the back of my neck rose. That night on Philae, it had been dark. His face had been hard to make out, but I remembered the blond hair shining like silver in the moonlight. And his low-pitched voice.

My throat was dry. I couldn't remember the last time I'd had anything to drink. "Inez Olivera."

"I see," he remarked, his tone polite. He might have been inquiring after my health. The hair on my arms stood on end. "So, it's not Elvira Montenegro? The other one insists that's *her* name, but she could be lying."

I shook my head, feeling sick. Since arriving in Egypt, I'd given my cousin's name on more than one occasion. Foolish, foolish mistake. "I'm the one you want. Please let Elvira go."

"Where is your mother?"

"I don't know."

He raised his hand and smacked me across the face. The sound reverberated in the tomb. I tasted blood in my mouth.

Whit used his elbow to slam the face of the one holding him down. He jumped to his feet, eyes feral. "Touch her again and I will end your miserable life."

"Do you think you're in any position to be issuing threats?" the tall man asked mildly. He jerked his head in the direction of his companion—who had a gun aimed at the level of my heart.

Whit stilled, scowling. And once again, the three men clutched at Whit.

The tall man returned his attention to me. "I'll ask again. Where is your mother?"

I licked my dry and cracked lips. "I don't know."

He hit me in the stomach and my breath wheezed out of me. I bent forward, tears gathering in my eyes. Whit howled, struggling anew.

"One more time," the tall man said quietly. "If you don't tell me where she is, I'll seal the tomb. Think carefully before you answer. Where is your mother?"

I thought about lying. A dozen probable locations were on the tip of my tongue and I only had to choose one far, far away—

"If I find out you've lied to me," he said in that same terrifying, quiet voice, "I'll shoot your cousin. Your mother, Inez?"

I straightened, and wiped the blood from my mouth using the fabric covering my shoulder. "I don't know."

The man's eyes shone in the candlelight. They were a warm brown, the color of well-worn leather.

"Suit yourself. But know this—your cousin will share your fate."

"Let her go!" I yelled. "She doesn't know anything, she's only just arrived. *Please*."

The tall man ignored me, while the other three released Whit. He slumped to the ground, his face battered and bruised. The sound of stone scraping against stone crashed around us, the room darkening inch by slow inch.

And then silence.

We were trapped.

CAPÍTULO TREINTA Y CINCO

I sunk next to Whit, tugging at my bindings, but there was no give. He mumbled against the packed dirt floor, lying on his side, his long legs drawn close to his chest. Slowly he opened his eyes. They were bloodshot.

"How bad are you hurt?"

"Bad," he wheezed.

"Can you sit up?"

"Not at the moment."

I slumped next to his knees, resting my arm on top of his thigh. He grunted in response. "They've sealed the entrance."

"I heard," he muttered. "Can you come closer?"

"Why?"

"I need to know what they've done to you."

Whit's voice was lethal, and the hair on the back of my neck stood on end. I leaned forward and he squinted up at me. His bloodshot gaze ran over every curve of my face, resting on my sore cheek. Rage radiated from him in widening ripples, charging the air around us.

He let out a foul curse.

The lone candle on one of the crates flickered ominously, casting moving shadows against the rock. If we could somehow cut free from the ropes, we might be able to find something practical to use inside one of the boxes or barrels. The walls seemed to press closer. A tight fist around my lungs. I knew we were in danger of losing light and air, but I didn't know how much time that left us. The image of a dwindling hourglass scored itself in my mind. Every time I blinked, the level of sand lowered.

"Would one of my hat pins be useful to pierce through the rope?"

He shook his head and slowly sat up, groaning. "I don't think so. What else do you have hidden in your hair?"

"Nothing else, I'm afraid."

Whit glanced down at his shoes. "I wish they hadn't found my blade."

"What are we going to do, Whit?" I asked softly. "How will we get out of this?"

"I might be able to wiggle out of the rope," he said. "I was awake when they tied the knot, and I kept my elbows apart when they secured it."

"I don't know what that means."

"There's a margin of slack," he explained, the muscles in his arms rippling as he worked on his bindings. "If I stretch and pull at the rope by moving my wrists, I can release some of the tension."

"That's a neat trick. Where did you learn it?"

A shadow of grief crossed his face, as if he'd walked under a rain cloud. "A friend taught me in case I were ever abducted."

"Have you been?"

A lock of hair fell over his forehead. I wanted to smooth it back. "Until now, no," he said.

"What happened to your friend?"

Whit paused for a hairsbreadth before continuing. "He died."

I wanted to press him more but his expression shuttered, and instinct told me to hold back. He fell silent as he continued to work on the rope, muttering one foul word after another. He wore none of his charming facade; instead I stared at someone who was no stranger to surviving. A seasoned fighter with none of the polish in a ballroom. We were far from the rules of society, from expectations and duty. This was the Whit I knew had existed all along, the one he had hidden because it showed him at his most vulnerable. The youngest son with a failed military career.

"Olivera," Whit whispered. "I think I've done it, by God."

He stood, the rope unraveling, and then he hunched down to untie my knots. I was dizzy with relief. "Gracias."

"Don't thank me just yet," he said, helping me to my feet. "We still have to find a way out of here." He looked down at the gash on his arm, staining his linen shirt. "But first, if you'll sacrifice your petticoat . . ."

I leaned down and ripped a long stretch of fabric. Whit took it from me and in one fluid movement, he used his teeth and left hand to wrap it around his wound, securing it into a makeshift bandage. He'd done it in less than a minute, as if he'd taken care of scrapes and knife stabbings a thousand times.

Whit clutched at his side as he walked to the entrance. I followed after him, knowing there was no way on Earth that we'd manage to roll the stone away with only our combined efforts. He must have come up with the same conclusion because he angrily turned away.

"Bastards," he snarled.

"Let's look through the crates," I suggested.

Whit took one stack and I took another. The first lid I lifted showed nothing inside. My throat tightened as I moved to the second and then the third with the same results.

"Nothing," Whit said.

"Me too."

We both looked at the barrels and then silently looked through them, too.

We came up empty.

The magnitude of our situation hit me full in the face and my knees gave out. Whit let out a sharp sound and rushed toward me, dropping onto the ground and pulling me into his lap. I didn't know I was crying until he wiped at the tears dripping down to my chin.

"Easy, Inez," he whispered. "I have you."

I leaned against him and he wrapped his arms around me. I breathed in his scent, mingled with sweat and blood, and it felt so real to me. He was full of strength and vitality and *life* and in a matter of hours, all that energy would be taken from him. I couldn't stand it.

"I think we're doomed," I murmured against his chest. "Have you come to the same conclusion?"

His arms tightened around me.

Minutes passed, the only noise in the tomb coming from our quiet breaths mingling together in the dark.

"You asked me once why I was dishonorably discharged."

I lifted my head. "And you're finally going to tell me now that we're going to die?"

"Sweetheart, do you want to hear this or not?"

I laid my head back down, the endearment working like a balm. Whit removed my hairpin and plucked my hat off my head. He cast it aside.

"I was stationed at Khartoum," he began. "Under General Charles George Gordon. Do you know who that is?"

I shook my head. "Is that who the gun belongs to?"

Whit nodded. "The bastards stole it from me." His fingers crept up and he smoothed my curls away from my face. "He had an impossible task," he continued. "The Mahdis were fast approaching, intending to take control over the city, but Gordon held his ground. Britain ordered him to evacuate, but he wouldn't, and instead he sent women, children, and the sick up into Egypt to escape from the attacks on Khartoum. All told, over two thousand five hundred people were removed from the city and into safety. Over time, the surrounding British-occupied cities surrendered to the Mahdis, and Khartoum was left isolated and vulnerable."

I lifted my head and pulled away far enough so I could stare at Whit's face as he recounted his tale.

"Gordon continued to hold the city, refusing to leave. He forced me to meet the rescue mission he knew was coming, and to help guide them back to the city. I went kicking and screaming, and eventually met up with the British officers attempting to navigate the Nile." His mouth twisted into distaste. "The head of the relief force, Wolesley, decided to hire *Canadians* instead of Egyptians to pilot the river, and wasted *months* waiting for them to arrive all the way from *North America*."

He clenched his fists against my thigh.

I gently prodded, not wanting him to lock up. "What happened then, Whit?"

"I told them I would go up ahead on my own," Whit said softly. "But Wolesley refused. Forbade me from coming to General Gordon's defense.

So, I disobeyed the Crown, and snuck away from camp. Made the trek up the Nile on my own. Traveled through where the fighting had left bones. Humans, horses, camels. All sizes. What a waste of life." His voice dropped to an anguished whisper. "I went as fast as I could, but in the end it didn't matter. I arrived two days too late. The Mahdis beheaded General Gordon on the palace steps. A week later, I was dishonorably discharged for desertion."

He lifted his head, his blue eyes shining with an unholy light. "I would have made the same decision. I only wish I would have done it earlier. Maybe I could have helped him, saved him."

For a year, he'd been carrying the guilt of something that wasn't his. It had burdened him when it wasn't his to own. I understood why he hid behind a mask that tried to convince everyone that he didn't care about the world or what happened to it. I wanted to take off the weight as if it were a tangible thing, just so he could be free to let himself *feel* again. "He would have stayed behind, regardless of if you were there, Whit."

"I wasn't there when he needed me."

"You went to get help," I said. "He knew you would have done anything to help him. You *did* everything you could—to your own detriment." I caressed the hollow of his throat. I knew what it cost him, to reveal something that he felt tremendous shame about. Something he would have carried alone. "I think you're more decent than you think. Practically a hero."

"The military judge didn't think so."

"I don't care what he thinks." I softened my voice. "Thank you for telling me."

"Well, I wouldn't have, if it weren't near certain that we're doomed."

I shook my head. That was part of the reason. Maybe I would have believed him before, but he'd told me a story to slow the ebb of panic that threatened to swallow me whole. "You said it to comfort me."

"Yes." He swallowed hard. "And I wanted someone to know the truth."

"I never thought it would end this way," I whispered. "Whit, at some point they'll have to contact my mother. When she hears about what they've done, she'll come running."

He didn't reply. He didn't have to. I knew he didn't believe me.

"She'll be here. If she didn't care about me, she would have never sent me those tickets and warned me. I'm her weakness, remember? Her vulnerable underbelly."

"We're talking about a lot of money, Olivera."

"She'll come. You'll see."

Whit gave me a sad smile. My bottom lip wobbled, and Whit immediately reached forward, softly dragging his thumb across it. "*Don't.*"

Warmth filled my belly, and for the first time I was aware of our proximity, my weight on his long legs, the strength of his arms enveloping me, the tantalizing brush of his breath against my brow. We were both still, as if recognizing the danger of moving, how it might shatter the spell. My pulse jumped as our eyes locked. He regarded me with a gentle look, one I'd never seen, one I didn't think he was capable of. I gave in to the impulse I'd been fighting and smoothed the errant lock of hair from his brow. He shut his eyes against the caress, his breath catching.

When he opened them next, his expression blazed in sudden decision.

"Inez," he whispered slowly. "You'll have to forgive me for what I do next."

The moment his mouth covered mine, every thought, every worry fled from my mind. He tugged me closer, his arms digging into my lower back. One hand glided upward, holding the back of my head, threading his fingers through my messy hair. He kissed me deeper, and I melted against him. I swept my hands across the width of his shoulders and he shivered under my touch. He coaxed my mouth to open, touched his tongue to mine in a delicious sweep. I moaned, and he caught the sound, holding me tighter. A sharp tug pulled, deep in my belly, as I shifted to get closer. He made an approving noise at the back of his throat, and his hands cupped my rear, and he pulled me against him.

My eyes flew open when I felt how much he wanted me.

Whit pulled away enough to read my expression, a tender smile bending his mouth. I was flushed, my blood pitched to feverish heights.

"I've never had a friend like you," he said. "That day on the dock, you walked away from me, leaving behind almost everything you owned with the most insufferable smirk on your face. My God, you surprised the hell out of me." He kissed me, pulling my bottom lip into his mouth. "When you made me run after your bloody carriage, I couldn't believe you had that much nerve."

I laughed, and he kissed me again. He drew me close, and he palmed my breast, his thumb brushing across sensitive skin over my shirt, and I shivered.

"Do you kiss all of your friends like this?" I asked, breathless.

"Did you know you taste like roses?" he whispered against my lips.

I shook my head, dizzy from his touch, the strength of his arms wrapped tight around me. The hard plane of his chest made me feel safe, as if he'd protect me from whatever happened next. I kissed him, knowing there'd never be another chance. I kissed him, knowing it would be the last.

The flame of the candle went out.

We froze, our breaths mingling together in the dark. Whit wrapped both arms around me, our chests pressed so close together not even a secret could pass through. A sob worked its way up my throat, coming out in a muffled gasp. Tears dripped down my face, and Whit kissed each one.

"Is this it, Whit?" I whispered.

He squeezed me and pressed his lips against mine lightly. "If it is, this is where I want to be."

We were fused together in the pitch black. Whit idly dragged his palm up and down my back, and the only sound came from our soft breathing and the scuttling of some insect across the stone. We traded kisses in the deep shadows, distracting me from the terror inching closer as the hours dragged, minute by slow minute. I lost all sense of time. In my whole life, I'd never known such darkness. It was cold and infinite.

A muffled sound came from the entrance.

I turned my head, my pulse leaping in my throat. "Did you hear that?"

Whit hauled us to our feet and we felt our way to the stone barring the exit. "Who's there?" he called.

Another muffled shout from the other side. I looked at Whit and smiled, relief sinking in my bones so fully, I almost crashed to the ground. "It's Mamá!"

Whit shook his head uncertainly. "I don't think so."

"I know it's her. I told you she would come."

Whit furrowed his brow, and pressed closer to the entrance, angling his ear nearer and listening intently. I crept forward but he neatly maneuvered me behind him. A loud noise sparked from without. Whit pivoted and threw his arms around me, pushing me backward and behind one of the stacks of crates.

The blast enveloped us.

CAPÍTULO TREINTA Y SEIS

A horrible ringing sounded in my ear, persistent like a buzzing mosquito. Whit's arms bracketed my head, his long body shielding me from the barrage of rocks and pebbles scattering around us. He flinched and I reached up and touched the side of his face. He leaned into my hand, his eyes clenched tight.

Gingerly, he lifted himself off me, his jaw locked, his expression pinched.

"Whit, are you all right?"

He grunted.

I sat up and crawled toward him, trying to see where he'd been hurt. Gently, I placed his head in my lap. A figure drew close. My palms were covered in sweat, trembling. My mother had come for me. She had made it in time.

"¿Mamá?" I croaked. "¡Mamá!"

"It's not"—Whit coughed—"your"—another cough—"mother."

The figure rushed forward. I turned my head to meet the dusty face of Tío Ricardo. He stood over us, panting, a gun in his hand. Sand covered him from head to foot. He'd lost his hat at some point. My uncle stared down at me with an unfathomable expression on his face, hard and unblinking.

As if he weren't seeing me at all.

My mother hadn't come. A sob worked its way up my throat. I wasn't her weakness after all.

"*Inez*," my uncle breathed. "*Inez*."

Whit hauled us both to our feet, swaying slightly.

Tío Ricardo stepped forward and helped steady him with his free hand. In the other, he held a pistol. "How bad are you hurt?"

"Some bruising, I'd guess," Whit gasped, eyes watering. "Nothing broken. I can walk . . . or run if you *really* need me to."

"I really need you to. They will have heard the blast. We have to go right now before they return."

We followed him, my heart beating wildly against my ribs. We ran through a tunnel, the walls close, holding memories from centuries past. Whit stayed at my side, gripping my hand and helping me navigate the debris littering the ground. None of this looked familiar.

"Where are we?"

"The Valley of the Kings," Tío Ricardo tossed over his shoulder, picking his way through the rubble. We emerged in sunlight. I blinked, waiting for my eyes to readjust to the hot glare. Tío Ricardo immediately began the descent to the bottom of the stony hill, covered in dry sand and sharp boulders. I looked behind me, startled to find an immense rocky cliff rising up from the desert floor. We'd come out of a tunnel that had led to the tomb, hidden deep in the limestone. There were several gaping holes dotting the facade of the mountain and I stopped, my gaze narrowing. My cousin might be trapped in one of the tombs.

"Hurry," Tío Ricardo yelled. He'd reached the bottom and turned, glaring up at us where we stood at the top of the switchback.

"No," I yelled down. "We can't leave without Elvira. She's here somewhere—"

A gunshot rang out.

I let out a terrible scream as my uncle was catapulted off his feet and flung backward. Blood bloomed on his left arm. I ran down the pebbled slope of the hill, and tripped over my long skirt.

Whit was next to me in an instant, and dragged me up to my feet. I shrugged him off and kept moving, and then I fell again onto my knees next to my uncle's prone body.

"¡Tío!"

He blinked up at me, his eyes dazed and out of focus. I ripped the hem of my skirt and pressed the fabric against his wound.

"*Shit*," Whit said, bending to pick up my uncle's pistol. "Here they come."

Four men approached on horseback, the sound roaring in the valley. They formed a half circle around us, one man pulling at the reins of his horse, looking down at me in cold fury. I wouldn't have recognized him. He wore dark clothing, his hair slicked back with too much pomade. He'd removed the spectacles and foppish smile.

The American businessman who shyly asked me to dinner and delivered me mail.

Mr. Burton.

His associates, including the tall blond man, had their weapons already drawn and aimed at every one of us.

"Mr. Hayes, please do me the honor of lowering your gun," Mr. Burton said. "Good, now kick it away from you. Any more tricks up your sleeve? Knives and that sort of thing? No? Fine."

Then Mr. Burton turned his attention to me. The force of his cold fury nearly knocked me over.

"Stand up and away from Ricardo, Inez," he said, his voice devoid of any warmth. He dismounted on the left side of his horse, and his companions followed suit, their guns still trained on us.

I recognized the burly man, the mean line of muscle that corded his arms. The other two, the tall blond and the other with a thick beard, drew near Whit. One of them held Whit's revolver, the general's initials carved along the side.

"If you can keep your hands up, I'd be most grateful," Mr. Burton said. Whit complied with a grimace.

"What is this?" I asked.

"Stand up, Inez," Mr. Burton said. "And move away from your uncle."

"But he's hurt. Please, let me help him."

"I wasn't aware you were a physician," Mr. Burton said coldly. He pulled out his pistol and aimed it at my heart. "I won't repeat myself. Stand up."

"Stand up, Olivera," Whit said, his face paling.

I prepared to stand but my uncle gripped my wrist. His eyes widened slightly, and then flicked downward, toward his necktie. Without stopping to think, I pulled at the knot, and it loosened. I stood, slipping the fabric off his neck, and quickly stuffed it inside the pocket of my dress.

I stepped away from my uncle, thinking fast. It wasn't a weapon but it was something.

"Bring the girl," Mr. Burton said to the burly man. He brushed past, knocking into my shoulder. I teetered on my feet, and barely managed to stay upright.

Whit swung around, snarling. The burly man laughed, and disappeared into one of the tunnels visible on the rocky surface.

"It seems burying you alive wasn't enough of a motivator," Mr. Burton said.

"What do you want?" I exploded.

"I want the artifacts your mother stole from me. I want to know where she went. You both worked together on Philae; she clearly trusted you."

"She left me behind, and took the treasure. I don't know where she went. The last person who saw her is that tall gentleman standing next to you."

"The bitch double-crossed us the minute we arrived in Cairo," the blond spat out.

Mr. Burton cocked his gun, and Whit immediately stood in front of me. "Lower it," he growled. "She's telling you the truth. She doesn't know her mother's whereabouts."

"Oh, I believe her *now*," Mr. Burton said. "But fortunately my plan worked to draw forward the person who knows the answer to my question." He pointed to my uncle. "The bullet grazed him, sit him up."

Two of Mr. Burton's companions dismounted and strode to Ricardo and dragged him up to his knees. Blood stained his cotton shirt, and he flinched at the rough movement.

"We'll wait a moment until we're all together," Mr. Burton said.

Whit's gaze flickered from Mr. Burton to the rest of the men surrounding us. His shoulders were tense, hands clenched into a fist. The burly man appeared at the head of the tunnel, a slight figure hunched by his side. I gasped, and started to move forward—

"Make sure she doesn't go anywhere, Mr. Hunt, if you please," Mr. Burton said.

One of the men propping up Ricardo darted toward me, but Whit intercepted him. "Stand back."

I immediately stopped out of terror for Whit. I didn't like the way Mr. Burton's goons sized him up, as if he were disposable. Mr. Burton eyed me shrewdly, and I looked away, furious that I had given away my feelings for Whit.

The burly man approached, dragging Elvira down the side of the rocky hill. A bruise marred her cheek and her eyes were red-rimmed, as if she'd been crying. Someone had gagged her with a thick rope. The material had rubbed her skin raw. Fury bubbled in my veins, threatening to spill over, but Mr. Burton still had his weapon aimed straight at me.

"Elvira," I said raggedly.

She met my gaze. In the span of twenty-four hours, she'd lost something vital. The ability to look at the world and see promise. Now she looked at the world and it scared her. I wanted to tell her that it would be all right, but I didn't want to lie to her.

"Where is your sister?" Mr. Burton turned toward my uncle. "You know her better than anyone."

The words came out slowly, each one pulled out of my uncle as if with pliers. "Not as well as I thought."

"You suspected her involvement with The Company," Mr. Burton said. "And I know you followed her to the warehouse, Mr. Hayes. Where could she have gone? Because she's not in Cairo."

My uncle flinched. Something had clearly occurred to him.

"Tell me," Mr. Burton said.

"I will once you release my nieces, and Whit. They have nothing to do with this."

Mr. Burton narrowed his gaze. "Seems highly unlikely."

"It's the truth."

There was a long pause while Mr. Burton and my uncle stared at each other in silence.

"Do you know what I think?" he asked softly. "I think you know how much money you can make by hoarding all of the treasures yourself. You want what Lourdes stole as much as I do."

"First," Tío Ricardo said, somehow still managing to sound disgusted while panting, "they aren't treasures, they are objects with historical significance to Egyptians—"

Mr. Burton sliced the air with his hand. "I don't give a damn. Believe me when I tell you that you'd much rather deal with me than with my associate. He won't take your refusal as kindly as I have done."

I blinked at the revelation. "There's someone else?"

"Everyone works for someone, my dear," Mr. Burton said. "Ricardo. The location."

"Release them first."

Mr. Burton had a manic gleam glowing in his eyes. He waved the gun, first at Elvira and then at Whit. "Are you really going to let them die?"

My mind was still unable to connect how this man was the same foppish, kind gentleman who had delivered our mail, who had asked me to dinner. They couldn't be the same, and yet they were. Mr. Burton beckoned the burly man with his index finger, and Elvira was dragged forward, squirming.

Mr. Burton said, "I will shoot her."

"Boss said not to harm the girl," the burly man said uneasily.

Elvira flinched as Mr. Burton caressed her cheek. "So he did. But that was before he knew we had the spare."

I gasped as if I'd been kicked in the stomach.

"Thomas," Tío Ricardo said coaxingly. "I'll tell you once—"

Mr. Burton lifted his weapon to Elvira's temple. She yelled, the sound low and muffled, full of horror. Time seemed to stall as her head swung in my direction, her eyes wide with terror meeting mine. My heart wrenched in my chest. In an instant, memories assailed me. One after another.

Elvira on her sixteenth birthday, standing in the middle of my mother's garden, for once still and patient as I painted her writing in her journal.

A blink, and I was nine years old at the dinner table, and she was sneakily eating the boiled carrots off my plate because she knew I hated them, and I'd get in trouble for not finishing every last bite.

Another blink, and Elvira was sitting close to my side the night I'd read my uncle's letter for the first time. She'd hugged me while I cried myself to sleep.

I blinked again, and I was back in the desert, and the horrifying sight assaulted my vision once more. The barrel of the gun pressed close to her temple.

My uncle and I spoke at once.

"Wait, *no*," I said. "Por favor, no—"

"Stop! I'll tell you—"

Whit lunged forward.

Mr. Burton fired. The sound carried to every corner of my body, filled me with so much despair, I screamed.

And screamed.

And screamed.

Blood and bone splattered across my face. Elvira slumped to the ground in a pool of red. Tears stabbed my eyes as I rushed to her side, my vision blurred and tinted red. Anger inflamed my blood. Her beautiful face was unrecognizable. Destroyed in a second. Her life snuffed out from one moment to the next.

I gripped my hair, unable to keep quiet. Unable to stop screaming. Grief distracted me. I didn't realize the danger I was in until I caught the scent of Mr. Burton's expensive cologne. He knelt beside me, his gun cocked and ready, aimed for my heart.

The bullet would shatter it. I'd never survive.

Whit turned his anguished face toward me. Despair carved deep lines across his brow. I moved my hand, my fingers hovering above my pocket.

"Ricardo," Mr. Burton murmured, his attention on my uncle. "She's next. The location? And you better not lie."

Slowly, I pulled out my uncle's necktie. Whit tracked my movement. I met his gaze and he subtly dipped his chin.

"Por favor," Ricardo said, his voice hoarse. "I can only make a guess."

"Fine," Mr. Burton said. "Let's have your guess, then."

"I think she could be in Amarna," my uncle said.

"Why?" Mr. Burton asked, his voice cold.

"She might be after a hidden tomb," he said. When Mr. Burton didn't lower his gun, my uncle added quickly, "Nefertiti."

"Nefertiti," Mr. Burton repeated. "Was she the one—"

I wrung out the necktie at Mr. Burton's face, scalding water covering his brow and cheeks and eyes. He fell back, screaming, covering his face with his hands. Boiling water dropped to the ground, sizzling on the hot sand. I whipped the fabric again and more water flung in his direction, drenching his dark pants and shirt. Behind me, the sounds of fighting reached my ears: fists smacking flesh and bone, grunts and muffled cursing. I turned around in time to see Whit throw a punch at one of the men.

The burly man approached Whit, his gun raised—

"Watch out!" I cried.

Whit dropped as the shot zipped past his head. His hand reached for the rifle and he flipped onto his back and fired at the burly man's stomach. The man dropped hard and heavy to the sand. I swayed on my feet, the scent of metal thick in the air. Sweat dripped down my back. I tried not to look at Elvira's still form, her yellow dress bunched around her thighs.

"You bitch," came a gargled voice.

Mr. Burton yanked me backward, pressed me close to his damp chest. He clapped a hand hard across my mouth. His skin was blotchy and red, angry blisters forming up and down his arm. Whit jumped to his feet, lifting the rifle at eye level, and peered through the peep sight. In a blur of motion, he slid the gun forward and back, and fired.

The sound deafened me for one long, terrifying moment. A burst of wind brushed against the side of my face.

Mr. Burton flew backward.

I turned to find him on the ground, spread-eagled, a single gaping hole between his brows.

"I warned you," Whit said coldly. Then he raced forward and pulled me into a tight embrace. "Are you all right?"

I didn't know how to answer that question. My words came out hushed. "I'm not hurt."

But I wasn't all right.

CAPÍTULO TREINTA Y SIETE

I stood in the balcony of my parents' suite, the moonlight casting the city of a thousand minarets in a silver glow. I had cried myself to sleep. I had a nightmare and cried again. I woke up, and knew there were hours yet until the dawn.

Grief refused me sleep.

The night had turned cold. Winter had settled over the land, and a chill skimmed down my spine and I shivered. I turned away, closed the doors behind me with shaking hands. The bedroom seemed too far away for another step, and so I sank onto the couch. The trinket box rested on the wooden coffee table. Absently, I leaned forward and cradled it in the palm of my hands.

A memory crashed into me. The worst one yet.

Cleopatra's quarters turned upside down by Roman soldiers. The ingredients for her spells destroyed and burned. Bottles of tonics emptied and dumped out the window. Her power stripped away as she faced the emperor, her maids crying in horror.

Her emotions flooded me. Rage. Despair. Sorrow to have lost everything.

The desire to be left alone in peace with her lover.

I blinked and the moment passed, the memory vanishing like mist. The quiet in the room thundered in my ears. I had finally left my uncle to rest, but energy curled tight under my skin.

I wanted to hunt my mother down.

Wherever she was, I would find her. She would pay for what she stole from me.

My uncle slept like the dead. I'd tried to make him comfortable, pulling the bedding up under his chin, but he'd restlessly shoved them off in his feverish sleep. I sat in a chair by his bed at Shepheard's. His room was disorderly and crowded with books and rolled-up maps, several trunks and clothing heaped into piles around the floor.

My mind was full of blood.

No matter how long I sat in the bathtub that morning, I couldn't rid myself of the sand crusted under my nails, embedded in my ears and hair. I couldn't get clean enough. I couldn't scrub the image of Elvira's face from flashing across my mind. The despair on her face right before she died.

Her death was *my* fault.

She'd come after me, followed me, and I'd failed to protect her. How could I ever forgive myself? She ought never to have gotten involved in my mess. She trusted me to look after her. I should have barred the door so she couldn't have left my hotel room. I ought to have woken up before her and anticipated her doomed decision to go down to the lobby.

I ought to have known what my mother was.

But I hadn't, and she was gone.

I pressed my palm against my mouth, trying to keep myself from crying out. I didn't want to wake my uncle. I slumped against the seat and tried to keep my eyes open. I hadn't slept or eaten anything in . . . oh, I had no idea.

One day turned into another and then on the second day, my uncle finally opened his eyes. He stared unblinking in the dimly lit room. Whit had come in earlier, and he'd sat with me while I hovered over my uncle, wiping his brow with cloths that I'd dipped in cool water.

"Hola, Tío." I stood and went and sat by his side on the bed. "How do you feel?"

"What happened?"

"You were treated in Thebes and then brought back to the hotel in Cairo. The local authorities arrested the men who kidnapped us. Whit and I had to"—my voice broke—"leave Elvira in a cemetery in Thebes. I didn't know what else to do with . . . her body. They told me that I could always move her coffin wherever it needed to go. I suppose that means Argentina. My aunt will want to have her close."

Whit stood and laid a hand on my shoulder, his thumb drawing circles.

My uncle regarded me with a tender and grief-stricken expression. "I'm so sorry, Inez. I never meant for any of this to happen."

I met his gaze squarely. "I want to know all of it. I deserve the truth."

He nodded, his throat working hard. "I've been excavating alongside Abdullah for a little over two decades. Your mother began acting strange early on. She claimed to be bored at the dig sites, so she stayed behind in Cairo, finding her own amusements. She started lying to me, became obsessed with searching for alchemical documents, of all things."

My eyes flickered to Whit, but his expression revealed nothing of his thoughts. My uncle continued with his account. "As the years went on, she'd make excuses and not join us at all at various dig sites. Your father grew concerned, but he loved what he was doing and so turned a blind eye to her behavior. Cayo was always too passive when it came to my sister."

"Go on," I said. "What happened next?"

My uncle lowered his eyes. "During this last season, your father and I had to come back to Cairo unexpectedly. When I was on my way to a meeting with Maspero, I saw your mother with a group of men who I knew to be Curators for The Company, thanks to Whit's sleuthing. I tried to warn her, but she refused to listen. I think that was when your father suspected she was having an affair. Your father started acting strange, hiding things from me, not trusting me."

Whit moved away from me and sat on the bed next to my uncle. He replaced the washcloth across Tío Ricardo's brow with another.

"When he might have found Cleopatra's tomb," I said, "did he mail something for me from Philae?"

Tío Ricardo nodded. "Yes, I think so. We had a lot of tourists coming and going on the island. He would have had opportunity."

I nodded. "There's something I still don't understand. Why didn't Papá come to you? Why were you angry with him?"

"I campaigned hard for Cayo to forgive your mother for the affair,"

Ricardo said quietly. "The scandal would have destroyed Lourdes, and I still thought I could help her. We argued constantly, to the point where he became paranoid, believing I was involved with her schemes."

I licked my lips. "He didn't trust you. That's why he sent me the ring."

"I believe so."

"What happened then?"

"Your parents left. In all likelihood back to Cairo. That was the last I'd seen of them."

"Where my father *presumably* died," I said.

"Why presumably?" Whit asked.

"Because my mother is a liar," I said. The last line of his letter to me was seared into my mind. *Please never stop looking for me.* I would not let him down. "What if my father is alive somewhere? He could be kept anywhere."

"Olivera," Whit said softly, his eyes kind and full of sympathy.

"He might be alive," I insisted. I turned away from him, wanting to hold on to hope that my father still lived. It was foolish. It was almost impossible. But it could be true. "Tell me the rest of it, Tío."

"When your parents didn't come back for weeks, when my letters were unanswered, I left Philae and came back here." Tears gathered at the corners of his eyes. "Inez, I searched everywhere for them, but they'd disappeared. No one knew where your parents were. I feared The Company might have murdered them both. After weeks of searching, I had to come up with a plausible story for their absence."

"Which is when you wrote to me."

He nodded sadly.

"Meanwhile, my mother was preparing to frame you for my father's alleged murder. She left behind a letter for someone to find, addressed to Monsieur Maspero, warning him that you were dangerous and involved with criminals."

"Then," Whit said, picking up the narrative, "she must have come to Philae, hoping you'd discover the tomb since her husband had."

"I led her right to it," I said bitterly. "She took the treasure, and then double-crossed Mr. Burton, whose *associate* came up with the plan to kidnap me in retribution, hoping to make a trade."

"Whoever the associate is, they must have deep ties to The Company."

"Isn't it obvious?" I said bitterly. "It must be Mr. Sterling."

Whit shook his head. "Or it could be Sir Evelyn. He did plant a spy on Philae."

"Whom you never discovered," my uncle said sourly.

"I questioned all viable suspects," Whit said icily. "Discreetly, of course. No one seemed like our culprit."

We were getting away from the real issue. We weren't on Philae, and Elvira was dead. That's all I cared about. "It's my fault Elvira died, Tío. Do you have any idea where my mother could have gone? Could she really be in Amarna?"

"How could you have known Elvira would come after you?"

"Because she always did," I said. Anguish tied up my stomach in knots. "She always did what I did. And Mamá offered her up for slaughter in my stead." I leaned forward, my gaze intent on my uncle. "But I will make this right, Tío. I'll get the artifacts back, I'll make my—"

"I don't care about the artifacts!" Tío Ricardo shouted, his voice rising, butting through my thoughts. "I care about your safety." He reached for my hand and I let him take it. "Inez, you have to go home."

"If you think I'll leave after all this, then you're sorely mistaken." Rage bloomed in my chest, thundered in my ears. "I'm not leaving until my mother pays for what she's done. Elvira *died*. I can't—I won't *ever* let that go. She knows the truth about Papá and I will never give up on him. Not as long as I'm breathing. Mamá has to be stopped, and I'll be the one to do it."

"But—" my uncle began.

"You said it yourself," I cut in, impatient. "She's probably after another tomb, more artifacts. Alchemical documents. Who knows how many others will be hurt by her actions? Killed? Do you want that on your conscience? Because I certainly don't."

"Fine, stay then," Tío Ricardo said with some of his former coldness. "I don't know where you'll live, but you're welcome to continue in Egypt if you wish to."

I blinked at him, confused. "What do you mean, where I'll live? I'm going to remain at Shepheard's. With all of you."

"In what room? With what money?"

Anger rioted in my blood. My voice shook from it. "With *my* money. I'm an heiress, aren't I? I ought to have enough money to buy a kingdom. Surely there's money for me to arrange for continued accommodations."

Whit looked between us, deep lines creasing his brow. "A *kingdom*?"

"Inez," my uncle said, his tone lethal. "Your money is mine until you marry."

I blinked, sure I misheard. "Do you remember the first letter you sent me?"

"Of course I do," he snapped.

"You gave *me* control over my fortune. Those were your very words, or were you lying to me again?"

His eyes blazed furiously. "I said you could have an allowance. Besides, that was before you barged into my affairs—"

"*Barged?*"

"That was before you endangered your life in the most foolish of ways, before I knew how lousy a judge of character you are. Trusting the wrong people, recklessly putting your safety at risk, nearly drowning in the Nile. You've put me through enough; you've put yourself through enough. Go home, Inez."

I inhaled sharply. "Tío—"

"Without money, you won't last in a foreign country, Inez," he said, his voice implacable. "I will not help you destroy your life."

 ## WHIT

The telegram had been waiting for me when we returned to Shepheard's. It was not from whom I expected. She had never written to me before. Not even once. I didn't expect her to cut me out of her life. But she had. Thoroughly.

The devil damn me.

I sat in a trance out on the balcony of my narrow hotel room, fixating on the busy street below, but not really seeing it. The noise rose up, familiar but dim, my mind already hazy from drink. Whiskey, I thought. I squinted at the bottle, the label swimming across my vision.

Right. Whiskey. Hello, old friend.

It was fire going down my throat. It would be hell going back up. I wasn't stopping until I met oblivion. Because I could still see Inez's face far too clearly in my mind. I could still remember how she tasted.

It had been a mistake to kiss her.

What if my plan didn't work? Fear worked like acid at the back of my throat. I raced to the water closet in my room and vomited. After rinsing out my mouth, I stumbled back to the narrow desk in my room, thinking about choices and how I didn't have any.

I had stayed in Egypt if only for the mere illusion of independence. In search of something that might change my fate. But this entire time, I'd been looking in the wrong place. In the back of my mind, I knew there was an expiration date. My parents would snap their fingers, expecting obedience. And I would give it because they knew my weakness.

My time had run out, and now duty had rung its final bell.

The blank sheet of paper at my elbow stared up at me. It was stark and impatient. Again, I thought of my plan and how it could work if I didn't somehow fuck it up. Which was a very real possibility. I grabbed the pen and wrote one line, and then my family's home address. Sweat dampened my brow. They'll be thrilled to hear from me. Their wayward son delivering on his promise.

I stuffed the note in an envelope, and scrawled my brother's name, flinging the pen away. It rolled out of sight, clamoring to the street below. Jolly. Someone got a new present.

The knock came five minutes later. I stumbled into my room, still carrying a handle of the whiskey, and blinked, looking around. There was only supposed to be one bed. Someone rapped on the door again, louder, and I answered it, scowling.

"You asked for someone to come up?"

I thrust the envelope to the hotel attendant. He was young, his grin fading when he took in my expression. Ali, I think his name was. "Deliver this to the telegraph office." I was surprised I could still speak coherently. That wouldn't do.

"The address?"

"Don't you know it already?" I asked bitterly. "I've sent several of these over the past few days."

Ali blinked. "I don't recall the address, sir."

"The ninth circle of hell, England."

"Sorry?"

I leaned against the frame and sighed. "It's in there."

"Very good, sir. It will be sent first thing tomorrow morning."

"Brilliant."

"Would that be all?"

I glanced down at the bottle, and nodded. There were still several inches of the amber liquid. Plenty. Ali scurried down the hall.

"Shokran," I muttered, and slammed the door. I took a long pull, barely tasting the rich smoke of the liquor.

It was done.

CAPÍTULO TREINTA Y OCHO

I woke up the next morning, furious. My uncle had effectively cut me off, had reduced me to begging. My mother was going to get away with murder, and one day soon, I'd have to face my aunt and explain to her how it was all my fault. I stared at my wan face in the mirror hanging above the basin in the water closet. Mamá's scarf with its brightly woven flowers seemed to mock me. I had kept it as a reminder for what she had done to me. It was around my neck as a battle flag and I would not take it off until I found her.

I tore my gaze away, anger simmering in my veins, as I slammed the door to the water closet behind me. Without ceremony, I opened my luggage and began throwing everything I had into it. Trust my uncle to book me passage for the first boat leaving Egypt and heading straight to Argentina.

A sudden knock disrupted my furious thoughts.

I crossed the room and opened the door. "It's you."

"Well observed." Whit sagged against the doorframe at the sight of me. Until I saw his face, I hadn't realized that I was waiting for him. We hadn't spoken about our time in the cave, and what it meant.

"Can I come in?"

I opened the door wider to let him pass. He brushed past, his familiar scent wrapping around me, but mixed with something else. My nose wrinkled as the smell of whiskey wafted in the air. It clung to him like a second skin.

"You've been drinking."

He let out a bark of laughter. It didn't sound remotely friendly. "You're absolutely brilliant this morning, Olivera."

Disappointment pressed down onto my shoulders. His walls were up, and I didn't understand why, and my confusion only made my eyes burn. In no world would *this* Whit call me *sweetheart*. I averted my gaze, not wanting him to see how his behavior was affecting me. Tension crackled between us.

"Inez," he said softly. "Look at me."

I had to force myself to lift my chin. We stared at each other from across the living space, his hands tucked deep into his pockets.

"Why are you standing all the way over there?" I asked.

Whit visibly weighed his response, his attention flickering across my trunk, and asked carefully, "What are you doing?"

I didn't like the stonelike quality to his face. Closed off and remote. It reminded me of a fortress. The person who had held me in the darkness was long gone. That person who had comforted me, kissed me desperately, saved my life.

This person before me was a stranger.

Perhaps that was his point. My words came out stiff. "What does it look like I'm doing? I'm packing. My uncle is sending me away."

"You're just going to give up," he said flatly. "After what your mother has done to Elvira, your father? After what she stole from Abdullah and your uncle?"

His questions grated against my skin. Guilt and shame washed over me.

"Didn't you hear him?" I asked, not bothering to cover up the bitter taste coating my tongue. "I have no money. None until I wed. What else can I do but go home? I have to see my aunt anyway. And I suppose I could find someone to marry. The son of the consul. Ernesto." I let out a harsh laugh, wanting to hurt him in the same way he was clearly trying to hurt me. "My mother would approve."

"Is that what you want to do?" he demanded.

"What else can I do?"

"You can't marry him." He lifted his hand and rubbed his eyes. They were bloodshot, tired, and red-rimmed. But when he focused on me again, his blue gaze seared.

"Why not?"

"Because," he said in a husky whisper, "he won't kiss you the way I will."

The ground seemed to shift under my feet. I didn't understand how he could say something like that to me, but stand so far away. As if that moment in the cave had never happened. "What are you saying?"

"I'm saying," Whit said in that same husky whisper. It drew goosebumps up and down my arms. He walked forward, every step seeming to roar in my ears. He bent his arm and reached for my waist, pulling me flush against the long line of his body. A soft gasp worked its way out of my mouth. Whit dipped his chin, his lips an inch from mine. His breath whispered against my cheek, the smoky scent of whiskey between us.

"Marry me instead."

EPÍLOGO

*P*orter looked out onto the Mediterranean Sea, the telegram clenched
in his hand. The paper was creased from frequent reading, but still
he held on to it as if it were a lifeline. He supposed that it was. His fellow
passengers were crowding the deck, every one of them eager for the first
sight of Alexandria's port. He read the short message for the hundredth
time.

INEZ FELL FOR IT.

It had been an abysmal crossing. But it didn't matter anymore.
Whit had kept his word.
And now it was time to collect.

AUTHOR'S NOTE

My first glimpse of this story, the first spark, was of a young woman, sailing to Egypt—but not for tourism. I sensed she had a story to tell, and I was particularly interested in exploring a young woman in a position of relative privilege who decides to boldly stand for something against the common ideals of the time period. Inez knows that she can't—and shouldn't—take on the governing forces in Egypt, but she can fight in her own corner, even if that means against her own mother.

While *What the River Knows* is a historical fantasy, I wanted to ground it with as many details from the late 1800s as possible. Egypt saw a sharp increase in tourists from all over the world and Cairo became a metropolitan city, with new hotels springing up every decade, welcoming royalty, dignitaries, explorers, entrepreneurs, missionaries, and countless people from all over the globe looking for work and a new start. It was a time of colonial expansion, imperial rule, and also a pivotal moment in archaeology.

After Britain bombarded Alexandria, many Egyptians lost their government jobs to foreigners, and they were also disallowed from studying their own heritage and ancestry. It would take decades before Egyptians took their place in the pursuit of archaeology, and meanwhile unrestricted tourism often resulted in the desecration and pillage of temples, monuments, and tombs. Statues became lawn ornaments for stately homes. Millions of artifacts disappeared, the majority of which Egypt has never seen again.

In *What the River Knows*, I included two historical figures who played a significant role in the 1880s, with the hope that they would provide a glimpse into the unsettling attitudes of non-Egyptians who held powerful offices in Egypt. Monsieur Gaston Maspero was a French Egyptologist who was the director general of excavations and antiquities for the Egyptian government. He allowed duplicates to leave the country, despite legislation that had restricted Egyptian artifacts from leaving its borders since 1835. This system, known as partage, greatly benefited museums and educational institutions that sponsored British archaeological projects because it paved the way for them to receive countless archaeological finds. For many Egyptians, it meant these finds were inaccessible—sometimes permanently. Infamously, Maspero established the sales room at the Egyptian Museum, allowing tourists to buy legitimate historical artifacts.

Sir Evelyn Baring, or Lord Cromer as he was later known, served as the controller general in Egypt, overseeing its finances and governance. His politics were appalling, particularly his belief in the Western world's superiority over Egypt, and his insistence that Egyptians were not capable of governing themselves. His policies barred many Egyptians from receiving higher education, men and women alike. As for the latter, he sought to discredit female professionals at every turn. To me, he's a villain, and he showed up in my book as one. I took liberties with his dialogue and his actions, but I hoped to portray the spirit of his unseemly arguments as accurately as possible, with as much care and sensitivity as possible, too.

Whit's experience in the British military was inspired by the real-life rescue attempt of General Charles Gordon in Khartoum, but for the sake of fiction I moved up the events surrounding his death by about three years. There are a variety of conflicting sources regarding his last days, but the general consensus was that he was able to evacuate some two thousand women, children, and sick or wounded soldiers out of Khartoum before his death. In Gordon, I fictionalized a softened, fatherlike figure for Whit, while in reality the man himself, sometimes romanticized as a martyr and saint in the eyes of the British, was complicated. But in the framework of this historical fantasy, he fit as a background character who had cared for Whit.

The 1880s were an exciting time for photography, and I hope you'll forgive my including a Kodak. It was the first portable camera, allowing anyone to snap a picture with a click of a button, but wasn't in widespread use until 1888—though the patent was filed in 1884!

My last note is on the spelling of colloquial Egyptian Arabic. There is no standard or uniform Romanized version, and as a result, spelling differs from region to region and in different time periods. For example, *shokran,* "thank you," can also be spelled as *shukran,* depending on where you're from. I ended up using the Egyptian Arabic spelling as it was taught to me by Egyptian friends and Egyptologists.

Incidentally, Egyptian Arabic differs wildly from that of other Arabic-speaking nations. It's said that other countries have no trouble understanding Egyptian Arabic, which tends to be more informal, while an Egyptian might have trouble understanding Arabic from other Arab nations. The reason behind this is because most Arabic films and TV shows are filmed in Egypt, and as such, Egyptian Arabic is widely understood.

ACKNOWLEDGMENTS

My fascination with Egypt started when I was a little girl. I devoured books on the subject, fiction and nonfiction alike. For years, I dreamed of visiting and getting lost in the city streets of Cairo and exploring ancient temples, and standing in front of the pyramids. When Inez drifted into my mind, dressed in black and pretending to be a widow, I just knew she was sailing to Egypt.

The rest, as they say, is history.

This book would have been impossible without the guidance, input, and help from so many, and I'm incredibly grateful for the support. To Sarah Landis, thank you so much for believing in this story, and for finding it the perfect home.

Eileen Rothschild, my wonderful editor, I'm so glad this book and I were in your thoughtful hands. Thank you for reading and reading and reading again. This story is so much stronger with your wisdom and insight. I still remember when I first told you about the tomb scene where Inez and Whit were trapped, while I walked up and down the grocery store parking lot. You heard my excitement and love for this story even then. Thank you for helping me bring this book to life.

An enormous thank you to the Wednesday Books team because there is so much that happens behind the scenes to bring a book to life and I'm so grateful for all that you do. To the marketing team: Brant Janeway and

Lexi Neuville (who made my day by emailing me her shocked reaction to the ending—sorry, not sorry, Lexi!). To Mary Moates (publicist), Melanie Sanders (production editor), Devan Norman (interior designer), thank you, thank you!! To Kerri Resnick, cover designer extraordinaire, you are a genius. To Lisa Bonvissuto, endlessly patient with all of my emails and questions. A *huge* thank you to Micaela Alcaino, who illustrated the cover of my dreams!! I'm so thankful for you and our friendship, amiga!

In October 2021, my dream to visit Egypt came true. I had the incredible opportunity to travel to Egypt on a research trip for three weeks, taking care to see and eat what my characters would have eaten and seen. Whenever I could, I stayed in hotels or ate at restaurants that existed in 1884 (a dream come true). I'm indebted to Adel Abuelhagog and Egyptologist Nabil Reda's guidance and patience as they answered question after question, taking me to one temple after another (and their favorite places to eat).

During my trip, I traveled on a dahabeeyah up the Nile for six days, and I'll never forget the experience. A huge thank-you to the wonderful crew: Reis Ahmed, Adam, Hassan, Mahmood, Magarak, Hamdy, Husam, Mahmood, Ramadan, Asmaell, Shiku, and Mohammed. They taught me to sail, invited me into the kitchen, and sent me away with bags of spices and recipes. I'm forever grateful for the wonderful memories.

A heartfelt thanks to Egyptologist Dr. Chris Naunton, who read the manuscript and gave such incredible and valuable feedback. Thank you for sending me email after email filled with notes, suggestions, and pictures of mummies. Classicist Katherine Livingston's insight into archaeology was fantastic. Thanks for the thorough reading and feedback, and the textbook recommendation!

To Kristin Dwyer, once again saving me on writing emotion, thank you. To Mimi Matthews, who read from a historical lens—thanks for reminding me Inez would need accessible buttons to get in and out of her dresses. Alexandra Bracken, a huge thank-you for reading and for your feedback, particularly on the magic system. You are so inspiring! Thanks to Natalie Faria and Jordan Gray for being such wonderful beta readers.

Thanks to Kerri Maniscalco, who spent an hour on the phone with me to help me brainstorm a particularly thorny scene. A big thank-you to Adrienne Young, who helped me brainstorm my way out of plot tangles.

To Rebecca Ross, my stoutest cheerleader, my first reader, drafting partner, and critique partner. This story will always make me think of you. Thanks for seeing the possibility from the first sentence, for coming with me to Egypt through the pages of this book. I'm so thankful we're in this together. And now we're editor/imprint sisters! ☺

And to Stephanie Garber, who loved this idea from the very beginning and knew what it could be. Thank you so much for reading the entire manuscript at a moment's notice, for telling me everything I did right, but more important, for your honesty when I lost my way. Your support will forever mean the world to me. I can't wait to bake a thousand pumpkin-flavored things with you.

To all of the wonderful authors who blurbed *What the River Knows*: Ava Reid, Elizabeth Lim, Mary E. Pearson, Amélie Wen Zhao, Stephanie Garber, Rebecca Ross, Rachel Griffin, Heather Fawcett, Jodi Picoult, and J. Elle. Reading your gushing emails gave me so much joy.

A million thanks to Emily Henry, who listened to me despair on how to handle the romance in this story I don't know how many times. Thanks for distracting me with an impromptu Sherry Thomas book club session. Reader, if you've made it this far, please pick up *The Luckiest Lady in London*. You're welcome.

I'm incredibly lucky to have wonderful support in my family, friends, and writing community. They cheer me on, and celebrate my wins, and stick with me through the ups and downs. You all know who you are, and I love you all so much.

To my parents, thanks for fostering a love of reading in me at such a young age. For fostering a love of Egypt as a little girl, and for not blinking when, as a seven-year-old, I said I wanted to be an Egyptologist. I'm a storyteller because of you both.

Rodrigo, read this one. I think you'll enjoy it. ☺

Andrew James Davis, the love of my life. Thanks for not blinking an eye when I said I wanted to go to Egypt. For three weeks. In *October*. Also known as the most beautiful month in Asheville, when all the leaves turn red and gold. When I was terrified to write this book, scared I'd get it wrong somehow, you reminded me that I was doing the very best that I could, and that I was human. Thank you for reminding me that I wrote from my heart. You were right. I absolutely did. Here's to more Octobers in our favorite city. I love, love, love you.

And to Jesus, for loving me where I am.